WOULD LIKE TO MEET

Would Like to Meet

~~UNTITLED~~

Rachel Winters

G. P. PUTNAM'S SONS
NEW YORK

PUTNAM
— EST. 1838 —

G. P. Putnam's Sons
Publishers Since 1838
An imprint of Penguin Random House LLC
penguinrandomhouse.com

ISBN 9780525542315

Printed in the United States of America
1   3   5   7   9   10   8   6   4   2

BOOK DESIGN BY KRISTIN DEL ROSARIO

Title page art: Coffee ring by Monash/Shutterstock.com
Interior art: Emoji by Cosmic_Design/Shutterstock.com

For anyone who's ever been told
they're not good enough
(you are)

WOULD LIKE TO MEET

Prologue

FADE IN

INT: GIL'S COFFEE HOUSE, EAST DULWICH—
SUNDAY, DECEMBER 2, UNGODLY HOUR (10 A.M.)

EVIE SUMMERS—late twenties, freckled, red
curls down to her shoulders, a bright
yellow 1950s-style tea dress, Doc Martens—
stands in front of the counter, tapping her
foot, clearly full of nervous energy.

The barista was taking his time with my order, and I silently thanked his dedication to the art of a well-squeezed orange. I glanced at his "Hello! My name is" badge. *Xan.* One of those names that announces the next generation is here, and they craft organic juice like it's a meditative experience. As the queue grew longer behind me, my orange juice was achieving Zen.

For once, though, I didn't mind holding anyone else up—today I needed Xan to take his sweet time so I could gear myself up for what I was about to do.

"Want me to add in a little something extra to make it special?"

Only if it's vodka, Xan. "What did you have in mind?"

"'The magic ingredient—perfect for hangovers." Xan unfurled his fingers, revealing an egg. I waved at him to stick it in the blender—it wasn't like I was planning to drink it.

By now, my hands were shaking, which would certainly help make what I was about to do look like an accident. I took a few deep breaths. *You can do this, Evie Summers,* I told myself sternly.

Though, if I was going to do this properly, I had to come away with the poor guy's name, and, if it went really well, his number.

I checked my phone while Xan blended and saw the JEMS group chat was active.

JEREMY: is she doing it? Evie, Evie, Evie. Are you doing it? TELL ME YOU ARE DOING IT

SARAH: Mar, have you sorted out the table centers yet?

JEREMY: Sarah, you want the BRIDEZILLA chat thread. This one is for more important things

MARIA: GUYS. Evie, are you sure you want to do this? I mean, god, I hope you do it, but are you sure?

"Ta-da!" Xan said, brandishing my juice. My heart convulsed. It was time.

EVIE: I'm going in

Even this early on a Sunday, the Southeast London café was packed. Ahead of me lay an obstacle course. Crisply dressed teenagers straight out of tube ads for online fashion sites everyone is too old for. Laptop users pretending they hadn't already finished the coffee they were still nursing. Yummy Mummies with perfect, doll-like kids. And him—Ramones Guy.

I'd chosen him as my mark from the table where I'd perched earlier with my laptop so that I could see everyone who entered the café. He'd sat near the big Christmas tree. Late twenties, cute, bearded, wearing a Ramones T-shirt under a checked shirt, and more student than adult (*i.e.*, just my type).

He'd arrived on his own, he wasn't wearing a wedding ring, he didn't have any children—basically, he'd achieved the bare-minimum requirements for a potential love interest. Lucky him.

Though, if I were being honest, he didn't just tick some boxes—I genuinely found him attractive, which was making me even more nervous. Because these days, my approach to finding someone I liked was to imagine the life we might have together and then never speak to them. *Not* what I was about to do.

I emerged from the cluster of tables a few steps away from my target. He was leaning over his book—*How Not to Grow Up!* by Richard Herring—which gave me pause. Is that something my love interest would read? But I couldn't afford to be choosy, so I started to close the gap between us.

Three more steps.

Two.

One.

I was right by him. He was even cuter close up.

Now or never.

I held the juice out as I approached, heart simultaneously in my throat and rapping so hard against my ribs it felt like it was trying to escape.

Come on, come on, NOW!

Ramones Guy laughed at something he'd just read . . . and I walked straight past him.

Damn it. I couldn't do it. But I also couldn't back out.

Because, just maybe, I was about to meet the man of my dreams. We'd lock eyes and, in that instant, we'd both know we were about to start the rest of our lives together, just like in a film. Though right now, holding an orange juice with an egg in it, I felt as far from the silver screen as it was possible to get.

I'd been walking as slowly as possible, but now I was back at my table. I'd sat at the communal one, and in my absence a man and his daughter had joined me. Him: midthirties, neat, dark hair, reading the Sunday paper, with the look of someone with IT in his job title. Her: cute, slightly wonky pigtails, red-rimmed glasses, about seven years old. Her legs were swinging as she read her book. I had a vague feeling I'd seen them in here before.

I got out my phone as I hovered by my laptop.

EVIE: I couldn't do it. Why did I think I could? And isn't it your responsibility as my friends to stop me from doing something that's clearly bonkers?

SARAH: you can do whatever you put your mind to. Though, yes, it is absolutely bonkers

JEREMY: Evie, don't you dare back out now. Go get your Hugh Grant

MARIA: you can do this, Evie! Take a deep breath and try again. We believe in you!

JEREMY: do it for love! At least, do it for us

For the most part, my best friends were sane, intelligent people, and it made me feel better to be reminded that even they had encouraged me to do this.

Besides, they were right. I *could* do it. Or, rather, I had to.

I'd delayed long enough. In that brief pause before I turned back, the man at my table looked up at me, as if wondering about my behavior. I tried to seem like I'd simply forgotten something and needed to go back for it. *Which people do all the time, thank you very much.*

This time I took a shorter route, which meant squeezing past the cabal of perfectly turned-out mothers.

Two neatly dressed, wide-eyed children were blocking my path, one white-blond, the other with straight dark hair, both looking like they'd answered a casting call for "children that could haunt your nightmares."

"Sorry, I just need to get past. Thanks. So if you could . . ." My drink dribbled down my wrist and I hastily straightened the glass before any more escaped. *Imagine a* Notting Hill *where, instead of spilling his drink on Julia Roberts, Hugh Grant simply flattened his empty cup against her chest.*

"*Please* move," I pleaded quietly. They smiled. "Please?" I said, a little louder, flicking my gaze toward Ramones Guy to check that he hadn't left.

One of the mothers—blond, wearing ironic high-waisted "mom jeans" and box-fresh sneakers—leaned away from her conversation with her friend with the gleaming ponytail to appraise me. "Is everything okay?"

My cheeks immediately started to burn. "Everything is fine! Sorry. I just need to get past."

People at nearby tables were starting to look up.

Ponytail shook her head. "Our children make their own decisions. Vendetta, Justice, what do you want to do?"

Good Lord. The children looked at me and then held hands.

The curse of having red hair, pale skin, and freckles is that your body turns traitor at the slightest provocation. I knew without looking that my chest and neck would be covered in red blotches. "You're like a carrot! Look, Mummy, she's a carrot!" the girl—Justice?—exclaimed.

The boy's face crumpled as he wailed, "Does she have a rash? Is she contagious?"

"Clever word, Detty. No, the lady is just a little bit embarrassed!"

"I'm scared," Justice said.

Now all five mothers were looking at me and I forced a smile, wishing I had the courage to tell them they were raising their children to one day become other children's traumatic high-school experiences.

Instead, face and chest still glowing, I swiveled to edge around their table. The mothers all watched me struggle past, while Justice, Vendetta, and the other Children of the Café (I assumed their names were Regret, Huge Mistake, and Grave Error) burst into high giggles.

Ramones Guy was back in my line of sight. This time I was definitely going to do it. I'd walk straight toward him, eyes on my phone as if I wasn't paying attention, and "accidentally" bump into him. Then we'd have a really cute "how we met" story. A meet-cute.

Of course, the thing about not looking where you're going is that knocking into someone is fairly inevitable. You just can't always choose who.

The next five seconds happened in excruciatingly slow motion.

Five. I kept my eyes on my screen, held my glass high, and picked up speed.

Four. At the last possible moment, I looked up.

Three. My smile was shy; his eyes were filled with horror.

Two. Because he had just been joined by his tiny granny, whom he was now clutching protectively to his chest.

One. I smacked into him, compressing her between our two bodies as the orange juice left the glass.

Everything came back into sharp focus. I pulled away, heart hammering, and was relieved to discover they were both dry. His sweet old granny was safe.

"I am *so* sorry. Are you both all right?"

"No thanks to you, you clumsy cow," Granny said. Ramones Guy glared. I sighed. Something told me the two of us were not meant to be.

I was about to offer more help, but unfortunately, what goes up must come down. And the sudden outraged screams told me exactly where.

"Justice! Are you okay? Speak to Mummy!"

Oh, no. I turned around, still holding the empty glass.

Little Justice's white-blond hair was now a bright orange as her mother frantically wiped at the sodden strands, her pointed face absolutely dripping. Detty was grinning as he watched his sobbing friend.

"I'm really, truly sor—" I tried to say.

"Is she okay?" Detty's mother interrupted, from a safe distance.

"No, she is not okay. For sodding's sake, Janet, pass me a moist towelette."

Then something seemed to occur to Justice's mother and she turned to where I stood, clutching the glass in both hands. She rubbed the juice between her fingers.

"What, *exactly*," she said to me, "is in this?"

My voice came out strangled. "Oranges, that's all." She relaxed a little. "And an egg."

She shrieked and began wiping at her daughter even more furiously, blond bob swinging.

Another mother called out, "Oh my God, Suze. Is she vegan?"

Every part of me was on fire. "Can I help at all? Here, I'll get napkins." I ran back to my table, feeling a little hysterical. Both the dad and the daughter had their heads down, reading, the only two people in the whole café who were oblivious to what was happening. Their napkins were at the edge of the table closest to me. I put down the glass and grabbed them. As I did, the daughter raised her eyes . . . and winked. I was too flustered to respond.

Suze snatched the napkins from me without comment, holding them in front of her daughter's mouth.

"Out!"

Justice stuck out her tongue, and I swear she looked right at me as she did it. Suze started to wipe at it, her movements punctuating her words. "She. Is. Allergic. To. Egg. If she ingests even a tiny amount, she—" As if on cue, Justice went pale, then hiccuped.

"Justice, tell Mummy you didn't swallow."

The little girl burped once. Twice.

This wasn't actually going to happen, was it? I held my breath and seriously considered running out of the café, leaving my laptop and bag behind.

"Mummy, is *she* contagious?" precious little Detty asked.

Justice looked like she was about to cough, only . . . she didn't.

What can only be described as a gleaming fountain of sick shot out of her mouth with such force that when it hit Detty's face he was knocked backward by a foot.

The whole café froze, silent but for the deafening sound of dripping coming from Detty.

Even though it was awful—truly, inescapably awful—and I felt terrible as the little girl's projectile vomit once again managed to target Detty's upturned face, a very tiny, unforgivable part of me thought: *And* that's *why she's called Justice.*

I emerged from the restroom, where I'd been hiding only after the mothers and their children had finally left, thoroughly outraged and promising they wouldn't be back. Xan had waved off my offer to help him clean up—apparently the mothers had been driving him and the rest of the staff crazy for weeks with their campaign against the gender-neutral bathrooms. He'd even made me a fresh coffee, which was waiting for me back at my table. I gave him a grateful wave.

The dad and his kid were still there—I'd been hoping they'd have gone so I didn't have to face anyone. The only sensible thing to do was down the coffee, pack up my belongings, and never return.

As I sat back behind my laptop, using it as a shield, I risked a glance around the café. It had more or less settled back down.

It was almost like nothing had happened.

Except that I'd think about today every time I closed my eyes to sleep for the next ten years.

JEREMY: well??? How did it go? Did you land Hugh Grant?

SARAH: OMG Evie, tell me you didn't actually go through with it, you weirdo

MARIA: I'm here if you need to talk

I flipped my phone over. It was too soon to relive the trauma.

Picking up the coffee, I faced my blank screen. Now all I had to do was write about what just happened in agonizing detail, which was, after all, why I'd done it in the first place.

As I started to type, I felt the peculiar itch of someone staring at me.

The little girl. She appeared to be waiting for me to say something. I pushed my hair over my shoulder and leaned toward my laptop, hoping she'd get bored. She inched closer.

"Well?" she said, impatiently. "How did we do?"

"I'm sorry?" I asked her, baffled.

"Anette," the man cautioned distractedly, gently tugging his daughter to his side. "Leave the young lady alone." *Young lady!* Something about the way he said this made me prickle. As if he were the only adult at the table.

She pulled away from him and he moved his hands in quick succession—sign language, I realized, spotting her hearing aids. His daughter ignored him. "We pretended we didn't see what happened," she told me. Adding, presumably for clarity, "With the vomiting."

Her dad appeared riveted by the travel section.

"It was all *his* idea," she continued. "He said you'd be embarrassed enough." The man turned his page. "*So?* Did we do well?" It took me a moment to respond. I knew I should feel mortified—especially when her dad clearly thought I was an idiot—but her earnestness was touching.

"You did," I assured her. "Thank you." She beamed, though her dad remained focused on his paper. He was probably sympathetic toward the families I'd just traumatized. "But as bad as it was for me, it was worse for them. Those poor children, and their mothers—"

She was already shaking her head, the ends of her pigtails hitting her glasses. "They are *literally* our mortal enemies. We've been trying to think of ways to get them to stop coming here for *weeks*."

"I bet you didn't think of that one," I said wryly.

She grinned. "I'm Anette," she said. "This is my dad." She elbowed him.

After a slight pause, he held out his hand. "Ben," he said stiffly.

"Evie," I replied, giving him my best "I'm completely normal" smile. My hand was briefly swallowed by his before he returned to his paper.

Anette leaned forward, peering at me as if I was the most interesting thing in the room.

"You've been the best thing to happen in here in ages," she declared.

"That's very sweet," I replied, deciding to take this as a compliment. Somehow I didn't think her dad agreed. "But today was a complete one-off, I promise. I *never* do things like that."

For whatever reason, this earned me Ben's full attention. He looked at me, hooded brown eyes flashing with something like amusement. "Really?" he said. "Then why was that the second time we've seen you spill your drink on someone in this café?"

Chapter 1

Code Red

INT: A BASEMENT BAR IN SOHO—FRIDAY,
NOVEMBER 16, 10 P.M.

EVIE stands in a small crowd of well-
dressed twentysomethings, holding a scuffed
plastic "glass" of house white wine,
nodding in time to the conversation
happening around her. She checks her phone,
too tipsy to be anywhere near as
surreptitious as she thinks she's being.

Two Weeks Earlier

SARAH: I'm going to email the presentation to you all to help
your planning session next weekend. Check your inboxes!

MARIA: we really don't mind planning your hen do ourselves

JEREMY: which isn't to say that we don't mind planning your
hen do

SARAH: but this way you'll KNOW I'll love it. While we're on my
wedding, can we talk about your plus one situation, Evie?

I slipped my phone back into my bag. Sarah had been trying to
get me to talk about my "plus-one situation" since she got engaged.
As if I had some sort of condition that I'd been ignoring.

As I turned my attention back to the two achingly trendy young women with me in the bar, I noticed two things: 1) Their beautiful, pristine, untouched-by-worry baby skin. And 2) That I was much tipsier than I realized, despite sticking to my strict three-drink rule.

That was the curse of the assistant drinks. Once a month, every assistant working in TV and film talent agencies met in a different yet equally terrible bar in Central London to "network" (*i.e.*, gossip). There was never any food available at these events, though there was always an abundance of a very particular type of white wine (the cheapest). I could only assume everyone else here was too young to have experienced hangovers as adults, and were therefore blissfully unaware of what it's like to wake up feeling like every single one of your twenty-nine years has smacked you in the face.

Myself, on the other hand . . . I had an egg sandwich in my satchel that I was dying to eat, but hadn't yet found an appropriate moment. While my practical side was telling me I needed something to line my stomach, I also conceded that normal people probably don't bring their own sandwiches to networking events.

One of the girls, Jodi, swept the curtain of blond hair from her face and gave me a little smile that made *me* feel like the young one. I had the feeling she'd just asked me a question. She was an assistant at one of the biggest talent agencies in the business, and one of those people who collected gossip like it was currency.

"What was that, sorry?" I squeezed my plastic wine cup tightly. It wasn't that long ago that I'd had someone by my side at these events.

"I'm whisking young Geraldine here around to introduce her to the cool kids," Jodi said. She had one of those drawling London accents that made me feel more northern with every syllable.

I turned to the teen with round glasses. Most of her long hair was pulled up into a messy bun, leaving the rest down in the sort of tangled waves that said "Just *look* at how much I don't care about my appearance." Beneath her overalls she wore a white T-shirt with

GRETA GERWIG across it in large black lettering. I immediately wanted one, though I'd never be cool enough to pull it off.

"Who are you interning with?" I asked.

There was a moment of silence.

"Evie, you big nerd," laughed Jodi. "She's an assistant."

"But she's a kid!" I clamped my mouth shut, as if that could somehow take back my words.

Geraldine let out a low, throaty laugh and placed a hand on her chest. "*Thank you*. I'm almost prehistoric in assistant years." She dropped her voice to a whisper. "I'm actually *twenty-three*. I was worried everyone would think I was too old."

"You don't look a day over twenty-one" was Jodi's automatic response. I wanted to take Geraldine by the shoulders and tell her she was so young she was practically brand-new. Instead, I took another sip of my wine.

"Geraldine's at Geoffrey and Turner," Jodi said, with a significance that I studiously ignored.

Geoffrey and Turner was a small but respected agency for screen and TV writers. A few years ago they'd been the William Jonathan Montgomery & Sons Agency for Screenwriters' direct rivals. But lately, they'd become the agency of choice for writers looking for prestige, and we had . . . Well, someday we'd get back on track again.

"One of Geraldine's new colleagues, Ritchie, is an old friend of yours, isn't he, Evie?" Jodi pressed. Nothing got by her. Since she'd found out I'd known him back when he was plain old *Ricky*, she never missed an opportunity to dig for more information. My ex was what was known in the industry as a unicorn, *i.e.*, a single man. Putting him firmly on Jodi's gossip radar. I could have told her that Ricky was the kind of guy who'd make you feel like the luckiest person in the world. Until you were no longer what he wanted. Instead, I kept my smile fixed, as usual giving her nothing.

"Ritchie's amazing," Geraldine gushed. "I'm sure he's going to be made an agent any day now. Everything about him says 'meteoric rise.'"

"Well, he was hardly going to remain an assistant forever," Jodi said, then put a hand on my arm. "Don't worry, you'll get there. You just have a unique situation."

Jodi wasn't wrong, but that wasn't what I was upset about. *They wouldn't really promote him yet, would they?* My throat tightened.

"Where do you work?" Geraldine asked me. I sighed, snapping myself out of it. She'd find out sooner or later anyway.

"William Jonathan Montgomery and Sons," I said.

Geraldine's eyes widened. "Oh, you're *that* Evie."

When you were the longest-serving assistant in the industry, word tended to get around.

It was a relief when they decided they needed a refill and headed back to the bar. I pulled out my phone again, wishing it was next Friday already so my friends could be here. Sometimes the miles between us felt more numerous than I could count.

EVIE: HELP ME I AM SURROUNDED MY CHILDREN

MARIA: where are you?

EVIE: assistant drinks

EVIE: *BY children

JEREMY: is Dicky there?

EVIE: no. He only socializes with agents now

SARAH: it's good for her. IT'S GOOD FOR YOUR CAREER, EVIE

JEREMY: indoor voices, Sarah

MARIA: you're an agent in all but name, Evie. You've shown your face. Why don't you head home? Take care of yourself

I tucked the phone away without responding to Maria. As difficult as I sometimes found these events, I had to attend them if I had any hope of one day progressing beyond assistant. Everyone was here with the same purpose: desperate to say the right thing, speak to the right people, make those all-important connections. I used to feel the same way, back when I'd first moved down to London. Just not about agenting.

If my dad could see me now.

He'd be proud, I knew; he'd just be surprised to see me on this side of the business. Wanting to represent screenwriters, instead of being one. He'd wonder what had happened to the girl who'd declared, at the age of twelve, that she was going to be the next Nora Ephron or Dorothy Taylor, who'd acted like writing was as essential as food, or air. Of course, he'd never know what the first agent I ever showed my work to told me.

You just don't have what it takes.

A small shudder ran through me. Normally I could quell any thoughts about my writing days, but something about this evening had made it harder. *Seven years as an assistant. Happy anniversary, Evie.* Still, I always told myself I was lucky. I couldn't follow my own dream, so now I helped other screenwriters follow theirs. It would all be worthwhile once I was made agent. Monty always told me I wasn't quite ready yet. I just had to find a way to make him see what I was made of.

I squeezed up to the bar beside Jodi to put my empty cup down, just in time to catch the end of what Geraldine was saying.

"I'd *never* stay in a job for that long." She spotted me standing there. "No offense," she added quickly.

"It isn't Evie's fault," Jodi said. "Her boss, Monty, is a bit of a joke." I bristled at this. Monty was what was known in the industry as the Old Guard. One of the last bastions of the days when most deals were sealed in the bars of private members' clubs. He could still charm a producer when he needed to, but the world had moved on. The tide of enthusiastic young people entering the industry all came with an innate understanding of *content*. A word that made Monty break out in hives.

"He's brilliant at what he does," I said, knowing I was defending my own experience as much as his.

"We all know your real reason for staying. The work perk." Jodi pronounced it "werk" and the age gap between us became a gulf. "A certain Oscar-winning screenwriter Monty must have solid dirt on to have kept hold of him for so long."

Jodi knew about all the poachable writers as a matter of principle. Though there were some things even she didn't know about Monty's prize client.

Geraldine's eyes gleamed. "You're not talking about Ezra Chester, are you? *Oh my God*, what's he like? Is he as hot as he looks on Instagram? It's so *cute* he's dating Monica Reed. She's like *ten* years older than him, which is so not something he cares about. How's his big film coming along? Didn't he donate half his fee to charity? Tell me *everything*."

Ezra had become an instant industry darling after winning a screenwriting Oscar three years ago, but it was only when he started dating Hollywood royalty Monica Reed that he claimed celebrity status. Thanks to his appearing on various gossip pages and hotlists, his Instagram account now had more than three hundred thousand followers. It helped that he looked like he belonged on the screen, rather than behind it.

"I can't really say much about the film," I said, smiling to soften my words.

"You're hilarious, Evie," Jodi said, and suddenly I was back in high school, being mocked for putting my hand up in class. "We're all friends here. You can at least tell us if the rumors are true. Does the great Ezra Chester have writer's block?"

"Not even close," I said, trying to ignore how the word "friends" had made something tighten in my chest. We'd seen each other once a month for the last year or so, ever since Jodi had started as an assistant. Did that qualify as a friendship? Part of me hoped it did, because since moving to London I'd found making new friends outside of work all but impossible. And yet . . . the one time the two of us had gone out for a drink, I'd dropped my guard and told her something personal. The next day an assistant I didn't know emailed me to recommend her grief counselor. We hadn't gone out again.

"His charity work is probably taking up his writing time," Geraldine said sympathetically. "He just spent one whole month in South America so he could meet all the children he's raising money for. I don't know how he does it."

"We wonder the same thing," I said neutrally, thinking of the artful shots of the vineyards he'd also managed to visit.

"Tell us something we *don't* know about Ezra, Evie," Jodi said, widening her eyes, as if we were both irritated by Geraldine. Co-conspirators.

"Well," I said, still light-headed from too much cheap booze on an empty stomach. "The truth is that Ezra . . ." I saw Jodi hold her breath. My phone buzzed.

I paused, realizing how easy it would be to tell them too much; all I had to do was explain why my friends back home call him NOB. Ruining his and the agency's reputation in one fell swoop.

Much to their dismay, I reached into my bag, pulling out the sandwich to get to my phone. *Oh, what the hell.* I opened the packet and took a generous bite. People who think being an agent is a glamorous career path haven't seen me catching the last train home cradling a loaf of bread so I can eat toast in bed. Jodi cleared her throat, looking embarrassed for me. "Well? Come on, Evie, share."

"Okay," I relented. "The truth is . . ." I paused to quickly polish off the sandwich. They took an impatient step closer. "His next project is going to blow you all away."

A beat. Their faces filled with disbelief. "Right," said Jodi flatly, and this time I was the one left in the cold as she and Geraldine exchanged looks.

That's the thing about being an assistant for seven years. You get really, really good at it.

Ezra might be a NOB, but no one here was ever going to find out why.

I tucked the empty packet back into my bag and retrieved my phone. I had several missed calls from Monty. Knowing him, it could be anything from a client crisis to wanting a suit dry-cleaned.

For once, I was grateful he was high-maintenance. "I'm so sorry, but I have to run. I'm needed back at the office."

Geraldine checked the time on her waterproof Baby-G watch. "But it's after ten p.m.!" she said, bewildered. "On a *Friday*."

I gave her my sweetest smile. "Welcome to agenting."

"Code Red. They've ambushed me." Monty's voice was a whisper but echoed oddly. "Did you tell them where I was tonight?"

"Who?" I dodged through the Friday-night Dean Street crowds.

"Sam-and-Max. They're here." Sam-and-Max were the producers for Ezra's new script. They did everything as if they were one person, like a hydra someone had tried to kill that had merely divided in two and continued its life as normal. I'd never met two more enthusiastically polite people. It seemed unlikely they'd approach Monty without any warning.

"Are you at the Ash?"

"Aha!" he hissed. "So you *did* tell them I was here."

I bit back my response. Monty was always at the private members-only club; he'd all but moved in. He spent more time at the Ash than at home, and anyone who knew even the slightest thing about Monty wouldn't look for him at the office.

"And they both just turned up?"

"Yes, they didn't even call first." A noise drowned out his next words. *Was that a flush?* "You need to get here. Code *Red*, Evelyn."

Monty had devised a code system for needing my help when he was with clients so that they didn't know he was calling for assistance. Amber meant "stand by for action." Green was for minor emergencies. Taxis that needed booking, that sort of thing. The severity of a Code Red situation was unpredictable. The last one had involved a client choking on a meatball, and Monty had been too drunk to remember that I'd gone home for the weekend and couldn't perform the Heimlich maneuver from Sheffield. The client had, despite this, survived.

"I need an extraction." It was also worth bearing in mind that Monty could be dramatic. We worked with screenwriters, not spies. *"Shit."* For a few seconds, I could hear only women's voices in the background.

"Monty? Is everything okay?"

"Hang on," he whispered. The voices faded. "Come and get me out of here!"

"I'm on my way. Which room are you in?" The club was based in Mayfair and its seven floors included a rooftop pool and a health spa.

Monty mumbled something about wombles talking.

"Sorry, I don't think I caught that."

"I said I'M IN THE WOMEN'S TOILET."

"Then, er, leave?" I suggested helpfully.

"I'd love to, only I'm STUCK, Evelyn. I'm bloody *stuck*."

As I headed for the tube, I was immensely glad I'd eaten that egg sandwich. Something told me I'd better be sober for this.

Chapter 2

Stuck

INT: THIRD-FLOOR BAR, THE ASH, PRIVATE
MEMBERS' CLUB—FRIDAY, NOVEMBER 16,
11:02 P.M.

The bar's color scheme is ironically bright
and garish. There are several giant film
canisters on the ceiling from which reels
of filmstrip hang down. A purple curtain
with lime-green tassels hangs between the
bar and the restaurant beyond. A blond-
haired waiter in a crisp usher's uniform
stands next to the curtain. He huffs a
filmstrip out of his face and appears to be
listening.

"Please, I *have* to get across the restaurant without being seen."

The blond waiter clasped his hands, his smile bland and practiced, well-versed in handling the eccentricities of the Ash's clientele. "Miss Summers, I appreciate you're Monty's assistant, but this is highly unorthodox. We wouldn't want to disturb our other guests."

Monty was a founding member of the club, hence the first-name basis, so the staff knew who I was even though he wouldn't pay for an additional membership fee. As a nonmember, my rights were limited. I tried my best to look like someone worth helping.

Given that I was currently wrapped in a curtain, this was a struggle.

From my vantage point I could see Sam-and-Max sitting at a table on either side of an empty chair I assumed had been Monty's before he'd spotted them coming into the room and hidden in the nearest restroom.

If the producers saw me, they'd know for sure that Monty was still in the building. Somehow, I needed to get past them and help Monty escape without them noticing.

"You're welcome to sit in the bar while you wait for Monty."

I hugged the material closer to me, trying desperately to decide what to do. The producers could be here for only one thing. Eighteen months ago, Ezra Chester had signed a contract with Sam-and-Max's up-and-coming film company, Intrepid Productions, to write their next film—a romantic comedy. They'd wanted the hottest new talent behind their project. Enter Ezra and his Oscar-winning kudos. The fact that this rom-com would be the first follow-up to his major success, the ultimate tearjerker *A Heart Lies Bleeding*, made him all the more alluring.

When the original deadline whizzed past with no sign of the script, they'd been very understanding, especially when Monty had explained to them that Ezra's grandmother had just passed away. But then Ezra missed the next deadline, and the next . . . and the producers had stepped up their game.

Since then Sam-and-Max have been pursuing the script with a cheerfulness bordering on aggression. Looking at them now, dressed in identical blue suits, worry on their blandly good-looking faces, I wondered why they wanted to meet with Monty so badly they'd broken his cardinal rule (no surprise meetings). Was it because what Ezra had managed to write was actually terrible? The tiniest part of me hoped this was true . . .

Because there was something Sam-and-Max couldn't know about their beloved screenwriter. The same something I would never tell the Jodis or the Geraldines of the world.

The truth was that Ezra Chester—Academy Award winner, charitable heartthrob, and industry darling—was an arrogant, insufferable arse.

My friends had taken to calling him Number One Boychild (NOB for short) after he'd stormed out of a meeting because I'd gotten his coffee order wrong, and then refused to return until Monty promised him cocktails. The meeting had been about his charity for underprivileged children, several of whom had been in the room at the time. It was a testament to Monty's PR skills that NOB's charity work had anyone fooled about his real nature. Now I had to be incredibly careful never to call him NOB to his infuriatingly beautiful face.

Thinking about him gave me an idea. "I promise I'll move, if you wouldn't mind doing one small thing for Monty," I said, because the waiter wouldn't be able to refuse one of the Ash's founding members.

He looked both relieved and concerned. "I can't do anything that will upset the other patrons," he cautioned.

"Look." I tried to keep the desperation from my voice. "The truth is if I screw this up, my boss will use it as another reason not to promote me. *Please.*" I shuffled toward him as much as the curtain would allow. "Do I look like the kind of woman who has other options?"

He shook his head—*insulting*—and I gave him what I hoped was a reassuring smile before explaining exactly what I needed him to do.

"Is Mr. Montgomery here? Mr. Chester has just arrived and is waiting in the VIP area downstairs."

The waiter was standing within earshot of Sam-and-Max while talking to his colleague.

"Come on, come on," I prayed.

I saw them sit up straighter, exchange a look, stand, and head as one toward where I was hidden. I shrank back behind the curtain, one of its tassels tickling my nose.

Their footsteps faded away down the stairs and I counted to ten before slipping out and heading for the door on the opposite side of the room, trying not to feel as out of place as I must have looked with my mussed hair and Doc Martens.

The women's toilet was lit by a vaguely apologetic kind of lighting designed to make you feel you were stepping into something illicit. I could just about make out beveled pink tiles, a lot of chrome, and products that probably cost more than a month's salary.

There was only one stall in use. "Monty?" I called hesitantly.

"Evelyn? What took you so long?" Monty's cut-glass accent held an edge of hysteria.

"You can come out now, it's clear."

"Yes, why didn't I think of that?" He rattled the door from the inside. "That's right—I'm stuck."

For a moment we both pushed back and forth, which only succeeded in establishing that he was right. "I think it's the lock," said Monty.

"I'm going to have to get someone."

Monty made a strangled sound. "I'll be the talk of the club! Can't you jimmy it a bit . . . ?" He went quiet as the main door opened. An older woman breezed in. I smiled at her and pulled out my phone to send a quick message to JEMS, hoping someone would be up after midnight.

EVIE: does anyone know how to unjam a toilet door?

Jeremy worked as an attorney and often kept odd hours. Maria was an editor for a monthly food magazine, a job that rarely necessitated an all-nighter, apart from when she left dough to rise. Sarah worked in HR and finished at 5:30 p.m. on the dot, because her time-management skills were a force to be reckoned with. She was probably fast asleep.

I saw a response pop up and almost sagged with relief—until I read it.

JEREMY: why would it be covered in jam?

EVIE: 😵 Are you still working?

JEREMY: just for some of my freebie clients. Homeless guy arrested for begging outside M&S. Thank goodness a diligent officer prevented such a terrible crime

JEREMY: wait, are you stuck in a toilet?

EVIE: not me. Monty

JEREMY: . . .

EVIE: stop laughing, please. This is serious

JEREMY: sorry. If Sarah was up she'd probably have some annoyingly useful solutions. Have you tried putting soap on the hinges?

EVIE: right now, I'll try anything

JEREMY: you could try leaving him there

"Do you mind?" I looked up from my phone to find the woman smiling and gesturing to my sink. Now I recognized her. She was a Dame, over seventy, and fiercely chic. Ramrod-straight neck and shoulders, cropped white hair, and loose, flowing clothes, with a silk scarf draped elegantly over one shoulder. She exuded grace and poise. I blinked at her in awe, then realized she was still waiting.

I stood back. "Sorry, I'm just waiting for my friend."

The unmistakable sound of a man urinating filled the room. The lady looked up from reapplying her lipstick and I studied the end of my braid intensely. The noise continued.

Of course Monty would get stuck in the one place where needing the toilet wasn't actually a problem and still choose to go at the worst possible moment.

And he really was going. And going. The woman was basically film royalty, and right now she was having to listen to Monty emptying his bladder with gusto.

The tiniest of trickles from the stall echoed around the room. Finally, finally, the sound trailed off. The lady capped her lipstick before turning to go, tucking her bag under one stylish arm.

She paused with a hand on the door. *Oh, God.*

"Sometimes," said the Dame, "you just need a really good piss."

As the door closed behind her, I relaxed against the sink, a snort of laughter finally escaping me.

"I fail to see how this is funny," said Monty.

"Sorry, I'm just getting soap to put on the hinges, but—"

"Whatever you're doing, do it quickly. There's a good girl."

"But is soap really our best—"

"*Now*, Evelyn."

I plucked the expensive-looking bottle of liquid soap off the shelf and returned to the stall. As I looked for the door's hinges, I decided to take advantage of the fact that I literally had a captive audience. "Monty," I said. "Why don't you want to meet with Sam-and-Max?"

Silence from the stall.

"Is it the pages?" He'd told me NOB was making progress. Not that he'd let me read the draft for myself.

"Actually, you can call someone after all."

"Sam-and-Max are out there, but if you think that's the best thing to do—"

"No, no," he said hastily.

"What do they want to meet about, Monty?" I asked gently, pumping the liquid on the hinges.

A long pause.

I rattled the door, muttering, "It's just *so* stuck. I really should go and get help . . ."

There came a heavy sigh from the stall. I heard the toilet creak as Monty took a seat. "They want Ezra to sign an addendum stating he'll deliver the full script within three months. They won't accept the partial; I've tried. They've mentioned lawyers."

It was a generous offer, as far as ultimatums went, especially considering they'd been getting the runaround for over a year. Monty had assured everyone that NOB was writing, so what was the issue? Perhaps NOB had taken offense at the formality. Every other extension had been a "gentleman's agreement."

"Is Ezra being resistant?" There was the tiniest of gaps between the door and the frame where the lock was, and I could just about see the bolt. I pumped some soap in there too.

Another pause. "I didn't want to risk stifling his creativity by mentioning the new deadline."

Translation: Monty had wimped out of telling NOB he could no longer take his sweet time. I took a deep breath. "He doesn't know he only has three months to finish the script?"

"It's worse than that, Evelyn," said Monty, irritable now. "If he doesn't deliver, they want their money back, all of it. If that happens, we're screwed."

I frowned. Could it really be that bad? For the last few years, as Monty devoted more and more of his time to maintaining NOB's benevolent public image, I'd been handling most of the agency's negotiations. I had a good idea how much we were bringing in, even though Monty kept most of the company financials to himself. "I thought we were doing fine," I said, trying to keep the frus-

tration out of my voice. If he'd made me an agent, I could have been
helping more.

"You really should know more about how the business works by
now, Evelyn." I pushed my indignation down, knowing from experience that there would be nothing gained from pointing out that he
purposefully withheld information from me. "We're being squeezed
out by bigger agencies every day. There's no room for the little man
anymore. Ezra's our one ace, and without him, we're done. We are
both out of a job if he doesn't deliver."

"We're *what*?" I squeezed the bottle too hard and the pump
head came off in my hands. The whole thing slipped from my fingers, bouncing off the dark slate tiles and spraying its contents
everywhere.

"No script," enunciated Monty, "no job."

For a moment I just stood there, absorbing this, soap dripping
from my fingers. After this long, the agency felt like home. I knew
that my friends thought I had Stockholm syndrome, given all the
stories they'd heard me tell about Monty over the years. Yet to me,
my job was more than dealing with Monty's eccentricities. It was
being able to make the perfect pairing between one of our writers
and a producer or an incredible production company. It was the
hours I'd spent in that cramped office editing scripts, completely
lost in helping a writer find their way. The edits that weren't strictly
a part of our service—I just loved doing them. It was a demanding
job, but I'd made it my own. I didn't know what I'd do without it.
I didn't know who I would *be* without it. Now, that was a sobering
thought.

"Ezra needs to sign that addendum," I said without thinking.

"*Does* he?" Monty's voice was heavy with sarcasm. "Whatever
would I do without my sage assist—" He stopped abruptly. "You
know," he said, his tone suddenly airy, "it's a shame. Before all this
unpleasantness, I was going to talk to you about stepping up."

What was he saying? *Had he been considering making me an agent?*

Rap rap rap. I jumped.

"Hello? Miss Summers? Are you still in there?" I recognized the voice of the waiter I'd spoken to earlier. He was outside the door. "I have two gentlemen here who are asking to see Monty." He coughed. "For some reason, they were under the impression he might be in our VIP area, and the maître d' is rather touchy about uninvited guests." I winced guiltily. "I'm terribly sorry, but he's really quite insistent that you help us resolve the . . . *misunderstanding*, so that they can leave."

"They can't see me stuck in here. Get me out, get me out!" Monty hissed.

"Just one minute!" I called to the waiter. "Monty," I said more quietly, "I'm going to need you to push from your side when I say. Okay? Just trust me." I steadied my feet.

Rap rap rap.

"Hurry up, will you!"

"Okay," I told him. "On three. One. Two . . ."

"Madam! I must insist you come out now, or I'm going to have to come in."

A few things happened in quick succession.

First, Monty panicked. Rather than waiting for me to say "three," he shoved forcefully against his side of the door. Completely unprepared, my hands slipped off the handle and I had to catch myself against the next stall. As if on cue, the blond waiter rushed into the room, flanked by Sam-and-Max. Which of course was when the stall door sprang open and Monty flew out, gliding across the wet floor like he'd been shot from a cannon.

He tripped and sprawled onto the tiles, landing at the waiter's feet. To his credit, Monty leaped up impressively fast. He was a sweaty mess, but he brushed his waistcoat down, smoothed his hair back, and tried very hard not to look like he'd just exited a women's restroom stall at thirty miles per hour. He almost pulled it off.

"Sam, Max, what a surprise. I was just helping my assistant. *Toilet troubles*," he said, sotto voice, gesturing to where I stood.

I turned so pink I blended in with the wall.

"Glad we caught you," said possibly Sam, shock melting away as his default positivity took over. "Almost literally, eh? Ha, ha. We just wanted to chat about the addendum, as you promised you'd have it signed by today." *By today?* How long had Monty been sitting on this?

Monty waved a hand as if it was nothing. "My assistant is handling it. She has a meeting with Ezra first thing Monday. He can't wait to share the pages."

I stared at him. *I do?* There had to be a mistake. NOB wouldn't listen to me. For him, I had only two functions: 1) Book the meetings, and 2) Force him to attend them. After getting him there, my job was done, leaving Monty to swan in for all the expensive meals and drinking sessions he used to slip boring things into the conversation, like when might the script NOB had been paid to write actually materialize.

Monty's smile was full of easy reassurance. For the producers' benefit, not mine. "I've already got him to agree to sign, so don't worry, it's only the paperwork," he said to me, the very image of a wise, benevolent agent placating a nervous underling. Part of this job was not reacting when your boss told a blatant lie. "All you need to do is hand him the pen." His pale blue eyes flashed. "It's all good practice for your next step."

"Next step?" I repeated. Almost imperceptibly, Monty nodded. "Of course," I said smoothly as my heart sped up. He'd been serious earlier. He might actually promote me. *If* the agency survived.

"Now, was there anything else?" Monty said, tugging at his shirt cuffs and giving Sam-and-Max his signature smile as if everything was settled.

"Just one more thing." Sam-and-Max looked Monty up and down. "What's that you're covered in?"

Monty's smile faltered as he looked down at his sopping-wet front.

The waiter picked up the empty bottle from the floor. It was squashed from being under Monty's foot. "That would be body oil, sir."

Silence followed this statement.

In the light filtering in from the restaurant, I could see a glistening snail trail leading from the toilet door to where Monty now stood, drenched in oil. *Oh, no.* I had picked up the wrong bottle. *Why would a private members' club have body oil in the rest—Ugh.* I shuddered. Judging by the deeply uncomfortable expressions on Sam-and-Max's faces, they were clearly a few steps ahead of me.

"You know what?" one of the producers said. "This looks like a bad time."

At that, Monty recovered himself. "Then maybe next time," he said, with as much dignity as he could muster, "you'll call first."

Chapter 3

--- --- --- --- ---

NOB

EXT: A BEAUTIFUL TREE-LINED STREET IN SOUTH
KENSINGTON—MONDAY, NOVEMBER 19, 8:55 A.M.

EVIE is holding two takeaway coffees in a
tray as she squeezes past a gleaming red
sports car parked across the pavement. She
climbs up stone steps to a large dark green
front door and glances back at the car,
rolling her eyes. Her cheeks are flushed as
she squares her shoulders, puts on a
determined expression, and prepares to
knock.

My fingers were left grasping air as the door flew open and the coffees lurched with the unexpected motion. I managed to steady them, expecting to see NOB, only for a tall strawberry blonde to stride out and stop just short of treading on me. I had a weird sense of familiarity, despite not knowing her, before my brain caught up with my eyes. She was Monica Reed, the Yorkshire-born Hollywood darling. My breath caught in my throat. She'd dated NOB on and off for the last few years—though God only knows what the attraction was. He was a boychild, and she was the woman who'd stormed into Hollywood demanding equal pay and diverse roles for women over the age of thirty-five. It was safe to say I was a bit of a fan.

I'd seen NOB's various partners come and go over the years. His type was blondes in their early twenties. Monica was different. Regal, statuesque . . . older than him. Her yoga gear showed off her incredible figure, and her wavy shoulder-length hair gleamed rose-gold in the wintry morning light. She caught me staring and I blushed.

The tail end of an L.A.-inflected apology drifted down the hallway. It was the kind of voice that sounded well traveled, the voice of someone who had experienced more of the world than you ever would, and taken the pictures with sedated tigers to prove it. The vocal equivalent of a Tinder profile.

"Mon, babe, this isn't another brushoff, I promise. There's no one else. I have a meeting I can't avoid. Believe me, I've tried."

Of course NOB would call Monica Reed *babe*. The actress favored to win her second Oscar for her upcoming film *The Con*, a period piece set in a convent in which the nuns run an illegal gin distillery. I'd heard she'd become fluent in Italian just for that one role.

I smiled shyly at her.

She looked me over. "It's okay, Ez, I believe you. It's *clearly* just a work thing," she called back to him.

Ouch. So maybe they were better matched than I realized.

"Then believe me when I say my agent's assistant is a total pain in my arse," NOB said from the hallway. He was rustling around for something. "She emailed about this meeting on Friday while we were at the club. If she ever got a life, I'd be able to enjoy mine." NOB's tousled blond hair came into view as he handed Monica a set of keys. "Oh, hi, Stevie." He couldn't have appeared less concerned about my overhearing, probably because that had been his exact reply to me at the time.

He'd chosen to wear pajama bottoms and nothing else for our meeting. If my heart skipped at the sight of his muscled chest, visible V, and ridiculous "just stepped out of a yacht catalog" good looks, then I decided to forgive myself. He might be an arse, but he was certainly pretty.

"Evie," I corrected, a few seconds too late. Then, just to make absolutely sure I had no dignity left: "And I was out on Friday too." *You big jerk.*

NOB draped an arm around Monica's shoulders. Just two ridiculously good-looking human beings, generously adding to the amount of beauty in the world simply by being in it. Standing there in my 1950s-style dress, beautifully handmade by my mum, I felt I was from a different world entirely.

"You're leaking, by the way," Monica said, shifting her Birkin higher on her shoulder.

I glanced down. The coffee had pooled in the cardboard tray and was dripping all over my Doc Martens. "Shit," I said. *Very professional, Evie.* "Sorry," I added.

NOB looked amused.

"At least they're wipe-clean," Monica said. Then, turning away from me, she pulled NOB toward her and gave him a kiss that would have absolutely scandalized the nun she was playing. Dabbing her lips, she slipped a large pair of sunglasses on and strode down the steps.

"I'll message you," NOB called after her. She held up a hand in acknowledgment.

He looked back at me with irritation. "What do you want?"

I held my smile. "I'm here for our meeting."

"Where's Monty?"

I'd been very clear this was my meeting. "It's just me. And I have coffee. Can I come in?" I lifted the tray. "I've got a soggy bottom."

He let that statement hang for a moment before lifting his eyebrows. "Well, nobody likes a soggy bottom."

I kept my smile while I died a little inside.

NOB nodded at the coffee. "Is one of those a decaf triple-shot soy latte?"

"Of course."

"Then come on in." He walked away, leaving me to follow him. *Right, Evie. Get it together. You can do this.* My job depended on it. And maybe my promotion.

If I got NOB to sign *and* agree to finish the script on time, then maybe I would finally, *finally,* be made an agent. I could expand the agency's remit from white male screenwriters by bringing in, well, anyone else really, but I longed to work with incredible female screenwriters. No more putting all our eggs in one NOB-shaped basket. So to speak.

In the sleek black kitchen, trying to avoid multiple reflections of my face in the mirrored tiles, I handed NOB his coffee and dumped the tray in the recycling.

NOB took a swig and winced. "This is terrible."

"That's decaf for you." I fished the bag of sticky muffins out of my satchel and went to offer him one. He caught it before I could put it on the gleaming black marble of the breakfast bar.

"Hey!" NOB held the muffin away from his sculpted chest like its calories might contaminate him. He flipped the lid on his trash can and threw it in. "This is a gluten-free household."

I swallowed the considerable bite I'd just taken, and he watched me with a look of disgust that I assumed masked a desperate longing for carbs. "Your new place is lovely," I said into the silence.

NOB shrugged, his eyes shifting elsewhere. "I had it remodeled by the same designer Tom uses." I kept my expression neutral. If NOB was anyone else, I would have asked who Tom was. But he was NOB, so he meant Tom Cruise. He looked over my left shoulder as he said, distantly, "She's really intuitive." I followed his gaze and realized he'd caught his own eye in one of the reflective tiles.

"I can tell."

NOB had split his time between L.A. and London since winning the Oscar for his first—and only—film a few years ago. I wondered if this new house meant he was back in London permanently. The moving boxes would suggest that was the case.

He poured his coffee into the sink with a grimace. "So, what's Monty sent *you* for?" he asked, reminding me of how little he thought of me. I'd schooled myself to ignore NOB's insults over the years. I worked hard at the agency. Monty spent all his time attending to NOB—a full-time job—so I took care of his other clients. Which was fine. Since the Breakup, I'd had more time to dedicate to the agency anyway. My friends cautioned me about maintaining a healthy work/life balance, but they didn't factor in that "life" mostly consisted of takeout pizza and Netflix.

"I'm here to discuss your script for Intrepid," I said, feeling less terrible about the news I was preparing to deliver. NOB turned his back on me and cranked up a coffee machine that looked as if it had been modeled on the ridiculous sports car he'd parked across the pavement.

"The producers," I said, raising my voice to compensate for the coffee machine revving its engine, "are really excited to see the script. And they recognize that you've been—"

"What?"

"You've been—"

"Can't hear you."

"WORKING HARD ON IT."

The machine fell silent just as my shout rang out across the kitchen. NOB still had his back to me but his shoulders were hitched up as if he was laughing. He turned his head slightly. "Did you say something?" He waited for me to open my mouth and hit a button on the machine. Steam noisily filled the kitchen until the air was misted and damp. I felt my scalp itch. My hair never did well in heat. It expanded like a marshmallow in hot chocolate.

Not to be deterred, I raised my voice again. "They've given us an extension on the latest deadline." *That you missed, six months ago.* "It's very GENEROUS." The machine fell silent. "You have three—" Then it roared as NOB used 850 horsepower to produce a single shot of decaf coffee.

But rather than drink it, he left the espresso on the side. I eyed it with annoyance.

He grabbed a glass from a cupboard. Wiping crumbs from my hands, I pulled the paperwork from my satchel and followed after him. "All you need to do is sign this. It's a straightforward adden—" *Crrrk!* Now he was filling up the glass with ice from the dispenser on the fridge. "It's an addendum saying you agree to DELIVER THE FULL SCRIPT IN THREE MONTHS."

I believe NOB heard me that time. He paused, very briefly, before pouring the ice into a smoothie maker. He returned to open the fridge and, after a moment of rustling around, tossed something toward me.

"Catch."

I found myself winded by a bag of avocados, which is possibly the most middle-class thing that's ever happened to me. NOB nudged the door shut with his gym-sculpted bottom, his arms laden with various fruits and vegetables, which he promptly loaded into the blender.

"If you could just look at the addendum . . ."

He held out his hand. I sighed with relief and went to give him the folder, but he shook his head. *"Avocados,"* he said, as if I was stupid. I slammed them into his hand, perhaps slightly harder than necessary.

With deft fingers, he began to peel and slice, removing the stones with a knife and a flick of his wrist.

"If you could just"—he chopped as though the work surface had offended him—"agree to the wording."

I shoved the folder under his nose and opened it to reveal . . . nothing. He raised perfect golden brows at me. I looked around, panicked, before seeing the copies of the addendum under NOB's foot. I bent down to tug the pages free and they tore almost in two as they came away. I stood too quickly, only to find myself nose-to-nose with NOB. This close, I could see that the dazzling blue of his left eye contained a burst of hazel.

He smirked. Then, waiting for the exact moment I was going to try to speak again, he pressed the button on the smoothie maker. "Please could you—" *Wrrr.*

"You need to sign—" *Wrrrrrrrr.*

I snapped my hand out and covered the button, breathing hard. His fingers touched mine, still trying to press, but I remained where I was. "You have three months," I said firmly as I held out the torn copies of the addendum. "It's very generous, considering how delayed we are."

The royal "we": agency-speak for "definitely you, but we don't want to appear to be saying this is all your fault." Which it was. Though Monty's mollycoddling hadn't exactly helped.

"All you need to do is sign it, and I'll leave you to your juicing."

"I see." At last, NOB picked up his espresso cup and took a sip. It still had the label on the bottom. Like everything else here, it was new. I wondered why NOB had moved back. Had L.A. not worked out the way he'd hoped?

For a while, NOB had been the go-to writer for every film director wanting to make their name. Yet he hadn't produced a follow-up to *A Heart Lies Bleeding*. It was a small industry. He had the weight of expectation on his shoulders. After such an extraordinary success, he must feel like he had a lot to prove.

Maybe all this attitude was really a response to that pressure. "It must be hard—"

"The thing is, Stevie"—I bit my tongue this time—"I'm not signing that."

Or I'd just let his bare chest go to my head.

Still, I kept my tone soft. "Unfortunately, you have to. If you don't"—I dropped the bombshell he must have known was coming—"they'll cancel the contract outright. You'll be obligated to give them their money back. This addendum at least gives you more time, and a chance to deliver."

"I don't need time," he said petulantly. "I'm not signing."

I took several deep, calming breaths. In all the years of overblown coffee orders, high-end restaurant bookings, arranging his "I only do first class" travel, and his dedication to not even once getting my name right, NOB had never broken me.

He wasn't about to now. I kept my professional mask firmly in place and reminded myself that he didn't know the whole agency was at stake.

I tried a different tactic. "Think of all the time you've put into it so far. What's three more months?" I'd heard every excuse in the book for not writing. Sometimes they just needed to know you were in their corner. "I'm here to help you finish in any way I can."

NOB smirked and opened his mouth. "I heard it," I snapped, before he could say the kind of thing that, until recently, assistants had been putting up with for years.

He shrugged. "Luckily, I don't need your help."

"And why's that?"

"Well, the thing is, Stevie." He tossed back the smoothie. "I haven't even started writing it."

Chapter 4

The Challenge

INT: A KITCHEN FILLED WITH REFLECTIVE
SURFACES—MONDAY, NOVEMBER 19, ONE MINUTE
POST-BOMBSHELL

EVIE stands in front of NOB, one hand on
the kitchen counter to brace herself, as
two expressions war for dominance on her
face—bland professionalism and complete
outrage. NOB pours himself another
smoothie, oblivious to EVIE's gurning.

I fought to remain calm, but when I spoke all the understanding left my voice. *"What?"* The entire agency was at stake, and he hadn't typed a single word? "Monty said—"

He laughed as he drained his drink. "Old Monts said I was writing?"

Now I knew why Monty had been so cagey about showing anyone those pages. "But . . . you knew exactly what you were signing up for." I could feel the heat spreading up my neck.

"I've changed my mind." He wiped his hands and then leaned toward me. "Oscar winners," NOB said, *"don't* write rom-coms."

My mouth went dry. I was going to lose my job because a man who hadn't even managed to get dressed for a meeting had decided he was too good to write a romantic comedy? *"Oscar winners,"* I hissed, "wear clothes to meetings. *Oscar winners* look at someone when they're speaking to them. *Oscar winners* write the damn script they've been paid for."

There was a moment of complete silence, during which NOB seemed to be mentally recalibrating. His gaze sharpened on me and, for the first time possibly ever, he really *looked* at me.

Oh, no. Oh, no. Oh, no. All my internal alert systems were firing, and my skin reacted by turning a deep and ferocious crimson. *What did I just do?* Goodbye promotion.

NOB flashed his perfect white teeth at me. "Well, well, Evie Summers. There you are."

I blinked. Of all the responses I might have expected . . .

"I . . . What?"

NOB folded his arms across his chest, the movement accentuating his carefully honed muscles. "Five years of knowing you—"

"Seven." (*Oh, God, Evie, just stop talking.*)

A quirk of his brow. "All these years of knowing you and this is the first time I've seen the real you."

Of all the patronizing . . . As he looked at me, I suddenly had an inkling of what it might feel like to have the attention of someone like NOB. He was, though I would never admit it to him, ludicrously good-looking. Golden skin, sky-blue eyes, cheekbones for days, a jawline that was movie-star straight and firm . . .

What a shame all that beauty was wasted on a wanker.

"Actually," I said imperiously, "the real me is far more polite."

NOB pulled out one of the stools at the breakfast bar and gestured to it. For a moment I wanted to refuse, but my knees were trembling too hard and I collapsed gracelessly onto the black leather.

"I'd love to hear more about all these Oscar winners you know so well," he said, still standing. "But first, let's be real. I won't write a *rom-com*. It's not my brand."

As long as we were being real . . . "Why not?" He had signed up to write one, after all. And while the massive upfront fee and months of being relentlessly wined and dined (aka The Full Monty Special) had certainly helped, he'd known the brief from the start: The producers wanted a modern twist on the "meet-cute"—that moment in a romantic comedy when the two love interests meet for the first time. They used the term frequently, as if showing off their knowledge of the genre.

NOB sneered. "I write real life, not fantasy. Romantic comedies are meaningless make-believe for people too stupid to realize they're being fed a pack of lies about love." He looked at me distractedly. "Your hair is very big," he said.

I touched it. The curls had separated in the heat and steam from the espresso machine. There was no saving it, so I shrugged, recognizing a distraction tactic. "Rom-coms give people hope when they need it most." I flashed back to all the times I'd rage-watched *You've Got Mail* post-Breakup so I could throw things at Tom Hanks's face. *Not relevant.* "They have heart, and meaning, and they help people."

"You're talking like you think they're realistic."

"I do, actually." Or I had, once. Not that he needed to know that. I used to love how Ricky would say the way we'd met was a meet-cute. Not destiny, but something like it. I'd stumbled into an alley, during one particularly overwhelming assistant drinks, needing some air, only to meet a guy doing the same thing from the bar opposite. If it had been a few minutes earlier for either one of us, we'd never have met, never known that our person was, for a brief window of time, only a few meters away.

I exhaled slowly. The pain from the Breakup had dulled over the last twelve months, but occasionally it could still surprise me.

NOB snorted, clearly mistaking my expression for misty-eyed whimsy.

"That's cute," he said. "I don't do *cute*, and that's all those hack producers want. I write movies about the kind of love people recognize. Obsessive, needy, toxic, *real* love, not *meet-cutes*."

Movie. One movie. Singular. But this wasn't the moment to remind him of that.

"*A Heart Lies Bleeding* is beautiful, but it's not the only kind of love story out there," I insisted, aware of how painfully earnest I sounded.

"You watched my movie," he said, leaning back against the unit. "And you liked it?"

It ended with both characters unable to admit that their relationship has disintegrated beyond repair and staying together anyway. It had made me sob so hard I had to follow it with a Disney marathon just to feel like there was light left in the world.

"Of course. But people need *The Proposal* just as much as they need *A Heart Lies Bleeding*. A good meet-cute shows us it's possible for a single moment to change everything for the better."

NOB shook his head. "Please. No one's ever met anyone the way they do in those movies. The coincidences. The clichés. In real life if someone spilled a drink on you, you'd be pissed off, maybe sue them if it's a hot one, not fall for them. Real love can't be contrived."

"Tell that to Tinder," I said tiredly. Not for the first time, I marveled at the irony of a bunch of men appointing NOB the new Nora Ephron.

He slid the creased addendum pages back toward me. "Tell the producers I'm not signing. I'd rather return the money than risk my reputation on this trash." NOB turned away from me, pouring himself another smoothie from the machine. "My life coach will be here at ten. You can let yourself out." As quickly as that, I'd been dismissed. It was like a spotlight had been turned off.

I picked up the papers, knowing I had no choice but to tell Monty I'd failed to even get us three more months.

"I told Monty from day one I didn't want to do this," NOB said as I walked away. "He shouldn't be surprised."

"Then why agree to write it in the first place?" I snapped, turning. The words were out before I could stop them, and I found I didn't care. If the agency was going under anyway, what did I have to lose?

NOB ignored me, leaving me to stand there, getting angrier and angrier. It was his stupid ego that had got us all into this mess, agreeing to write something when he couldn't actually . . .

Wait. Was that it? Could it be that the great and powerful NOB had writer's block after all?

It made a terrible sense. What if he'd had every intention of writing the rom-com . . . but *couldn't*? NOB had been hailed as one of Hollywood's hottest new talents, yet in the three years since he'd won his Oscar he hadn't given Monty a single script to sell. Monty would excuse him, saying that greatness couldn't be rushed. But then Sam-and-Max had come along offering him their next project. What if he'd signed on to show Hollywood he was still hot property . . . only to find rom-coms weren't the easy ride he'd imagined?

Time to test this theory.

"I know how you can write this rom-com."

NOB glanced around as if in surprise. "Oh, you're still here?" he said.

"Just listen. In three months' time, you could have a finished script, just like you originally agreed. You keep the money. Sam-and-Max sing your praises in Hollywood. We all walk away happy." NOB rolled his eyes. "Or," I said, going straight for his weak spot, "we cancel the contract and send out the release before the end of the week."

"Release?"

"To get ahead of any announcement from Intrepid," I said

airily. "The producers will want to publicize that they're looking for a new writer and that Ezra Chester is off the project."

NOB wouldn't just be the award-winning screenwriter with no follow-up. He'd be the man who couldn't write a rom-com. *It doesn't seem like such a silly genre now, does it?*

For a few seconds, he said nothing, his eyes going distant. Then his attention snapped back to me.

I held my breath.

"I know I'm going to regret saying this," he said. My heart did a preemptive victory jig. "But I'm listening."

Thank you, NOB's ego.

The genre wasn't the real problem, it was his *excuse*. I just needed to find a way to get him writing. I'd start with coaxing him to admit he was wrong about rom-coms. Given his scorn for meet-cutes, all I had to do was show him it *was* possible to meet someone exactly the way Harry met Sally . . .

How hard could that be?

"If I prove it's possible for people to meet exactly like they do in rom-coms, you can sign the addendum and write the script secure in the knowledge that the genre is realistic and completely *on brand* for you."

He narrowed his eyes. "How exactly would you do that?" I walked carefully toward him across the kitchen, as if he were a wild animal and not a screenwriter refusing to admit he has writer's block. *Same difference.*

"The producers want a new kind of meet-cute," I said slowly, thinking it through. "I'll bring you real-life examples of couples meeting each other just like in a film." I was sure I could find stories. When you were single, the Internet was full of them. "Ones that will show you you're being . . ." *Arrogant. Willfully ignorant. An asshat.* "*Short-sighted* about the genre."

NOB was thoroughly unimpressed. "Anyone can Google, Red."

As I glared at the nickname, an idea started to form. A ridiculous, totally foolish idea.

Because he was right: What I was offering wasn't enough. It wasn't just about getting him to sign the addendum so he could put off the inevitable humiliation for three months. I had to get him to *write*. For that, he'd need inspiration. And lots of it.

"I'll do it, then," I said.

He blinked. "Do what, exactly?"

"I'll be your living proof. Sign that addendum and *I'll* meet someone exactly like they do in rom-coms. I'll re-create the meet-cutes from those films. The road trips. The holidays. The chance encounters. I'll keep going until one of them works."

But you can't even meet someone through Tinder, my voice of reason pointed out. I shushed it.

NOB looked me up and down with a sly smile. "So what you're saying is, if even *you* can meet someone that way, I have to believe it's possible."

I put the addendum down on the breakfast table. "So what *you're* saying is we have a deal?"

His golden brows quirked. "Steady on, Red."

"Evie."

"Signing that will just give me three more months of the producers and Monty being on my back, distracting me."

"That's what I'm here for," I said, trying not to sound too eager. *I'll show Monty what I'm capable of.* "Tell them I'm assisting you. I'll keep them at bay."

NOB studied the wall behind me for a moment. "Say you do meet someone. How will I know you're telling the truth? You could just bribe someone to say he fell for you. And you'd have to find someone pretty quickly to give me time to write a whole script."

"All valid concerns," I said, quickly retrieving pad and pen from my bag. "So let's talk terms."

"Isn't that what the addendum's for?"

"The addendum is for your deal with Intrepid. *This* is for the deal between us."

I wrote down, *If Evie Summers ("The Assistant") can prove to* ~~N~~ *Ezra Chester ("The Screenwriter")—*

"What did you just cross out?"

"Nothing."

—that the "Romantic Comedy" genre is realistic by meeting some-one the same way people do in rom-coms (i.e., through a "meet-cute"), then he will submit the full script to Intrepid Productions by their deadline of February 18 of next year.

NOB leaned over my shoulder. "You have to fall in love with them too."

Surely he's not serious? "This is about *meeting* someone."

"Exactly." He was clearly enjoying himself. "You meet someone, and you both fall in love. Isn't that the rom-com way? You have to find Mr. Happy Ending. Otherwise, no deal."

My fingers tightened on the pen. *This is your life he's talking about.* It had been a year since Ricky. I didn't know if I was ready to meet someone, never mind like this.

But surely NOB was only trying to make things difficult. Right now, I just needed him to sign. Then I'd get him writing. *Worry about the love part later.*

"Fine." I made the amendment with a flutter of apprehension. Though if he was going to get his way, I'd get mine.

The Screenwriter agrees to start work on the script from the mo-ment he signs the addendum, I wrote. *And will send his pages to The Assistant on a regular basis.*

The amusement faded. "What?"

"Just making sure you can get it finished on time," I said. "Oth-erwise it wouldn't be responsible of me to let you sign this. Plus, I'll need proof you're actually writing."

He folded his arms, something unreadable slipping into his eyes. "I'll start writing, but there will be no happy ending from me until you get yours. And the pages will go to Monts. He's my agent, last time I checked."

I faltered, then made the change. *As long as he writes the script, that's all that matters.* The agency would be safe, and so would my promotion.

"Here." He plucked the pen from my fingers. With brisk strokes he wrote, *The Assistant agrees to write detailed reports on every meet-cute for The Screenwriter.*

"I'll need proof you're actually doing it," he mimicked me, right down to the accent.

Snatching the pen back, I went to cross the line out—and hesitated. *This could work in my favor.* He probably thought the reports would keep me busy and off his back. But maybe one of these "reports" would be exactly what he needed to kick-start his writing.

"There's just one more thing," I said, and wrote: *The Screenwriter and The Assistant agree that the above arrangement will never be disclosed to Monty.*

If Monty ever found out how tenuous the agreement was—an understatement, if there ever was one—he'd be furious. He'd assured the producers that he had everything under control. If he discovered that the deal was resting on his assistant's love life, he'd be humiliated. Forget about the fact that I'd succeeded where he had failed. I'd be fired before NOB even had the chance to miss the new deadline. Better that he believed NOB was writing of his own volition. It would be one less thing for me to worry about.

"Keeping secrets from your boss, Red? You're just full of surprises today." NOB considered me. "You know you're only going to prove that rom-coms are bullshit, don't you?"

"A lot can happen in three months," I said.

"Agreed." An expression flitted across his face, but it was gone too quickly to catch.

"Are we done?"

I held out my hand. He took it. "I need to hear you say it."

"Red," said NOB. "If you can prove it's possible to fall in love like they do in those movies, I'll write the damn script."

I pushed our handwritten agreement and the copies of the addendum over. He hesitated, just a little, before signing them.

"Maybe I was wrong about you, Red. You're not so boring after all."

That's not the only thing you're wrong about, I thought.

Because whether he liked it or not, I was going to get him to finish that *damn script.* No matter what it took.

Chapter 5

The Moral Support

EXT: EVIE'S FLAT, EAST DULWICH—FRIDAY,
NOVEMBER 23, 8:30 P.M.

EVIE rushes up the tiled path in her tiny
garden and opens her front door, shrugging
a canvas bag higher on her shoulder. It
clinks. A bunch of basil and a baguette are
poking out of the top. Once inside the
compact hallway, she wriggles her key into
the lock of a second door while hastily
scrolling through her phone messages.

MARIA: Evie darling, we have arrived at your flat. We're just
outside

JEREMY: why aren't you answering? Tell us you're in there. This
weekend is going to be painful enough planning She Who
Must Not Be Named's hen do without having to deal with your
flatmate alone

SARAH: did my instructions come through?

JEREMY: oh, hi, Voldemort. Yes, we received the 19-page
PowerPoint presentation and reading list. Thrilled to be
included in the acknowledgments section

MARIA: let us innnnnnn

YOU HAVE 10 MISSED CALLS FROM MARIA NOWAK

MARIA: hello, it's your best friends here, who are hoping you are just around the corner because Jane is in and it sounds like she has company. Whoever she's with is having a VERY good time

JEREMY: we're guessing it's not you

MARIA: Evie Doris Summers where ARE you?

JEREMY: don't do this to us, Evie. Oh, God, Jane is coming

JEREMY: and now she's heading toward the door

I'd tried so hard to be on time for their visit. When they'd been here last, Monty had declared a Code Red (out-of-town client lost in Underground) and they'd been halfway through dessert by the time I'd made it to the restaurant.

This time I was late because Sam-and-Max had confirmed receipt of the addendum, and Monty had wanted to talk to me about it. He hadn't hidden his surprise when I'd returned to the office with NOB's signature on Monday, even holding the (slightly wrinkled) pages up to the light as if checking their authenticity. "You've taken on a lot of responsibility, Evelyn," he'd said eventually, smoothing out the paper. "See that it pays off and in three months' time, we'll be celebrating more than the finished script." He'd smiled at my hopeful expression, then brought me down to earth by giving me half a dozen contracts to check "urgently" before I left.

I entered the living room to see Jeremy, head in hands, his curly hair falling over his forehead and his usually crisp clothes rumpled on his slender frame as if to echo his despair. And Maria, nodding at whatever my flatmate Jane was saying, thick dark hair pulled back into a ponytail as she clutched an empty wineglass like it was the only thing nailed down in a storm. An expression of forced politeness wrestled with wide-eyed horror on her pretty face as Jane finished a particularly animated story that involved the kind of miming you don't see at kids' birthday parties.

"—and that's when it fell out on the floor!"

Maria flinched.

I shook the bag so they could hear telltale clinking, and Jeremy leaped up. "Oh, Evie, thank God, I hate you, you goddess." He bent to embrace me. "Jane was just explaining why she took so long letting us into the flat." Jane smiled behind him. I grabbed Maria next, trying not to show the tears that sprang to my eyes at seeing them. I wished Sarah could be here too, but this weekend was for planning the hen do we all had to pretend she hadn't already planned herself.

I hid my expression from Jeremy, but Maria, being Maria, caught sight of it and held on to me a little longer.

"It's so good to see you never do this to us again," she said in one breath. Jeremy had already taken the bag from me and was filling a spare glass.

"Jane," I said, taking it from him gratefully, "you have a date to get to, don't you?"

Jane stood in one sinuous movement, her black hair gleaming under the light. "I do. He's in the bedroom. I'll see *you* later." This last part was aimed at Jeremy, who raised his wineglass.

"Still gay, Jane."

"Still interested." She smiled, then slunk out.

Jeremy shook his head. "Does anyone else feel both appalled *and* slightly confused about themselves?"

"Are you still working late every night?" Maria asked me, her tone casual.

Jeremy poured more wine. "I mean, obviously I'm going to drink enough to forget most of what she just described, but part of me still hopes to be Jane when I grow up."

"Just tonight," I said to her.

"Evie," she reprimanded, seeing through the fib. I knew Maria wasn't mad at me; she was hurt. We barely saw each other, and I hadn't been there to greet them on time. Again. I'd promised them a meal after their journey, and now it was after eight and the vegetables I'd bought at lunch were wilting in the bag. I couldn't bring myself to tell her that I'd been finishing off the pile of contracts so I could please Monty. She'd insist, again, that I needed to leave the agency. Maria was full of all kinds of love, and her tough love packed a punch.

"I'm fine, I promise," I insisted.

Out of all my friends, Maria had known me the longest, and at times like this, those years showed. I still remembered the day the little girl with the thick, dark hair and huge gray eyes helped me up when some other kids had pushed me over on the playground. She's been my protector ever since. Two became three in high school, when we had Jeremy's acerbic wit to get us through. Sarah joined us when we all started at Sheffield University. She lived with us in student halls and—possibly because no one else could cope with her—she became a firm part of our group. The four of us were close, but Maria probably knew me better than I knew myself.

To my relief, she didn't push further. She sat down next to Jeremy, and I eased into my favorite chair, hoping that would be the end of it. I rested my wine on the well-worn arm, where it slipped on something. When I wiped at whatever it was, Jeremy let out a gagging sound. I looked over at him, wondering what was wrong as I rubbed my fingers together. My friends both sat there with vaguely guilty expressions. "What?"

Maria grimaced. "Oh, sweetie. You missed the beginning of Jane's story. The part that took place on that chair."

Jeremy tipped back his wine. "It was bad. As in burn-the-chair bad."

"RIP chair, good knowing you." They clinked their glasses.

"Oh, *God*." I sprang up and flew to the door. "Jane!" I hollered as I hurried down the hallway to the kitchen to scrub my hands.

Her music dipped. "Yes, my duck?"

Before responding, I ran through my calming mantra: *She hasn't increased the rent in three years. She hasn't increased the rent in three years.* Jane's lifestyle wasn't usually an issue. We'd set some ground rules early on to avoid any mishaps. Namely, I got sex-free communal spaces and Jane could have her nightly visitors, which I'd know about only through her jaw-droppingly filthy stories and on those occasions when she used the dishwasher to sterilize her sex toys. She had a reassuringly high bar for hygiene, but that isn't a comfort when you reach in for a cup first thing in the morning and pull out a dildo.

"You promised no sex in the living room."

She leaned out of her bedroom wearing some extremely complicated-looking underwear. "Of course, my darling! We only *began* in the living room." Well, that was some relief, at least. "We finished in the kitchen."

I recoiled, then grabbed the sponge to wipe down every surface.

I could hear the rumbles of a deep baritone drifting from Jane's open door.

"One more thing," Jane sang out. "Trev promises he'll replace the sponge."

- - - - - - - - - -

"Are you really going to do it?" Maria leaned forward over her plate to bite into her takeout pizza. The moment they'd heard the full story about my deal with NOB, Sarah's military-grade hen do presentation had been abandoned ("Absolute No-Nos for the Perfect Hen!! 1) NO penises. Jeremy: *That's me out.* (a) not on springs, (b) or inflatable,

(c) *especially* not edible. (d) Jeremy, your penis doesn't count. Jeremy: *Exactly which category does she think my penis falls into?*)

Jeremy waved his wineglass. "Just so we're clear: You're going to try and fall in love within the next three months by re-creating meet-cutes from rom-coms?"

"This is for my career, Jem, not my love life. I just need to get NOB through his writer's block. I'm hoping then he won't be as hung up on the love thing." Silence. "In case there's any doubt, I do know this is completely bonkers."

"He's such a . . . a *nob!*" Maria said forcefully. She was the sweetest, kindest, most forgiving person I knew. And she hated NOB with a fire even I couldn't muster. "Evie, are you absolutely sure you want to go through with this? Don't let NOB force you into something you aren't ready for. He'd never ask this of a guy."

"Yes, put yourself first. Be careful," Jeremy intoned dutifully.

"I know how it sounds, but aside from the love part, the deal was entirely my idea. It's not just about saving the agency. Monty's promised to promote me to agent if NOB writes the script."

"He really said that?" Maria asked.

I nodded, understanding the doubt in her voice. "He's never even hinted at it before." It was part of the reason my friends found it so hard to understand why I stayed working for him, but agent positions were rare, and though I'd gone for interviews, I'd never made it to the second round. I had to prove to Monty—and, if I was being honest, to myself—that I was good enough before I could move on. Ricky had always got that. I wished they could too.

Jeremy exchanged a look with Maria. I suddenly got the feeling they'd been discussing me at length on the journey here.

"What?" I said, feeling a little ambushed.

Maria went first. "Ever since Dicky, we've noticed that you've been putting even more of your energy into work." They'd been calling Ricky that since the night of the Breakup. I loved them for it, even if I couldn't bring myself to do the same. "We want to make sure you have time left for yourself. Maybe even for real-life dating."

That gave me pause. I hadn't realized my lack of dating had them concerned. They came from two different ends of the dating spectrum from me. Jeremy was rarely without a date, and Maria had never been on one. She and David had been together since they were sixteen. To her, the dating jungle was more of a well-maintained patio.

Though from the sounds of things, it was my complete lack of *anything* post-Breakup that worried them.

"We know how much your career means to you, and having this job helped you at a really bad time," she said, ever so gently. I'd started at the agency not long after my dad died, and she was right. It had filled up the worst of those days. "But maybe a break would do you good. You could do anything you wanted to. Even start writing again." After Dad, my friends had tried to keep me writing. They'd never fully understood why I couldn't get back to the version of me who'd stay up all night feverishly typing, who'd push all her favorite films on them, encouraging them to treat dialogue like it was art. I'd never found the right way to tell them what that agent had told me. It was just too awful. "We're concerned you aren't taking care of yourself down here."

I busied myself by grabbing another slice of pizza. Sometimes I worried that my friends believed I existed in a state of arrested development. Like there were still some tick boxes I hadn't checked in order to become a full-fledged adult, as they had with their mortgages, savings accounts, and sensible life choices.

Maria sensed my distress. "We're just saying that you don't have to spend what's left of your spare time outside of work doing this. You don't need to put your personal life on the line for a man like NOB, or for Monty. He should be the one doing everything he can to save his agency."

Jeremy leaned over and put his hand on my head. "What Maria is saying, dearest Evie, is that we only wish you knew your worth. Because to us you are priceless."

My eyes filled with tears for the second time that evening, and I nodded, swallowing a few times before finally speaking. "Thank you for caring. It means a lot, really. But I want to go through with this. I am going to get that promotion. Plus"—I gave them a small grin—"anything is better than Tinder."

My friends pulled me in for a hug and I held on tightly to their arms.

"Right," Jeremy said, sitting back. "Have we finished with the considerate-friends bit for now?"

"To due diligence," said Maria, raising her glass.

"Great." Jeremy scooted forward, grabbed his overnight bag from the side of the sofa, and pulled out a large rolled-up notepad. "Because we made you a list."

Moments later, he had the pad propped up with a series of colored markers laid out on the coffee table. The first sheet said *Sarah's Hen Do!* in Maria's handwriting.

"Ugh. No." Jeremy flipped over the page.

I felt a flash of guilt at our absolute lack of planning.

"If you're determined to do this," explained Maria, "then we are here for you a hundred percent. You will get that NOB to write the script."

"Evie," Jeremy said grandly, uncapping a pink marker and turning the pad around to reveal what was written on it. "We are going to help you fall in love."

Chapter 6

The List

```
INT: LIVING ROOM—FRIDAY, NOVEMBER 23,
10:15 P.M.

EVIE is sitting on the carpet, leaning
against the black velvet couch, a glass of
wine halfway to her mouth. JEREMY is
kneeling in front of a large notepad with
The Challenge! written on it, arms splayed
in a ta-da gesture. MARIA is sitting on the
sofa behind EVIE. She's giving little
encouraging gestures to JEREMY that EVIE
can't see.
```

"Not that I don't fully appreciate your efforts, but I meant what I said. I only agreed to the love part to get NOB to sign. I have no intention of actually falling for someone." Not after Ricky.

"Sure, we know that," said Jeremy, glancing behind me at Maria. He drew a line under *The Challenge!* "But hear us out. Evie Summers, from the very moment you agreed to this deal with NOB, you entered the Challenge meet-cute. As seen in *10 Things I Hate About You* (RIP Heath Ledger, too beautiful for this world), *She's All That*, and *How to Lose a Guy in Ten Days*. To the uncultured, very different films. But they each come down to the same thing: a challenge is issued, followed by inevitable misunderstandings, brutal betrayals, and, ultimately, love." He wrote *Love* on the pad. "The Challenge meet-cute often overlaps with the 'love to hate you' romcom, but then we realized the only person you hate is NOB."

"It's funny to think," Maria chipped in, "but if this was an actual rom-com, you'd end up with the arrogant writer who, it would turn out, was only using his massive ego to hide an endearing lack of confidence." There was a moment of stunned silence in which we both stared at her. "I'm kidding! You'd never fall for that cockhat."

"Drunk Maria, everybody," toasted Jeremy.

I raised my glass too, as my brain helpfully reminded me of NOB's sculpted chest. *Stupid brain.*

Jeremy powered on. "Now, as per any self-respecting Challenge meet-cute, there's a deadline. You've got three months. You said you need to send regular 'progress reports' to NOB to keep him inspired. To help you stay on track, I present to you your carefully curated meet-cutes, chosen by the experts." He waved the tip of the pen between himself and Maria. I gave him a pointed look. Jeremy was the biggest cynic I knew. "What? So I have watched a few rom-coms, no big deal. Your choices are . . ." He hit the board with the tip of the marker. "The Road Trip: *When Harry Met Sally. Elizabethtown. Thelma and Louise.*"

"Pass on that last one. I want to meet someone, not drive with them off a cliff."

"Isn't that all relationships?" Maria and I both rolled our eyes. "Okay, fine, but no more vetoes."

"It's not even a rom-com!"

"Hush, now, remember your gratitude." That told me. Jeremy flipped the page. "Then there's the Holiday Romance. Also doubles as the Christmas rom-com. Most famously: *The Holiday. Love Actually. Bridget Jones's Diary. A Christmas Prince.* Don't give me that look. I wasn't one of the people Netflix called out for watching it twice a day for two weeks." He avoided our eyes as he revealed the next page.

It bore the words *Big Finale??* in giant letters. "We'll come back to that." He turned over to a list that looked a little more "drank wine on train."

"'Stalk Someone'?"

"*While You Were Sleeping.* A stone-cold classic," said Jeremy.

"I don't intend to get arrested, Jem." I moved on to the next one. "'The One Where They Meet in a Bookshop'?" I read out.

Jeremy started to tick off on his fingers. "*You've Got Mail, When Harry Met Sally—*"

"You've already used that one."

"Venn diagram," called Maria. Jeremy flipped to a very complicated-looking series of overlapping circles with headings like "Christmas" and "Hugh Grant," filled in with various rom-coms from pre–golden age to now. It was a work of drunken genius. "There's some overlap."

"I can see that," I said, beginning to smile.

The living room door flew open. "Darlings!"

Jeremy reached for the wine bottle.

"Jane!" I said loudly, aware of how the room must look. "How was your date?"

"I'll tell you in the morning."

A pair of arms snaked around her slender waist and a dark-haired man peered over her shoulder into the room. He was gorgeous, like a young Antonio Banderas. All three of us gawped. Sometimes I thought Jane's relationship spectrum was like a beautiful prism, albeit one that had to be dishwasher-safe.

"I'm Trev," he said in a broad East End accent. "Jane's told me loads about you." One might think he'd be talking about me, Jane's flatmate, but he was looking at Jeremy when he spoke.

"Not as much as we heard about you," Jeremy muttered into his glass.

"We just wanted to pop in and ask you about the courgettes

you've put in the fridge." Trev nudged her. "And the aubergine. Are you planning on using them . . . ?"

I held up some pizza. "We decided to stay out of the kitchen. You're welcome to eat them."

Jeremy, who'd been busy rolling up a slice, stopped to shake his head vigorously at me. "Duck," said Jane. "We won't be eating them."

It took me a few seconds to get it. "But they're organic," I said, as if that mattered.

Trev nibbled Jane's ear. "Be right back."

Jane's eyes slid to the pad. "What are you darlings up to?"

Maria gamely stepped in. "We were just trying to think of ways Evie could meet someone in a bookshop," she said.

"You're dating again?" Jane asked me. "How thrilling! Though hardly anyone meets organically anymore."

Speaking of organic, Trev had returned with my vegetables and—unaccountably—a spiralizer.

"What about a book group?" he suggested, munching on the end of a carrot.

Jane tugged it away from his mouth. "Don't waste them. Oh, I know! My friend raves about the one in the Dusty Bookshelf in Peckham. Says it's an absolute scream. It's got such a fun name. What *is* it . . . ?"

I exchanged looks with my friends, but what was the worst that could happen? It was a book group. Jeremy wrote it down.

"How did you two meet?" Maria asked her. Jeremy switched his pizza for more wine.

"Mustache dating app," Jane said promptly.

We all looked as one to Trev's bare upper lip. *"Must Dash,"* Jane enunciated. "It's an app for commuters who want a quick fu—"

"How lovely," Maria interjected.

We were treated to a live demonstration of the "dash" part of the app as Trev chased Jane down the hallway with the courgette.

I closed the door so we couldn't hear anything. "Okay," I said, returning to the list. "So I've got my list of meet-cutes for inspiration. Now show me your plan for the big finale."

I don't think I'd ever seen two people look more pleased with themselves.

Jeremy held up his phone, showing he'd been busy on JEMS.

SARAH: is this hen do-related? Tell me you're not getting distracted!

"Wait, not that one." He scrolled down.

SARAH: got it. Right, count me in for the wedding one.

"What does she mean?"

"That Sarah's wedding is finally going to be useful for something."

"Jeremy," Maria chastised automatically. Still our conscience, even when tipsy.

Jeremy pointed to the middle of the Venn diagram, where the word *Wedding!* was made barely legible by the overlapping circles. "Approximately ninety-five percent of rom-coms feature a wedding, maybe more, I haven't actually done the math. *The Wedding Planner. 27 Dresses. My Best Friend's Wedding.* Having the wedding as your end point is literally the most rom-com thing you could possibly do. This," said Jeremy, spreading his hands, "is your grand finale."

Maria was beaming encouragingly. "Sarah's going to find you the perfect date." She paused at my expression. "She's going to find you *a* date."

"It's Sarah's day, I can't make it about me!"

Jeremy snorted. "Every day is Sarah's day. With this one she's just legitimized it. The wedding is just before your deadline, Evie. It's perfect timing. If you haven't succeeded by then, who better to make sure you do than an obsessive, aggressively organized control freak? Our questionable friendship is finally going to pay off. Evie, my dear, do it for all of us."

I looked to Maria, who shrugged. "Sarah seems happy about it . . ."

"Okay, okay, you win."

Jeremy came back to sit between us on the sofa and we all looked at the word *Wedding!* at the center of the pad.

"I'm really doing it," I said, slightly dazed. "I'm going to live as if I'm in a rom-com for three months."

If I was truly honest, I knew I feared the very thing my friends believed this challenge might be good for. *Am I risking falling in love again?* Ricky's final words to me were at the back of my mind. *I think you're great, Evie,* he'd said. *It's just me. I want more.* It was the ultimate "It's not you, it's me" breakup, only I was still left feeling like I'd failed to be what he wanted. I wasn't grieving anymore, not exactly; but some things linger.

"To Evie," Jeremy declared, as we clinked our glasses, "and her love life."

"Career," I corrected. "And here's to my brilliant friends proving, with a little manipulation, real life can be like the movies."

Jeremy held two books from the coffee table over my lap like they were a director's clapper board, bringing them together with a snap. *"Action."*

Chapter 7

The Drink Spill Takes One and Two

From: Evelyn.Summers@WJM.co.uk
To: JEMS
Subject: IT WENT REALLY BADLY WRONG
November 26, 10:30 a.m.

Hi guys, so I'm about to send You Know Who the details of
my first meet-cute attempt—The Drink Spill.

I've attached what I've written. Do you think it reads okay?
I'll be honest, I chickened out a bit. I was sitting at one of
the communal tables. I had a cup of water and I was next
to a guy I think was my age (he was a hipster, but who's
judging?).

FYI, spilling your drink on a complete stranger is MUCH
harder than it sounds. It took me two attempts to knock it
all the way over, I was so nervous (DO YOU REALIZE HOW
INSANE THIS MAKES YOU LOOK?). When I did finally get

the courage to tip it, it went all over his vintage Rubik's cube
and some of the colored stickers peeled right off.
MORTIFIED.

Much love,
That person in the café you don't want to sit next to
xxx

- - - - - - - - - -

From: Evelyn.Summers@WJM.co.uk
To: TheEzraChester@ezrachester.com
Subject: HIGHLY CONFIDENTIAL: The Drink Spill
November 26, 11:00 a.m.

Dear Ezra,

As per our agreement, I am delighted to be attaching my
first meet-cute report. I'd be grateful if you could please
confirm receipt and let me know that you've started writing.

Best wishes,
Evie

EVIE SUMMERS
ASSISTANT TO WILLIAM JONATHAN MONTGOMERY III
THE WILLIAM JONATHAN MONTGOMERY & SONS AGENCY FOR
SCREENWRITERS

- - - - - - - - - -

From: TheEzraChester@ezrachester.com
To: Evelyn.Summers@WJM.co.uk
Subject: Re: HIGHLY CONFIDENTIAL: The Drink Spill (WTF?)
November 27, 2:34 p.m.

Dear Red,

This was so fucking boring. Do we really have to go through three months of you spilling drinks on strangers and apologizing to them to prove I'm right?

Kind regards,
E

- - - - - - - - - -

From: Evelyn.Summers@WJM.co.uk
To: TheEzraChester@ezrachester.com
Subject: Re: HIGHLY CONFIDENTIAL: The Drink Spill (haven't you seen *Notting Hill*?)
November 27, 7:46 p.m.

Dear Ezra,

I'm sorry to hear you found it boring. Please remember there is still plenty of time for me to meet someone and prove you wrong. I'll send my next report shortly. Looking forward to seeing your first pages.

EVIE

- - - - - - - - - -

From: TheEzraChester@ezrachester.com
To: Evelyn.Summers@WJM.co.uk
Subject: Re: HIGHLY CONFIDENTIAL: The Drink Spill (why would I have seen that?)
November 28, 1:06 p.m.

Red, I'm not joking, I'm not writing anything if this is the kind of drivel you're going to send me. Please remember that even dramas have to keep their audience awake. I assume from this that rom-coms don't have the same standards.

- - - - - - - - - -

From: Evelyn.Summers@WJM.co.uk
To: TheEzraChester@ezrachester.com
Subject: HIGHLY CONFIDENTIAL: The Drink Spill Take 2
(has the package I sent you arrived?)
December 2, 2:56 p.m.

Dear Ezra,

Given the disappointment you expressed at my first attempt, I have given this meet-cute another go. Please find it attached. It's not long, so you could at least try to stay awake.

Fingers crossed,
Evie

- - - - - - - - - -

From: TheEzraChester@ezrachester.com
To: Evelyn.Summers@WJM.co.uk
Subject: Re: HIGHLY CONFIDENTIAL: The Drink Spill Take 2
(yes, but no one owns a DVD player anymore so I put it in the trash)
December 2, 3:06 p.m.

This is more like it, Red. When the kid spewed, I honestly thought this had to be bullshit so I rang the café. Fairly sure they've put you on a watch list.

I changed my mind. I can't wait to hear about your next "meet-cute."

Humbly yours,
E

- - - - - - - - - -

From: Monty@WJM.co.uk
To: Evelyn.Summers@WJM.co.uk
Subject: Progress update
December 3, 11:45 a.m.

Dear Evelyn,

Can you give me an update re: the script? I'm stepping back to allow Ezra the space to create. You should see this as an opportunity. There could be a great future ahead of you.

Of course, for that to happen, the agency does need to still be here.

Best,
Monty

WILLIAM JONATHAN MONTGOMERY III
THE WILLIAM JONATHAN MONTGOMERY & SONS AGENCY FOR SCREENWRITERS

- - - - - - - - - -

From: Evelyn.Summers@WJM.co.uk
To: TheEzraChester@ezrachester.com
Subject: Re: HIGHLY CONFIDENTIAL: The Drink Spill Take 2
(www.netflix.co.uk/nottinghill)
December 3, 1:15 p.m.

I'm sure the pages you're about to send Monty will make the
whole thing worthwhile.

P.S. I've attached a comprehensive list of the best rom-coms
for you to watch to address your alarming lack of cultural
knowledge. Consider this an education. I trust you'll find
them inspiring.

Chapter 8

The Other Shoe

EXT: GIL'S COFFEE HOUSE, EAST DULWICH,
SUNDAY, DECEMBER 9, 10 A.M.

It's pouring rain. EVIE hurries past the
door to Gil's, holding a red umbrella but
still soaked through. The café next door is
closed for refurbishment. She spins around,
looking for another option. The torrential
rain makes it all but impossible to see, so
she dashes back to Gil's. Despite the
weather, she hesitates at the door.

It had been only a week since I'd made a child projectile-vomit in this café. Could I really go back? An ice-cold droplet of rain found its way down my neck, and I had my answer.

It wasn't like I could go home, I reminded myself as I opened the door. In the territory negotiations for the flat, I'd got sex-free Saturdays and Jane had claimed Sundays so she could have sleepovers. Not that anyone did much sleeping. I needed somewhere I could write up my latest meet-cute "report" for NOB in peace. He hadn't sent Monty any pages even after approving of my second Drink Spill, but I wasn't panicking yet. It had been only a few weeks, and I hadn't expected him to break through his writer's block straight away. NOB needed more inspiration to get him going, and that's what I was giving him. Even if, so far, that had entailed humiliating myself all over London.

I headed to the counter, telling myself no one would recognize me. My dad always said that everyone was too busy worrying about themselves to give a damn about anybody else. I kept this in mind as I checked to make sure the Yummy Mummies had stuck to their promise never to return. They weren't there. *Thank God.*

Xan was serving. I ordered a coffee and toast, my heart kicking up a beat.

"Sure, mate, coming right up." Xan smiled. I was fairly sure he was the type of person who used "mate" indiscriminately. If the guy who'd had to clean up the mess didn't remember me, no one would.

While he made the coffee, I scoped the café for a free table. There were two familiar faces at the back. Ben and Anette were sitting where they'd been the week before, both with their heads down, reading. I exhaled slowly.

The sound of a cup hitting the counter made me turn back around.

It was an orange juice.

I looked at it for a long moment.

Xan stood behind it with a big grin on his face.

"I thought you might like to try our new special." He produced a blackboard with a handwritten message on it.

The "Not Suitable for Children" Surprise! (spoiler: contains egg)

His expression wavered as he caught sight of mine and he quickly replaced the juice with a coffee.

"It's given us a break from the pumpkin-spice lattes," he said, slightly apologetically.

I took the coffee with the tiniest of thank-yous. I'd made a mistake. I should never have come back here. A throat cleared behind me.

Anette and Ben were both standing there. They were holding

juice. Anette nudged her dad to hold his up higher. She grinned, oblivious to his discomfort.

"We've come to help you find this funny," she said.

Anette insisted I join them again, leaving me with no choice but to set up my laptop next to them at the table. I had the distinct impression the invite wasn't mutual when Ben immediately opened his paper. He was wearing a shirt beneath his jumper, which seemed overly formal for a weekend. I concentrated on writing my latest report, determined to show him I wasn't here to intrude on their breakfast.

Anette didn't have the same concerns. "Have you done another meet-cute yet?"

I tried not to look over at her dad. I'd told them the absolute bare minimum last week after Ben had called me out on what I was doing.

Before I could reply, Ben said, "Anette, leave Evie alone." He made a movement with his hands and I saw his daughter track this and pull a face. Her small hands moved in response, and he lifted the edge of his mouth. Anette tucked a strand of dark hair behind her ear and the hearing aid there.

"Okay, I'll play," Ben replied out loud. "But I get to choose this time."

They put their heads together and spoke in hushed tones, occasionally punctuating their conversation with more sign language.

I turned back to my report. It was a recap of the Damsel-in-Distress meet-cute (not the most progressive rom-com trope but it worked in *The Wedding Planner*). Like my first two attempts, it hadn't exactly gone to plan. I could already picture NOB's reaction. So far, the meet-cutes had served only to amuse him. *All this humiliation better be worth it.*

It wasn't just the act of doing the meet-cutes that was proving tricky; it was writing about them. I hadn't considered that sending NOB the reports would feel like anything close to writing again. Yet when NOB had said he was bored by my first attempt, an old hurt had flared. I used to lose hours to writing, whole days going by in a blink. My dad would always be my first reader, his measured feedback helping me to polish off the edges. Then Dad died, and that agent had rejected the first script I'd written without his help. Maria used to say the urge to write would come back to me eventually. But every time I faced the blank screen, all that returned were the agent's words. *You just don't have what it takes.* Now I had no choice but to write without my first reader there to guide me. And every word I put on the page felt like taking tentative steps out onto ice.

My phone buzzed, yanking me back into the café. I turned it over, expecting it to be JEMS, but then I saw the message, and the nickname.

UNKNOWN NUMBER: So, Red, have you made any more children vomit? I have to say, I found that incredibly motivating. More so than the list you sent of all the rom-coms I'm never going to watch. Eagerly awaiting the next update

He was just as infuriating by text as he was in person.

RED: who is this, sorry?

NOB: Just how many devastatingly attractive screenwriters do you know, Red?

RED: none

NOB: Very funny, Stevie

RED: oh. It's you. Shouldn't you be writing?

NOB: So demanding. I want more of these reports from you first. I like seeing you inflicting yourself on people other than me for a change. Plus, your writing isn't half bad, Red

RED: neither is your distraction technique. We had a deal

NOB: Exactly, so what's next?

I glanced up as Anette giggled. She was holding what looked like a professional camera. I would have assumed it was her dad's, except the strap was rainbow-colored, and there was something in the way she handled it that told me it was hers.

She took a picture of Ben. He smiled for her, willing but awkward. I dropped my gaze back to my phone, wondering why they were here alone again. Maybe Sunday breakfast was their official father/daughter time. They seemed so close. They were strangers to me, but there was something about them that felt familiar.

Flash. I blinked to find Anette lowering her camera, grinning at me. "Do you want to play too?"

Ben opened his mouth as if to protest, but I got there first. "What's the game?" I asked, not entirely sure what had come over me. It was painfully clear her dad didn't want me to join them. For some reason, this made me want to more.

Anette beamed. "It's called Bad Lamp Random," she said. Then she repeated herself without any sound.

"Bad Lip Reading," Ben supplied quietly.

"Here, we'll show you. You have to pick someone, like those two over there." Anette pointed toward an elderly couple a few tables over. Ben gently pushed her extended finger down. "Watch this." She squinted over at them. I could see the couple talking, but across the crowded café, it was impossible to hear them.

"Oh, I am going to the shops to buy cheese," Anette said, deepening her voice. There was a pause. *"Dad,"* she urged.

"Do I always have to be the woman?"

"Yes," she said. "And do it properly."

He glanced at me, before shifting his attention to the couple. "Why are you obsessed with cheese?" he said, his voice higher than usual. I held a hand over my smile.

"Cheese is great," said Anette in that same deep voice. "And so are bees," she added, when the old man carried on talking.

Ben and Anette were perfectly matching the couple's exchange, speeding up their own responses or slowing them down to coincide with the movements of their mouths. You could almost believe they really were lip-reading, except it was complete nonsense.

"You've never mentioned bees before," said Ben in his falsetto.

The man made an irate gesture toward a waiter. "Get me some bees!" Anette shouted, leaving Ben to wince as the couple looked over and we all ducked our heads.

"That was brilliant," I said under my breath.

"Dad made it up."

Ben shook out his paper, indicating the game was over, the tips of his ears pink.

His daughter took the opportunity to edge closer to me, a gleam in her eye. "So, *did* you do another meet-cute for NOB?"

Had I really used NOB's nickname last week? I'd been so flustered, I could barely recall exactly what I'd told them. No wonder Ben didn't want me there.

"His name's actually Ezra," I said hastily, looking over at Ben. He turned his page, oblivious. *Fine.* "Your mother is going to think I'm a bad influence," I said to Anette.

Now Ben's head snapped up. *What did I say?*

But Anette was smiling at me. "I think she would have bloody loved you," she said.

It took me a second to register the past tense, and then, with a jolt, I knew why Anette and Ben were here alone.

"Anette," Ben reprimanded. "Remember what we said? You may swear only in French. I want people to think we're cultured."

"*Merde,*" said Anette.

"Better."

"I'm sorry," I said softly to Ben. Maybe there was something in my tone that let him know, in my own way, I understood. He lifted his eyes to mine and, for the first time, smiled at me. He placed a gentle kiss on the side of Anette's head.

Watching them both, an impulse struck me. "I know it's not strictly a breakfast drink, but what would you say to a hot chocolate?" My dad and I used to drink them together all the time.

"A big fat yes!" Anette said, at the same time as Ben replied, "We're fine, thank you."

Anette jutted her chin at her dad and spoke to him with her quick fingers.

"Yes, that would be very kind, thank you," he amended.

It felt something like progress. I emailed NOB the meet-cute and went to order.

The woman in front of me in the queue had a long, honey-blond ponytail that she kept swishing in my face. It took me a second to register that she was one of the mums who'd been here last week. She caught sight of me and I froze for a moment, unsure what to say.

"Samantha," she said, adjusting the strap on the yoga mat slung over her shoulder.

"Evie," I replied, warily.

"Oh, don't worry about that little thing last week. That wasn't the first time Justice has cleared a room." Her laugh was high and fluting. I gave her a weak smile.

She ordered a skinny flat white from Xan. "I can't help but notice you're sitting with Mr. Tall, Dark, and Brooding over there."

I forced myself not to look back at my table. "I'm sorry?"

"Oh, it's just a little joke between me and some of the other mums. Our kids all go to the same school." She chewed her lip. "Can I give you some advice?"

"Sure." I doubted I could stop her. I ordered the hot chocolates from Xan, requesting extra marshmallows on one of them.

"He's not really dating material." Her tone was almost apologetic. "I went for a drink with him once after my divorce, and it was *super* awkward. He barely said two words the whole night unless it was about that little girl of his. Not that I'm judging. Maybe he just wasn't ready, you know? Especially after how his wife died. Or maybe he's just like that. Some men are." She plucked her flat white off the counter. "Just thought I'd save you some time."

Before I could tell her she'd got the wrong impression, she'd flounced off, ponytail swinging. I lifted the tray of hot chocolates. *How* had *his wife died?* a small part of me wondered, before dismissing the thought. *Definitely not my business.*

"So," Anette said, once I'd divvied out the hot chocolates. Ben looked at his with a little frown before carrying on reading. I'd given him the one with the most marshmallows. He seemed like he needed it. "*Now* can you tell us about your last meet-cute?"

Describing it to NOB was one thing—there was something about writing it down that at least put some distance between myself and the humiliation. The idea of saying it out loud was different. And yet Anette's expression was wide open. There wasn't a trace of judgment to be seen.

I glanced over at Ben—he was once more absorbed in his reading, his mug now pulled close. When he didn't protest, I told her about the Damsel in Distress, describing how I'd walked up and down the street for half an hour in heels that pinched my feet before spotting a mark—checked shirt, woolly hat, beard. Not quite Matthew McConaughey, but far more my type. I'd waited until he was a few feet away, then I'd stepped onto a sewer grid cover and jammed my heel between the slots.

"You pretended you were stuck?" Anette asked, thrilled.

"I gave quite the performance. He didn't even stop. That's when I realized."

"What?" she asked, mesmerized.

"I really was stuck." My heel had been fully wedged between the bars. "And while I'd been busy trying to get a guy's attention, workmen had arrived to fix the road. They were all taking bets on how many safety barriers they could put around me before I noticed. They managed to completely cordon me off."

Anette burst out laughing.

"I had to leave my shoe behind," I told her, relieved to find that I could smile about it now too. "They lent me a spare work boot so I could get home."

"Is all that true?" asked Ben suddenly, voice tinged with disbelief.

How long has he been listening? I lifted the plastic bag containing the boot to show him. "Behold the proof. I'm returning it on my way home."

Ben blinked, a muscle twitching in his cheek.

"It will all be worthwhile if the meet-cutes inspire Ezra," I said, a little tartly.

"As long as it's worthwhile," Ben replied.

I folded my arms. "Look, if it was up to me I'd meet someone because we'd be the only two people who'd booked tickets for a *Brick Park* showing at the Prince Charles Cinema, but that's never going to happen."

"What's *Brick Park*?" Anette asked. Her dad was studying me, his dark eyebrows slightly raised.

I focused on her. "Only the best film no one's ever heard of," I smiled. "It's from the fifties. Dorothy Taylor was a screenwriting genius, but she only ever wrote one film." From the moment my dad had introduced me to *Brick Park*, that was it for me. I'd wanted to be a screenwriter so I could write a film that made people even half as happy as *Brick Park* made us. My dad gave me my first laptop, telling me, "Whatever you write, Evie, 'Make it mean something.'" It was our favorite quote from the movie. It was hard to remember sometimes that I'd once genuinely believed I could produce something worthwhile.

"What happens when you do meet someone?" Ben asked unexpectedly.

"Then NOB has to write the script," I replied, realizing when Anette giggled that I'd once again used his nickname. "And I get promoted to agent."

"And what about him?" he pressed.

"NO—Ezra?" I stumbled.

"The man you meet through one of these meet-cutes. As far as he's concerned, it's all real, isn't it?"

Anette looked between us both as I paused to choose my next words. I'd told my friends I wasn't doing this for love. The truth was, I hadn't let myself think that far ahead. I thought I'd found my happy ending with Ricky, and look how that turned out. I couldn't admit this to Ben, so I shrugged. "I just need to find someone willing to say he's fallen for me," I said tightly. "I'm not looking for 'the One,' just something NOB will find believable. It doesn't need to be earth-shatteringly real for either of us."

A beat. "Right," said Ben. He returned to the travel section, as if I was dismissed.

Anette made what looked like a *K* symbol under her dad's nose, using two fingers and a thumb. After a moment, he returned it. She leaned back as if satisfied, swinging her legs.

"*I* think you're brilliant," she told me.

I clinked my mug against hers. Who needed Ben's approval, anyway?

The woman in the queue couldn't have been more right about him.

NOB: Your dialogue's improving. Though, you do know that you can give up at any point, don't you, Sewerella? I'm starting to think I'm the only one taking our deal seriously. Two months to fall head over heels, and you're already one shoe down. Tick-tock, Red

Chapter 9

The One Where They Meet in a Bookshop

```
EXT: THE DUSTY BOOKSHELF—Wednesday,
December 12, 7:30 P.M.

EVIE stands in front of a bookshop. The
window frames are painted midnight blue.
A wooden sign hangs above the door in
matching blue with silver lettering,
declaring it THE DUSTY BOOKSHELF. There are
Christmas lights in the window display,
flashing languidly on and off, illuminating
the books. EVIE's nose is bright pink. Her
braided hair pokes out from beneath her
thick green woolen hat as she peers into
the shop.
```

It is a truth universally acknowledged that the moment the words "What's the worst that can happen?" are uttered, a dozen possibilities pop into existence. Yet, as I stood outside the Dusty Bookshelf, on a side street in Peckham, those were the words I repeated to myself.

I'd gotten the time and details from Jane, who hadn't known what this month's book was but promised the group would be an *absolute hotbed of romance*! When I'd asked her what kind of books they read she'd told me, "Fantasy, mostly. You know, werewolves and whatnot." I hoped that meant horror and sci-fi too, because I was at least familiar with those as film genres.

As I stood in front of the window of the warmly lit shop, my stomach tipped like a funfair ride heading over a drop. Assistant drinks aside, it had been a while since I'd done anything social without Ricky by my side. *How did I end up with an introvert?* He'd smile, vowing to stick by me all night.

I steeled myself. I had to do this. It had been over three weeks, and the only thing I'd managed to get out of NOB was requests for more meet-cutes. My only consolation was that he was insisting I was helping him to write. I just wished I could believe him.

I pushed the door open.

Inside, a woman sat reading behind a till at a desk that groaned beneath a pile of books. The place was beautiful. Wooden shelves were crammed with books old and new, fairy lights had been wound around the rafters, and the furniture was mismatched, with lamps in every conceivable nook and cranny.

"Hi," I said hesitantly.

The woman took a second to finish her page before looking up at me. "We're closed," she said.

"I'm here for the book group." The woman leaned back in her chair and took off her glasses to appraise me.

"Well," she said after a pause, "it takes all sorts. Follow me."

Flustered, I trailed behind her, trying to keep track of her bobbing bun as we zigzagged between shelves until we must have been at the very back of the shop. The shelves gave way to a small, book-lined space filled with people, a variety of chairs, and an old stained table bearing wine. *Oh, thank God.*

"One of yours," the woman announced, and then left me there.

- - - - - - - - - -

There was a tall black woman in long red boots near the table, perhaps a few years older than me. "White or red?" she asked. She sounded American.

Nerves had hold of my tongue.

"I'm Steph," she added.

"Evie."

She pushed a glass of white into my hands. "Drink this, it always helps the first time."

"I like to think of it as social lubrication!" A man stepped out from behind her. Steph gave him an affectionate look and a glass of red. He was slight and neat-looking, midsixties, with a knitted vest top over a short-sleeved shirt. "Gabe," he said. "What brings you to our little corner of the world?"

"Somehow our notice keeps getting removed from the window," Steph added. "Though someone keeps putting it back." Gabe grinned.

"People can be weirdly snobbish about genre fiction," I said.

"You should try writing it. Whenever I explain what I do for a living, people act like I've grown an extra head," said Steph.

"How fitting," I said, and was rewarded by Steph's red-lipped smile. I wanted to ask her more about what she was working on, but a woman with thick corn-colored hair clinked her pink nails against her glass and indicated for us all to take our seats.

"Welcome, my fellow explorers." Her gaze alighted on me. "Oh, I do *love* seeing a new member."

A few titters as people turned to look at me. I beetrooted on the spot.

There was a pause in which I realized slightly too late that that was my cue to introduce myself. "Evie!" I shouted in a misguided bid to compensate for the delay.

"Welcome *Evie!* I'm Meagan. We can't wait to hear what you thought of December's book choice." This was absolutely the moment any normal person would speak up and admit that they hadn't had time to find out what the book was, never mind read it. However, my friends had insisted I follow one rule while doing the meet-cutes: no taking a backseat in my own movie. Meaning: I had to take part in the book discussion, even though I hadn't read the book.

As I looked around at the faces in the circle, my heart started to drop. Of the dozen people there, there was one man. Gabe. I'd come here assuming most science fiction and fantasy fans were men, but clearly I was wrong.

A throat cleared behind us, and Meagan beamed. "Come in, come in." We turned to see a latecomer. It was a man who was about my age.

The curious looks everyone gave him told me he was a first-timer too. He unwound his scarf and took off his hat to reveal a shock of thick ash-blond hair. *Oh, hello.*

Newly Arrived Potential Love Interest had the kind of stubble that said "not arrogant about my appearance" yet also "edgy enough to be sexy," and wore super-cute round tortoiseshell glasses. *Just like Ricky.* I nudged the thought away, and the pang that came with it.

Meagan pulled a chair in next to her and gestured to it. "Tom, take a seat. I was so pleased to get your email about joining us today. Everyone, say hi to Tom." I was definitely not alone in eyeing him. We all chorused a hello, some of us louder and far more obvious than others.

Tom smiled as he passed me. Despite definitely not doing this for love, there was nothing wrong with finding him attractive.

"So, the first question is for one of our new members. Evie." *Thanks, Meagan.* "Are you new to the genre?"

At least we'd started with an easy one. I cleared my throat, trying to sound confident. "I used to read it more when I was younger." Steph's eyebrows shot up. "Not that I ever grew out of it," I added hastily. I was relieved to see a few smiles at this. "It's just that it's hard to find time to read these days."

A few of the women nodded in agreement.

Meagan beamed. "Thank you, Evie. What did everyone think of the book? Amanda?"

She looked to a woman in a crisp trouser suit.

"Far better than last month's choice," Amanda replied. "The feminist subgenre holds no interest for me. Give me a real man anytime. No offense to your writing, Steph."

"By 'real men,' I assume you mean the kind who need a compliant woman to validate the size of their—"

"Now, ladies, we all have our specialist interests," interrupted Meagan. "Remember what we say?" Everyone except Tom and me joined in with her next words.

"There's a subgenre for everyone."

He caught my eye and smiled, which sent a welcome thrill down to my toes. *Steady on, Evie.*

"Evie, what's yours? Don't feel embarrassed, there are no wrong answers here."

Oh, God. I thought back to everything I knew about genre fiction. I knew only film genres, so picked the one I felt safest with. "Horror," I said. There were so many great female writers: Kathryn Bigelow. Karen Walton. Diablo Cody. "The scarier, the better."

A few mouths dropped open. I guess even among open-minded genre fans, horror was still looked down on.

Meagan was nodding slowly, a frown dimpling her forehead. "Like I said, you're among friends, you'll find no judgment here." This last part seemed to be aimed at the room, and some of the ladies shrugged as if acquiescing.

I relaxed. Another question down. If the next person to answer revealed a bit about the damn book, I'd have half a chance.

"Evie." Good Lord, this was torture. Was she doing it on purpose? Surely it was Tom's turn at some point. I felt like I'd somehow been rumbled and she was determined to get me to admit it. But how on earth could she possibly know? "Sorry, we will get on to everyone else, but I'd just love to know what you thought about *that* scene between the pirate and his stepmother."

At least now I had some details. "Well," I said, stretching out the moment to give myself more time to think. Insightful yet vague. I could do this. I drank more wine. "I found it very moving."

She tilted her head. "Even the scene where they *dueled* belowdecks?"

I hesitated, but now that I'd stated my opinion, I had to stand by it or it would look weird. "Especially then."

"And when his sister joined them?"

"It was a bold choice, but I thought the writer handled it very well."

"And the climax?"

"Very satisfying."

"Really got the juices flowing." This from an older woman with stylishly large glasses and a blunt-cut fringe. "A real highlight."

But Meagan wasn't done with me. "Thank you, Heather, but I think we'd all love to know Evie's favorite scene."

I fanned my face, the room seeming uncomfortably hot, and Steph jumped in. "Personally, the one with Princess Esmerelda and the pirate king on the treasure island was smoking—"

Meagan held up a hand. "Thanks, but it's Evie's turn to speak."

"That was mine too." I gave Steph a grateful smile and decided to hazard a safe guess. "Especially when they finally found out where the treasure was buried."

For some reason, Heather cackled at that. "It certainly surprised Esmerelda to find it there," she said.

I looked around the room. *Am I missing something?*

"And what did you make of Esmerelda?" Meagan asked me.

Damn it, Meagan! I became determined not to let her beat me. Giving critical feedback was the part of my job I loved most. "I found her incredibly relatable. It was refreshing to see a female character handled with such emotional intelligence. I haven't seen two more kindred souls since Jane Eyre and Mr. Rochester." I felt a little burst of triumph. *Take that, Meagan!*

Tom seemed to be suppressing a smile and Steph had the strangest expression on her face.

Meagan, at last, managed to speak. "Thank you, Evie, for that . . . *unique* insight into the dragon princess." Wait, *dragon*?

"Gabe, we all know you're fond of the *dueling* scenes—what's your take?"

He rubbed his hands together and put one slim finger next to his chin in thought. I took a sip of wine, glad of the reprieve. "I have to say, when the pirate king and Esmerelda finally got their cocks out"—I coughed as the wine went down the wrong way—"I thought it couldn't get any better. Then when it was revealed that dragons have *two* cocks, the book went straight into my top ten!" There was the sound of a book dropping, and the bookseller who'd been returning it to its shelf gaped at us before pulling her cardigan around herself and hurrying off.

"Now, Gabe. You know we like to keep things less blue here out of respect for our neighbors." Meagan eyed the retreating bookseller. "Remember to substitute the more colorful words."

"Fine, fine. So, I thought the *dueling* scene where Esmerelda's second *wand* shot flavored *sparks* was absolutely smashing. It was the single most *exotic* thing I'd ever read."

I returned my empty glass to the table, fighting the urge to grab my coat and run with every fiber of my being. If there was the slightest chance I could salvage any part of this evening by speaking to Tom, then I had to try.

Tom was browsing the bookshelves. I had to hope he'd see the funny side. There had definitely been moments when we'd caught each other's eye.

Before I could get to him, Steph appeared in front of me and topped up my wine. "Sorry about Meagan—she sussed you out from the start, didn't she? She's just a stickler for making sure we've all read the book. Sometimes people just turn up for the free wine."

"Imagine that!" said Heather, appearing with two glasses.

"She was kind of right in my case," I said, still thrumming with embarrassment. "I can't really blame her for being annoyed."

The other members—I now realized why there had been titters at the word—were chatting, but I spied a few of them glancing our way.

"Don't worry about them. You aren't the first person to wander accidentally into a Banging Books session," said Heather.

"I guess the clue is in the name." I had been foolish to think any book group Jane recommended could be anything but *exotic* in nature.

"When you called the climax 'very satisfying,'" snorted Heather, the large beads of her necklace catching in the light.

Despite my lingering embarrassment, I found myself laughing too.

"The look on your face when you finally realized!" said Steph, wiping at her eyes.

As our laughter gradually subsided, I asked, "What was the book called?"

"Taken by Dragons: A Jolly Rogerer Adventure."

We lost it again.

"Why *did* you join us?" Steph asked.

I blushed. "It's going to sound silly, but . . . to meet someone."

"Oh, honey," Steph said, following my gaze to Tom. "Then what are you still talking to us for?"

- - - - - - - - - -

I stood next to Tom, pretending to look at the books.

"So, that was . . ." said Tom, in a soft London accent.

"It was definitely a first," I replied.

We smiled at each other. His teeth were slightly crooked at the front.

"I didn't quite know what to expect when I arrived," he admitted.

"Fewer wands," I said.

"You didn't read the book, did you?"

"Do you think anyone noticed?" I joked.

"There's always next time," he replied.

"Will you be back?" I was genuinely curious.

"Maybe," he nodded. "Would you come again?"

"Maybe," I echoed with a smile. "A part of me is a little curious to read the book."

"I really hope you like it."

"Why's that?" I asked.

We were interrupted by Meagan calling everyone's attention to her. "Thanks again for coming, everybody." Laughter, which I now understood. "We didn't want to say anything at the beginning in case it stymied the conversation, but I am thrilled to say that the author himself, Mr. T. Mingle, has been with us all evening. He's here to answer all your burning questions."

I looked at Tom in alarm while everyone gathered around us. "It's okay," he said as I was elbowed farther back by eager members. "Even my girlfriend thinks it's weird. I've lost count of the number of *wands* I've been asked to put my signature on."

Chapter 10

- - - - - - - -

Mash-Up

```
INT: GIL'S COFFEE HOUSE, EAST DULWICH—
SUNDAY, DECEMBER 16, 10 A.M.

EVIE enters the café, glancing around for a
spare table. She spots BEN and ANETTE at
the same table they were at the week before
and ducks her head, making her way to a
bench occupied by laptop users.
```

"Evie!" Anette's piping voice cut clear across the café. There was no way I could ignore it.

I braced myself, then found myself smiling. She was holding up a mug of hot chocolate. I signaled that I'd head over after I ordered breakfast.

If Ben saw fit to pass further judgment on my activities this week, next Sunday I'd try somewhere new. I needed somewhere to write up my meet-cutes. Not that they were getting me anywhere yet, romantically or otherwise. NOB still hadn't sent any pages to Monty, and it was making my boss twitchy. Last week, he'd advised that I "at least attempt" to get NOB to send us proof he was writing. Stating, without any trace of self-awareness, "That's what any good agent would do." To keep Monty distracted, I'd sifted through the agency's ginormous slush pile—the mountain of screenplays sent to us by writers hoping for representation. He was seldom happier than when he was explaining to me exactly why the ones I'd chosen weren't up to the agency's standards (*i.e.*, they were by women). It cheered him up at least, and allowed me time to concentrate on the meet-cutes.

Ben didn't look up when I reached their table. He was absorbed in an issue of *National Geographic*. Anette had saved me the chair between them.

"Hold it right there . . ." Anette said as I opened my laptop. She was holding her camera. I stuck out my tongue for the photo. "Now chop chop," she told me, opening her book. "That meet-cute isn't going to write about itself."

The blank page. One of the biggest obstacles a writer has to face, along with everything on the Internet. NOB was still pushing me to use more dialogue and it was making the writing process even more of a challenge. *Come on, Evie. You'll never get NOB to keep reading these if you don't use a boychild-friendly format.*

I began the Bookshop meet-cute like I was delivering bad news, jabbing reluctantly at the keys. Then, when I got to Meagan's lines as she tried to catch me out for having not read the book, something happened. It felt like catching up with myself, as if I'd been lagging behind. It wasn't exactly like it used to be, but I found a rhythm that helped the words come a little easier.

When I checked the time, almost an hour had flown by. I became aware of someone looking at me. *Anette,* I thought.

It was Ben.

"What?" I asked, startled.

"Nothing," he said quickly, and went back to his magazine, the tips of his ears now pink.

When I next looked up, Ben was resting his chin on his upturned palm; his other arm was draped over his long legs, completely engrossed in an article. *Good,* I thought.

I couldn't help but notice a smudge of red glitter on his nose. His face wasn't quite as somber when he was lost in concentration. Dark brows, intelligent eyes, crooked smile—not that I'd seen it very often—an angular, neatly shaved jawline and near-black hair that looked like it might curl if it was allowed to grow longer. Teamed with his clothing—a shirt and jumper again—it was like he was trying his best to be a stock image for "A Sensible Adult Man."

My phone lit up. I tugged my attention away from him.

MARIA: did you sort the manor for Sarah's hen?

EVIE: all done! Just need to confirm it with our deposit, if you guys don't mind dropping your share into my account

MARIA: you star! I'll nudge Jem. How are the meet-cutes?

EVIE: mortifying as ever. And guess who's back in Gil's?

MARIA: Ben? His daughter sounded lovely, though. Maybe you caught him on a bad day

EVIE: that's every Sunday so far.

I'd told my friends about Ben after his interrogation last time had caught me off guard and I'd needed a reality check. *Was what I was doing okay?* They'd told me not to let his reaction prevent me from doing the meet-cutes. I suspected they really meant "Don't let his reaction stop you from meeting someone." At least this week he'd spoken even less than usual.

I glanced up from my phone, frowning, sensing something was a little off. I observed Ben and Anette for a moment, trying to figure out what was bothering me. They were both reading, but there was something strained about the silence. Anette had been all smiles for me, but now her mouth was set in a stubborn line. She had her back turned to Ben, who was also angled away from her.

Ben and Anette weren't speaking to each other.

None of your business, Evie. I tried to go back to the message I was writing to NOB, but the silence grew too loud.

"Is everything all right?" I asked.

They both looked up in unison.

"It's totally fine," Anette smiled at me. "By the way, Evie, please could you ask my father if I can have another drink?"

"That depends on whether she's going to apologize," Ben said coolly.

"Is he going to let his only daughter *die* of *thirst*?" Anette said.

Ben turned his page. "He's certainly considering it."

"How about Evie doesn't do anything until someone tells her what's going on," I said in my best no-nonsense voice.

"Nothing, except *he* wants my whole school to laugh at me." Anette folded her arms, tucking her chin into her chest.

Her dad scowled. "It's not my fault. I did my best."

"I'm not doing it."

"Doing what?" I asked.

"The stupid school play," Anette said.

"Anette," Ben said levelly. "It's a great part. Everyone else has to wear a costume."

"Yeah, but not *this* costume."

"I give up," he said, exasperated.

"What's the play?" I asked. I shouldn't intrude, but seeing them at odds just felt wrong.

When Anette didn't answer, Ben replied for her. *"Peter Pan."*

Anette made a furious sign, which Ben returned.

They glared at each other before both jutting their chins in opposite directions. I hid a smile.

"I love *Peter Pan*," I said.

Anette raised her dark eyes to mine.

"Really?"

Now I did smile. "My dad used to read it to me all the time. I still have the book. It's one of the greatest stories ever written, and you're going to be in the play?" I poured awe into my voice. "What part?"

"Tinker Bell," Anette said, her tone unimpressed.

"Tink." I sighed. "That's lucky."

"Why?"

"She gets all the cool lines, and she swears a *lot*." I couldn't think of anyone better to play the tempestuous fairy I'd loved growing up.

"See, you're already halfway there," Ben told his daughter.

She set her chin. "I'm signing my lines. What if everyone's looking at me in that stupid costume and I mess up?"

Ben's brown eyes softened.

"Do you know the sign for 'silly ass'?" I was rewarded with the tiniest of smiles.

"Mrs. Clarke doesn't like swearing," Anette said.

"Does *Mrs. Clarke* know the sign for 'silly ass'?" I asked.

The smile widened as she shook her head. I thought I saw some of the tension leave Ben's broad shoulders.

"There's just one *huge* problem." She tossed her dad a look. "Tell her."

Ben cleared his throat. "The play's a 'mash-up.'" Ben used the term like it exhausted him. "They've made it into a musical."

"*Not* the Disney one." Anette covered her eyes. "Show her."

Ben gave his daughter a look before reaching into a dark bag by his feet.

I understood where the streak of red glitter had come from as he extracted what must surely be Anette's costume. It was a very sad-looking pair of glittery wings and a raggedy tutu stiff with glitter glue. Handmade, by the looks of it, with a certain try-hard enthusiasm if not a great deal of skill.

"Chloe was better at this stuff," Ben said, picking at a particularly large clump of glitter. *His wife,* I assumed, noting how easily he spoke of her—it took a long time to turn that corner. "I was hoping her grandmother might be able to salvage it."

"It's definitely creative," I assured him. "The colors alone . . ." For some reason, he'd chosen red, white, and blue rather than the traditional Tink green. As I squinted, I realized it was a pattern. The wings each bore a wobbly glitter-glue Union Jack.

"What's the other half of the mash-up?" I asked.

Ben's reply was resigned. "It's the Spice Girls."

"Mum, I have a clothing emergency," I said. I was standing in the back entrance to Gil's, where it was quieter, my duffel coat done up against the cold.

"My favorite kind!" my mum exclaimed down the phone. It was one of the many things I loved about Mary Summers: no preamble required.

I explained about Anette's costume, and how she might feel more confident if it was beautiful. "Her dad really tried," I said. "But we're in need of an expert." My mum made most of my dresses. Her skill with a needle was unparalleled, and had not been passed down through the gene pool. I preferred super glue to thread.

"I'd love to, pet. Though isn't there anyone else around to help?" That was my mum: subtle as a brick.

"He's a widower, mum," I said.

"A lost cause, then." My mum's voice was wry.

"That's not what I meant," I said, hastily. "Besides," I continued, before she got any ideas, "it's for Anette. There's just one more thing . . ." I explained what I had in mind, and my mum crowed with delight. "And they need the costume by Friday morning. Is that possible? I'll pay for the material."

"Pish posh. I'll have it to you by Thursday. That gives me time to finish off Aunty Margaret's Dorothy outfit. She's having a Wizard of Oz party for her sixty-fifth."

When I headed back inside, there was a woman with a yoga mat talking to Ben, her hand occasionally reaching out to touch his shoulder as if they were friends. Samantha. She didn't appear to be heeding her own advice from last weekend. Anette was now in the chair next to her dad, head down reading, seemingly oblivious to the woman's presence. Her hearing aids were now in the open case on the table. I decided to hover a few tables back until Samantha had gone, not particularly eager to encounter her again.

Plus, it gave me a chance to deal with NOB.

RED: what have one book group, dragon erotica, and a case of mistaken identity got in common?

NOB: Don't tease me, Red

I was taking a leaf from Monty's *Big Book of NOB*. So to speak. NOB was a master of evading difficult conversations. I'd have to force him to see me in person if I ever wanted to get anything out of him. Of course, NOB thrived on making that impossible. I couldn't afford to lure him in with a twenty-course tasting menu, but I did have something else he'd enjoy: my potential humiliation.

RED: the report is in your inbox. If you love my meet-cutes so much, It's time you joined me on one

"I really do think you should take my advice." Samantha's words cut across the café. "It's absolutely fine at home, just not in *public.*" It was harder to hear Ben's quiet response. Not that I was trying to, of course.

"Thanks, but it's like I said all those other times. No." His tone was flat. You could have drawn a straight line with his back. Samantha reached for him again but seemed to think better of it. I dropped my eyes to my phone, curious but wary of intruding.

NOB: unlike you, I have better things to do with my time

RED: I'm planning to do something that is highly likely to result in my very public humiliation

NOB: I can do next Friday morning at ten

RED: perfect. Dress warmly

Got you.

"I only want to help, Ben. But perhaps you're too busy focusing on other things, now you're dating again."

I looked up.

"Dating . . . ?" Ben trailed off. Samantha was eyeing my chair meaningfully, and I was very glad I wasn't in it. "I'm not dating her," Ben said abruptly, catching on. *Ouch, Ben. Try not to trip as you race to deny it.* "She's Anette's friend."

"Really, Ben, this is exactly the sort of thing I'm talking about. This is the same woman who caused absolute havoc in here a few weekends ago. After what happened with Justice, poor Suze hasn't been able to show her face anywhere since. Is she really the best influence for Anette? You daughter's never going to be—"

"Anette," Ben interrupted, a sharpness to his voice I hadn't heard before, "is going to be friends with this woman whether I like it or not. Even if she does insist on making a public spectacle of herself. In fact, that's exactly why she's—"

I didn't get to learn what I was, because a man chose that exact moment to try to squeeze past me and one of the toggles on my coat caught on his bag strap, carrying me along with him. By the time I'd extracted myself, Ben was ending the conversation.

"*Goodbye*, Samantha," he said, returning to his magazine. She looked affronted, then pretended to check the time on her phone and walked away like she had somewhere to be. Part of me almost felt sorry for her. *Almost.*

After Ben's questions last weekend, I shouldn't have been surprised to learn that he thought I was ridiculous for doing the meet-cutes. *Public spectacle*, indeed.

If I already knew, why does it sting?

Because after this morning I'd been thinking I might actually be getting somewhere with him.

I made a beeline for the table and started packing my things. "My mum will have the costume here by Thursday, will that work?" I said coolly.

"Perfect. The play's Friday afternoon," Ben said, closing his magazine. He looked tense. "Please pass on our thanks to your mother. Anette will be very grateful. She's just having some quiet time." He indicated his daughter, who was still reading. His attention remained on me as if waiting for something. I nodded my understanding, and his shoulders seemed to relax. "Let me know how much it comes to."

"It's for Anette," I said. "I'll drop the costume off here first thing Friday morning."

"Evie," Ben said, as if to get my attention. "Thank you. This means . . . It means a lot to Anette. She was nervous about more than the costume. This is a big help."

"It's fine," I said tersely, just wanting to leave.

Anette looked up, a frown on her face. I opened and closed my hand in the sign for *goodbye*. She signed quickly to her dad; I caught a bit of what she said, as I'd been trying to learn a few signs, but not enough to understand. A line appeared between Ben's dark brows as he turned to me.

"Would you like to come to Anette's play?" he asked.

I looked between them both, at Anette's hopeful expression and Ben's guarded one.

"Are you sure?" I asked, quite certain he wouldn't want me to go, and yet still finding myself wanting to.

He frowned, as if confused by my question. "Yes," he said.

I gave Anette a big smile and signed *Thank you*. She looked thrilled; Ben's feelings were less clear as he studied me. Not that it mattered what he thought. I'd be going for her.

Besides, it's not every day you get to see a Spice Girls/*Peter Pan* mash-up.

Chapter 11

Not-a-Pervert Paul

SARAH: I don't think you should do it

JEREMY: DON'T LISTEN TO HER, EVIE

SARAH: so far she's made a child vomit and accidentally joined an erotic book group—what makes you think doing a road trip with an ACTUAL STRANGER will be any better? Get the train home for Christmas like everyone else

EVIE: the Road Trip meet-cute has to be a long car journey with a guy. I know the meet-cutes have been a bit of a disaster so far, but if I'm going to get NOB writing, I need to hold up my end of the deal

JEREMY: you mean the part where you meet someone and fall in love?

EVIE: thanks for the recap, Jem. Guys, will you help me find my Harry?

SARAH: fine. But knowing you, he'll probably be an ax murderer or something

MARIA: Operation "Find Evie Someone Who Isn't an Ax Murderer" is now in progress. Everyone share my post!

SARAH: done

JEREMY: only with friends, right, Sarah? Not the whole world?

SARAH: yes, Jeremy, I'm not the disaster here

EVIE: hey!

JEREMY: Sarah just shared with everyone

SARAH: I didn't, did I? I'm doing this while on a conference call with the caterer, the florist, and the venue manager, so forgive me if you don't have 100 percent of my attention

EVIE: don't worry, Sarah. I'm sure any friends of your friends are just fine

JEREMY: bless your little heart, Evie

SARAH: I think I just shared it again

MARIA: speaking of oversharing, NOB made it into the gossip columns this week. Hang on, I'll send the link

MONICA REED "DEEPLY UNHAPPY"

A close source told *Bitch About It* that the Oscar winner, 44, is finally ready to throw her boy toy out of the pram. Mum of two Reed has been dating one-hit wonder Ezra Chester, 33, on and off for a year now. Reed's friends are concerned: "It's her first fling after her divorce and she's clearly deeply unhappy. The last thing she needs is another child to take care of."

MARIA: it's about damn time. She deserves so much better.

JEREMY: I adore catty Maria

MARIA: it's my release

SARAH: I've found someone!

JEREMY: I've changed my mind. The road trip is a terrible plan. Don't do it

SARAH: he's lovely, I promise. Absolutely definitely not a pervert!

JEREMY: it's not reassuring when you have to say it, Sarah

MARIA: hush, Jem. You know what she means. That was quick, Sarah. Who is he? A friend?

SARAH: in a way

JEREMY: now I'm reassured

EVIE: right now, I'll take anyone

SARAH: good, because I've already sent him your number

UNKNOWN NUMBER: Er, hi, this is weird, but do you know Sarah? She said you were offering lifts to Sheffield at Christmas?

EVIE: hi! What's your name, sorry? Yes, it's more of a car share, is that okay? Do you have a car?

UNKNOWN NUMBER: Sorry, haha! It's Paul. I don't have a car.

EVIE: hi Paul. No worries. We can hire one. Do you have a license?

NOTAPERVERTPAUL: Yes, though there might be a small issue that means I can't actually drive. I can explain when we meet.

NOTAPERVERTPAUL: Are you there?

NOTAPERVERTPAUL: Hello? Are you ignoring me? If you are, don't worry. I don't mind.

NOTAPERVERTPAUL: It's just that it's Christmas, and Sarah said you were giving free lifts but if you've changed your mind just let me know. It's the polite thing to do. No need to be an arsehole. Haha!

EVIE: sorry for the delay, I was on the tube heading home from work

NOTAPERVERTPAUL: It's late to be just finishing work, but no worries.

EVIE: I really was on the tube, Paul

- - - - - - - - - -

EVIE: Sarah, who is Paul?

SARAH: You know my friend Michelle from work?

JEREMY: no

MARIA: the one who went missing?

SARAH: it turned out she just needed some time to herself. He's her ex

EVIE: Sarah!

SARAH: What?! I met him once and he looked rich

- - - - - - - - - -

EVIE: hi Paul, I'm so sorry, there's been a mistake. I'm really looking for someone with a car. Sorry to waste your time

NOTAPERVERTPAUL: I thought you were a saddo looking for a boyfriend.

EVIE: bye Paul

- - - - - - - - - -

EVIE: it's a no to Paul

MARIA: don't worry, I've found you a guy—the lovely Graeme. His mum lives next door to mine and he's driving home for Christmas too. Operation Road Trip meet-cute is a go! I can't wait to have you up here for a whole week

EVIE: thank you! Sorry Sarah

- - - - - - - - - -

SARAH: to be honest you've probably dodged a bullet. Besides, I already have the solution to your plus one situation. MY WEDDING. I'm going to find you the perfect man

JEREMY: #TeamGraeme

- - - - - - - - - -

YOU MISSED A CALL TODAY AT 12:14 A.M. FROM NOTAPERVERTPAUL

YOU MISSED A CALL TODAY AT 01:34 A.M. FROM NOTAPERVERTPAUL

YOU MISSED A CALL TODAY AT 03:17 A.M. FROM NOTAPERVERTPAUL

NOTAPERVERTPAUL: I'm so sorry, Evie, it looks like my cat fell asleep on my phone and butt-dialed you a few times. But while we're here, can we talk about that lift?

YOU BLOCKED NOTAPERVERTPAUL

Chapter 12

WLTM

EXT: SOUTHBANK CENTRE BOOK MARKET—FRIDAY,
DECEMBER 21, 11 A.M.

EVIE is browsing the stacks of secondhand
books laid out on wooden tables in the
shadow of Waterloo Bridge. She's too
absorbed to notice a man stepping up behind
her until he tugs on one of the pigtails
sticking out from beneath her woolly hat.

I whipped my head around to see NOB, clearly hungover. For NOB, this meant he was wearing sunglasses in winter, rather than reconsidering his life choices like any normal human being.

"You're late," I said.

"You're lucky I came at all." NOB had a large coffee in one hand; his other was shoved deep into his coat pocket. He was wearing a gray beanie that hung loosely off the back of his head and was about as practical as a paper crown against the bitter December weather. Though his Canada Goose parka looked toasty enough.

When I'd told NOB what time to meet, I'd accounted for the fact that his clock ran at least an hour later than everyone else's, and he'd still managed to be late enough to throw off my day. This morning I'd dropped Anette's costume off at Gil's to find she'd left something with Xan for me. My ticket to her play. *Peter Pan: "For Every Boy and Every Girl!"*

The start time was 12:30 p.m. today, and Anette's school was an hour away, meaning I'd have to finish here pretty quickly if I was going to make it. But I couldn't leave without getting NOB to agree to send Monty some proof that he was writing. All week Monty had been holed up in the Ash, his go-to comfort place. The only contact I'd had from him were the increasingly hysterical messages about the script. I needed to send him something from NOB to calm him down—and to prove his faith in me wasn't misplaced.

I tried to hand NOB what remained of my breakfast doughnuts. "I don't do carbs. Why are we meeting here?"

"You'll see." I made him take them from me anyway. "And live a little."

He chucked the bag into a trash can under the bookstall, pulling a face as he wiped his hands. "So, on the meet-cute scale, from projectile-vomiting to dragon cocks, where does this one sit?"

A woman pulled her child away to another stall, ignoring my mouthed *I'm sorry*. I glared at NOB, who gave me a look that said he couldn't have cared less. My phone buzzed. I knew who it would be without looking. Somehow the alert from Monty's message came with an edge of hysteria.

MONTY: Can you look into how to sell an office? Might as well start preparing ourselves.

I put my phone away. "Hand," I said. After a pause, NOB held out his palm. I gave him a small stack of business cards, keeping the rest for myself.

"Nice mittens," he said, spotting them dangling from my sleeve.

I indicated his chapped fingers. "It's function over fashion."

"I'm well aware of where you stand when it comes to fashion." He took a sip of his coffee as he peered at what was printed on the cards.

Evie WLTM you

He flipped the top one over. It had my number on the back.

"WLTM. Will. Losers. Text. Me?"

I pulled a face at him as I moved to the opposite side of the stall. *"Would Like to Meet.* It's an old personal ads term," I replied. I'd thought it was appropriate, given I was attempting to meet someone the old-fashioned way, without an app. "They're for the books." I made sure no one was watching, then picked up a water-damaged edition of Donna Tartt's *The Secret History.* I slipped one of the cards inside before snapping it shut and putting it back. I spotted Kerouac's *On the Road* and put one in there too.

"What *are* you doing?"

"It's the Fate meet-cute," I told him. Shuffling along, I slid another card into a book with a sticker announcing it was a literary prizewinner. "I leave my name and number in random books around London, and if a guy happens to contact me after coming across my details, it must be fate. I'll arrange for us to meet." Providing he wasn't a weirdo. I assumed there wouldn't be very many who weren't, but Jeremy had insisted I try it anyway. His love of John Cusack films apparently extended to *Serendipity.*

NOB seemed skeptical. "Sounds like your fate is to meet a bunch of perverts."

I pulled a copy of *The Iliad* from under a pile of James Pattersons.

"Do perverts read the classics?"

"Exclusively." NOB yawned. He downed the rest of his coffee and left the empty cup next to one of the many NO FLYERING signs stapled along the edge of the bookstall. I dropped his cup into the trash, looking nervously toward the hulk of a man who ran the stand. He kept walking between the bookstalls like a bouncer, glaring at anyone who dared to treat his business like a library.

"This is what I skipped my morning vinyasa for? I thought I was going to see a meet-cute in action. I'm not your lackey, Red. You need to up your game. We're at the one-month mark, and *somehow* you still haven't convinced anyone to fall for you. At this rate, that script is never going to get finished."

It was the perfect opening. "I'm more concerned with it getting started."

There was a pause. "Pay attention, Red." He flashed those perfect white teeth of his. "We have work to do." He picked up a tattered copy of *The Da Vinci Code* and put one of my cards inside before moving on to the next table. I tugged it back out of the pages.

"*Red,*" he admonished, catching me.

"What?" I asked, wide-eyed.

NOB smirked, selecting a book with an illustration of a woman on the front. She was bursting out of an impractically small bikini, and I wasn't sure what the man dressed as a PI was up to behind her, but she appeared to be enjoying it. *Private Intentions*, the title read.

He smiled sweetly and pushed my card in. "Oh, we're in luck. Sequels." He locked his eyes with mine as he slid a card into each. I didn't give him the satisfaction of a reaction.

It was time to hurry this along.

"That's secondhand erotica, you know," I said.

NOB wiped his hand on his coat. "And I'm done." He turned his back to me and I quickly retrieved all of his cards before following him to the other stall.

"You agreed to send Monty some pages," I reminded him, taking care to not sound as annoyed as I felt. When it came to NOB's writer's block, softly-softly was best. "That's the deal." His face darkened, but I was prepared for this. "Or," I offered, "you could keep him happy if you just send him your idea." Any good negotiator knows you don't concede, you compromise. "If you haven't come up with one yet, I can help. That's what I'm here for, remember?" *Come on, NOB, just admit that's why you haven't written the pages.*

"I don't need your help." NOB wrinkled his nose. "Are you done looking for Mr. Pretentious yet? I have things to be doing."

"Quit it," I told him. He raised his brows over his glasses. "We are going to have an actual conversation for once. I've done everything we agreed. Now it's your turn. Monty has been asking you for your pages, right? And he's going to keep asking, if you don't give him *something* to convince him and the producers you're writing." I paused. "And what do you mean, Mr. Pretentious?"

"What's that book you're holding?" NOB said.

I flushed. "*Ulysses.*"

The worst thing was, I knew full well that every book I'd stuck a card into was one of Ricky's favorites. *What am I doing?* NOB shook his head, then tapped some cards into a bunch of YA books and a *Beano* annual.

"Mr. Pretentious," NOB said. "The kind of man who reads literary fiction to make up for his lack of personality. In other words: bloody dull. Is that really what you're looking for?"

I stalled. Was he really describing Ricky? He *had* always made a point of reading in public. I stared at the books in dismay. It was like I was determined to repeat myself, like some kind of relationship *Groundhog Day.*

"Speaking of, what's your next meet-cute after this?" NOB asked, tapping more cards into a stack of Stephen Kings.

"It's the Road Trip meet-cute," I said, trying to focus. "I'm heading home for Christmas." I leaned across him to grab a Terry Pratchett, just as he was reaching for a stack of children's books near me. I collided against his chest (just as firm as I'd imagined).

Blushing, I straightened. NOB lowered his glasses to look at me. Irritatingly, the hangover had mellowed the blue of his eyes to the color of a fresh spring sky. He flipped them back in place and grabbed a Tom Clancy. "I'm heading to Monica's for Christmas," he said conversationally. "She has an estate just outside of Harrogate. Isn't that your neck of the woods?"

So that gossip column was wrong about their breakup. Not that it mattered. "I'm from *Sheffield*," I said. "And I know you're trying to distract me. I've sent you plenty of meet-cutes, and you only need to think of one. If you need inspiration, I have this great Venn diagram…"

"I told you, I don't need your help." Behind his glasses, NOB's expression was indecipherable.

"Don't you?" I slammed down Michael McIntyre's autobiography. "Then next time Monty asks me where your pages are, I'm going to tell him the truth. That you haven't written a damn word. We'd be better off telling the producers that now."

It was a risk to threaten this, but I was banking hard on NOB's desire to continue to put off any kind of public announcement. I stormed off, silently counting down. *Three, two, one.*

I was halfway across the bookstalls when he called, "You're assuming I don't already have one."

I spun around. "What do you mean?"

He was still putting my cards into books.

"I mean," NOB said, "that I do have an idea."

"You do?" I asked, hurrying back to him. *NOB had broken through his writer's block?*

"Yes."

"And you're writing?"

"Yes."

"*You,*" I said. We were standing almost toe-to-toe. "You are an infuriating man, you know that, don't you?"

A sly grin. "Yes," he said.

Dazed, I reached out for a familiar-looking book.

"The thing is," he told me, "I need more time to get the pages to Monts."

"I'll buy you time. All you need to do is tell me what your film is about." I couldn't let myself believe him until I had proof.

"*Oi!*" The shout rang out across the stalls.

"Oi, you!" It was the stall owner, and he was coming straight toward us. "What are you doing? No flyering the books! How many times?" He started to push past people to get to us.

"Come on, Red," NOB said. "*Run.*" Before I could react, he grabbed my hand, sending the remaining cards flying and pulling me along with him as he dodged through the throngs of book browsers.

"Come back here!"

"Not bloody likely!" NOB called, swiping an armful of books from a stall into the man's path like he was in a very British action movie.

We ducked between some Christmas trees for sale and out the other side, running as fast as we could until we were away from the bridge and heading along the South Bank, weaving between tourists and not stopping until we reached the railing overlooking the Thames.

I leaned on it, breathless. *You're still holding NOB's hand.* I let it go and clutched my aching side.

"Has . . . he . . . gone?" I panted.

NOB had barely broken a sweat. "Luckily for us he was a big fella, though we were neck and neck for a while there. Have you ever run before?"

I glowered at him, throat burning too much for a retort.

"This was fun." NOB eyed me. "We should get a coffee. I know a place."

The play, I thought, followed by: *NOB has just volunteered to spend more time with you.* He'd come up with an idea for his script. We could talk about it. No distractions. After a month of nothing, finally, *finally*, we were getting somewhere.

Bzzz. My phone. It would be Monty again, probably asking

about selling my desk on eBay. NOB was about to give me what I needed to assure him I was doing my job. I thought of Anette as Tink, looking for me in the crowd. Ben's disapproval when he realized I'd let her down. But what choice did I have?

"Okay," I replied, the feeling of elation fading.

"What's that?" NOB said, pointing. I was still holding the book.

It was a ragged paperback of *Peter Pan*, the spine so creased it resembled layers of sediment. *Loved*, I thought. Like the beautiful edition I had on my shelf, the one my dad had read to me a hundred times.

"I have to go," I said, wonderingly.

If I hurry, I might still make it.

"What about our coffee?" NOB said.

"I do want to talk about your script, there's just somewhere I need to be."

"My script? That's for Monts, Red," NOB said. "He's my agent, remember? I just really need a coffee."

I couldn't help myself. I laughed. He was nothing if not consistent. "Just promise you'll tell Monty your idea *today*," I told him, walking away. "It will keep him off your back." *And mine.*

"I have somewhere to be too," he called after me. "I have a hot brunette to collect."

"I hope you both have a lovely time."

"We will," he hollered.

It wasn't until I was heading into Waterloo station that I thought: *But isn't Monica strawberry blond?*

Chapter 13

Wind, Actually

INT: EAST DULWICH ACADEMY—FRIDAY,
DECEMBER 21, 12:45 P.M.

EVIE is pacing in front of a set of double
doors with covered windows. There's a note
tacked to the door showing a cartoon of a
person falling off a pirate ship and the
words *Tick-tock! Latecomers walk the plank!*
A gray-haired man sits at the ticket desk,
looking pointedly at his watch.

I peeled down the edge of the paper covering the window to peek inside the auditorium. The man at the desk cleared his throat. "Not yet," he told me.

I'd got here at 12:31 p.m., but he'd insisted I wait until Peter Pan had finished singing "Spice Up Your Life" to the Darling children before heading to my seat.

The man tutted and I realized my phone was buzzing. Monty again. *Of course* NOB hadn't spoken to him. What had I expected? Resigned, I checked the message.

It took me a moment to process it.

He'd sent me a picture of a freshly popped bottle of champagne, along with a rambling message.

NOB *had* sent Monty his idea—and the producers loved it.

I exhaled shakily as I read the message a few more times to make sure I wasn't mistaken. It was true. *At last.* I could relax.

Applause drifted through the doors. "Now?" I asked.

"You're in the Baby block, seat D43," the man called after me as I rushed inside. "Look for the pink carpet!"

The curtain had lowered for a set change, the glittering pirate ship on its surface shimmering as people moved unseen behind it.

"Excuse me, excuse me, so sorry, thanks so much." I squeezed my way along the row until I got to the only spare seat.

It was next to Ben.

You're here for Anette, I told myself firmly, sitting down.

The chairs were packed close together and the warmth from Ben's body radiated all down my right side. I shifted in my seat.

"I didn't think you were coming." His words were clipped.

"I got held up," I whispered back.

"Shhh!" a woman in front of us hissed.

The curtain lifted and a girl appeared onstage in her nightgown. I focused on her, determined to ignore Ben. "Oh my God. Is Justice *Wendy?*"

I should probably have been prepared for this possibility. Samantha had told me she and the other mums knew Ben from their kids' school.

"Yes," Ben said, something like amusement in his voice.

"Shhhh!" The same woman again. I gave her an apologetic smile.

Peter Pan appeared at the window.

"Is that *Detty?*" I exclaimed, sinking down into my chair.

"Shhhh!"

"Unfortunately."

Why have I come? As if to remind me, Anette walked onto the stage.

Someone offstage ushered her farther forward and, slowly, she padded to the front, hands buried in the many layers of her skirt, Union Jack wings dazzling. My mother had worked her magic. I held my breath as a spotlight lit her, accompanied by a tinkling sound. *Come on, Anette. You can do this!*

Her dad leaned forward in his chair.

"What's that, Tink?" Detty asked, for the second time.

When she still didn't respond, Ben held his hand up high in the symbol for *okay*. I'd looked it up, curious, after I'd seen Anette use it in Gil's. Anette spotted her dad first, then me. Her face relaxed.

Okay, she signed back, hand close to her chest. She pressed something on her bodice and her blue skirts lit up with the tiny star-shaped fairy lights my mum had threaded through the layers. There was a collective *ahhh* from the audience.

My breath caught when I saw the gloves I'd asked my mum to make. They were covered in silver crystals that flashed when Anette moved her hands. She started to sign, slowly at first, then picking up speed.

Finally, she smiled.

Ben was sitting so close that when he turned to me, I could see his brown eyes had warm amber tones in them, like whiskey held up to the light.

"Now everyone can see her shine," I said.

When the curtain fell for the interval, Ben and I sat in silence.

"I'm going to assume," I said eventually, "that Anette does not like Justice."

"Well, she didn't stop at 'silly ass,'" Ben agreed.

I hadn't needed to be able to read sign language to figure out that Anette wasn't exactly sticking to the script. It was perfectly clear in the way that Ben had gone from watching his daughter with a fierce pride to burying his head in his hands whenever she appeared onstage.

Detty had been oblivious, "translating" her signs for the audience exactly as they were written. Anette would most probably have got away with it completely, had it not been for the row of kids Ben told me were from East Dulwich Academy's sign language class, who'd spent the entire time in peals of laughter.

"To be fair," I said, smiling a little, "the audience was probably distracted."

"*Peter Pan* meets the Spice Girls does make for a striking mash-up." Ben's tone was bone dry.

"I'm not sure the wind machine was strictly necessary." It had almost blown several of the "Spice Boys" clean off the stage.

"I think it was their ode to nineties pop music."

"What lyrics did the Spice Boys sing to 'Wannabe'?"

"'If you wanna be my mother, you've got to get with my friends.'"

I caught his eye and we both smiled. Then I remembered what he'd said to Samantha about me last weekend.

"It was really great seeing Anette so confident," I said, keeping us on common ground. She had been prancing all over the stage by the end of the first act, completely stealing the show.

"I haven't seen her like that for years. Not since before Chloe . . ." He trailed off, and suddenly it didn't seem to matter that he didn't like me.

"How long has it been?" I asked gently.

"Almost three years." I'd put money on him knowing the actual amount of time, right down to the day. "We're okay. Christmases are still . . ."

"Christmases are tough," I finished.

A beat. "You lost someone too," he said softly.

I didn't normally like to talk about it. "My dad," I said, indicating the room. "Being here reminds me of him, actually. He used to come to all my film screenings when I was a student. My equivalent of the school play," I explained. "I'd never sit with him in the audience. I'd peek into the room during the film so I could see his reaction. He always had this look. Like he was proud, but also the tiniest bit sad. I never really figured it out."

"Ah," said Ben. "The 'How did I help create such a wonder and why is she growing up so quickly?' look. A dad specialty."

I smiled. "Is that what that was?"

His eyes crinkled.

"Chloe must have loved seeing Anette perform," I said, encouraged.

Ben looked away. "This was her first time on stage." When he fell silent, I thought maybe I'd overstepped, but then he spoke again. "Normally, whenever Anette does something new, that's when I miss Chloe the most. When it feels most unfair. But tonight, Anette has never seemed more like her. Her mum practically grew up on stage. She would have loved seeing Anette up there, bad language and all. Plus," he said, lifting the corner of his mouth, "she was a really big fan of the Spice Girls." I smiled with him. Then he gestured to the stage and said, "How can I think Chloe isn't here when Anette is right there?"

It was the most Ben had ever said to me. It made me wonder if I'd misunderstood something last weekend.

"Ben, I—"

"Ben! I thought that was you." A woman had swiveled round in her seat to face us, cutting off whatever Ben might have said next. Her face lit with obvious interest. It occurred to me that, to her, Ben was an eligible single dad. The school-gates equivalent of the film industry unicorn. *Tall, dark and brooding,* as Samantha had so thoughtlessly put it. Ben, for his part, didn't seem to notice. "Aren't you our official photographer?"

I felt him tense beside me, though his voice was polite. "Not anymore, Ann."

"Well, you're used to a bit more excitement than a school play, no doubt."

"I was always glad to do it," Ben replied. "I'm just no longer a photographer."

"But aren't you always off up a mountain somewhere?"

There was a pause. "I . . . I work for the local council now."

"Then whose camera is that?" The woman stabbed a finger toward the one sticking out of the canvas bag at his feet. It had a rainbow strap.

"Mine," I said, picking it up. I'd never seen him quite so rattled. It made me want to rescue him. "I specialize in selfies, mainly, so I'm not sure I'd be much help either."

To demonstrate, I angled the camera toward us both. "Smile, Ben." It flashed in our faces. Ben blinked rapidly.

"Okay." Ann's smile took on a polite edge. "Well, Ben, if you ever change your mind . . ."

Ben nodded, relieved. It was only when she'd turned back around again that I felt him ease up.

"Thank you," he said, quietly.

"It was nothing." I couldn't shake the thought of him being a photographer. *What made you give that up, Ben?* The man was a puzzle, one I had no business solving.

We both spotted them at the same time: a group of parents gathered at the front of the stage, looking over the audience. *At us,* I realized with a start. I recognized Justice's and Detty's mothers, who did not look pleased, and Samantha, who did. They were standing around a tall woman in her fifties with a severe bob that swung as she headed over to us.

"Ben." The woman had an air of reluctant duty. She wore a black shift dress and platform boots. I guessed we'd found the Spice Girls fan. "Can we have a quick word before the second half starts?" The gaggle of parents still stood by the stage, all taking enormous care to look like they weren't staring.

"Yes, Mrs. Clarke," Ben said, tucking in his chin like he was in trouble. "Just tell me what you want, what you really, really want."

I bit back a surprised laugh. Mrs. Clarke didn't look as if she appreciated the humor.

Up onstage, Anette's head appeared between the curtains. As soon as she caught sight of her teacher with her dad, she disappeared.

Ben sighed. "I've got to go catch myself a fairy."

When the curtain closed for the final time, I stood to leave, lifting my satchel. It was heavier than usual, reminding me of what was inside. Whatever had transpired backstage had kept Ben occupied for the rest of the performance. I badly wanted to find Anette, but that meant risking bumping into a certain group of parents.

"Evie!" Anette was pushing her way toward me through the throng, still in her costume and trailing glitter. "You came!" she squealed. The red ribbon was missing from one of her pigtails.

"You were spectacular," I told her.

"I have some apologies to make," she said, as if repeating dutifully a line that she'd been given.

I bent low so I could whisper in her ear. "Tink would have been proud."

She grinned. "My dad said to come and get you. He's backstage with my head teacher. Come on, I'll show you." She grabbed my hand and danced ahead of me, taking me up the steps and onto the stage.

We pushed through the curtain and stepped onto the dimly lit set. "Wait for me *right here*," she told me, positioning me next to the wooden pirate ship and backing away. "Dad wants to speak to you."

"Wait, Anette!" I called after her, sure she was mistaken, but she'd vanished into the wings.

Several minutes passed as I listened to parents attempting to round up their children behind the thin partition at the back of the stage.

Finally I heard footsteps.

"Anette?" It was Ben, looking harassed.

"It's just me," I called.

Ben picked his way through the Spice Boys' den toward me. As he stepped over Tiger Spice's canoe, his shoe got caught. I reached out to steady him as he extricated himself.

"Hi," Ben said.

"You wanted me?" I said.

He frowned, studying my face as he took a step closer. "I thought you wanted me?"

I shook my head, puzzled, then caught sight of a bunch of mistletoe strung up on the bow of the pirate ship. It was tied there with red ribbon. Anette.

Was she trying to set us up? Surely not. And yet—this could be a scene straight out of *Love Actually*.

I flushed, praying Ben didn't follow my gaze, so of course he did.

"Ah," he said. "Evie, I—"

A blast of air hit me from behind like I'd been whacked with a pillow. Unable to grab hold of anything in time, I smacked bodily into Ben. He tried to peel me off, but I could get no more than a few inches away before I was sent careening back into his chest. He opened his mouth as if to say something, only to inhale the end of my braid.

"Justice Merriweather, the wind machine is not a toy!" Mrs. Clarke bellowed as Ben choked. The wind abruptly shut off and a piercing giggle rang out, followed by racing footsteps.

We quickly disentangled ourselves, Ben straightening his shirt and wiping his mouth. A smile tugged at my lips as I pulled my cardigan down from around my shoulders. Then I saw his expression.

"Evie," he said gravely, "I need you to know. I'm not interested in being any part of what you're doing."

I stared at him, shocked. "I'm sorry?"

Ben indicated the machine, the mistletoe. "This is a meet-cute, isn't it?"

Did he seriously think I'd set all this up for him?

"Believe me, Ben," I snapped, cheeks burning. "You'd be the last person I'd want to meet." I couldn't bring myself to tell him that his daughter was behind this when she'd only been trying to help. I yanked at my satchel, pulling out the gift I'd brought with me, the reason I was late to the play. "Here, for Anette. This is what I came back here for."

Ben took it from me, touching the edge of the large bow that was wrapped around the metallic-green paper. "It's secondhand," I said, as I turned to leave, knowing he'd have no idea what it was I had given him. "But loved. I wanted Anette to have it."

I found a sheepish Anette standing in the wings. She threw herself at my legs. "Happy Christmas, Evie. I'm glad we met you."

"I'm glad I met you too," I said, throat tight. I didn't look back at Ben.

This time there was no mistaking the message. Ben thought I was a complete fool, and his opinion of me wasn't changing any time soon.

Chapter 14

Ramblin' Man

EXT: A STREET OF CONVERTED TERRACES, EAST
DULWICH—SUNDAY, DECEMBER 23, NOON

It's sleeting as EVIE struggles out of her
front door, pulling a suitcase. A tall,
balding man with a paunch visible through
his windbreaker—GRAEME—runs up to her and
takes her case. He opens the door to the
passenger side of his blue Škoda to usher
EVIE inside before trying to fit the
suitcase in the cramped boot. This is
taking some time.

"Are you okay?" I called to Graeme again as he huffed and puffed.

"No worries, all tickety-boo here!" he said. It was quite lovely to hear a Sheffield burr, although it was a shame about the "tickety-boo."

"I'm really sorry I was a bit late," I called.

"It would have been nice to miss the traffic," Graeme said, voice strained. He slammed the trunk shut with enough force to shake the car.

When he shunted his tall frame into the driver's seat, I saw the sleet had pasted his remaining hair to his scalp.

"I'll go first, then, shall I?" he said brightly, tapping the wheel. *You were the one who put me in the passenger seat, Graeme.* I smiled. Maria wouldn't be happy to know I'd written off the Road Trip meet-cute before the key was even in the ignition.

Maybe he just makes a bad first impression.

EVIE: you can stop worrying

MARIA: I'm not, I promise!

SARAH: I still think my choice would have been better

JEREMY: yes, if only Evie had chosen someone who DEFINITELY WASN'T A PERVERT

EVIE: right guys, I'm going to talk to him. No backseating. Wish me luck . . .

"So, this is weird, isn't it?" said Graeme as we made our way over Vauxhall Bridge. The Thames was slate gray and resolutely grim.

"A little," I said, smiling at him. Maybe this wouldn't be so bad. *When Harry Met Sally* was one of my all-time favorites, and in some small way, I was getting to live it. I had a list of conversation topics all ready to go to ensure our journey was rom-com-worthy.

"It's just under five hours, traffic pending," Graeme said. "Of course, it would have been less if we'd set off when we'd planned."

"Right," I said. We were definitely going to need that list. As I went to retrieve it from my phone, a message popped up.

NOB: How's the road trip? Is Garry as thrilling as he sounds?

RED: it's Graeme. And haven't you got more pressing things to be concerned with? A script, perhaps?

NOB: I take it that's a no.

I tucked my phone under my thigh, frustrated. NOB still hadn't told me what his script was about, and I couldn't bring myself to ask Monty. I didn't want my boss to lose faith in me. Given that I was supposed to be the one helping NOB to write, it might seem a little surprising that I didn't know what he was actually writing. At least the producers were happy. Sam-and-Max had been so thrilled with NOB's idea, they'd scheduled a meeting for January 2 to discuss what he'd written so far. Of course, as NOB hadn't yet produced any pages, this was set to be a very short meeting.

I tried to relax. Having an actual idea put NOB one step closer to finishing the script. I just needed to keep doing everything I could to find Mr. Happy Ending so NOB had no excuse not to write. And, if that failed, I'd chain him to his desk, professionalism be damned.

There was a rustling, followed by a stench so godawful, I gagged. "What's *that?*"

"Oh, do you want some?" Graeme asked, his left hand stuck in a plastic bag that contained something that had surely been dead for a while. "It's dried fish. I've just been to Iceland. I love traveling, don't you?"

I wound down the window, gulping in the fresh air.

Half an hour later, Graeme was still sulking about having to throw out the fish. I hadn't been able to stop heaving, and he hadn't wanted to risk his upholstery.

"Maria said you're a data analyst," I said to soothe him. "What does that involve?" This was not on my list of conversation topics, but I doubted Graeme was in the mood to decide whether he'd rather have nipples for toes or toes for nipples (Jeremy's contribution).

"This and that," said Graeme. "Maria said you had an interesting job. A film agent, or something. What's that like? Have you met George Clooney?"

He was trying, at least.

"I'm an assistant," I replied.

"Behind every great man and all that," he said, flipping the radio on to a preset channel. I eyed him. Had he meant that?

He'd put a chat show on. The host was one of those professional dissenters who enjoy taking vile standpoints and watching Twitter explode. The moment they mentioned "undesirables" I switched it to a pop radio station. Graeme turned it straight back, using a button on the steering wheel.

"Driver's choice," he said, with clenched-teeth joviality.

EVIE: Maria, my darling, how well do you know Graeme?

MARIA: I know his mum—she's lovely. Is everything OK?

EVIE: I'm sure it will be fine

I remembered what was in my pocket. I'd been late this morning because I'd gone to Gil's to write, determined not to be put off by Ben's attitude toward me. I'd even sat next to him and Anette (at her request, of course). After his assumption at Anette's play, I'd decided it would serve him right if I wrote NOB a report as if I had intended it to be a meet-cute after all, with Ben in the starring role. It had been cathartic, almost like how writing used to feel. Then I'd put together a list of films for Anette to watch over Christmas, while pointedly ignoring Ben—the closest we'd come to interacting was when he'd reminded Anette that she had a Christmas present for me.

It was a USB stick containing a road trip playlist.

"May I?" Not waiting for permission, I stuck it into the slot on the dash.

"Hi, Evie, it's Anette here," came her lilting voice through the speakers.

"What is this?" Graeme asked.

"It's a gift from—"

"And Ben." I stopped, astonished as his deep voice rolled through the car.

"*Meet* your *cute* road trip playlist," Anette continued.

"Is there a small chance Evie might miss your meaning?" Ben cleared his throat. "Because, sometimes, people can misunderstand."

"And then they act like giant doofuses."

"Thanks, Anette." His tone was wry but assenting. "I promise to be less of a doofus from now on."

Was I hearing this right? Ben no longer thought I'd concocted an elaborate scheme to kiss him? I wished he'd said something at Gil's this morning. Though, to be fair, I had been ignoring him. Speaking of fair . . . I felt a flash of shame, remembering that I'd sent NOB the meet-cute report.

"Is this guy one of your exes?" Graeme asked, intruding on my thoughts.

"No," I said. "He's . . ." It was too complicated to explain. "They're just some friends."

"Playlists are Dad's specialty," Anette continued. "So lie back."

"Keeping your eyes on the road," said Ben.

"And who knows what might happen."

I sang along to the entirety of "The Circle of Life" and Meatloaf's "Objects in the Rear View Mirror May Appear Closer Than They Are" before realizing I was waiting to see if there were any more messages from Ben between the songs.

What am I doing? Playlist or not, the man clearly thought I was completely bonkers for doing the meet-cutes. Right now, I thought he might be right.

"Can you reach into the back for my water? I really need it," said Graeme. "If only I'd brought my earplugs too! Ha, ha." I handed him the bottle and got my phone out to distract myself and give Graeme a break from my off-key warbling.

NOB: Entertain me. My hot brunette is proving beauty is only
skin deep. Absolutely zero conversation. No fun at all

Had Monica dyed her hair? It seemed such a cruel thing to say
about her, but that was NOB for you. Maybe the gossip columns
were right after all and they were going through a rough patch. She
really could do better.

EVIE: Graeme's a total riot

NOB: Bull. You're stuck in the same traffic I am and you ran out
of conversation 10 junctions back

My first thought was *Traffic?* Graeme would be thrilled. Followed by *Hang on a minute.*

EVIE: you're on the M1??

NOB: I'm spending Christmas at Monica's, remember? You
never listen. Tell me about your meet-cute

So much for that rough patch.

EVIE: it's going brilliantly. Have you picked your lead character's
name? I'm thinking Graeme

NOB: No woman in the history of rom-coms has gone weak at
the knees for a Graeme

EVIE: Jude Law in THE HOLIDAY. Ha!

Outside, the sleet turned to rain. Fluorescent ribbons of rear
lights trailed into the distance ahead of us.

"Traffic." Graeme smiled triumphantly. "I told you so."

"You certainly did." *Come on, Evie. Give him a chance.* "How will you spend Christmas?"

"Helping my mam. She'll be wondering why I'm so late. She'd have no one without me." Graeme slurped his water. "Being single means I have time for her," he continued, glancing over. He coughed. "Not that I wouldn't make sacrifices for the right person. The problem is"—he waved his bottle, face ruddy in the glow of the brake lights—"there's a reason so many women are single."

Now, there's a statement that's never ended well.

"Will you just look at that rain," I said. The raindrops were fat, full things that burst against the window, sending great cascades of water over the glass. "Kissing weather," I murmured softly.

He coughed loudly. "What's that?"

"Nothing." It was movie rain. The kind that soaked you through. When there's no point using an umbrella because there isn't a single part of you that isn't drenched. *Four Weddings and a Funeral* popped into my mind, and that infamous line from Andie MacDowell.

Graeme shook his now-empty bottle and plonked it into his lap, sighing. "What's that?" he cried suddenly, shooting forward in his seat and straining against his belt.

"What?" I asked, alarmed, searching the traffic ahead of us.

He sat back. "It was a *bird*," he said, as if it were obvious.

"Are you okay?" I eyed him warily. His hair was all over the place and I was starting to think the redness in his cheeks wasn't entirely down to the glare of the traffic.

Graeme's eyes went wide and he tossed the empty bottle into the back. "I'm fine, why?" He thought for a moment. "I do need a wee-wee." *I'm sorry, the grown man just said what?* "Let's pull into the next service station. Aha!" He bounced up and down. "This one coming up is my favorite."

My breath hitched as a smell filled my nostrils.

"Are you eating more of that fish?" I asked, glancing to check for the bag.

He coughed. "You made me throw it away, remember?"

"Then what's—"

A loud noise ripped through the car, followed, just a second too late, by another cough.

I closed my eyes briefly, understanding. This cycle continued for a few more minutes, each time Graeme getting worse and worse at timing his coughs until he might as well have given up altogether.

I wound down the window. The GPS had corrected its estimate of when we'd arrive. Our destination was now five hours ahead of us. Until then: hell.

MARIA: how's it going?!

EVIE: we're at his favorite service station

MARIA: so he's quirky

EVIE: it's Milton Keynes, home of the concrete cows

SARAH: give him a chance, Evie

EVIE: he's also a misogynistic arsehole

MARIA: oh god! I'm so sorry, Evie. I thought he was a good one. I even told him you were single

EVIE: to be fair, I think romance is the furthest thing from his mind. He just announced he was going to "clear the pipes"

I shouldn't be mad at Maria for setting me up with Graeme. It's just that she wasn't the one who was stuck in a car with a man who genuinely believed he had successfully disguised his farts. I sent my mum my new arrival time, thinking longingly of the moment I'd be pulling onto my old street. We weren't getting back before nine. I shivered, turning the heat up.

Rat-a-tat-tat.

A very damp-looking Graeme waved at me through the glass. Thinking we were swapping seats, I got out and stood back to let him past.

Which was when Graeme grabbed me by the shoulders and snogged me like his mouth was a plunger trying to unblock a drain.

My response was pure reflex and entirely justifiable.

Graeme jerked back. "You bit me!" he said, astonished. He stuck his tongue out. "Is it bleeding? Why would you do that?"

"You shoved your tongue into my mouth!" *Was that . . . dead fish? Ugh!*

"I was being *romantic*. You were the one going on about it being kissing weather!"

Great, so now that was ruined for me. "*Consent* is romantic, Graeme." I wiped the drizzle from my eyes, breathing hard and seriously considering leaving him there. "Just get in the car," I said finally, climbing into the driver's seat. A minute later, he got in beside me.

He produced a new bottle of water, moaning as he sipped it. I turned the music up. His fingers moved toward the radio.

"No," I said shortly. He dropped his hand. Twisting away from me, he curled up in his seat, clutching his water like a teddy bear. Unbelievably, he started to snore.

I enjoyed almost an hour of relative peace before he woke up. "The problem with women like you," he declared, startling me, "is that you never go for the nice guys. It's always the arsh-holes. Then you complain to *ush* when they treat you badly." His tongue must really be swollen. *Good.*

I checked the GPS again. Four hours to go.

A sensible person would have kept the peace. I wasn't feeling particularly sensible. "The problem with nice guys, Graeme," I said, "is that they don't realize they're the arseholes."

"The problem with—"

"See?"

He glared at me, gulping his water like it was an act of defiance. Ahead of us, the traffic was finally starting to break up. I accelerated, feeling freedom was at last on the horizon, when the car engine let out a rattle.

What was that?

The whole car shuddered. Was something burning?

"Graeme, when was the last time you checked your oil?"

"Shorry, *Mum*. 'Graeme, have you checked your oil?' 'Graeme, why are you making your female colleagues uncomfortable?' Women always ashk such irritating questions."

Black smoke billowed out from under the hood and all the warning lights went off on the dash.

"Whoopsh!" Graeme said. The car juddered and his hand jerked, spilling his drink over me. Which was when I realized the water was, in fact, vodka.

Chapter 15

The Arsh-hole

EXT: THE HARD SHOULDER, M1—SUNDAY,
DECEMBER 23, 5:42 P.M.

A fire engine's flashing lights turn the
night an artificial orange as police
officers wave a slow procession of cars
past the hard shoulder. An ambulance pulls
away from the scene just as a tow truck
arrives. EVIE is wrapped in a silver space
blanket and is talking to an officer.
GRAEME is also wrapped in a blanket,
arguing with the firemen.

"Are you okay, miss?" asked the concerned police officer, her eyes on Graeme. "Your partner seems agitated."

"I'm fine, thank you," I said, shivering in the drizzling rain. "And he's not my partner." I hadn't told her that we were actually complete strangers and that I'd orchestrated the road trip to get a screenwriter to write a rom-com. She already suspected I was drunk.

I returned the Breathalyzer. She checked it. "Thank you, miss. Everything looks fine. We just had to be sure."

"I completely understand," I said. I had, after all, been covered in vodka.

She left me to go and rescue the firemen from Graeme. I sat down heavily on the barrier, exhausted and wanting nothing more than to be with my mum eating homemade mince pies with steaming-hot mulled wine. It was looking highly unlikely that I was going to get home now, and tomorrow was Christmas Eve.

My cold fingers could barely type.

RED: you were right

NOB: I know. Wait. Have you tried faking an orgasm?

NOB: Red?

RED: I'm on the hard shoulder on the M1, while Graeme— who's drunk, by the way—shouts at a fireman for hosing his engine because it was on fire. So in short: no

NOB: you're not the ones driving that blue piece of crap, are you?

My heart hammered as I glanced up at the blue Skoda, which Graeme was currently draped over, much to the annoyance of the people from roadside assistance. *Yes, why?* I typed out. No response.

The Skoda had been successfully attached to the tow truck and Graeme scraped off its hood when the red sports car pulled up onto the hard shoulder.

I squinted at its tinted windows, wondering what kind of person drove their car onto the scene of an emergency.

The passenger window started to slide down, revealing blond hair styled to look effortless, achingly blue eyes, and an irritatingly beautiful, extremely welcome face.

"Hey, Red."

Am I really seeing this? NOB. On the side of the M1. My heart was a hummingbird in my chest.

He grinned and leaned over the empty seat to open the passenger door.

"What are the odds that you were the pain in my arse in all this traffic, Red?" he said, eyes sparkling with amusement. "Get the hell in."

"Are you really here to pick me up?" My voice shook as I leaned into the warm interior.

"What else?" he said. "Hurry up, you're dripping on the leather."

"Is there room for one more?" I pointed at Graeme, who was sitting a little farther down, hugging his luggage. The tow guys had refused to take him with them. He was an arsehole, but it was late, and it was Christmas, and his mother was waiting up for him.

"That depends." He raised his eyebrows suggestively. "Am I dropping him off at yours?"

"Two streets over." *Five at the most.*

"Fine. If my hairy friend doesn't mind." NOB indicated the backseat. If it could even be called that. It was a minuscule leather shelf made all the smaller by the absolutely ginormous hound occupying it.

"What's that?" My frozen brain couldn't keep up. It definitely wasn't Monica.

"Red, meet Ziggy. Ziggy, Red." NOB grinned at me. *Wait.* So this was his "hot brunette"? Did he know what I'd been assuming?

The mocking grin suggested he did.

It had taken so long to wrestle the drunk middle-aged man and two sodden pieces of luggage into NOB's sleek yet tiny car that when we finally set off, the traffic was almost clear.

"Thank you," I said, wondering if those two words could possibly be big enough to contain my gratitude. Christmas felt like it was back on, and it was all thanks to *NOB*. "This really means—"

"So *you* must be the arsehole," Graeme piped up from the back. NOB raised his brows. "What?"

I angled my head to glare at Graeme. He was pushing at Ziggy to claim some more room. The dog barely even noticed. "Women always choose the arsehole. *You.*" He jabbed a finger at me. "Just don't come crying to me when he dumps you."

"Ziggy," said NOB calmly. "Down."

With a great huff of air, the giant hound lay out flat, smothering Graeme, who yelped and scrambled upright, gasping for air.

I couldn't look at NOB. "He's drunk," I explained.

"I noticed."

"And another thing!" Silence. I looked back to find Graeme fast asleep, head resting on the mound of Ziggy's back.

"I already said thank you, didn't I?"

"Thank me with your report," he replied.

I rolled my eyes. *Still NOB.*

Once I could feel my hands again, I messaged my mum, followed by JEMS, to let them know I was delayed but okay.

MARIA: Evie, I'm so sorry. I can't believe it. I've just got his mother to talk. She said he's been fired. Something about drunken misconduct in the workplace and a Twitter rant

JEREMY: Sarah, don't you dare say it

SARAH: Evie has been through hell. I'm hardly going to mention that Paul was clearly the better choice, now, am I?

JEREMY: that's it. No more hen do. I think we can all agree that's fair

MARIA: how are you getting home?

EVIE: you'll never believe me

"Don't take this the wrong way," I said to NOB. "But why the rescue?"

"We have a deal, don't we?"

"As far as I know it doesn't involve roadside assistance."

"Red, you needed help. I was close by." A pause. "I'm really not that much of an arsehole."

"Graeme would disagree."

He laughed. I busied myself by letting my hair out of its braid so that it could dry in frizzy ringlets, wondering at these new versions of him. NOB, the dog owner. NOB, the rescuer.

"What?" I asked, when NOB glanced over at me.

"Nothing." This time, his eyes lingered a little longer. "You look good with your hair down."

"Thanks," I said, startled. *What is going on?* It meant nothing. To NOB, flirting was like breathing. If that's even what it was.

The music dipped as his phone connected with Bluetooth. *Babe calling*, said the display on the dash. NOB's mouth flattened, the perfect line of his jaw tensing. He canceled the call.

I wondered at this as I patted Ziggy. "Is he Monica's?" The dog hadn't been at NOB's house when I'd visited.

NOB snorted. "Monica can't stand him. He's been in quarantine since L.A., and she's not that happy he made it out. I'm taking him to a kennels, where at least he'll have a better Christmas than me." NOB reached around and ruffled Ziggy's ears. *Babe calling*, the dash told us again. Another jab of his finger to end the call.

"Is everything okay?" I asked.

"Peachy," NOB said, his tone short. I let the silence stretch. "You're insufferable, you know that? Fine. Monica's kids are spending Christmas with us. She sprang it on me this morning."

"And they're . . . how old?" I was unable to resist asking.

He arched an eyebrow at me. "Old enough to think their mother could do better than a 'one-hit wonder.'"

"They'll have plenty to be impressed with soon," I said. "The producers loved your idea. Just wait until you have the script to show them." His beautiful features held an expression that looked an aw-ful lot like doubt, and I felt a flutter of anxiety. "We should talk about the meeting in January."

"I got your meet-cute this morning," he said, sidestepping. "I knew straight away you were wasting your time with Dull Dad."

After everything that had happened, I'd almost forgotten I'd sent it. "He's called *Ben*, and you can just ignore that one," I said, flushing with guilt. The playlist was tucked up safe in my pocket.

"Don't worry," NOB said. "The guy was pretty forgettable. So, when will I get your report for the road trip?"

"As soon as you send some pages to Monty," I said, more irrita-bly than I'd intended.

Silence. He kept his eyes firmly on the road. "That idea I sent Monts," he said at last. "The truth is, Red . . . I couldn't have come up with it without you." He shook his head. "It's those damn meet-cutes. They've helped more than you could know." He'd said some-thing similar before. And yet, if this were true, then where were the pages? "But"—he looked over at me—"I just get the sense . . ."

"What?"

"That you're holding back when you write them." He shrugged. "Don't. You're a good writer, Red. If you want to have any hope of getting me to finish this thing, you need to be all in."

I eyed his chiseled profile, wondering at his words. I'd been tell-ing myself that I was the only one taking our deal seriously, and NOB—*NOB*—had seen right through me.

Because he was right. Even though I'd felt myself loosening up more and more with each report, there was still a voice in my head telling me I wasn't a real writer, reining me in. I'd made this deal with NOB to get him to write. If he was telling the truth, and the reports were genuinely inspiring him, then what was I so afraid of? That I'd find out NOB was mocking me when he said how good my writing was?

Or that I might actually enjoy writing again?

"Okay," I said, and his smile was strangely relieved. I put steel in my voice. "But you need to deliver some pages first."

"It's a deal."

Ziggy stuck his head between our seats, whining for attention.

"Sorry, buddy," NOB said, patting him. "We'll catch up after Christmas."

I buried my fingers in the dog's fur, sad to think of him alone over the holidays so soon after being in quarantine. "You know, I could look after Ziggy for the week," I said slowly. "It's the least I can do, after you rescued me. At Christmas my mum's policy is the more the merrier." Though Ziggy was probably a little more than she'd be expecting.

Heaven forbid NOB be grateful. "At your *mum's*?" he asked, clearly skeptical.

"Well, it's not the Four Seasons, but it's hardly *Emmerdale*," I shot back.

He let out a laugh. "You have to know what you're taking on, that's all. Ziggy is a dog that needs a lot of space. And he's vegan." There was tentative hope in his voice.

"Anything for my savior," I said, patting Ziggy.

"Savior! I like that."

"I meant the dog."

I found myself blinking back tears when I saw my mother's little end terrace all lit up with twinkling lights. *Home,* they said with each blink. NOB killed the engine and the temperature drop felt like a bubble had burst.

"Are you sure you're going to be all right with . . . ?"

Graeme let out a large fart mid-snore. There was no follow-up cough this time.

"I'll get sleeping beauty home."

"You've got his mum's address."

I realized I was dragging this out. It felt like we'd established some sort of truce over the last few hours, one that I thought would end when I got out of his car.

"Ziggy's stuff is in the bag in the back." We left it unsaid that he could have moved that bag to make more room for Graeme. "Send pictures so I know he's alive."

"Every day," I promised. "Right, I guess I'd better . . ."

NOB leaned toward me. I briefly caught a scent of honey and cream before he pressed the button for the trunk.

"It's been fun," he said.

As I pulled my case from the trunk, it bumped against the backseat.

"Evie!" Graeme poked his head above the headrests, startling me. "Wait. I . . . I'm sorry. It's been a bad time. I'm a good guy, really, I promise. Can I help you with your case?"

"Graeme," I said. "You're about to witness firsthand that women don't always choose the arsehole." His bloodshot eyes filled with hope. I slammed the trunk shut.

As I turned toward my mum's house, I found NOB standing in my way. Flakes of snow began to drift down from silvery clouds.

"Forgetting something?" NOB asked.

"Am I?"

He handed me Ziggy's lead and pushed a vast black bag onto my shoulder. I stumbled forward under the sudden weight, grasping NOB's chest. He caught my forearms and leaned in so his lips were beside my ear.

"Are you falling for me, Red?" he said, and grinned. Snow landed on my upturned face, melting on my lips. As his eyes searched mine, his cocky expression faded. It was the first time I'd seen him anything less than certain.

He blinked, pulling back first. "Don't forget," said NOB, and this time his smile seemed forced, "to send me your report."

"No problem," I told him, oddly shaken. "You know exactly what to do to get it." I yanked the handle up on my case. "Thanks again for the rescue. Don't worry about Ziggy, he'll be fine. Fatter, probably, but fine." I turned and walked away.

Opening the front door, I stepped into the warmth and familiar smells of my mum's house and snapped on the hall light.

Maria, Sarah and Jeremy were all standing in my mum's hallway with huge grins on their faces.

"Mary, she's home!" Jeremy called into the living room. "And she's brought some kind of hairy beast." Before I could react, they all rushed toward me at once.

This, I thought, hugging them fiercely, all thoughts of NOB chased away, *this is Christmas.*

Chapter 16

A Hot Brunette

From: Evelyn.Summers@WJM.co.uk
To: TheEzraChester@ezrachester.com
Subject: HIGHLY CONFIDENTIAL: Merry Christmas
December 25, 7:39 p.m.

Dear Ezra,

You'll notice in the attached picture that Ziggy really enjoyed (our) Christmas dinner. We took our eyes off him for one minute and the next thing we knew he was mounting the turkey.

I thought you said he was vegan?

Happy Christmas. I hope the kids are treating you well. And if not, just think, in less than two months you'll have a script to show them.

Must go before Jeremy finally kills Sarah. They're playing Pictionary despite our strict No Pictionary Rule, instigated after "Boobgate 2015" when Sarah drunkenly misread the card and instead of a *beast* drew a *breast*. Jeremy still celebrates the anniversary of her shouting "It's a BOOOOB" at the end of her minute.

Evie x

- - - - - - - - - -

From: Evelyn.Summers@WJM.co.uk
To: TheEzraChester@ezrachester.com
Subject: HIGHLY CONFIDENTIAL: Ziggy Stardust (are you even reading these?)
December 26, 3:02 p.m.

Dear Ezra,

Apologies for my email yesterday. I blame the bucks fizz.

I am attaching today's photo of Ziggy. Yes, my mum *has* dressed him as his namesake, David Bowie. You'll be glad to hear he took it all in his stride.

Best wishes,
Evie

- - - - - - - - - -

From: Evelyn.Summers@WJM.co.uk
To: TheEzraChester@ezrachester.com
Subject: HIGHLY CONFIDENTIAL: Furry fiend (Remember: January 2)
December 27, 2:56 p.m.

Dear Ezra,

We are officially in countdown-to-deadline mode. I know I don't need to remind you when Monty and the producers are meeting (it's January 2). And I especially don't need to remind you that I won't send my Road Trip report until you deliver those pages. I really mean it, Ezra.

Before I write this next bit, my mum wants me to assure you that we have loved having Ziggy here.

You'll notice today's picture of Ziggy features a sign that says THINGS I HAVE EATEN.

Here's a working list:

• ham
• a brand-new sneaker (the left one)
• a turkey
• two pairs of slippers
• Jamie Oliver's *15-Minute Meals*
• a Victoria sponge cake
• more ham
• the majority of a throw pillow
• next door's garden gnome
• next door's letter of complaint
• even more ham

Things Ziggy did not eat:

• anything remotely vegan

All the best,
Evie (and Mary) Summers

P.S. January 2

- - - - - - - - - -

From: Evelyn.Summers@WJM.co.uk
To: TheEzraChester@ezrachester.com
Subject: HIGHLY CONFIDENTIAL: Christmas Limbo (SEND
THE DAMN PAGES ALREADY)
December 28, 8:04 p.m.

Ezra,

I WAS going to write to tell you about how my mum
introduced Ziggy to our tradition of "Christmas Limbo," which
she does evry year between Christmas and new year. She
gets pople around, makes a shed ton of margaritas and
challenges everyone to a limbo competition. As you'll see frm
the picture, Ziggy enjoyed his go and made off with the stick!

INSTEAD, what I'm going to say is this, because it's
Christmas, and because TEQUILA.

I know EXACARLY what you're doing, Mr. Oscar-winning
Screenwriter. You're using the fact that I'm being super-chill
and withholding my latest rapport as an EXCUSE NOT TO
WRITE.

So here's my belabored Christmas present to you: it's the
Road Trip meet-cute. I wrote it on Christmas eve because
sober Evie is a big greek. You're a brilliant write, so WRITER
ALREADY. Doesn't even have to be loads. Just send Monty
SOMTHING.

No more excuses.

Bye,
Evie Xx

- - - - - - - - - -

From: Evelyn.Summers@WJM.co.uk
To: TheEzraChester@ezrachester.com
Subject: HIGHLY CONFIDENTIAL: Apologies
December 29, 10:02 a.m.

Dear Ezra,

I just wanted to apologize for the content of my email yesterday. It was unprofessional and, if it's any consolation at all, I am absolutely mortified and I feel dreadful—both because of the content of my email and the sheer volume of tequila.

I'd be very grateful if you could please disregard it completely. Apart from the bit about the pages.

You really need to deliver those.

All the best,
Evie

- - - - - - - - - -

From: TheEzraChester@ezrachester.com
To: Evelyn.Summers@WJM.co.uk
Subject: You're an absurd human being, you know that, don't you?
December 30, 3:20 a.m.

I've sent Monts Act One.

Call it a belabored Christmas present.

E.x

Chapter 17

Sleepless in Sheffield

INT: EVIE'S CHILDHOOD BEDROOM—MONDAY,
DECEMBER 31, 7:34 P.M.

EVIE is wearing a nightgown and is halfway
through styling her hair with a curling
iron. The walls are covered in peeling film
posters—*Waitress*, *Gentlemen Prefer Blondes*,
You've Got Mail, *Brick Park*, *Singin' in the
Rain*, *Tootsie*, *Sleepless in Seattle*. The
old, disused fireplace is piled high with
DVDs.

My mum pushed the door open with her slippered foot, holding two glasses of fizz. She passed one to me. Ziggy padded in after her, huffed into my lap, and lay down heavily on my feet.

"Happy New Year's Eve, pet." We clinked. "Did you get everything booked for Sarah's hen do?"

"Pretty much." I still had the manor booking to confirm, but that only required a quick email.

"Great." My mum sipped her prosecco. "Then we can chat about your next meet-cute."

I groaned. "I'm running late, Mum. The taxi will be here soon."

My friends and I were spending our New Year's Eve in The Wick, in honor of our student days. Maria had insisted we all dress exactly as we'd have done at university. I was wearing an old blue-and-white polka-dot 1950s dress with huge underskirts. I hadn't styled my hair for years, but back then I went full 1950s pin-up in Dorothy Taylor fangirl mode.

"Maybe I can help you plan it."

Before I could protest, my mum picked up my curling iron and began to separate the back of my hair into sections, just like she used to. She caught my eye in the mirror and smiled.

When I was dropped off before Christmas by NOB himself, bane of her daughter's working life, my mother had eagerly pried every detail from me about the deal I'd made with him and the meet-cutes. Any normal mother might focus on the fact that her only daughter was, for a very questionable reason, trying to meet a man. The only thing my mum had said was "I don't care what sort of man you meet, my pet, as long as he has kind eyes." Then she'd asked me when I'd be going back to the erotic fiction book group. When I'd explained that I'd gone only for the meet-cute, she'd said, "Evie, my pet, some of the best friends I ever made after your dad passed were in my book group. They loved a bit of smut too. All the best people do."

As she tried to coax my curls into slightly sleeker ones, my phone lit up with its own bit of smut.

UNKNOWN NUMBER: Hey found yr number in a John Grisham, would luv to get 2 know u better. Will u be my xmas ho ho ho?

For the last week I'd been getting almost daily messages from strangers who'd found my cards. Apparently, Christmas made a lot of people extremely horny. Which I guess explained *Love Actually*.

I deleted the message before my mum could read it and tell me I should give him a chance. We had very different approaches to life in general. She was always trying new things and avoided routine as much as possible. I, on the other hand, valued my safety and sanity. Or, at least, I had. As soon as these three months were up, my life could go back to normal. All Netflix and no chill. *Is that really what you want?* a little voice asked.

"It was supposed to be the Holiday Romance meet-cute," I told her, trying not to pay this thought too much attention.

"Oooh."

"But I can't afford to go away."

"Ah."

I'd been really hoping to book a beautiful cottage somewhere. A break and a meet-cute in one. But I'd used all my savings for Sarah's hen do.

"How about staying somewhere in the Yorkshire countryside?" my mum suggested.

"My budget might just about cover a tent, and that's hardly rom-com material."

"Did you know that the cottage in *The Holiday* was a set? It was basically cardboard!" my mother said.

"Well, I couldn't afford to stay in that either."

My phone buzzed. Dreading more messages from London's bookish sex pests, I flipped it over.

UNKNOWN NUMBER: hi Evie. I found one of your cards in a book.

No mention of what they wanted me to do to their candy cane. I considered it for a moment before deciding to reply. I really did need another meet-cute.

EVIE: thanks for getting in touch

I bit my lip, then wrote:

EVIE: if you don't mind me asking, what book did you find it in?

It would have been impolite to ask outright if they were a weirdo. *Unknown Number is typing* flickered on and off.

UNKNOWN NUMBER: Peter Pan.

I didn't remember putting a card in the book before I'd returned it to the book stand, but I'd been flustered after accidentally stealing it when NOB and I . . . *Don't think about NOB.* He'd sent his pages to Monty—*that's* what mattered. The meeting in two days' time was going to go fine. My friends and I were going to celebrate tonight with champagne.

Just don't think about your email. Do NOT think about that email . . .

EVIE: may I ask your name?

"I stayed in a cottage just like the one in that film with some girlfriends a while back," my mother mused as she tugged at a stubborn curl. "Absolutely perfect for a holiday romance," she winked. "*And* cheap as chips."

"A cottage?" I said distractedly.

UNKNOWN NUMBER: it's Ben.

What? Ben? Surely not *Ben* Ben.
Of course it wasn't. It was a coincidence, that was all.

EVIE: hi Ben. Nice to meet you

"What was it called now? Honeysuckle Cottage," she said, answering her own question. "It was exactly as you imagine a cottage should look, if you know what I mean." My mum took my phone and peered over her glasses as she did a quick search for it. "Oh," she said, holding it away from her. "Ben is sorry for how he acted at his daughter's play. Was he disappointed with her costume?"

"*What?*" I read the message.

BEN: I wanted to tell you how much I liked you and that I'm
sorry for being super-rude at my daughter's play.

I caught my breath. It *was* him. What was going on? Was he *drunk*? Not that I could judge after my recent antics . . .

EVIE: are you OK, Ben?

BEN: I'm great! When we see each other again I might not say
we spoke. I'm very mystrious.

"Pet?" My mother broke me out of my daze. Ben *liked* me? I wasn't quite sure how I should feel about that. Relieved?

More like puzzled. He might have made me a playlist but that didn't explain him suddenly wanting to be friends.

"Anette's costume was perfect," I told her, still trying to figure him out. My mother made an interested noise and I shot her a glance. "He was referring to the fact that he made absolutely sure I knew he wasn't the man I was looking for with my meet-cutes."

"Did he? So why is he messaging now?"

An excellent question.

EVIE: are you sure you're OK?

BEN: a big fat yes.

"Well, he's certainly put a smile on your face."
"It's not him," I told her, still grinning.

BEN: Anette, are you using messenger on my tablet?

BEN: merde.

I could picture them both at home: Anette sneaking the tablet into her room, Ben probably reading somewhere, seeing the app on his phone light up.

BEN: I'm sorry to have bothered you. Don't worry, my daughter will be suitably punished. Anette, no catfishing for a week.

EVIE: Ben, it's me. Evie

A few seconds passed. Either he was wrestling the tablet away from Anette or he didn't want to respond.

BEN: Anette said she's very sorry for SLEEPLESS IN SEATTLE-ing you.

That's what she was doing. The widowed dad. The kid. Anette was still trying to set me and her dad up. It was sweet, if completely and utterly misguided.

BEN: she found a card of yours in the book you gave her. I wanted to talk to you about that.

My grin faltered. A flush spread across my skin. I'd been finding those stupid cards all week. Did he seriously think I'd somehow orchestrated this after what he'd said to me at Anette's play?

"Urrgh!" I groaned, jabbing out a reply as my mum put the finishes to my hair, humming to herself.

> EVIE: that was an accident, Ben. I can promise you I'm not
> going to rope you into having a meet-cute with me anytime
> soon
>
> BEN: I just wanted to thank you for the book. It meant a lot to
> Anette.

Oh. *Merde.* Outside, my taxi beeped its horn. My mother kissed my hot cheek.

"I'll just tell the driver you'll be a few more minutes," she said, taking Ziggy and leaving me to it.

> EVIE: you're welcome. I'm very glad she liked it
>
> BEN: was it yours?

At first, I hesitated. Then:

> EVIE: yes

I wriggled into my dress, trying to imagine what Ben was thinking right now. That it was silly? I *loved* that book. It meant more to me than anything else I owned, and yet giving it to Anette had felt right. I looked at the framed photo on my vanity table. My dad with his arm around my shoulders, a proud grin on his face. It was taken on my fourteenth birthday, and in it I'm gripping a boxed laptop, cheeks flushed with both happiness and the reluctance of having to pose.

BEN: you made her Christmas.

I caught sight of my smile in the mirror—almost silly with happiness.

BEN: and I really am sorry about being super-rude at Anette's play.

EVIE: apology accepted. Safe to say we're both good at jumping to conclusions. Did you have a good Christmas, Ben?

BEN: we ate far too much and watched all the films you recommended.

BEN: it was the best one in some time.

My breath caught. There was something about the thought of just the two of them laid out on the sofa in front of the TV, watching all my favorite films on Christmas day, that squeezed at my heart. Another message popped up when I was halfway into my duffel coat. It was a link to "You Were Meant for Me" from *Singin' in the Rain*, one of the films on the list. I shook my head.

EVIE: hi Anette

BEN: hi Evie!

BEN: say goodbye, Anette.

BEN: we'll be back at Gil's again from next week!!

EVIE: I'll see you both then

BEN: see you soon, Evie.

As I got into the taxi, my phone buzzed in my hand. *Was it Ben again?* But it was just a message from Monty.

MONTY: I could have sworn you said you had everything under control, Evelyn. So where the devil are Ezra's pages?

Chapter 18

New Year's Evie

INT: THE WICK AT BOTH ENDS—MONDAY,
DECEMBER 31, 11:45 P.M.

EVIE and MARIA are sitting at a table full
of empty glasses in the packed-out bar.
There's a DJ playing. Green lights strobe
over people's heads as they dance. EVIE is
clutching her phone. MARIA, dressed fully
in black with heavily kohled eyes and dark
lips, rests her head in her hands.

"Have you seen this?" I shouted over the music.

I was thumbing through NOB's Instagram.

"How long have those two been at the bar?" Maria asked, sounding tired.

I scrolled past images of an impeccably dressed Christmas tree. Mountains of perfectly wrapped presents with foiled paper and elegant gauzy ribbon. NOB in a yoga pose, balanced on his head, bare-chested, muscles tense and glistening . . .

"It's only four shots of tequila," she grumbled.

I stopped at a slightly out-of-focus shot of a woman with her face partly obscured by a white mug. Soft waves of strawberry-blond hair falling to her shoulders, long woolen socks pulled up to her knees, a gray cashmere jumper on her slender frame. Monica. The image was tagged #loveofmylife #blessed #bestchristmasever.

I shoved it beneath Maria's nose.

"If he's had enough time for daily posts, he could at least write one page—one *measly* little page—of the script. Instead, he's living a hashtag blessed life while I'm stuck with receiving messages from perverts. You know, it's not even that he hasn't written anything."

"It's that he lied," intoned Maria, her black fingernails pressing into her cheek as she rubbed her face wearily.

"Exactly!" I said, picking up my glass before remembering it was empty.

"Don't let him stop you from enjoying yourself tonight." There was a note of warning in my friend's voice.

"How can I when he's swanning around Yorkshire doing yoga with hashtag gazelle legs?"

"Oh my God, *Evie*," Maria said, exasperated.

I looked at her. "Is something wrong?" I asked.

"Is she still going on about the cockhat?" Jeremy appeared with a tray, towering over Sarah, who had her arm around his waist. The pink and yellow glitter that had been on her eyelids at the start of the night had now migrated to her thick blond hair.

"My heroes," Maria said, reaching in. "It's your turn to deal with her."

"No, you don't." Sarah slapped her hand away and allocated us each a shot and a slice of lime, placing the salt dead center on the table.

"I'm not that bad, am I?"

"Evie, we are moments away from midnight. We're all together. You're *I Love Lucy*. Maria's Wednesday Addams. Sarah's dressed as a fairy—did you really use to wear that?"

"At least I'm not in spandex!" Sarah said, tugging at her wings. Jeremy's lean figure was encased in head-to-toe neon, like a cyclist who'd gone clubbing.

"It was a phase. Let's just *enjoy* this," he insisted. The DJ lowered the music and began the countdown. *Ten.*

There was a roar of noise as everyone shouted along with him.

"Is everyone sick to death of me?" I asked, looking at my friends.

"Not *you*." Maria linked my arm. "But I am hashtag done with deconstructing NOB's latest Instagram post."

My friends were poised with their shots. In that moment, in these outfits, we could have been us from ten years ago.

Nine.

Jeremy was right. I was wasting precious time.

Eight.

"Lick," Jeremy commanded. We did and all dutifully held out the backs of our hands as he made a circle of salt over them.

Seven.

"To still being young. Ish." Jeremy held up his shot.

Six.

"To having the best friends who plan me the perfect hen do, *and* to single-handedly pulling off the wedding of the year." Sarah paused. "And to becoming a stepmummy."

Five.

"To . . ." I thought about what it was that I really wanted. Jeremy fluttered his fingers to hurry me along. "To getting NOB to write that damn script."

Four.

"To falling in love," Maria said, holding her shot high. "Just like in the movies."

"Three. Two. One," Jeremy finished before I could protest. We all tossed back the tequila.

"Happy New Year," I said, wondering what it would bring.

"Hey, hey you, do you know what you are?" I was in a stall, sitting on the toilet lid, skirts bunched up around me, the cold plastic sticking to the backs of my thighs. I had a number of tequila shots in me, all competing to be the one that convinced me this would be a good idea.

"Do *you* know what time it is?" NOB's voice was tired.

"It's definitely after midnight," I said. He wasn't going to change the subject that easily. "And you're a NO—annoying." I stopped myself just in time.

"You're . . . drunk, aren't you?" He perked up. "How drunk?"

"Drunk enough!" I hollered. There was a flush from the stall next to me.

"Are you in a toilet?"

"No." The hand dryer came on.

"Really, Red—" NOB's voice became muffled. *"It's nothing, just Eddy, you know what he's like. I'll be right back, babe."* A door closed. "Have you only called to tell me I'm annoying?" he asked. "I'm picking Ziggy up tomorrow. Couldn't it have waited?"

"No!" I'd forgotten that. "I'm also calling because you haven't delivered—" I held my mouth close to the speaker. "LIKE YOU PROMISED. You lied to me."

"You wouldn't leave me alone. What else was I supposed to do?"

"Deliver the pages!"

"No one works over Christmas."

I heard some girls giggling and lowered my voice. "I do!"

He sighed. "If it makes you feel any better, I've had a rotten holiday."

"Liar." It did, a little.

NOB didn't reply straight away. There was a soft grating sound, like he was running his hands over his designer stubble. "You think you're the only one driving me nuts about my writing?"

I screwed up my nose. "Monty?"

"Him too."

None of this mattered. "I started writing again, *properly*, for you, and *you* promised to write the pages," I insisted. "So what's the problem?"

He made a strangled noise in the back of his throat. "You should be concentrating on getting someone to fall for you, not hassling me."

"Why is everyone so hung up on that?" I gripped the toilet seat. I felt like a kid in a wave pool, only instead of water, it was tequila.

"Isn't it the whole point?" NOB reminded me. I hiccuped sadly. "Look, your last meet-cute report was your best yet. I knew there was a great writer in there somewhere. Is that what you need to hear?"

"What I *need to hear* is that you haven't just been stringing me along this whole time. Because . . ." I leaned my head against the graffiti-covered cubicle, the fight leaving me on my next breath. "Because I'm going to lose my job if you don't deliver."

A pause. "Is that true?"

"Yes," I said, with a prickling certainty that I wasn't supposed to have told him this. "Surprise! Mr. Center of the Universe discovers he's exactly as important as he thinks he is. Without you, the agency's toast. It's time to bring home the bacon. Monty's meeting with the producers on . . ." I squinted.

"The second," he prompted.

"Send him some pages by then."

"It's New Year's Eve, Red, when am I supposed to—"

"Enough!" I pushed myself upright, not wanting to hear another excuse. He'd *promised* me. If I write more, he'd write too. Suddenly, everything seemed crystal clear. I was doing the meet-cutes to get him to write. He wasn't writing. Ergo: no more meet-cutes. *Brilliant logic, Evie,* I congratulated myself, trying to ignore the feeling I was missing something vital. "No more meet-cutes!" I declared out loud, and it felt *good.* "I'm serious."

"Seriously drunk, you mean," he dismissed.

"I'm both," I assured him. "If you aren't going to write, what's the point? No writing, no meet-cutes."

"We still have an agreement, Red." There was an edge to his voice. "You're not even close to winning this yet. And what about your job?"

Ah. That.

"What job?" I asked, on a bit of a roll. "No script, no job." Alarm fluttered wonkily in my chest, as if it were drunk too. *This is going well, isn't it?* I was sticking it to NOB, showing him he couldn't mess me around any longer.

"What would the producers say if they found out you'd got me to sign under false pretenses?"

"If you don't deliver, you can tell them everything for all I care. Including the fact that their writer is an irritating, contract-breaking, egotistical, selfish *NOB*!"

With that, I hung up, trembling with adrenaline. I'd done it. I'd finally told NOB exactly what I thought of him. And I definitely felt better for it.

"Evie?" It was Jeremy. "It's time to go! Maria's started singing, and we all know what that means."

I opened the door, still shaking. My friends were standing in front of the sinks, all supporting one another. They grinned blearily at me.

"One maca, two maca, three macarena."

"I don't think those are the words, darling."

Maria stopped singing. "Swevie, are you okay?"

The triumph was draining away like a tide pulling out, gradually, and then it was gone.

I held on to the doorframe. "I think . . . I might have just lost my job."

I sat bolt upright in bed.

"Shit. Shit. Shit. Shit." I scrambled for my phone to check, just in case it had been a dream, but the evidence was in the call logs. I'd rung NOB ten times—*ten*—before he'd finally picked up just after three a.m. The conversation came back to me in pieces. I'd called him *NOB*. I'd said I would lose my job if he didn't write. I'd all but told him to make sure I did.

There were a ton of unread messages. Some were from my friends. The rest were from Monty.

MONTY: You promised you'd get him to send his pages on time, Evelyn. Where are they?

MONTY: I should never have let you handle this responsibility. If we don't have anything by tomorrow, it's all over.

Oh God, the meeting with Sam-and-Max. I threw myself face-down on my sheets. Then I lifted my head, remembering. NOB was coming over today to collect Ziggy. *I'm going to have to face him.*

No. It was a good thing, sort of. I could talk to him, maybe even salvage this mess.

The doorbell sounded.

"Evie, your friend's here!" my mum called.

"Shit! Shit, shit, shit!" I yanked on some jeans and a jumper and hurtled down the stairs, stomach lurching.

My mum was waiting by the door with Ziggy. I gave the big hound a hug, burying my face in his fur. "I'm going to miss him."

"Me too," she said.

"Promise you'll behave," I told her, standing.

"Why wouldn't I?"

There was a funny feeling in my stomach that was one part hangover, two parts dread.

My mother hovered eagerly behind me. I counted to three before opening the latch.

It wasn't NOB.

Standing on the doorstep, in a fur gilet over a dark purple jacket, was Monica Reed, looking tall and regal like a misplaced royal. She was wearing sunglasses, presumably in case anyone was expecting to spot the Oscar-winning actress on New Year's Day in Crosspool.

"Oh, my," my mum said, leaning forward. "It's an honor." *Oh, no. She wasn't, was she?* She was. Mary Summers was bowing. I turned to Monica and smiled.

"I'm here for the dog," said Monica, holding out her palm. I gave her Ziggy's lead before my mum could attempt to kiss the back of her hand.

She grimaced. "What's that?" My mum had gone back inside and was now waddling toward us with the huge black bag. I hurried to take it from her.

"It's all his things. I've packed a snack. It's sausages," my mum said helpfully, holding out the clear plastic Baggie.

Monica pulled a face. "I'm vegan."

"They're for the dog," my mum replied, baffled.

"He's twice the size he was before Christmas. Ezzie will be furious." It was hard to tell with the glasses, but it seemed like the thought gave her a lot of pleasure.

"I'll give you a hand," I told Monica, shouldering the bag.

"Great." She handed Ziggy's lead back to me and spun on her booted heel.

"So lovely to meet you, pet," my mum called after her.

I followed Monica, still hoping for a quick word with Ezra. A gleaming white Land Rover was parked at the curb.

"Where's Ezra?" I asked, an unpleasant twist in my stomach that had nothing to do with my hangover.

"Ezzie's already gone ahead to London," Monica said. Ezzie's *what*? She opened the passenger door. I gave Ziggy one last rub before he climbed into the footwell. "Aren't you the assistant?" she asked. I saw her slip him one of the sausages. "Shouldn't you know this?"

"Know what?" I asked.

"Ezzie wanted to meet with Monty before seeing the producers tomorrow."

Cold dread surged through me. Surely Monty would have told

me if I had to organize a meeting for today? I tugged my phone from my pocket.

There was a new message from him, sent only minutes ago. It simply said: *Code Red.*

There weren't many things that would lead NOB to willingly organize his own meeting.

One. An assistant had told him that if he didn't deliver, he could tell Monty he'd never wanted to sign the addendum in the first place.

Two. Our conversation last night had convinced him to write some pages after all.

Three. *Oh, God. NOB's telling Monty everything.*

The world took on a soft edge. My vision narrowed to a point, like I was an old TV set shutting down. If Monty found out that the script—and the agency—depended on my love life, I could forget about a promotion; I'd be lucky to work in agenting again at all.

"Are you okay?" Monica asked, somewhat reluctantly.

The world snapped back into focus. She was climbing into the car.

What had NOB said last night? *You think you're the only one driving me nuts about my writing?* Maybe Monica wanted NOB to get the script done just as much as I did. "I hope Ezra's writing didn't get in the way of Christmas too much," I blurted out, hoping she'd tell me *something*.

She lowered her glasses, revealing light green eyes the color of vintage gems. "Ezra's writing?" she asked.

"The script." The words stuck in my throat, panic fluttering in my chest. "For Intrepid Productions."

"You really have no idea, do you?" There was pity in her voice. She dropped her glasses back into place. "Right," she said, as if to herself. "That's enough." The door slammed shut before I could respond.

Well, that was hardly reassuring.

Chapter 19

A Cheeky Nando's

EXT: CHINATOWN, LONDON—TUESDAY, JANUARY 1,
7:30 P.M.

EVIE yanks her suitcase over the cobbled
street, passing closed restaurants, mittens
dangling from her cuffs. Overhead, lanterns
swing in the breeze. There are a few people
around, but the streets are mostly empty.
Her eyes are glued to her phone. She just
about manages to avoid colliding with a
tourist.

I skidded around a corner, sliding a little on black ice. *Right, Evie, probably time to calm down.* NOB hadn't responded to any of the messages I'd sent on my train ride here. The only message I'd received had been another Code Red from Monty, telling me I had to come straight to the office.

There were any number of scenarios that would explain why Monty could possibly want to see me at this hour. They all ended with Monty wanting to fire me.

My phone lit up again.

It was NOB. *Oh, thank God.*

NOB: Where's the fire, Red?

RED: didn't you get my messages?

NOB: All 300 of them, yes

RED: then you know our deal is still on

NOB: That's not what you said last night

Shit. I rattled my keys in the lock but the door wouldn't budge. Monty had slid the dead bolt across on the inside. *What is going on?*

EVELYN: hi Monty, I'm here, but I can't get inside

EVELYN: it's very cold out! Are you still there?

EVELYN: hello?

MONTY: I NEED YOU TO GET SOME THINGS FROM TESCO.

EVELYN: didn't you want to talk to me first? You did say Code Red

MONTY: BLEACH. AND CARPET CLEANER.

MONTY: AND SOME PAPER TOWELS. AND GLOVES.

MONTY: AND AIR FRESHENER.

He was going to fire me. Or worse.

EVIE: guys, I think my boss is going to murder me

MARIA: are you at work?!

EVIE: in Tesco, buying Monty the things he needs to clean up when he's done with me. The checkout assistant is giving me the eye

JEREMY: ask her for some tarpaulin

EVIE: NOB had a meeting with Monty today. I think he's told him about our agreement. My heart might explode

MARIA: try not to worry. It could be absolutely anything

EVIE: OK. I'm back at the office now. Wish me luck

SARAH: can everyone just take a second to appreciate the fact that I'M GETTING MARRIED THIS YEAR

JEREMY: Evie, send us proof of life as soon as you're done

Monty had removed the dead bolt this time. I pushed open the heavy front door, calling out a cautious "Hello?"

There was no response.

I left my case in the hall and headed slowly up the stairs with the bag of cleaning supplies, treading softly on the worn brown carpet. Usually the creaky old stairs gave me a sense of comfort and familiarity, but tonight they filled me with dread.

Creeeak. You're going to get fired. Creeeak. Monty is waiting upstairs and he's furious because NOB hasn't delivered and it's all your fault. Creeeak. You're carrying the stuff he's going to use to remove the evidence and they'll never find your body.

The main hallway was dark, lit only by the light in Monty's office. It had a window that looked out onto the corridor where my desk was, but the blinds were closed.

There was a smell that hadn't been here before Christmas. One that hit the back of my throat and stung my nostrils. With every step toward Monty's office, it grew stronger.

"Monty?"

My poor hungover stomach could barely handle it.

I held my breath and pushed open the door.

Monty was sitting on the floor, hands clasped, staring at an upturned Nando's bag between his splayed legs. There were two open bottles of champagne on his desk. One had red lipstick on the rim.

He looked up at me with unfocused eyes. "EVELYN, THANK GOD. I'M AFRAID I'M IN A BIT OF A PICKLE."

Well, that explained the messages. Drunk Monty always spoke in caps lock.

"What happened?" I asked, trying my best not to breathe through my nose.

"MY DATE." He saw me wince and lowered his voice to a whisper. "*My date.* I wanted to . . . 'show off' the office, but it turned out she very much had—*hic*—other plans." Other than the lipstick on the bottle, I couldn't see any sign of her.

"Why did you want to see me?" I asked.

He lurched suddenly to his feet. "I had a meeting with Ezra. He told me the news."

"News?"

"Then we went for a cheeky Nando's."

"You and Ezra?" I asked, mystified, trying to imagine them eating chicken together.

"Me and my *date*."

"And what happened *before* then, Monty?"

"Well, we were getting on really well. She kept checking I was okay with getting frisky." I closed my eyes briefly. "She was helping me celebrate the brilliant news."

Wait. "What brilliant news?" I asked, hardly daring to hope.

"Aren't you listening? Ezra's written the first act. And the pages . . ." Monty raised his voice and threw his arm out as if addressing a crowd. "The pages are STUPENDOUS. He's outdone himself."

For a moment, I couldn't respond. Was this *true*? I sank to the rug, leaving Monty standing.

"I wouldn't sit there."

"But . . . the Code Red."

"It is VERY hard to find a decent restaurant that's open on New Year's Day."

That was it? That's the emergency I'd spent all day fretting about?

On the plus side, I hadn't lost my job. NOB was writing. Our deal was working.

"Can I read the pages?"

Monty's expression performed several acrobatics before landing in a frown. He waggled a finger at me. "*You* have to wait. He said he's at a delicate . . . a delicate junction. Top-level eyes only until it's done." *Will Monty* ever *see me as more than just his assistant?* "Right now, you have an important job to do."

"I know, get him to finish it," I said. Monty frowned at this. "Wait, if everything's fine, why the second Code Red?"

"That's what I've been trying to tell you," Monty huffed. He leaned over the Nando's bag, hands on his hips. "My *date*."

I suddenly dreaded finding out what was beneath that bag.

"If ANYONE asks if they can 'cop a feel of you,' say *no*," Monty advised gravely. "Of course *I* said: Why not? Then we started to . . ." He waggled his fingers. I blanched. *DO NOT PICTURE MONTY NAKED.* "Just when I thought we were going to get down to it, she pushed me out of the way and—" He bent down and, in the manner of a waiter lifting a tray to reveal a hot dish, whipped off the bag. "Got down to it."

There was a poo nestled in the white fur rug.

"Funny old world, eh?" said Monty. "You know," he added thoughtfully, "maybe she wasn't saying 'cop a feel of ya' after all."

The bag of cleaning products helped me guess where his thoughts had gone next. *Is this all he thinks I'm useful for?* I'd always wondered what my limit would be when it came to doing exactly what Monty asked of me. As I looked at the rug, I thought, *This is it.*

"You," Monty said abruptly. He swayed and I stood to steady

him. "You are so good. I never say that, do I?" Was he . . . compli-menting me? *Now?* His voice went very high. "Whhhy don't I say that? You are so good at cleaning up my messes." He nodded, eyes closing as he leaned into me and I nudged him upright with a heavy sigh. "It's good to know," said Monty sleepily, "that I can always rely on you. Funny thing is . . . I didn't have anyone else to call."

Oh, Monty. I looked at his nodding head, the paunch that hadn't been there a few years ago, the gray in his hair, and I knew I was going to do what I always did.

I was literally going to take Monty's shit.

"Come on," I said. "Let's get you home."

MARIA: hey lovely, is everything OK?

EVIE: yes, it's all fine. My job is safe for now. NOB's writing and Monty celebrated a bit too hard, that's all

SARAH: so you're not dead??

EVIE: god no, sorry! No casualties—unless you count the rug. Quick question. Do you know the term for someone with a poo fetish? It's coprophilia. Jane helpfully confirmed

MARIA: OK. Firstly, YOU GOT NOB TO WRITE! I hope you're proud of yourself, my love. Secondly, I know you don't like me saying this, but you work for total shitbags

Chapter 20

Anywhere, or Shrewksbury

INT: GIL'S COFFEE HOUSE—SUNDAY, JANUARY 6,
10 A.M.

EVIE sits at her usual table with her
laptop open and a spread of papers
around her—printouts from SARAH's hen do
PowerPoint presentation. She picks up
pages and checks them while firing
messages off on her phone.

JEREMY: did Linda RSVP?

SARAH: for the last time, Jeremy, not everyone who works in
HR is called Linda

EVIE: Beth's coming, don't worry!

SARAH: good. She's my biggest work rival, and she's still single.
I love her, but if she doesn't spend the whole weekend sick
with jealousy, what's the point? And I'm not worried!! I know
you guys will have done everything you can to make sure my
hen do is absolutely perfect

JEREMY: I think I speak for all of us when I say how much we're
looking forward to this weekend

Everything was sorted—largely thanks to Jeremy and Maria.
I'd budgeted to buy them many thank-you drinks throughout the

weekend. Hopefully the Michelin-starred restaurant had some affordable house-wine options. The only thing I had to do now was make sure I didn't have to work during the hen do. Which meant no meet-cute this week.

Unfortunately, NOB hadn't taken "I'm busy" as an acceptable excuse for skipping one. Now that he'd finally delivered, he was taking immense pleasure in reminding me that I was now the one holding him up. *No meet-cutes, no writing,* he'd said, echoing my drunken declaration. He'd been demanding the next one ever since the meeting with the producers last week, which I hadn't been "top level" enough to attend ("Next time," Monty had told me, with a wink). Luckily, I'd received live updates:

NOB: FYI, Monty's taking the credit for getting these pages out of me. You'll be relieved to know I'm not correcting him

NOB: Red? Are you still mad at me? I would have just told you I'd written the pages, but it was more fun this way

NOB: Are you sure you don't want Monts to know about our deal before things get really embarrassing for him?

RED: don't you dare

NOB: There you are. Where's my next meet-cute? The producers want Act Two before the end of the month. What should I tell them, Red?

I told myself it was fine that Monty had taken the credit. If anything, it meant he thought I was doing a good job. So good in fact, he happily passed it off as his own work. His mood had greatly improved since NOB had delivered. Not only was NOB writing with very little effort on his part, but Monty had discovered a brilliant new talent, Alessandro Russo, on the slush pile. Or, as it's more commonly known, his desk. Where I'd put his script with the rest of my suggestions. *This won't happen again once you're promoted.* I just needed to suck it up and wait a little bit longer.

I sent Maria and Jeremy a quick message.

EVIE: thanks so much for sorting everything

MARIA: you got us Shrewksbury Manor for a steal, all is forgiven

JEREMY: wine also helps with forgiveness

I pulled up the manor's website to look at our rooms again. Despite the cost, I was looking forward to spending a weekend in luxury with my friends. And Linda. *Beth.*

Damn it, Jeremy.

I might not have helped with the planning anywhere near as much as I should, but at least I'd negotiated a third off when I'd booked . . .

When I'd booked.

My heart slammed against my rib cage. Frantically, I opened my emails and scrolled through them. *Please, please, please, please.* Aha! There was the email from the manager questioning whether I'd meant champagne rather than prosecco on arrival. I *knew* I'd replied. Hadn't I?

Dread surged through me.

Slowly, I moved the cursor over to the drafts folder and clicked.

Dear Marjorie,

I am writing to confirm our booking with the deposit. And yes, I did mean prosecco. If you remember, I asked whether we could have the bride's favorite cocktail, Pornstar Martinis, but you didn't seem too keen . . .

Oh, no. Oh, no, oh, no, oh, no, oh, no.

I had to remain calm. There was every chance the rooms were still reserved. I raced outside to call the manor, squeezing past Ben and Anette as they arrived. Anette had a friend with her—a little girl wearing a woolen hat with ear flaps.

"That's our friend Evie," I heard Anette tell her friend as I scurried past. "Is she okay?" she asked her dad. I didn't catch his response, but it didn't take me long to find out the answer to that question.

I was most definitely not okay.

I sat back down at my laptop, staring unseeingly at the Shrewksbury Manor website with its unobtainable opulence. The manager had informed me that someone else had booked our suite—and they'd paid full price, she'd emphasized. There was nothing else available.

What have I done?

Ben looked up from his book. His dark brows rose, silently asking if I was all right. I nodded, knowing I must look ill. Anette tugged at her friend's hand-knitted jumper when she saw me. Despite myself, I was suddenly glad of them being here.

"Happy New Year, Evie! This is Bea. She just started drama club with me. Bea, this is our friend Evie."

I stuck a big smile on my face. "Hi, Bea, lovely to meet you."

"Enchantée," Bea said. Her hair was full of multicolored clips.

"How was your Road Trip meet cute? Did the playlist help?" Anette asked, barely pausing between questions.

"Worst one yet, unfortunately. Thank goodness I had your playlist. I don't know what I would have done without it. Thanks, Anette."

Anette appeared relieved. "Dad helped," she said generously.

"Then you both saved the day." The corner of Ben's mouth quirked up and I felt a rush of warmth.

Until I remembered what I'd done. *Oh, Sarah. I'm so sorry.*

"Anette, why don't you teach Bea Bad Lamp Random?" Ben suggested.

I shot him a grateful look and pulled up Sarah's presentation, racing through alternative options to the manor. Even if I booked elsewhere, my friends had spent over a month organizing all the activities in the presentation, and they were all in Shrewksbury village. How was I going to tell them? And how was I going to face Sarah? Her Mathers Meltdowns™ had been infamous at university, but it had been years since anyone had seen one. *That's because all of the witnesses are dead.*

I put my head in my hands, closing my eyes and breathing deeply.

"Evie," Ben said.

"Yes?"

"Are you okay?"

"I'm fine," I said, my voice muffled. Sarah was going to kill me. Maria would be furious. Jeremy . . . Well, Jeremy would probably throw a parade in my honor.

My phone buzzed. I turned to check it.

NOB: No more excuses. Where's my meet-cute?

I shoved the phone, sending it skidding to the other side of the table. There was movement in my periphery. Anette and Ben were having a rapid, silent conversation. Anette made a winglike shape with her arms. Ben nodded at her—*Okay, okay*—he signed, and she stopped, turning back to her friend.

"What is it, Evie?" he asked me. The back of my throat stung at his unexpectedly gentle tone.

"It's fine, really," I told him. "I've just ruined my best friend's hen do and I'm the world's worst friend, that's all. Please, go back to your book."

"Maybe I can help."

I raised my eyes to his. "You don't even know what I've done."

"Then tell me."

So I did, then waited for the inevitable judgment.

"When is it?"

"Next weekend."

"Where is it?"

"Shrewksbury."

"That's the middle of nowhere," said Ben.

"Yes," I said heavily.

Ben closed his book.

"I meant that you could have the hen do anywhere, as long as it's similar to Shrewksbury. Is that correct?"

"With Sarah, nothing's ever quite as simple as that." I pushed the presentation pages across the table toward him. He started to riffle through the top ones. He paused, then flipped through to the end, where the checklist of activities was. I couldn't look at it.

"Right," Ben said. Then he simply stood up and walked away. *So much for being less of a doofus.* I buried my head in my hands again.

"Do you want a hot chocolate, Evie?" Anette asked me a few minutes later.

"I'm okay, thank you," I mumbled into my sleeve.

"Too late," Ben said. There was a light thud and I looked up. He'd bought them for all of us.

"Do you have all the contact details for the bookings?" he asked.

I nodded, eyes still on my drink, then pulled up Maria's spreadsheet. "They're all here."

"And there definitely isn't an alternative venue nearby?"

"I've looked. The only way we could still do all the activities we've planned is if I hired a camper van, and my friend Sarah banned any form of camping back in 2006 after the four of us nearly drowned in a field in Scotland. Long story."

Ben leaned forward and retrieved my phone, handing it back to me. "Then brace yourself," he told me. "Are you ready? Here, take this."

He pushed the hot chocolate into my hands.

"You're going to cancel everything, the sooner the better."

I groaned loudly, though pressed my fingers gratefully around the warmth of the mug.

"There's good news."

"That seems unlikely."

"You've got this," he said simply. I looked at him. "From what I've seen, you can do anything you set your mind to. You're going to find somewhere new and rebook it all. And if you need help, I'm here. I've done this before."

"Organized hen dos?" I said, briefly stuck on the idea of Ben thinking I was capable of anything. *But you think I'm ridiculous.* Surely all this should just be compounding his view of me.

"Photography crews, mainly. Getting them places. Keeping them entertained. It was a lot like herding cats." Who *was* this man? "Trust me," Ben said. "Itinerary is my middle name." I gave him a small smile and he lifted a shoulder. "So, can I pitch in?"

Before today, Ben would have been the last person I'd want witnessing me be a complete catastrophe. Yet, he'd made it all sound so doable. Having an alternative weekend already lined up would certainly help when I delivered the news to my friends about what I'd done to the original. And Sarah's hen do wasn't going to be saved by wallowing.

"Okay," I said. "Let's do this."

"Then let's get canceling."

Less than an hour later, the perfect hen do that Jeremy and Maria had spent months organizing was no more. The only issue had been the Sunday spa treatments at Shrewksbury. They'd been paid for up front and were nonrefundable. Ben had tried too—and I'd heard him on the phone, brisk, polite, and impressively hard to say no to. Shrewksbury was firm. It meant that I'd need to save for the next few months to pay Jeremy and Maria back, but it was the least I could do.

"Now the fun part," Ben said lightly. I must have looked dubious. "We find a new venue. Then we each take half of the activities and rebook like for like. Where would your friend Sarah like to stay?"

Anything other than Shrewskbury Manor would pale in comparison for her.

"She's a little particular," I understated. "It would need to be absolutely perfect, like something out of a fairy tale." I shrugged apologetically. "That's her wedding theme," I clarified. "Bonus points if it's called something like Loganberry Lodge."

"Or Foxgloveington Hall," Ben offered.

"Honeysuckle Cottage," I smiled. *Wait.* I'd heard that somewhere. I racked my brains. My mum had told me about it on New Year's Eve. I'd been too distracted by Anette *Sleepless in Seattle*–ing me, I hadn't even looked it up.

What had she said? It was exactly how you imagine a cottage should be. There were only five of us, including Beth. We didn't necessarily need a manor . . .

Ben was now absorbed in dividing up the pages of the presentation. A curl of dark hair had fallen onto his forehead. It was longer than I'd seen it before. My fingers twitched, as if urging me to brush it back from his eyes. *Whoa, Evie.* Where had *that* come from? *The man thinks you're a fool, remember? He's probably helping you out of pity for Sarah.*

To distract myself, I searched for the cottage my mum had mentioned. It must be somewhere in Yorkshire . . . *Aha!*

The photos on the site were a little blurry, but the cottage itself was exactly as my mother had described. Picture-perfect. Built from roughly hewn gray stones, it had a snug thatched roof, beautiful sash windows, and a merry wooden door painted duck-egg blue. There were pale pink roses all up one side of the house, like it was delicately blushing. It was small—two up, two down—but still had enough rooms for all of us, and it really was "cheap as chips," as my mother had promised. It couldn't have been more ideal for a Holiday Romance meet-cute.

Hen do, I caught myself. This is for a hen do. This wasn't about me. This was about saving Sarah's weekend.

And it would be ideal for Sarah's hen.

Hope cautiously bloomed inside me. The cottage was, aptly, in Little Thrumpton, a village just like Shrewksbury. We could bring the luxury with us. Sarah was going to be disappointed about the manor, and I'd still have to face Maria and Jeremy, but it was either this or a field. It could just work. *Plus,* a little voice said, *you can kill two birds with one stone and keep NOB writing.*

Before I could change my mind, I said, "I've found it."

"See?" Ben said distractedly. I noticed the slide he was reading was the "no penises" policy. "You've got this."

While I was sorting the booking, Ben made two piles from the presentation slides. He pointed to the one nearest me. "Saturday activities." And the one near him. "Sunday."

I made a third pile with the accommodation slide page. "Booked," I said, and we shared a moment of joint appreciation for a good system.

Ten minutes later, Ben had found a replacement for the Olympic trainer Sarah had requested for our morning exercise class— Barbara's Bootcamp, he told me as he'd placed the page on the middle pile—and a woman who'd come to the cottage to do our nails and massages—Shelley's Shellacs. Little Thrumpton apparently prided itself on being twee.

I was still plotting out a new scavenger hunt. Luckily, the village boasted a large plot of land that was used for a maize maze (*It's Amaizeing!*). It was out of season but still open. Beth could just give Sarah a prize when she reached the middle. It wasn't a manor garden, but it would keep them occupied while we set up the cottage.

Ben glanced over at my phone, which had been buzzing relentlessly while we worked. I snatched it up.

NOB: I can't believe you're reneging on your side of the deal

NOB: Clearly you aren't taking this as seriously as I am

Not taking it seriously? Maybe I'd get more done if I didn't have to deal with the world's biggest ego needing attention every five seconds. *Enough interruptions.*

RED: I'm doing the Holiday Romance meet-cute this weekend at my friend's hen do. You can get back to your writing

NOB: You're using your friend's hen do for a meet-cute? Pretty ruthless, Red

NOB: I like it

I turned my phone over so I didn't have to see the screen. Was NOB right? I fully intended on making the entire weekend about Sarah—except, when we went for drinks in the evening I might happen to bump into some locals.

"How are you doing?" Ben asked.

I jumped, trying not to overthink how guilty I felt. "I think I've found a restaurant," I said, showing him the website.

"The Hangman's Daughter? Is it Michelin-starred?" He leaned over to look at my laptop. He smelled like fresh air and cinnamon.

"It's award-winning," I said.

Ben checked his tablet. "It's also the only one in the village that serves food."

"Then it's perfect," I declared, tossing the page of the presentation onto the growing "booked" pile.

Next, I found a local drawing class. Sarah had chosen Shrewksbury Manor not only because it was luxurious but because a local artist, Martine (no last name), held painting classes there on an extremely selective basis. Sarah wasn't remotely artistic, but Martine had once given a lesson to Kim Kardashian. The artist in Little Thrumpton couldn't claim that honor, but he was very relaxed when it came to alcohol being drunk during his class.

"Done!" Ben dropped his last page onto the pile. "What's next for you?"

"The cocktail class," I replied. "I thought I'd ask the restaurant if they could help."

As I made the call, he pulled up the website for the restaurant— did it look like more of a pub?—on his tablet. The drinks menu was just a photograph of the blackboard over the bar. "It does everything from Sex on the Beach to . . ." He paused. Someone picked up on the other end. "Slippery Nipples."

"Excuse me?" the person asked. I waved Ben quiet so I could ask about the private cocktail class.

"I don't suppose it's too late to look elsewhere?" he wondered aloud when I'd finished the conversation.

"Extremely," I said, adding the page to the pile and double-checking just to be sure. It was my last one. "I don't believe it . . . We've actually done it!" I held up my palm and Ben had already high-fived me before I could stop to think about who it was I was asking.

Who knew? I mused, turning my attention to the new itinerary. Having this to present to Jeremy and Maria would, I hoped, soften

the blow. Maybe then they'd stop speaking to me for only five to
ten years or so . . .

"Don't worry," Ben said, as if sensing I was starting to spiral.
"It's going to be okay."

"All thanks to you," I said.

"Are you kidding? You're the a-*maize*-ing one." He smiled when
I groaned, his hooded brown eyes lighting up. I smiled back, a few
seconds passing in easy silence.

Then I spotted something over his shoulder. Anette, grinning at
us. I hastened to gather up the pages. It was best not to encourage
her. Ben turned away too, rubbing the back of his neck.

When I opened up my bulging satchel to pack the pages inside,
I saw the box I'd put in there. I'd completely forgotten that I'd intended to spend some of this morning putting together a surprise
for Sarah.

Well, I'd certainly achieved that.

I pulled the box out and the lid came loose, a picture falling to
the floor. "Wait!" I said, but it was too late. Ben had picked it up.
The photo was of me and my friends, aged eighteen, at a fancy-
dress party. *Of course it had to be that one.* We'd gone as *Pretty
Woman.* Sarah was dressed as Julia Roberts before she took the
blond wig off. I was the "after," in a dressing gown with red curls
and a shy grin. Jeremy was our Richard Gere, sporting a thick gray
wig. Ben's mouth twitched.

"I was going to do a collage for Sarah," I explained, taking the
lid off the box to slip the photo back inside. I caught him glancing
at the rest of them, a curious expression on his face. Anette and her
friend leaned in too. There were more nights out. A series of me
bent over my laptop, writing, completely oblivious to whichever of
my friends was pulling their face behind me. Holidays we used to
all go on together. "Though I've run out of time."

I had some work to do this afternoon. One of our writers, Simon, had begged for a call to go through all the reasons why his current project was both the best thing he'd ever written and completely unsalvageable (he was a fifty-fifty client: fifty percent ego, fifty percent neurosis).

Anette waved her hands as though trying to signal something to Ben, but he didn't see her. "Actually . . ." he said. She stopped still, staring at him with a pleading expression. "I might be able to help with that too."

His daughter beamed.

Chapter 21

Cover It in Glitter

EXT: A DETACHED HOUSE, A CUL-DE-SAC,
SHEFFIELD—SATURDAY, JANUARY 12, 7:30 A.M.

SARAH runs out of the door, pulling a
bright pink suitcase behind her. Her
fiancé, JIM, wearing his dressing gown,
leans out for a kiss. She stands on her
tiptoes and pecks his cheek, then, spotting
her friend BETH arriving in a hot-pink Audi
TT, she throws her hands around Jim's neck
and snogs him. JEREMY pulls up next to Beth
in his boxy Vauxhall Corsa and stays
seated, leaving MARIA and EVIE to get out
of the car to greet SARAH.

"Happy hen do, Sarah!" called Maria, as we huddled to hug our diminutive friend.

"It's finally here!" Her grip was iron-tight with excitement. With Sarah, it's like someone took a very large person and condensed them down to make one that packed more of a punch. She was a neutron star of a woman.

Sarah introduced us to Beth, who had the kind of highlighted blond waves that sold hair products. The two of them were dressed in identical pink velour tracksuits.

"For the journey," Sarah said, in response to our looks. She waved at Jeremy, who rolled the window down. "Let's get this show on the road! I can't *wait* to find out where we're going."

"Yes, wherever could that be," Jeremy intoned.

My stomach swooped unpleasantly. I'd decided to tell my friends the truth after we'd dropped Sarah and Beth off for my version of the treasure hunt, and I was already sweating at the thought. Beth had never seen the original itinerary, but it seemed unlikely that Sarah hadn't told her about Shrewksbury being a possibility—after all, why would her best friends let her down?

I'd worry about Beth's reaction later.

Beep-beep.

"Don't keep Big Bertha waiting!" Jeremy called through the car window, patting his steering wheel lovingly. "Seat belts on?" he asked, once we were all in. "Then next stop: my own personal hell."

"Is he serious?" Beth asked from the back.

"You get used to him," said Sarah.

"I'll sort directions." I grabbed the GPS from the dash. Jeremy glanced at me—I was normally the last person to volunteer to navigate. The trouble was, I was the only one of us who knew where we were going.

- - - - - - - - - -

"Is someone going to explain why we've just dropped Sarah and Linda off in a field? Not that I didn't enjoy the look on their faces, but the treasure hunt was supposed to be in the manor gardens, no?"

I'd taken charge when we'd arrived at the maize maze—giving Beth the champagne for her and Sarah to drink on reaching the center, along with a map with walking directions to the artist's studios where we'd meet them in an hour. Beth had looked unsure, but on the surface, this was the exact same plan we'd had from the beginning: she was to accompany Sarah while we decorated the suite. Except there was no suite.

"Evie," prompted Maria from the back.

"Okay," I said, taking a big breath to prepare myself. "Don't be mad . . ."

"I'm not mad. Are you mad, Maria?" Jeremy was the first to speak once I'd finished explaining. "I'm really happy I spent a month of my life arranging a weekend that seemed designed to torture me, only to find out my friend has replaced it with something even less appealing."

"I'm so sorry. It was a stupid mistake, and I couldn't feel worse about it. We did our best to make sure the weekend still matched up to the one Sarah asked for. Maria?" I twisted in my seat to look back at her.

"I'm not mad," she assured me, though her voice was strained.

"'*We*'?" Jeremy picked up.

"That man I met, the one with the daughter. Ben."

"Hot Widower," Jeremy said.

"Yes. *No.* You can't call him that."

"I thought you didn't like him," Maria said.

"Well, I do. I think. I don't know. He's the reason I was able to pull all this together so quickly. Not that it isn't all well thought through, of course," I added hastily. "I've just emailed you both the new itinerary now so you can see for yourself."

Maria checked her phone. "It's all there," she confirmed for Jeremy. "We're still doing all the same activities."

"That's something, at least," he said. Then he shook his head. "What am I saying?"

"It's everything Sarah asked us for, I promise," I said eagerly. "Just about two hours west of where she's expecting it to be."

In the rearview mirror, Maria's gray eyes relaxed a little. "You've done your best. She has to understand that." I wasn't sure who Maria was trying to convince. "Where's the link to the accommodation?"

"It's really beautiful, just wait until you see it," I said, sending it over. It was a relief to have everything out in the open. *More or less.*

After a few seconds of silence, I asked, "Did you get it?"

"Evie." Maria's voice was eerily calm. "Tell me you didn't."

Jeremy kept his hands at ten and two on the wheel as he gave me a questioning glance.

"Didn't what?" I asked. *What have I missed?*

"The cottage, Evie. It looks just like the one in *The Holiday.* Don't tell me that you've made Sarah's hen do into one of your meet-cutes."

Whoops. Was it really that obvious? It made me wonder how much I'd been obsessing over the meet-cutes lately for this to be Maria's immediate conclusion. *Stellar self-awareness, Evie.*

"Trust me," I pleaded, stomach roiling with guilt. "I wouldn't have chosen it if it wasn't perfect for Sarah."

"Evie," said Jeremy. "You've hijacked Sarah's hen do to snare Jude Law. If every single part of the next two days isn't absolute perfection, it was nice knowing you, goodbye."

Huddled beneath Jeremy's umbrella, we all stared at what should have been my picture-perfect romantic-holiday-slash-fairy-tale cottage.

"Evie, darling," said Jeremy. "How old were those photographs you showed us?"

The paint on the splintered wooden frames and the front door was cracked and peeling, more corpse gray than duck-egg blue. The thatched roof drooped. One of the upstairs windows was boarded up and the other was broken, the torn edge of a lace curtain fluttering through the crack. Even the roses that had once climbed up the side of the house were now a cobweb of brittle sticks.

"Maybe it's better on the inside?" I said. A whole roost of

something dark and quick emerged from a gaping hole in the thatch and took to the sky.

"Bats," said Maria faintly. "The inside is full of bats."

"Not anymore," Jeremy deadpanned. "How did you find this?"

"My mum," I said faintly.

"Have you two recently fallen out?"

EVIE: Mum, how long ago did you stay in Honeysuckle Cottage?

MUM: Ooh, about twenty years! Why?

Oh, Mum. I took a picture of the cottage so I could try to get our money back later. "Come on. Let's see what we're dealing with."

I hurried down the overgrown path to the door, letting us inside with the key the owner had left under the mat. The cottage was bitterly cold. I reached for the light, feeling chipped laminate under my fingertips before flipping the switch. The lightbulb in the fringed shade flickered but held, casting fingers of shadow over the living room.

We were staying in a time capsule from the 1970s. The furniture was covered in at least two years' worth of thick gray dust, and the two floral sofas and dark green wing chair looked spongy with damp.

"Kitchen," said Maria. We all moved as one through the low doorway into the second room. Inside was a round pine table and four chairs—one of which was propped against the wall with a leg missing. The gas stove and the oven were both clearly broken. A collection of teapots shaped like faces watched us from the tops of the cupboards.

"Did you hear that?" Jeremy asked, cocking his head.

Maria and I froze, thinking about the bats. It was just the rain hitting a drain outside.

"Let's check out the fridge," I said. As long as that was working, we'd at least be able to keep the wine chilled. If not . . . It didn't bear thinking about. "Well?" No one moved.

"Jeremy," urged Maria.

He hunched up his shoulders a few times, preparing himself. Darting forward, he yanked open the door and jumped back.

The smell that drifted out was like nothing I'd ever encountered. "Shut the door, shut it!" Maria and I cried together, leaving Jeremy to slam it closed.

"Tell me that was cheese," Maria asked.

"Have I said how sorry I am?" I said.

"That's okay," said Jeremy generously, patting my head. "It's Sarah you should really be worried about."

"It *is* okay." Maria's voice was determinedly bright. "We're here now. I'll tell Sarah we'll meet her and Beth a little later after they've had their art class. Not at all ideal, but it can't be helped. We'll put the wine outside, it's cold enough. Jeremy, you check the bed situation. I'll clean. Evie can get the decorations up. Sarah will never even know it looked like this. Everything is going to be *just* fine."

Just over an hour later, we'd got the old boiler going. The surfaces were mostly free of dust. Jeremy had found musty but clean bedding in the airing cupboard and confirmed that the bats living in the attic couldn't get into the rest of the house.

I stepped back from hanging the sheet up in front of the projector. Ben had loaned me the equipment for the slideshow he'd made from all my photos. He told me he'd made slideshows before and that it would take "no time at all" to assemble mine. Given the amount of dust on the projector, I had a feeling it was the first time he'd done something like this in a while. And yet, he'd done it for me.

My friends gathered in the room behind me. We surveyed our work. With the candles now dotted around, the place looked almost . . .

"Well," said Jeremy. "You can't polish a turd."

"But you can cover it in glitter." I switched the light off. The flickering candles made it feel almost . . . Nope, still terrible. "Right. There's just one last thing we have to do before we go." This was met with groans. *"Drink,"* I said. They cheered and followed me into the kitchen. "Jem, can you check the cupboards for glasses?"

Maria had the itinerary out. "Okay, so they should be leaving the drawing class and heading for cocktail-making."

"Did either of you hear from them?"

"Nothing."

"Me neither." I allowed myself to relax a little. That seemed like a good sign.

"That sound is back," Jeremy said. He sniffed a half-eaten packet of digestives from the first set of cupboards. "Do you think Kate Winslet was this much of a slob?"

"Wine," I reminded him. The last thing I needed was to think about rom-coms.

"Nothing," Jeremy said, opening and closing the next set of cupboards. "Nothing. Nothing. Nothing." He went to the last two cupboards. "Pray with me," he said, as he flung them open.

A rat the size of a Yorkshire terrier leaped out at his face.

Chapter 22

Mathers Meltdown™

INT: THE HANGMAN'S DAUGHTER—SATURDAY,
JANUARY 12, 4:32 P.M.

The pub can be described only as a "local."
There are hundreds of horseshoes nailed to
one wall; the other walls are covered in a
vast collection of metal signs bearing
jokes and slogans that range from cutesy to
questionable. BETH and SARAH are sitting
around a stained table. SARAH is wearing a
silver "Bride" sash. Her expression is
closed as she takes in the dark pub, its
crackling fire, and the mostly male locals
staring at the two blondes in matching pink
tracksuits. The small entrance door opens
and JEREMY, MARIA, and EVIE enter, looking
nervous.

Jeremy took one look at the locals lining the tables along the walls. "I'll be at the bar," he announced, shaking out his umbrella. He still hadn't quite recovered from the rat.

"Ask about the cocktail class," I called after him.

The place was almost empty. Three men sat at separate tables along the far wall, each bearing the ruddy nose of the well-seasoned drinker. Two women eyed us distrustfully, their hair appearing to have been done by the same hairdresser, whose style book, like our cottage, dated from the 1970s: bouffant perms with stark blond streaks.

It was very clearly a pub, not a restaurant. Where had I brought us to?

"Evie," Maria said urgently, holding me back. She smiled for Sarah's sake, and showed me her phone. YOU HAVE 21 MISSED CALLS FROM SARAH MATHERS.

I quickly checked my own. I had fifteen, all spread out over the last few hours. There mustn't have been any reception at the cottage. And she wasn't the only person who'd tried to get in touch.

BEN: good luck with the hen do! Let me know how it goes.

NOB: Can't wait to hear about my meet-cute, Red

I sent NOB the picture of the cottage.

RED: I'm holding you responsible for this. I hope you're pleased. My friend's hen do is ruined

"Come on," Maria said, taking a breath. "Time to face the music."

Sarah and Beth had draped their soaking-wet pink jackets over the spare stools, leaving me and Maria no choice but to stand. Beth's arms were tightly folded. Her hair, which had been beautifully styled at the start of the day, was now expanding as it dried, like she'd been backcombed for a power ballad. There was a twig tangled in the thick strands. Sarah had tried to wrangle hers into a side pony, but most of it was refusing to stay in the hair elastic. She didn't look up straight away. Instead, she stirred her gin and tonic with a plastic spoon.

I swallowed tightly. "How was your day?"

"Sorry we couldn't join you sooner," Maria added.

Sarah tried to smooth her fringe down, but it sprang back up again. "Do you know," she said, "what an out-of-season maize maze is?" Beth huffed. "It's a field."

"Oh, Sarah," I said, feeling awful. "How was the art class, at least?"

Beth reached out a sympathetic hand toward Sarah. "It's okay, hon. I didn't want to say, because you were so sure they were booking her, but I did warn you. Martine doesn't just give classes to everyone. Even Kim had to pull strings."

"Just show them, Beth," Sarah snapped.

Beth pulled a roll of paper from the back of the seat and started to unravel it.

"Now, I'm not unreasonable," Sarah said. I tried very hard not to react. "But you do remember what I specifically said I didn't want for my hen do."

The picture gradually came into view as Beth tugged on the paper. It was like watching an image loading on the old dial-up Internet.

"What is . . ."

"*Oh.*"

Beth was still unrolling.

"Just how big *is* that thing?" Maria asked weakly.

"The artist gave us a life drawing class," Sarah said.

I couldn't look at her. "They can be very tasteful."

"He was the model."

"I come bearing drinks!" Jeremy called. "Holy *shit*, Linda, that's a big dick."

The other patrons bridged the gaps between their tables with shared glances. They did not look happy.

"What?" asked Jeremy. "*She* drew it."

"*Put it away*, Beth," Sarah told her. Beth started to wrestle it back into a roll. "Can we just go and check into the manor?" Sarah asked tiredly, rotating her shoulders. "I need a sauna and a swim to feel human again."

Beth had a self-satisfied smirk on her face as she looked at us, her brows slightly raised in a challenge. Sarah hadn't realized we weren't in Shrewksbury, and Beth hadn't corrected her.

"What's wrong?" Sarah said warily.

"I think she's talking to you, Evie." Jeremy perched on top of Beth's jacket. She yanked it out from under him.

"What on earth is *that*?" Sarah demanded. He'd placed a silver dinner tray on the table containing bottles of vodka, gin, and tequila; a carton of orange juice; and five glasses. One of them had a squashed paper umbrella in it.

"Oh, this? It's our bespoke cocktail-making class." Jeremy tilted his head at me. "It's DIY. They don't cater for hen dos, apparently."

My stomach plummeted as we all looked to the bar. Behind it stood a woman somewhere in her forties with wiry gray hair pulled back in a loose bun. Her mouth was set in a thin line, eyes full of blanket disapproval.

"Exactly what," said Sarah evenly, "is going on here?"

"I can explain . . ." I began.

"We all can," Maria said. She nudged Jeremy.

He poured some vodka into one of the water-stained glasses. "Sure, why not. The rat clearly wasn't punishment enough."

"No," I said, before Sarah could pick up on his comment. "This is entirely on me."

"Evie, it's okay," Maria said, but she couldn't hide her relief.

"For goodness' sake, one of you tell me," Sarah said.

I readied myself. "The thing is, Sarah—"

"This isn't Shrewksbury," Beth said triumphantly. "They've buggered up your hen do."

The thing about Mathers Meltdowns™ was that they never happened exactly when you expected them. Once the countdown was triggered, it was anybody's guess.

And from the look on Sarah's pinched white face as she sipped her gin, it had definitely been triggered. Soon she would turn a violent shade of puce, after that there'd be clenched fists, streams of angry tears, and, finally, a full-blown, eardrum-splitting tantrum of unpredictable length and reason.

"You lost," said Sarah slowly, "the manor booking?"

"I'll get us more mixers." Jeremy stood.

"You will stay right there," Sarah said.

Beth's eyes widened. "I have exactly what this hen do needs." She started fishing around in her handbag.

"So help me, Beth, if that's what I think it is . . ."

Beth's expression turned sulky. I thought I saw her put something in her pocket as she stood, tottering a little on her heels. The only mixer in her gin had been the cocktail umbrella. "I'm just going to go and ask about their vegetarian options for dinner."

"We're eating *here*? You've replaced Jorden's, a Michelin-starred restaurant, with a pub that only serves pies?" Sarah pointed to a sign that said: ASK US ABOUT OUR AWARD-WINNING PIES!

"They are award-winning," Jeremy said. In the silence that followed, he opened the tequila and began to fill each of our glasses.

"Is my hen do a joke to you?" Sarah asked quietly.

Maria and I immediately started to protest. Sarah held up her hand. *This is it,* I thought. The three of us braced ourselves.

But Sarah remained unnervingly calm. "I couldn't have been any clearer about what I wanted. Did you think it was funny to take everything I'd asked for and cobble together a sham version? You three are always running off together. I guess I just never expected you to leave me out of my own hen do!"

"Sarah, it's not like that at all," Maria said, horrified.

"It was all my fault," I insisted. "Maria and Jeremy did everything you asked for. I lost the booking, and I booked a cottage here because it looked like the one in *The Holiday*. I'm so unbelievably sorry."

Sarah placed her drink down.

"It's unbelievable, all right."

My friends and I exchanged looks over her head. There was a tremor in the air, like the calm before a storm. Mathers Meltdown™ imminent.

"I didn't mean it to turn out like this," I said desperately. "It's because NOB—"

"Evie," she said, with the force of a slap. *Here it comes.* Sarah took a huge breath and . . . released it slowly. "Don't you dare pin this on that man. This is all you. You could have done this any other weekend—why did you have to use *my* hen do?"

Maria reached over and took her hand. "Well done," she said softly.

"It's the therapy," Sarah said.

I think I would have preferred a tantrum. "I couldn't have afforded it otherwise!" My friends all jumped, and I lowered my voice, ashamed. "I'm sorry. I really wanted you to have your perfect hen, but you asked for such a lot, Sarah. I couldn't do both."

"Maria and David are still managing to go away in May. Jeremy is in New York over the summer. I can't have made all of you destitute."

Jeremy gave me a "You're on your own" look.

I folded my arms. It had taken me months to save for Sarah's weekend. My wage wasn't terrible at the agency, but it hadn't improved much over the years either. "You guys don't always understand what it's like to have to be careful with money," I said tightly. "You all have everything so together. Whenever I look at your lives, they make me feel like I'm several steps behind."

"Our lives?" Sarah said. Maria and Jeremy turned their astonished

gazes on me too. "Have you even considered that I might have wanted a decent hen do for a reason? I knew what I was getting when I agreed to marry Jim. I love him, but he comes as a package deal. He has two dogs, a mortgage with his ex-wife, terrible taste in clothes, and two children. So forgive me," said Sarah, "if, before I became a stepmum—and I will be *all in* for those boys, our honeymoon is at *Center Parcs*—I wanted a luxurious weekend and for everything to be all about me one last time. Was that too much to ask?"

I was lost for words. I'd assumed Sarah was just being her usual demanding self about the hen do. I knew that when she chose to be with Jim her life wouldn't exactly be straightforward, but I'd always thought she could cope with anything. I hadn't once asked her how she was doing with all the wedding preparations.

"Sarah's not the only one," Maria said tightly, and it was her turn to have our attention. "It might look like David and I have it together from the outside, but when I see your life, Evie, I really envy your freedom. When David talks about marriage and babies, it's like our entire life is laid out before us and it's on one track. You seem to have so many options in front of you."

"But you're always telling me I need to change things."

"Because you can," Maria said simply.

"I thought you and David were happy," I said softly. I'd never thought, not once, that my friend might be anything less than content in her relationship.

Maria smiled. "We are, as much as anyone is. And some of it's because we have each other, but mostly it takes a lot of work for it to look like we have everything together."

Jeremy nodded into his glass.

"No offense, Evie, but if I'm going to be jealous of anyone, it's Jeremy," Sarah said.

He spluttered. "I'm sorry, what?"

Sarah waved her hand. "Sometimes I think you're the only one of us who's got it right. Amazing job, that apartment, no urge to settle down."

"No urge to settle down? Try meeting someone when you spend every Saturday night in the office." Now Jeremy had our attention. "Evie, when you complain that your life is all work and Netflix, I sometimes look at you and think, *You have time for Netflix?*"

I was stricken. But Jeremy didn't *want* to find a partner, did he? Or, at least, he hadn't when we were younger. "I should have asked you how you were doing."

"We all should," Maria said.

"Oh." Jeremy shrugged. "Who am I to moan? At least my huge apartment keeps me warm at night. Evie only has her den of iniquity."

My friends and I looked at one another, and it occurred to me that while I'd been away in London, they'd been busy growing up.

"Evie," Sarah said at last. "Please don't take this as you being off the hook, but I am willing to accept that sometimes I might be a tiny little bit high-maintenance." None of us reacted. "About the wedding."

We immediately jumped in. "That's completely understandable," Maria soothed.

"There's so much pressure," I said.

We waited for Jeremy to take his turn. He poured himself some more tequila.

"What?" he asked. He sighed. "Fine. Sarah, you know we love you."

Sarah beamed, eyes a little watery. "Come on, then, hug me. I'm the one with my hen do ruined." Maria and I grabbed ahold of her, pulling Jeremy in too.

"Maria, you know you can come and stay with me whenever you like," I said.

"I know."

"Jeremy, now I know you've been trying to meet someone, I'll set you up with absolutely the perfect man," Sarah promised.

"Let's just focus on Evie. You know, the friend responsible for this disaster?"

"It really is awful, isn't it?" I said.

"Completely," Maria replied.

Sarah leaned back. "So what are you going to do about this, Evie?"

"Stop making everything about me?" I tried.

"That's a start, but I mean for the meet-cute," Sarah said. We all stared at her. "How are you planning to meet someone?"

"Sarah, I promise, I'm not anymore. This is your weekend."

"You're right. And you aren't allowed to have ruined it for nothing. Someone in this damned village has to be single." She stood, straightening her top. "I'm going to find him."

That's when we noticed that the bar had fallen completely silent. At first I thought it might be because we'd been too loud, but it wasn't us the locals were staring at.

"Oh, good, you're done. Let's have some fun!" Beth shouted. The HR manager was in the middle of the room, a gin in one hand and a giant inflatable penis in the other.

Chapter 23

Girl Alone

INT: THE FOX'S DEN—SATURDAY, JANUARY 12,
7:23 P.M.

The pub is a squat, windowless one-story
building. The room is square, with a pool
table at one end and a small bar at the
other. It's busier than the Hangman's
Daughter, but still half-empty. A bulldog
lies in the middle of the room, chewing a
pig's ear. As if in a halfhearted nod to
the name of the pub, a badly stuffed fox's
head snarls on the wall above a line of
mostly empty tables. Other than this, the
disco ball hanging from the center of the
ceiling is the only decoration.

"Do you know where Lawrence is?" Sarah asked the barman, zero-
ing in on him the moment we'd entered the pub. I found myself
admiring his perfectly shaped eyebrows.

Sarah had promised the Hangman's Daughter bartender we'd
take Beth and go if she could point us in the direction of any single
men in the village. The woman had told us we could find "that traitor" in the Fox's Den—apparently the more disreputable of the
village's two pubs—and then she'd spat. I hadn't taken this as a
good sign, but nothing could deter Sarah.

The barman eyed us, taking in Sarah's bridal sash and Beth's inflatable penis. "Lawrence won't be here until after nine." His tone didn't invite more questions.

Nevertheless, Sarah persisted. "And how old is Lawrence?"

This caused a perfectly arched brow to rise. "Old enough," the bartender replied.

"What gins do you have?" asked Beth, pushing forward. "I only drink Bombay Sapphire."

"We'll take doubles of whatever you've got," Jeremy told him, much to Beth's disgust. Sarah looked pointedly at the penis and her work colleague became suitably subdued.

"We have a No Hen Do policy," the barman warned us, eyes on the slowly deflating member of our group.

Sarah whipped off her sash and squeezed the inflatable in Beth's hands. "What hen do?" A sad whistle eased out of its tip as it sagged. The bartender sighed and went to get the glasses.

"Okay, here's the plan." We huddled around Sarah. "We're going to split up and ask around about Lawrence. Let's find out what we can before he gets here. Any questions?"

I raised my hand. "Do I have any choice in this?"

"Nope."

"I have a question," said Beth. "What's in it for me? I don't know her. I thought I'd paid for a luxurious spa weekend, not hunting down a cast member of *Last of the Summer Wine*. What?"

Sarah's nostrils flared. "We're finding Evie a date to my wedding," she said, in lieu of the much longer, and more questionable, explanation.

"Why should I care?"

"Because"—Sarah's eyes narrowed and she smiled sweetly—"if you help us, I'll make you a bridesmaid."

"Hold this." Beth handed Jeremy the inflatable, picked up her drink from the bar, and strode off into the pub.

"You aren't being serious about the bridesmaid thing, are you?" Maria said quietly.

"I told her, no penises," replied Sarah, sipping at her gin.

"I'll take my dress in a ten," Beth announced, throwing herself onto a chair. Jeremy was the only one of us who hadn't returned.

"What have you found out?" Sarah asked suspiciously. Everyone we'd asked had been evasive. They didn't seem to like outsiders, especially ones who asked questions.

Beth, apparently, had been more successful. She started ticking points off on her fingers. "He's from France, he's short, and he once worked at London Zoo as a penguin picker-upper." We all looked at her. "You know, when penguins try to watch planes and they overbalance?"

"Just how much gin have you had, Beth?" Sarah said.

"You mean it's not true?"

Maria hid her smile as I turned my laugh into a cough.

Sarah sighed. "At least he'll be here soon."

"Perhaps she shouldn't meet him at all then," Beth muttered. "Who'd want to start a relationship based on lies?"

"Does it seem busier?" said Maria. She was right; it was getting to be standing room only.

"Move over, move over!" Jeremy clambered back onto his chair, his coat bulging. "Here." He unzipped to reveal a bulky paper bag transparent with grease stains. "Courtesy of the Hangman's Daughter."

"What on earth . . . ?" Maria said.

"Pies!" Jeremy grinned.

We looked to Sarah for her reaction. After the minutest of pauses, she was the first one into the bag. We all followed suit. Beth wrinkled her nose until Jeremy handed her an individually wrapped cheese pie. She took it, slightly mollified.

"Evie, have you seen this?" Maria had her phone out. She wiped her screen clear of pastry flakes and showed me. It was the *Bitch About It* website.

MONICA REED TOSSES BOY TOY

"It's everywhere," she said. "They had a huge public row." Maria paused for dramatic effect. "He said he wasn't looking for a second mother, and she told *him* she didn't need a third child. She needed a partner who wasn't intimidated by a woman's success." I nodded, smiling for her, but I couldn't help feeling a little sorry for NOB. He was an arse, but a breakup was bad enough without the national media getting involved. Maria gave me a thoughtful look as she took her phone back.

There was a commotion on the other side of the room. As my friends all craned their necks to see, I got out my phone. There was another message from Ben, but I opened the chat thread with NOB first.

RED: are you OK? I saw the news

NOB: Why wouldn't I be?

RED: are you sure? Because I have a tried and tested Broken Heart Film Marathon I can recommend to you. Guaranteed to make you feel better

NOB: Thanks, Red. But it isn't broken. Tell me about the meet-cute

Fine. If he didn't want to talk about it, I wasn't going to push. Besides, I could cheer him up simply by telling him about my most recent attempt to meet someone.

RED: first of all, the cottage contained a giant rat

"What are these people doing now?" Jeremy asked, licking pastry from his thumb. I followed his gaze. A heavyset bald man had pushed two pool tables together and covered them with boards. People were starting to clear a space as if this was a normal occurrence. As he wheeled over some steps that had been against the back wall covered in a black cloth, Beth suddenly stood. "Just making a call!" she said, struggling past my chair. "I'm going to be the *best* bridesmaid."

NOB: What cottage?

I scrolled up so I could highlight the picture I'd sent him.
It wasn't there.
A sensation like ice water spread down my neck. I checked my sent items.
Ben. I'd sent *Ben* a message saying the ruined hen do was all his fault, and he'd replied.

BEN: right.

Oh, no. Time for some damage control. I'd just explain to him it was a simple mistake.
"Uh-oh," Jeremy said, making me look up. He shoved the remains of his pie into his mouth. I followed his gaze to see the heavyset man making his way over toward us.

Maria hastily tried to gather all our crumbs with the edge of her palm.

"Which one of you is looking for Lawrence?" the man grunted.

"That would be Evie here," said Sarah quickly.

The man's unimpressed eyes met mine.

"Come on, then."

I looked to my friends for help.

"No taking a backseat," said Jeremy.

"You'll be okay," Maria told me. She plucked my phone from my grasping fingers and gave me a little nudge. "We're right here."

Sarah raised her own phone. "Making sure there's a record of whatever happens."

Maybe they hadn't quite forgiven me.

Somewhat reluctantly, I followed the path the man cut across the bar—was *he* Lawrence? His arms dangled at his sides, propped up by vast muscles like swimming armbands. He wasn't my usual type, but, to keep Sarah happy, I should really be positive. Plus, I'd had a lot of gin.

The man led me to the covered pool tables. There was now a table and chair balanced on top of them. He held out his hand and I automatically took it. He shook me off, irritably. Apparently he'd just been gesturing for me to climb up the stairs. As I did, I saw that someone had placed a lit candle and a single red rose on the table. Was this about to be a very public first date? I glanced back at my traitorous friends, who waved me on.

When I was seated, a spotlight came on directly overhead. Everyone's eyes turned to me as music pounded out across the pub. The disco ball on the ceiling started to spin, and the black cloth was yanked from the stairs to reveal that they were glittering pink.

I was on a stage.

The bald man was now holding a microphone. "Ladies and

gentlemen, the Fox's Den is proud to present, back for good this time, our resident drag act and absolute queen, Lawrence of a Labia's famous Karaoke Singalong."

What?

A hush fell over the room and the crowd parted.

A stunning woman in a glittering black leotard, fishnets, huge blond hair and towering platforms strode toward the stage singing Shirley Bassey's "Big Spender." She glanced over at me, thick eyelashes closing in a wink.

It was the male bartender with the beautiful brows, dressed up to the nines.

The music dipped and she announced, "First, a confession." Her head bowed over the mic, nails glittering. "It's true. I was briefly seduced by the Hangman's Daughter." She deepened her voice. "I couldn't resist her pies." More laughter. "Now, I heard a rumor this redheaded minx has been asking after me all night. So, my dear." Lawrence placed one of her long, slender legs on the tabletop in a half-split. "Whatever would you like to do with me?"

I'm fairly sure I squeaked.

"How about you just tell me what song you'd like to sing?"

I stared beseechingly at my friends, but they were much too busy enjoying the show.

"Well?" Lawrence leaned the glittering microphone toward my mouth.

I said the first song that came to mind. "'Love Machine' by Girls Aloud."

She looked me up and down, lifting a tasseled shoulder. "All right." The music switched tracks. "Can everyone give a big hand for 'Love Machine' . . . by Girl Alone." Laughter rippled throughout the pub and my cheeks burned.

There was a rush of movement, and before I knew it, my friends were hurrying up the steps to join me.

"She's not alone!" shouted Maria, breathlessly. Sarah took the mic from the amused Lawrence and Jeremy pulled me to my feet.

"Come on, Nicola, let's show them how it's done."

But before we could follow through with that threat, a shout rang out across the room.

"What's all this, then?"

The whole pub fell silent, the music ending abruptly as a police officer pushed his way through the room to examine the questionable "stage" setup with his flashlight.

"Officer," said Lawrence of a Labia, the epitome of dignity. "However may we help you?"

"I'm not here for you," the man replied.

Beside me, Jeremy made a curious sound.

Which is when I saw the flashlight was sticking out of the officer's pants.

"Sarah Mathers," he shouted, yanking said pants off with one tug. "You've been a very naughty girl. Get up against the wall and spread 'em!"

\- - - - - - - - - -

My friends gathered behind me as I opened the door to the cottage. We stepped into the dark hallway.

"Now, Sarah," Jeremy said, stumbling a little. "You're about to see that Linda had the right idea, staying at the pub."

"*Linda* didn't have a choice," Sarah said darkly. "She knew my No Penises policy."

"Ready?" Maria and I reached for her hands, taking one each.

"I'm ready," she said bravely.

I took a deep breath and turned on the light.

Sarah breathed in sharply. "Oh, you guys."

The living room had been filled with rose-gold helium balloons, obscuring the damp ceiling, creating a forest of curling ribbons.

We all slowly stepped into the room.

Maria's face was full of awe. "What is this?" she asked me quietly.

Ribbons tickled my cheek. "I have no idea."

I turned the projector on, clearing the balloons that had drifted in front of the screen. The first picture was of us in our *Pretty Woman* fancy dress. Jeremy dimmed the lights. The balloons all took on a soft glow.

Who could have done this? The only other people who knew about this cottage were NOB and Ben. And NOB had come to my rescue before . . .

EVIE: was this you?

This time I sent the message to both men. Maria covered one of the sofas with a bedsheet, and my friends all gathered on it in front of the screen.

"Come on, Evie. We have wine." They oohed and aahed at the photographs, and I checked my phone.

BEN: the owner took delivery. You should be getting a refund
for the cottage.

"It was Ben," I said wonderingly. I'd hoped that was true, though he hadn't said anything about balloons when I'd picked up the projector from Gil's the day before. *Why would he . . .* With a sickening jolt, I realized he still believed I blamed him for the ruined hen do. With everything that had happened, I'd forgotten to explain myself. The balloons were an apology. *Oh, God.*

"I knew I liked him," Jeremy said.

"Don't get any ideas," I warned, as he pulled me down to sit beside him. "All this proves is that I really am ridiculous." I was going to have to explain myself to Ben. Dread twisted in my stomach, mixing with the alcohol.

> EVIE: I don't know what to say. Thank you, Ben. Sorry you felt you had to do this. I meant that message for stupid NOB, not you. NONE of this was your fault. If it helps at all, you've made Sarah's weekend!

"Ben is typing" reappeared and disappeared a few times.

> BEN: NOB? So the weekend was a meet-cute?

My first reaction was shame, then I immediately felt annoyed. It was one step forward, two steps back with him. Why did he have such a problem with me doing the meet-cutes?

> EVIE: I'm grateful for the balloons. And the photos. And for all of your help . . . But there's no need to get all Mr. Judgy

With that, I tossed my phone onto the carpet and turned back to my friends and the photos. Ben hadn't arranged the images in chronological order. As we watched, holding each other slightly tighter with each passing photo, themes started to emerge. Holidays, celebrations, graduations, mid-laughter shots, me and my laptop . . . Somewhere in the part of my brain that remained a few millimeters above alcohol level was the thought that this slideshow didn't look like something that had taken Ben "no time at all."

Knock knock knock.

We all stirred beneath the bedding on the sofa.

"What is it?" asked Maria. She held on to her head. "Are we moving?"

Jeremy was on the chair, wrapped up in a bedsheet like a chrysalis. He blinked sleepily at us.

"Evie, what heinous part of your plan is this?"

"It had better involve Deliveroo-ing a sausage butty," Sarah said.

Knock knock knock.

I frowned, struggling to recall the itinerary. "Oh, God, no," I realized. "It's Barbara's Bootcamp."

"No. Absolutely not," Jeremy said.

Pushing the duvet aside, I scrambled up, then braced myself as the room swayed.

"Evie," said Sarah. "I cannot cope with any more of this hen do. Tell them to go away."

"You wanted an exercise class!" I said, dismantling the pillow barricade we'd built last night to cover the gap beneath the door to prevent a visit from Jeremy's rat friend. "Anyway, you'll get pampered afterward. We have Shelley's Shellacs coming at eleven."

Jeremy cocked his head. "Do any of these sound like real things?"

I shot him an exasperated look as I pulled back the dead bolt on the front door.

"Evie." Sarah snuggled down into the duvet. "For all I care, you can tell Barbara to shove her bootcamp up her arse."

A man in a smart coat stood on the doorstep. Behind him, a black car idled in the road. He smiled, nose pink in the cold.

"Can I help you?" I asked, thinking, for one foolish moment, of that part in *The Holiday* when Jude Law appears on the doorstep.

"I'm here to take you to Shrewksbury Manor." His smile widened. "We should leave now if you want to make your spa appointments. Unless," he said questioningly, "you would prefer that I shoved them up my arse?"

Sarah scrambled to my side. "Spa?" she gasped. "*Shrewksbury* Spa? I don't care how you did this, Evie, but you finally got something right. Everyone, get your butts in that car!"

My woolly brain took its time putting it together. It was Ben again. *Ben* had done this. Rather than book replacement appointments, he'd hired a driver. *Shelley's Shellacs* indeed. That meant Sarah's entire Sunday was exactly as she'd hoped for.

"Hot Widower," whistled Jeremy from behind us.

Yes. Hot Widower. And how had I thanked him last night? By calling him Mr. Judgy. *Oh, Evie.*

Chapter 24

- - - - - - - - - - - - - - -

Turtles All the Way Down

INT: WILLIAM JONATHAN MONTGOMERY & SONS
AGENCY FOR SCREENWRITERS—TUESDAY,
JANUARY 15, 7:24 A.M.

EVIE is at her computer, lost to the world
as she types. The only light comes from her
desk lamp. At the end of the corridor,
MONTY's office is still dark. She picks up
her coffee and goes to take a drink, only
to realize the cup is empty.

I sighed, putting my cup back down again and scrolling through my inbox. There were still more than a hundred unread emails, not counting the hundreds of new queries from screenwriters hoping Monty would represent them. Or the pile of contracts on my desk that was now up to my nose. I'd spent yesterday writing up the Holiday Romance meet-cute, and, despite much of the weekend being a complete disaster, writing about it had felt like penance. I'd promised NOB I'd stop holding myself back when I wrote. I didn't have my dad to check my scripts anymore, so the only way I could let myself go was by pretending that no one else would see, that I was writing just for me. At some point, something must have clicked. Before I knew it, I'd lost an entire day to writing. As strange and wonderful as this was, it meant I was now playing catch-up with my work. It was going to take a week of late nights to get anywhere near back to normal. I just wished NOB understood.

To him, my full-time job was an inconvenience. The moment I'd sent him the Holiday Romance meet-cute, he'd demanded the next one.

NOB: It's your move Red

RED: this isn't a game

NOB: Then how come I'm winning?

Maddening though he was, he wasn't exactly wrong. The producers wanted Act Two from him by the end of January. I *should* be doing everything I could to ensure NOB sent it to them. Especially if I ever wanted my job to be anything more than answering all the emails Monty preferred to avoid.

My inbox pinged. Sarah. On the drive home, my friends had all volunteered new meet-cute ideas, so I was fairly sure everything was fine between us. Still, I opened her email with caution.

Evie, I want you to know that I've thought long and hard about this. I've decided to forgive you for ruining my hen do. You have your friend Ben to thank for my generosity, of course.

And the flowers you sent. I know they're probably from the money you saved on my weekend, but I appreciate the gesture all the same, what with you being so poor.

"You're welcome, Sarah," I murmured. I'd messaged Ben to thank him profusely for everything he'd done for Sarah, offering to reimburse him for the balloons and the Shrewksbury driver. His response had been "Don't worry about it." Which, try as I might, I couldn't decipher. It had felt like we were just getting somewhere with each other, then I had to go and prove his first impression of me entirely right.

> Also, I found another album on the USB stick with my photo collage. I assume it's Ben's, as it's his memory stick. You didn't say he was a photographer. From what little you have said, he seems to value his privacy. So to save you having to agonize over it, I've already looked at all the photos. You have a very talented friend!

There was a file-share link at the end of the message. I hovered my cursor over it. Despite Sarah's *thoughtfulness*, it still felt like it would be prying if I opened this folder. It could be personal—there might be old photos of his wife on there . . . I should respect his privacy.

I bit my lip.

The idea of finding out something—anything—about Ben was just too tempting.

I clicked. The file was huge. I set it to download in the background, jiggling my knees as I waited.

"Finally." It contained over a hundred images.

The first photograph was of a frozen lake. I relaxed a little. There was no reason to feel guilty about looking at a photo of a lake. It was hardly personal. As I clicked through to the next one, and the next, my relief sharpened into something like disappointment. Ben wasn't in any of them. The photographs looked like they'd been taken in Iceland, from the geysers, icy fjords and dark, rocky terrain. As I carried on clicking, I propped my chin on the palm of my hand, disappointment fading, lingering a little longer on each image. Through Ben's lens, the landscape had a life of its own.

"Oh, Ben," I murmured.

Every image was infused with a fierce love for the wildlife and landscape he'd captured. There was courage in the shot of the waterfall cascading over a crescent cliff into foaming waters. Awe for the blue icebergs slung along a black sand beach. I'd been wrong when I assumed they were just professional shots; all of these photographs were personal for Ben.

Why had he given up on this huge, incredible gift? Looking at these photos, I felt like I was finally getting to know the real him. Though, after the way I'd messed things up this weekend, there was a chance I'd never get to find out more. The thought made me inexplicably sad.

The sound of the front door opening shook me from my thoughts. Voices floated up the stairs. I went back to the album, thinking it was the accountants who shared our kitchen. Then I heard an unmistakable plummy tone. Monty.

I checked to see if I'd somehow lost track of time. It wasn't even eight a.m.

What? In seven years, the only time Monty had been in the office before ten was when he hadn't realized the clocks had changed. What possible reason could he have for being here at this time? It was early, even for me.

Monty reached the top of the stairs. "Good morning," I said, a little too late.

"Really, Evelyn, you could try to look a little less surprised," Monty said drily as he pushed past my chair.

Then his companion appeared, and my jaw slackened in shock.

"N . . . Ezra," I said, flustered at my near slip. I caught myself staring. With his expensively disheveled blond hair, ludicrously high cheekbones, and Hollywood smile, he seemed so out of place in our dingy office. I spent so much time being annoyed with him, it was easy sometimes to forget how absurdly pretty he was.

NOB didn't even look at me as he passed by. It was as if our relationship had reverted to where it was before our deal. It struck me how much it had changed over the last few months for this to actually sting. I used to think NOB was nothing more than an arse. Now I understood that he was just uncompromisingly himself with everyone. Of course, that did mean he was often just an arse, but he'd proven there was more to him than that. So, what was he playing at?

I sank low in my chair, tapping my pen furiously against my pad and glaring at his retreating back as if it could somehow give me the answers. What could the pair of them possibly be meeting about at this hour? And why didn't I know about it?

Just before he closed Monty's office door, NOB glanced back at me and winked.

I pretended to be typing, keeping one eye on Monty's window. NOB came into view, pacing the office and gesturing as he spoke. I could hear the occasional word through the thin walls. I thought I caught my name.

After my scare over the New Year, I'd made NOB promise once again that he wouldn't tell Monty about our deal. Given that drunk Evie had already let it slip to NOB that my job was at risk, I'd told him Monty would most likely fire me if he found out. He'd sworn he wouldn't say a word.

So what the hell was he doing?

NOB disappeared from sight and I leaned farther back in my chair. If I could just see Monty's reaction to whatever it was he was saying, I might have a clue about what was going on. I pushed my toe against the wall, tipping myself back a little. Just a little bit farther . . . A little bit more. *There.* I could see NOB again. He had something in his hand.

My chair wobbled alarmingly. I teetered, just for a second, before gravity took hold. NOB's gaze slid to the window and he watched as I tipped over backward, my headrest catching on the wall behind me and leaving me wedged at a ninety-degree angle with my legs in the air.

Monty stepped into view and scowled as if I'd done this on purpose. He pulled the cord on his blind. It fell halfway and stopped. He yanked it up and tried again. NOB stood behind him, amusement in his blue eyes as the blind seesawed up and down and I remained lodged in the corridor like an upended turtle. While Monty was distracted, I caught NOB's eye, smiled, and discreetly stuck two fingers up. NOB's brows shot up, and I gripped the arms of my chair before Monty could catch sight of his assistant flipping off his number-one client. *Was that really worth the risk, Evie?* Monty had managed to get only half the blind down when he gave up and stormed away.

I was upright and answering emails by the time NOB emerged from Monty's office. Once again, he didn't even look at me as he passed by. I stared after him, cold fingers of trepidation on my neck.

"Evelyn?" Monty called. "My office. Now."

When I entered, Monty seemed mesmerized by a small stack of paper on his desk.

"Is everything okay?"

He looked up, fingers dancing around the edges of the pages, as if checking that they were still there.

"It's Ezra," said Monty. "He's delivered Act Two."

For a moment, I couldn't speak. Then I heard myself saying, "But . . . he's *early.*"

"Well, it's not quite *complete* yet."

Ah. He'd at least delivered *something* though. "How is it?"

"Excellent," Monty replied, somewhat dreamily. I let out the breath I'd been holding. I should have been happy, and I was, but why did NOB have to be so infuriating about it? He could have at least told me he was writing. Instead, he'd once again cut me out. "I must confess, I didn't realize quite how much you were helping him." I was so distracted by the thought of beating NOB over the head with his own Oscar, I almost missed this. Monty. *Praising me.* His face brightened. "It's entirely different to *A Heart Lies Bleeding*, of course, but I think he really has something here, Evelyn."

Seeing Monty like this, it was easy to imagine him in the same chair fifteen years ago, back before years of indulgence had set in and the shine had worn off for him.

"I'd really love to read it," I said.

His attention snapped back to me, and I swear there was a hint of guilt in his expression. "He hasn't shown it to you?"

I shook my head.

Monty tightened his fingers around the edges of NOB's script. "All in due course." He pulled it closer to him. "We . . . We need to talk, Evelyn. Ezra has expressed some serious concerns about you."

I was too stunned to respond.

"About your workload."

"My . . . workload?"

Monty cleared his throat. "Ezra is concerned you might have distractions." By "distractions," I assumed NOB meant other writers, along with what little personal life I had left. *That arrogant, insufferable boychild.* "He's making good progress with the writing, and he wants to protect your time so you can spend more of it assisting him. Which is why I've made a decision." Monty paused. I held my breath, readying myself for whatever was to come. "I don't need to remind you how much is riding on this script. I'm counting on you to make sure he delivers the rest. Without distractions." Monty straightened a pen on his desk. "So I'll be making sure you can concentrate on your client."

"My what?"

Monty used his sleeve to dust a framed photograph of him with Richard Attenborough. "Do I really need to spell this out? At Ezra's request, I'm handing temporary responsibility for him over to you.

This does of course mean that you need to free up more of your time to spend on helping Ezra. As I'm sure I don't have to emphasize, he needs a certain amount of attention. Until his deadline, I'll be keeping an eye on your workload, and I'll even . . ." He mumbled something.

"I didn't quite hear—"

"I'll take on some of your work." Monty wheezed, as if I'd wrestled the words from him. "We really need him to keep writing, Evelyn. He's all we've got. With Alessandro out of the picture . . ." He trailed off.

"I thought things were going well?" I'd been relieved to see Monty going after someone new, even if I'd been the one to find him. Signing up Alessandro could have taken some of the pressure off us. I'd seen his short films—he was a talent to be reckoned with.

"He was being courted by another agent," Monty said, closing his eyes. This kind of thing happened all the time in the industry— if there was buzz around a new talent, agents would vie to represent them. Yet I could see this one had hit Monty hard. Part of me wondered whether things would be different if I'd been able to speak to Alessandro myself. *Next time.* "It turns out he didn't care enough about his career. He's signed with Geoffrey and Turner."

That explained it.

"I'm sorry, Monty," I said softly. Our mutual dislike of Geoffrey and Turner was always something we could agree on.

"He's gone with what's shiny. He'll soon learn his lesson." He seemed to shake himself out of it. "Hand me the Miller contract and your to-do list." It was one thing him saying he was going to do my work; it was another seeing him follow through. "Don't just stand there gawping, Ezra needs you."

I tried not to look too happy as I deposited the large stack of contracts on Monty's desk. He stared at the teetering pile with barely disguised horror. Then he took my pad from me and peered over my task list. "It's been a while since I've done any of this stuff. Then again, it's not exactly rocket science."

"That's just the first page," I said, leaning across the desk and flipping through the notebook for him.

He paled, then pushed his sleeves up. "You're witnessing a real agent at work. Now go on, get out of here."

"Just one thing," I said, pausing. "If I'm working with Ezra, I will need access to the expense account."

There was a message waiting for me when I got back to my desk.

NOB: You're welcome

RED: now you talk to me? You should have asked me first

NOB: I was keeping up appearances for Monts. I haven't forgotten what you said about your job being on the line. Only one month to go. You need to step it up if you want me to finish the script. How else are you going to meet someone on time?

I resisted the urge to throw my phone at the wall. He'd got so much praise for the script—surely he should want to finish it without the need for me to embarrass myself first?

NOB: You must know how much your reports are helping me by now. From now on, I need you to do at least two meet-cutes a week so I can get this done. You should be grateful. I'm doubling your chances of falling in love . . . and you need all the help you can get

I sat down heavily. Two meet-cutes a week? One had been more than enough. I wasn't sure I could handle doubling up on the humiliation. I waited for the familiar dread to appear at also having to double up on writing, only to find a prickle of anticipation there instead. *That's new.*

I wondered at NOB still insisting I had to fall in love. When I'd agreed to this deal, I'd thought if I could just get NOB to start writing, he'd finish and forget about the rest. But here he was, writing for the first time in years and still holding that part of the deal over me. He'd clearly broken through his writer's block, so why did I have to jump through that particular hoop? At least I had more time now. My friends had always said I'd meet someone if I worked less. I guess now I could find out if that was true.

RED: agreed . . . IF you send me your pages weekly from now on

NOB: How many times? I'll send them to my agent, Red

RED: correct me if I'm wrong . . . but isn't that me?

The three dots appeared and disappeared a few times, as though NOB had started his response and then changed his mind. Until finally:

NOB: When all this is over, we should go for a drink and work out all this sexual tension between us

I rolled my eyes at this. He was clearly trying to sidestep. And yet I couldn't help but think back to that moment we'd shared just before Christmas when NOB had dropped me off at my mum's. I'd slipped and he'd caught me, and, just for a second, it had almost seemed like there was something between us. I shook the memory away. *I'm clearly overtired.*

RED: two meet-cutes a week in exchange for sending me your pages weekly

NOB: Fine. I'll send them weekly. To Monty

He was promising weekly deliveries. No more anxiously waiting around until he deigned to share his pages with anyone. I'd got what I wanted here. Ultimately, to get my promotion, I just needed him to deliver. And to find Mr. Happy Ending.

RED: we have a deal

TAP TAP TAP. Monty was at the window, using two fingers to peer through the diagonal blind. He gestured at me and then toward the door. "Go on, *go*," he said, his voice muffled by the glass.

I wasn't sure what he expected me to be doing for NOB at nine a.m. on a Tuesday, but I collected my things anyway. I thought back to the list my friends and I had cooked up. If I could cope with two meet-cutes a week, could I push myself further? If I was to have any hope of fulfilling NOB's ridiculous stipulation of meeting Mr. Happy Ending, then the more meet-cutes I did, the better. It was time to take back control. *And,* I thought, sliding Monty's Amex card into my purse, *I might as well enjoy it.*

Chapter 25

Out of Office

From: Evelyn.Summers@WJM.co.uk
To: TheEzraChester@ezrachester.com
Subject: HIGHLY CONFIDENTIAL: The Queue Jump
meet-cute
January 16, 7:03 p.m.

Please find attached my attempt to re-create the meet-cute
from *Fools Rush In*.

To sum: I spent all day asking men if I could jump the queue
in front of them and trying to strike up conversations. There
are definitely some types of queue this works better for than
others. For example, the queue for the men's toilets. At
least you have a good excuse. Have you seen the queues
outside women's toilets?

I tried to jump the queue at the post office. Unfortunately,
the guy who let me in was trying to find out if it was possible
to post a live animal via recorded delivery. It is very hard to

flirt with a man carrying a snake in a box that he's determined to send to Australia.

Just in case you are wondering: yes, it is possible to send live animals via Royal Mail. It's just a shame waiting times at the Post Office are so long they're unlikely to survive the queue.

Best,
Evie

- - - - - - - - - -

From: Monty@WJM.co.uk
To: Evelyn.Summers@WJM.co.uk
Subject: Pitch query—URGENT
January 17, 1:45 p.m.

Dear Evelyn,

I'm pitching Michael Mayhew's latest to some producers this afternoon and I haven't got time to read it. I'm going with *The Handmaid's Tale* for fans of *Top Gear*. I'm keen to push the boundaries with this one.

Does this sound about right? Let me know before 2 p.m. if not.

Kind regards,
Monty

- - - - - - - - - -

From: TheEzraChester@ezrachester.com
To: Evelyn.Summers@WJM.co.uk
Subject: Must try harder
January 17, 5:43 p.m.

It isn't quantity over quality, Red. You're still holding
out on me. You promised you wouldn't do that anymore,
remember? You really aren't half bad. You should have
more confidence. So quit with all the description and give
me more dialogue already.

I'm going to need another meet-cute on my desk by the end
of the week.

E

From: Monty@WJM.co.uk
To: Evelyn.Summers@WJM.co.uk
Subject: Simon—URGENT
January 18, 11:32 a.m.

Dear Evelyn,

I have been on the phone to Simon for two hours now. I am
literally typing this while he's still talking. He only has one
more scene to write and he's having some kind of existential
crisis.

What do I do, Evelyn?

He's cataloging every negative comment he's ever received,
and he hasn't made it through his high-school years.

Help.

Kind regards,
Monty

- - - - - - - - - - -

From: Evelyn.Summers@WJM.co.uk
To: TheEzraChester@ezrachester.com
Subject: HIGHLY CONFIDENTIAL: The Trip
January 19, 5:15 p.m.

Is it really too hard for you to say "please," Ezra?

Please find attached the meet-cute from *The Lady Eve*. Not a rom-com, but it has a meet-cute that demanded to be honored. Though I'm not sure that's exactly what I did. It did enable me to try some of London's finest restaurants. What a pity I won't be allowed back to most of them.

It turns out that if you're going to try to trip someone in a restaurant, you need to stick your foot out quite far. I had my whole leg in the aisle before I got a man to trip over it. It makes it much harder to explain afterward, I can tell you.

In hindsight, I wish I'd chosen a restaurant without tablecloths. Because when people fall, they tend to grab everything they can on their way down. It was like one of those tablecloth tricks, except instead of all the food staying where it is, it ends up on the magician, who's just landed face-first in a seafood risotto.

I've documented every attempt I made at this meet-cute. The report is mainly dialogue. I trust it's more to your liking.

Best,
Evie

- - - - - - - - - -

From: TheEzraChester@ezrachester.com
To: Evelyn.Summers@WJM.co.uk
Subject: PLEASE
January 20, 1:12 a.m.

Yes, better. More like this, please. And now, please.

Ex

- - - - - - - - - -

From: Evelyn.Summers@WJM.co.uk
To: TheEzraChester@ezrachester.com
Subject line: HIGHLY CONFIDENTIAL: The Lift (AKA bonus
meet-cute)
January 22, 6:34 p.m.

Please find attached the *500 Days of Summer* Lift meet-
cute.

This took most of the day, three department stores, and
approximately 57 lift rides to achieve.

It's very hard to find someone listening to The Smiths loud
enough to sing along to, and (spoiler) I didn't.

I just had to go with what I got.

Here's a precis:

Me: *taps man on shoulder* Oh my goodness, is that . . .
Gloria Estefan?

Him: *blushing furiously* It's a Spotify mix. *Looks around at
other people in the lift.* It's completely random.

Me: *persisting* I LOVE this song

Guess what? It turns out his ideal woman *isn't* someone who knows all the lyrics to "Rhythm Is Gonna Get You."

You might not know this, but some older lifts still have emergency stop buttons. And if an elderly fellow passenger in said lift is, for example, prone to panicking, it doesn't take much for them to press it. A woman randomly bursting into song certainly does the trick.

It's been a week now. You've had three meet-cutes from me.

Time to send your pages.

Evie x

- - - - - - - - - -

From: TheEzraChester@ezrachester.com
To: Evelyn.Summers@WJM.co.uk
Subject: Re: HIGHLY CONFIDENTIAL: The Lift (AKA bonus meet-cute)
January 24, 2:20 a.m.

Your writing really is evocative, Red. Truly. It was like I was right there with you in the lift. Especially the part where the guy turned his music off and you still decided to finish the song.

I really felt exactly how long it took for the engineer to get you out.

Ex

P.S. Pages will be sent when they're good and ready.

- - - - - - - - - -

From: Monty@WJM.co.uk
To: Evelyn.Summers@WJM.co.uk
Subject: Email inbox full??? URGENT
January 24, 11:32 a.m.

I think there's something wrong with my inbox. It keeps telling me it's full. I had to delete emails just to send this one. Why are there so many?

Also, I'm not sure what your filing system is, so I've been putting contracts in any spare space I can find.

- - - - - - - - - -

From: Evelyn.Summers@WJM.co.uk
To: TheEzraChester@ezrachester.com
Subject: HIGHLY CONFIDENTIAL: We had a deal
January 24, 1:22 p.m.

Send them now, Ezra. No more meet-cutes until you do.

Though I am attaching the Department Store meet-cute from *Serendipity*, because when you've spent an entire day standing behind men who are clothes shopping and declaring you want to buy what they're buying, you want the humiliation to be worthwhile.

I know you can do this.

Evie

From: TheEzraChester@ezrachester.com
To: Evelyn.Summers@WJM.co.uk
Subject: OUT OF OFFICE
January 24, 1:22 p.m.

Hi, I'm currently drinking margaritas in an infinity pool and definitely won't be answering your email.

E

From: Evelyn.Summers@WJM.co.uk
To: TheEzraChester@ezrachester.com
Subject: Re: OUT OF OFFICE
January 24, 1:23 p.m.

This out-of-office better be a joke, Ezra! Our deal is that you send those pages. I've been embarrassing myself all over London, so the LEAST you can do is send Monty something.

Don't you dare ignore me.

Evie

From: Monty@WJM.co.uk
To: Evelyn.Summers@WJM.co.uk
Subject: URGENT
January 25, 12:42 p.m.

Dear Evelyn,

I'm sure you don't need me to remind you that the deadline for Ezra to submit the rest of Act Two to the producers is Thursday.

I've noticed that you've been using the expense account, so I assume all is going well.

Normally I'd offer to step in, as I do have a little more experience with these things. However, I must say I have been very impressed with you over the last few months. I'm starting to believe you might actually be capable of pulling this off after all.

I see great things ahead for you, Evelyn.

Best,
Monty

P.S. Unless the £100 gloves were bought to protect Ezra's hands while he typed, it would be prudent to return them.

- - - - - - - - - -

From: Evelyn.Summers@WJM.co.uk
To: TheEzraChester@ezrachester.com
Subject: Undeliverable: Re: Re: OUT OF OFFICE
January 25, 8:45 p.m.

Your message to TheEzraChester@ezrachester.com has been blocked by the user's profanity settings.

Chapter 26

- - - - - - - - - - - - - -

Mr. Judgy

```
INT: THE LORDSHIP PUB, EAST DULWICH—
SATURDAY, JANUARY 26, 10:30 P.M.

The pub is rammed. EVIE and STEPH are at
the packed bar, waiting to be served. They
both wriggle out of their wet coats in the
crowded space, shouting to each other over
the noise. They're almost at the front.
```

"Is it always this busy?" Steph called to me. I was jostled from behind and Steph and I surged closer to the bar, like flotsam on a tide.

I shrugged happily. "I've never been here before. Saturday night is usually prime Netflix time." I flushed. Clearly the wine we'd had with the meal had affected me more than I'd realized.

Steph grinned at me, tucking her straight, dark hair behind her ear.

"Oh, honey, thank God we got you out tonight."

It was strange, being out on the weekend, doubly so with someone new. After listening to my mum's typically sage advice about the book group, I'd gone back, having read the book this time (*Game of Bones*). Steph had once again provided the wine and made me feel welcome. It had taken me the best part of last week to pluck up the courage to ask her if she wanted to go out this evening. I was determined to make the most of having the time, for once. Making new friends as an adult is as nerve-racking as asking someone on a date. Getting their number is hard enough. Then you send that first message, hoping to hook them in with a bit of humor, and when they reply you hug yourself with joy and then hold off responding for an hour so you don't sound too needy.

"So, if you met someone in this bar, would it count as a meet-cute?" Steph asked. I'd told her everything about NOB and the challenge, including how he'd gone AWOL. I still had no idea where he was or when he'd be coming back. Act Two was due this Thursday, and he still wasn't responding to any of my emails or messages. I pushed my worry down.

The one good—great, amazing, *incredible*—thing from all of this was that after spending two weeks straight writing about meet-cute after meet-cute, I hadn't had the time to dwell too much on the fact I was writing again. I'd just written. And it had felt really good. I wasn't thinking about what this might mean quite yet. I didn't put too much pressure on this new, fragile, hopeful feeling.

"It would need an extra twist," I said. "Like in *Going the Distance* when Justin Long and Drew Barrymore find out they've been trying to beat each other's high scores on the arcade game in the bar." A space cleared in front of us and we eagerly forced ourselves forward. "Though, to be honest, I'm starting to worry I won't ever meet anyone."

"Trust me, I know the feeling," said Steph, flashing the bartender a smile. "My Tinder date last week asked me if I'd be interested in lactating."

Someone knocked heavily into us. "Sorry," I heard a man say in an Irish accent. "I'm usually far more coordinated. While I'm here, this is really none of my business, but I couldn't help overhearing that you're both dating the wrong kind of men." He was standing behind us with two overflowing pints in his hand, half of his chin-length blond hair pulled up in a bun.

"Thank goodness we had you to tell us." Steph dismissed him with a glance. "A bottle of rosé, please," she told the bartender. "House."

We made our way through the pub. Me clutching the wine to my chest and Steph holding the glasses up like they were beacons guiding our way through the crowd.

"I see a table!" But when we reached it there was already someone sitting on one of the four seats. Mr. Dating the Wrong Kind of Men.

His eyes brightened when he saw us—or, more specifically, Steph, who immediately turned on her red-booted heel.

"Hang on," he called. "We have two chairs going spare. You're welcome to them. Honestly, that was a bad first impression. You should really see my second."

Steph checked for my opinion. "It's this or standing," I said. She turned back around and placed the wine on his table.

"All right, let's see it, then," she said as she perched next to him.

The man grinned and sat up straight. "Marc. Recently single. Photographer. Top-notch guy when sober. Would never dream of asking you to lactate. That stool there is for my friend. One of those annoyingly handsome-and-doesn't-know-it-boy-scout types." He gave me a pointed look. "He's just helped me move out of my ex's." This last part was purely for Steph's benefit, and yet, completely on reflex, I started weighing up the situation for meet-cute potential. *Perhaps if I spilled my drink on the (presumably age-appropriate) boy scout . . .* Of course, NOB would have to be reading his emails for it to be worthwhile. "Now your turn. Tell me your names and the most interesting thing about you."

Steph poured wine up to the brim of my glass, suppressing a smile. "I'm Steph," she said. "I'm doing a thesis in feminist literature, which I fund by writing erotic fiction." Marc looked as impressed as I had earlier in the evening when she'd told me. "This is my friend Evie." I was trying to think of the best way to phrase "I watch a lot of Netflix" when Steph continued with "She works at a film agency. She's trying to fall in love the way they do in rom-coms, to get an asshole screenwriter to write one."

"I'm not really looking for love," I said, as if Marc needed or cared about the clarification. "I'm just doing it for my job." I took a huge gulp of wine, slightly mortified, and yet, at the same time, a little pleased that my life sounded a lot more interesting than I was used to.

Marc peered into his pint. "It's possible I've either drunk too much or not enough to understand what you've just said. Ah!" He waved to someone behind us. "Here he is." He looked to me again. "Truly, a wonderful human and the best friend a man could have."

My first thought was *Tall, curly black hair, soft brown eyes, dark expressive brows, great jawline* before realizing who I was describing.

"Ben?"

"Evie?" Ben stared at me as he slipped his phone into his pocket. I blushed furiously, glad he couldn't know what I'd just been thinking. *Meet-cute potential indeed.* Steph was looking at him too, intrigued. We hadn't got around to talking about Ben.

Marc gestured to the stool beside me and, after a noticeable pause, Ben sat down, eyes still on me.

"You already know each other? I thought you didn't get out anymore, pal. Have you been holding out on me?"

"We met at Gil's," Ben said quietly.

Marc's expression softened. "Ah, pal." He seemed to look at me anew. "Of all places."

There was a moment of silence following this, and I reached to fill it. "Steph, this is my Ben friend—my Ben—my friend *Ben*," I stumbled, causing Ben to raise those *dark expressive brows*. We hadn't spoken since last Sunday when I'd dropped off his projector at Gil's. It had been a flying visit because, in a less-than-courteous move, I'd hotfooted it out of there to do a meet-cute, unable to cope with facing him so soon after I'd called him *Mr. Judgy*. Anette must have somehow coerced him to pose for a selfie because an hour later I'd received a picture of them both drinking hot choco-

lates and the message *Good luck finding Mr. Happy Ending, Evie!*
I'd been feeling absolutely terrible for avoiding him ever since.

And now here he was, close enough to touch.

"You've already met my Marc," Ben said, as he held his hand
out to Steph. She shook it with a slow smile, giving him an appreciative once-over. I suppressed the strangest surge of possessiveness.
It's not like he actually is *your Ben.*

"We go way back." Marc drained half his beer. "Evie here was
about to tell us how she is definitely *not* trying to fall in love."

Ben didn't respond. I studied him, trying to work out if he was
annoyed at me.

Steph seemed to sense something was amiss. "Marc was just
about to tell us what kind of photographer he is."

"He was?" Marc said. She nodded encouragingly. "Look, I'm
not one to show off my equipment on the first date, but . . ." He
pulled a large camera out of the satchel hanging on his chair and
gave it to Steph.

"It's landscapes and wildlife mostly. *National Geographic* stuff. I
worked with Attenborough. Well." He blushed. "He wrote the intro
for a book containing one of my spreads." As he talked her through
the photos, I couldn't stop myself from looking at Ben, only to find
his eyes were on the camera. Had he once worked with Marc?

"Sissy Lately," Steph said, returning the camera. "That's my pen
name, if you're interested. You've shown me yours, only fair that I
show you mine. You have a considerable talent, Marc."

"You should see it in action." There was a rumble of thunder
from outside, provoking an appreciative drunken chorus from the
pub's clientele. "That reminds me, last orders are in twenty and
these guys do the best Dark and Stormys in southeast London."

Steph swiftly emptied the remains of the bottle into my glass. "The
weather gods have spoken. Let's go." They hopped off their stools.

"Here, big guy," Marc said, pushing the camera into Ben's

hands. "Jill almost gave it away with the rest of my stuff. My ex," he emphasized for Steph. "It's a sign." He spread his arms wide, walking backward into a group of drinkers. "You're coming on my next job—we need our boy scout back!"

"I gave this to you," Ben called after him. "And I have a job." But he'd already gone.

Leaving us alone together.

- - - - - - - - - -

Just relax, Evie. He might not even remember.

"So," Ben said. "Mr. Judgy."

"I was drunk," I said quickly, then winced at the defensiveness in my voice. I might have acted like a complete coward last Sunday, but I'd been trying to think of a way to thank Ben properly for everything since the hen do. A heartfelt apology seemed like a good place to start. "I really shouldn't have said that to you, and especially not after everything you did. I'm sorry. The thing is, those balloons, the slideshow, Shrewksbury—you made it a weekend Sarah is always going to remember." I smiled ruefully. "And not just because there were a *lot* of penises."

The edge of his mouth lifted, just a little. "You're very welcome," he said, and I let myself relax. Maybe I hadn't messed things up completely between us.

"I hope it was worth it." For a moment, I didn't know what he meant. "What happened with the hen do," he pressed. "The meet-cute you did for the screenwriter."

Mr. Judgy indeed, a small voice said, rather smugly. But this was supposed to be an apology, and it's not like I didn't deserve this. "If it makes you feel any better, I'm not even sure I'll be doing any more meet-cutes. NOB's gone."

"Gone?"

"AWOL. Disappeared. Vanished. Just when he was supposed to deliver the rest of Act Two."

"From what you've said, it's a miracle he's written anything at all."

"What are you, his biggest fan?" I snapped. *Rein it in, Evie.* At this rate, I was going to have to apologize for this apology.

"What I mean is," Ben persisted, "that you got him writing again. He clearly needs you. So call him on it." There was a challenge in his expression. "Refuse to do any more meet-cutes."

Why did he have such an issue with them? "Don't you think I've tried that?" Albeit drunkenly. "He doesn't take me seriously. He actually had me believing the meet-cutes were helping him write. That must sound ridiculous."

"Not at all," said Ben, and I looked up into his eyes, surprised. *Kind eyes,* I thought foolishly.

"Evie!" Steph rushed up to the table. "Do you have any change? Marc and I are trying to beat each other on the arcade machine." She gave me a meaningful look. Ben already had his wallet out, handing her what looked like a significant number of pounds.

"Good luck, Drew," I said. Steph winked and hurried off.

"Anette's started doing new things," Ben continued, when she'd gone. "Drama class. Making new friends. She really got her confidence after the play."

"That's wonderful," I replied, wondering where he was going with this.

"And it's all thanks to you. Seeing everything you've been doing, it made her want to be brave too." I'd never been called brave before. After running out on him last Sunday, I didn't feel I deserved to be. And while the meet-cutes generally required taking more than a few risks with my dignity, I always considered myself motivated by the fear of losing my job. "She told me she wanted to 'Be More Evie.'"

"She did?" I said wonderingly.

"She said I should be more Evie too." His eyes dropped to the camera, just briefly, before returning to mine. "That screenwriter would be lost without you, and he knows that. He needs you. Believe me. If he thinks you're really done with the deal, he'll come running."

I let Ben's words sink in. He sounded so sure. NOB *had* arranged it so I could do more meet-cutes. Would he have done that if he didn't need them?

In which case, how might he react if he genuinely thought he wasn't getting any more help from me? Would that be enough to make him stick to the deadline? Maybe even send *me* his pages, for a change? It would take more than the vague threat I'd issued on New Year's Eve. I needed to walk away from the deal.

For that, I'd have to be as brave as Anette believed I was. *Either that, or drunk.*

"Okay," I said to Ben. "No more meet-cutes." *For now.*

His smile lit up his face. "Then I believe this calls for more drinks." He headed off to the bar, his tall form cutting a path through the thinning crowd.

I got my phone out and wrote NOB a message I dearly hoped I wouldn't live to regret when I woke up, sober, tomorrow.

RED: you were right about rom-coms. They aren't realistic. I'm never going to find someone to fall in love with me. I'm going to tell Monty everything. I'm done. The deal is off

Ben was still at the bar when my phone lit up. I grabbed it.

UNKNOWN NUMBER: Hi there. I've just found your card. I think I really WLTM the girl who'd do something like this

I sank back in my chair, disappointed. I'd all but given up on the Fate meet-cute, after my X-rated Christmas messages. Could it be that someone normal had finally found one of my cards tucked into a book? I put my phone away without responding. I needed to stick to my decision: no more meet-cutes until NOB delivered. In the meantime, I just had to pray that NOB didn't talk to Monty about our deal, because I certainly wasn't planning to. It was a calculated risk, one I was willing to take if it got NOB to take me seriously. He knew my job was at stake if Monty found out. I *had* to hope this was enough for him to believe me.

Ben threaded his way back through the bar toward me. The tips of his ears were pink. I wondered if he'd checked in on our absent friends. He placed our drinks down—Dark and Stormys, I guessed, by the looks of them—a careful distance away from his camera, and I thought of the job offer Marc had made. Once again, Ben had helped me out, and so far I'd managed only a fumbled apology in return. Maybe there *was* something I could do for him.

Sometimes people just needed a nudge to get back on the right track.

I reached into my bag and pulled out the USB I'd been carrying around with me.

"You left some photos on here," I said.

He paused, the straw halfway to his mouth, emotions passing over his face almost too quickly to catch. Concern, maybe, as if he cared what I thought. And possibly even relief.

"They're incredible, Ben."

"Thank you." His tone was guarded.

There were so many questions I'd wanted to ask since seeing the pictures. I started with what I thought might be the easiest. "When did you stop?" I said gently.

A brief pause. "About three years ago." The same amount of time that had passed since his wife died. I doubted that was a coincidence.

Ding ding ding. "Last orders in five!" a barman called.

It was now or never.

Maybe if I hadn't seen those photos, or the way his eyes had lingered on the camera, this was where I would have stopped pushing. But I couldn't. Not before I'd told him something I very rarely told anyone. I owed him that.

"I used to want to be a writer." At my rushed words, he fell still, giving me his complete attention. "My dad and I would watch films together—we weren't picky. Romance. Musicals. Westerns. Thrillers. Dorothy Taylor's *Brick Park* was our favorite. I wanted to be like her so badly. I'd write all the time. I even studied screenwriting at university. Dad was on his way to a screening of one of my short films when it happened." I swallowed, remembering being annoyed at his lateness and wondering where he was, then getting Mum's call, and the world falling down. *Your dad's in hospital.* "They said it was a massive heart attack. It could have happened at any time." But it had happened when he was rushing to see my film.

"It wasn't your fault," Ben said, and I realized I'd fallen silent. "I know that's what people tell you, and it's hard to believe them, but it's true."

There was something about the way Ben said this that told me he very much understood how I'd felt. It made me wonder, again, what had happened to his wife.

"Thank you. I know," I said softly. "Luckily, I have really great friends who refused to let me think otherwise. They even tried to keep me writing. I managed for a while, but I was running on empty, I just didn't know it. My friends were all that was pushing me along. When I moved away to London, it was just me. It didn't take much for me to stop altogether." I swallowed, gathering myself for the next part.

"In the end, it only took one agent to tell me I wasn't good enough. These meet-cutes . . . They might not look like much from the outside, but writing about them for NOB has been like finally

moving forward, after spending a really long time standing still." I
paused, not wanting to push too hard. "Sometimes you can only
get where you need to go by taking small steps. You just have to be
willing to take a chance."

I searched his serious brown eyes, wondering if I'd done the
right thing telling him all this.

He surprised me by inching closer, until our knees touched.
"Evie. The meet-cutes, I didn't realize—"

A shout from near the bar cut him off. "Closing time! Thank
you, ladies, gents!"

"Hey, you guys!" Marc and Steph zigzagged toward us, linking
arms. Marc launched himself toward Ben, pinning him to his side
in a hug and nuzzling his head against his chest. "Steph said we just
had a *meet-cute*. Did you have one of those too?"

Was it quiet in here? Because Marc's words rang like tinnitus in
my ears.

"Time to put your coat on, Marc," Ben said evenly, extracting
himself.

I checked on Steph. Her footsteps were surprisingly steady as
she gathered her things.

"You're a great friend, you know that, don't you?" Marc said, as
Ben got him into his coat. "Ben! The guy who always shows up."
Marc looked green. "Though you might want to leave for this."

"Wait until we're outside, buddy." Ben gently but firmly shifted
him toward the door. "I'll even hold your hair back."

"Just a sec." Steph put a card into Marc's coat pocket, patting it.
"My number. Let's actually get to know each other."

Then she kissed my cheek, smelling of strawberries and rum.
"We should do this again. You good getting home?" I told her I was
just around the corner and she breezed out of the pub, trailing her
red scarf. I stared after her, slightly in awe.

Ben ushered Marc along, pausing briefly at the door. "We won't be at Gil's tomorrow, just so you know. I'll be picking Anette up from her grandparents'," he said. His expression was shuttered.

"I'll see you next week, then," I said, with an unexpected pang of disappointment. I tamped it down before he could see it on my face.

He nodded just as the door closed behind him.

What just changed? But I knew. The moment Marc had mentioned this being a meet-cute, Ben had shut down. Again. I yanked my mittens on. It wasn't like I was trying to have a meet-cute with *him*, so what was his problem?

As I pulled my duffel coat from the back of my chair, I saw the camera propped on Ben's seat. *Oh, no you don't.* If nothing else, I would reunite Ben with his camera. I grabbed it and hurried outside. It was pouring with rain. I shook out my red umbrella and stepped onto the street, squinting through the downpour. *There.* Ben had hailed a taxi and was trying to coax Marc into it. The rain had swept his dark hair into his eyes.

"Ben." I hurried up to him, placed the camera in his hands, then turned away before he could respond.

I'd taken only a few steps when I heard him call my name.

"Evie."

I turned around, shivering beneath a streetlamp as I clutched my umbrella, wondering what he could possibly want.

Flash. The whole street lit up, the rain slick and glittering. As I blinked away the light, I saw Ben lowering the camera. He looked down at it for a moment before lifting his eyes to meet mine.

"Small steps," he said.

Chapter 27

Bridesmaids Revisited

INT: EVIE'S BEDROOM, WEDNESDAY, JANUARY 30,
5:34 P.M.

EVIE is wearing tights and a nightgown as
she takes a garment bag out of a cardboard
delivery box and hangs it up on her
wardrobe door. Her room is tiny but neat.
There are framed film posters on the walls:
*Brick Park. When Harry Met Sally. Lost in
Translation. The Champ. A Room with a View.
Thelma & Louise. Juno.*

The bridesmaid dress felt heavier than I imagined it should. Sarah had chosen them before Christmas, but I hadn't been around, and rather than send me a picture, she'd wanted me to see it in person to "really get the benefit." She'd posted it out to me so we could both try on our dresses at the same time today, albeit at a distance of almost two hundred miles.

"Does it look okay?" Sarah's voice sounded tinny through the speakers of the laptop balanced on my bed. The camera quality from Jeremy's propped-up tablet was a little fuzzy, but I could see Jeremy and Maria both sitting on the small heart-shaped sofa at the bridal boutique in Sheffield, holding glasses of prosecco while they waited for us both to get ready. I wished I could have afforded to be there with them in person. Still, at least I had my own (plastic) glass of prosecco to get me through this.

"I'm still unzipping."

"It's so weird seeing you outside of work at this time," Jeremy said, his arms draped across his knees as he peered into the camera.

"You too," I told him. Now we all knew how crazy his hours had been getting, we'd been checking in with him more. "Monty's still taking work off me. Almost everything but my edits." It was almost like a dream job, except I was living a nightmare in which I hadn't told Monty that NOB was still out of contact. Or that I'd refused to keep doing the one thing that had apparently got him writing again.

I determinedly shook off my worries and grabbed the plastic flute from my desk. This was about Sarah, not me. I sipped the prosecco before approaching the bag. Jeremy's hints and Maria's stoicism implied that the bridesmaid dress had to be seen to be believed.

"So you told NOB that you're done?" asked Maria, as I yanked the zipper down and peeked inside. "Just like that?"

"Yep. Oh, my," I said. It was very . . . *peach*. Not exactly the tasteful rose gold Sarah had promised. At first I couldn't quite see the dress for ruffles. Then I realized the dress *was* the ruffles. I maneuvered it out of the bag and stepped back.

Maybe it would look better on.

"It must be nice having free time."

"I'm enjoying the break, actually. I forgot how many things there are to do in London. And," I added, a little shyly, "I've had time to think about how much I've enjoyed writing again. Even though it's only about the meet-cutes."

"Oh, Evie." This was from Jeremy, as Maria clung to his arm looking cautiously hopeful for me.

"Are you trying on that dress?" Sarah called from off-screen.

Obediently, I stepped out of camera range and shrugged out of the nightgown.

"I'm so, so pleased for you, Evie," Maria said.

"Same, but can we go back to the bit where Hot Widower took your photo?" Jeremy asked. I leaned in to the screen so he could see the look I was giving him.

"Has she got it on yet?" Sarah asked.

"Just a moment." I grunted as I attempted to locate the zipper. I felt like Katherine Heigl in *27 Dresses*, only I was wearing all of them at once.

"What's happening?" I heard Sarah's voice rising. "If it doesn't fit now, it's too late and I don't want to hear it."

"If you shimmy it round to the front, zip it up halfway, then twizzle it back round, it's easier." Maria's face was scrunched up in sympathy. I did as she said, wriggling and panting, then jumped up and down to coax the zipper upward.

"We can see you," Jeremy said. "As can our lovely assistant, Shannon." I spotted a dark-haired woman pausing as she topped up their glasses.

"Shit!" I waddled out of sight, pressing myself against my desk.

"So what happened after he took your picture?" Maria urged.

I winced, remembering how Marc had stumbled back out of the taxi, doubled over with cheeks bulging. "His friend threw up on his shoes."

"Lovely," Jeremy intoned. "And then?"

"Then Ben said, 'We should really stop meeting like this.'" Maria sighed.

"Hot Widower," Jeremy said appreciatively.

"Do I need to remind you he thinks I'm a ridiculous human being? And with good reason," I muttered.

"Do I need to remind you that this moment is about me?"

"Of course not!" I sang out to Sarah. The zipper moved another few inches and I did a slightly restricted victory dance. Just a little bit more and I was in. It snagged.

I was most definitely not in.

Sweat broke out on my forehead. What was this dress made out of, insulation?

"Have you considered the possibility that Hot Widower might be intimidated by the Hot Screenwriter you keep obsessing about?" Jeremy asked.

I paused at his words. "I am not obsessing about him, am I?" Silence from my laptop. "In three weeks' time I'll never speak his name again, I promise." I breathed out as the zipper finally slid all the way up. "Besides, you guys are assuming Ben likes me, and he doesn't. Not like that. We've barely made it to friendship stage."

More silence. I bent down to check that we were still connected. My friends looked out at me, expressions skeptical. They were too caught up in the fact that he'd all but saved Sarah's hen do. They just didn't know him like I did. It was like Marc said: Ben was the guy who showed up. He'd do it for anyone.

"Let's just focus on NOB," I told them.

"Let's focus on the *dress*," Sarah shrieked. "No, Shannon, I do not want to wear a *headband* on my wedding day."

"Welcome to our hell," Jeremy said to the camera.

"It might be a good idea to show Sarah your dress now," Maria added.

My phone buzzed.

"Just a moment." I smoothed some damp strands of hair from my forehead and read the message.

MONTY: Check your email, Evelyn.

Oh, God. Oh, God, oh, God, oh, God.
A bolt of absolute certainty shot through me: I'd blown it by telling NOB I was done. He'd spoken to Monty about the deal. He wasn't going to finish.

I opened the email.

From: Monty@WJM.co.uk
To: Evelyn.Summers@WJM.co.uk
Subject: FW: Re: WLTM
January 30, 5:04 p.m.

Just the ending to work on now, Evelyn.

Well done.

M

From: samandmax@intrepidproductions.com
To: Monty@WJM.com
Subject: Re: WLTM
January 30, 2019, 10:42 a.m.

This is GENIUS!* From all of us here at Intrepid Productions,
a huge hand to Mr. Ezra Chester for lighting up our lives
with such a big leap forward on the script.

The team has a poll going to guess who the lead's going to
end up with.

Waiting eagerly on the happy ending.

Atb,
Sam and Max
Intrepid Productions

*Small suggestion—are we sure on the title?

**One more suggestion: has he reconsidered that opening
scene yet. Bit far-fetched???

"Holy shit."

"You okay, hon?" Jeremy called to me.

"Is it the dress?" Sarah said.

"It's NOB," I replied, feeling light-headed. "He's just sent more pages to Monty. He's almost finished the script."

I read the email again. Did this mean pretending to quit had worked? Shaking my head in wonder, I sent a quick message.

EVIE: you were right. He's sent the pages. Thank you

"Congratulations!" Maria cheered. "So are the meet-cutes back on?"

Ah. My euphoria faded. "I guess so," I said. Though NOB still hadn't been in touch. I supposed I should just be happy he was writing. It occurred to me that I should reply to the WLTM message from Saturday. Besides, who knew? Maybe that stranger could be my Mr. Happy Ending. I was trying to ignore my inner cynic's laugh when my phone lit up.

BEN: it was all you. I knew you could do it.

I smiled. Could it be that, despite all our misunderstandings, Ben and I had finally made it to the friendship stage after all? Take that, Harry; Sally was right.

"Are you actually checking your phone right now? Is it a message from your dress, telling you whether it fits?" Sarah's voice was slippery with hysteria, a reminder of just what Jeremy and Maria had been dealing with in my absence. I put my phone down. After the hen do, I was still on probation as far as Sarah's forgiveness was concerned. Time to show her I was all in.

I sprang up off the bed.

Riiiiiiiip.

I froze, half bent over, my foot still on the trailing ruffle. I squeezed my eyes shut, willing it to be fine. *Shit!*

The entirety of the back of the dress had peeled off like the skin of an orange.

On the screen, Jeremy's eyes were wide, his glass part way to his mouth. "Oooh, are you in trouble now," he said.

"What, what is it?" Sarah asked.

"Nothing," Maria and I called. I got up close to the camera.

"Jeremy, if you dare breathe a word . . ." I hissed. I could see him thinking about it.

"No, not that *veil. I said a bit of bling, not visible from space.* Maria!"

My friend hopped off the couch to help Sarah.

Jeremy grinned. "Evie's ready," he said loudly. "And doesn't she look absolutely stunning?" It could be that he was still holding me accountable for the rat.

"I'm going first," said Sarah. "Turn the camera on me."

I hastily threw the trailing ruffle behind me. My mum would fix it for me before the big day, I told myself. Sarah would never know. *I hoped.* Because I couldn't let her down again.

Jeremy picked up the tablet and Sarah came into view, blurry at first and then in sharp focus. Her sleek blond hair was done up in a bun, a few artful wisps escaping. Thankfully, the bridesmaid dresses were bearing the brunt of Sarah's fairy-tale theme. Her dress was as elegant as I'd imagined. Ivory, with simple lines, strapless, hugging her compact figure and flaring out at the bottom in a fishtail, accented by a band of glittering crystals around her waist.

There was a moment of complete silence.

"Well, what do you think of me?" Sarah asked. "That's not your cue for a smart remark, Jeremy."

"Actually," I heard Jeremy say, his voice soft, "I was going to say you've never looked more beautiful."

I could hear Maria sniffling and a rustling sound, as if Jeremy had moved to put his arm around her.

"Oh, Sarah," I sighed, goose bumps dancing up my arms. Sarah had always said she'd be the first one of us to get married. Looking at her now, I couldn't have been happier for her that this was true. "It's perfect."

She preened. "I know." There was movement, and the camera was briefly compressed between my friends' bodies as they all embraced. I drank a bit more prosecco, feeling a million miles away.

I could just make out Sarah briskly wiping at her eyes before she shooed them away.

"Now, are you done messing around, Evie? Let me see you."

All three of my friends squeezed into view to assess me.

"Why don't you give us a twirl?" suggested Jeremy innocently.

A frayed edge of material had drifted to my hip. I did a little dance on the spot like I couldn't be happier, using my swaying arms to shift it behind me.

"I just love it so much!" I said.

Sarah's eyes glimmered. "I'm so glad. You know, I was thinking about my backup bridesmaid dress options all week, but you've decided it for me. Plus, these dresses go better with the cake. You look *adorable.*"

I stopped dancing. Maria gulped her prosecco and Jeremy beamed.

"Speaking of options," I said, "have you decided on Jeremy's outfit yet?"

Chapter 28

The Boy Who Never Grew Up

```
INT: THE ASH—SATURDAY, FEBRUARY 2,
7:30 P.M.

EVIE stands in the foyer of the Ash. There's
a giant Oscar-style award statue lounging in
one of the fluorescent-green spring-back
cinema chairs in the waiting area. The front
desk is a cinema ticket drop box. A girl
with pristine makeup stands behind it,
wearing an approximation of an usher's
uniform and a well-practiced smile.
```

I placed my recently purchased copy of *Peter Pan* on top of the front desk while I retrieved my brand-new membership card. Monty had ceremoniously bestowed it upon me last week after NOB had delivered, telling me I'd be using it soon enough for my own meetings. I should have been pleased, except it was an expensive reminder that I still hadn't heard from NOB. Yet here I was, doing another meet-cute, because it was the only way I could keep him writing.

When the attendant saw the name on the card, her eyes lit up. "Your guest is already upstairs waiting."

That was unexpected. They normally made the guests wait in the lounge. I checked my card as I put it back in my purse. Was this some sort of platinum membership package? It looked pretty regular to me. I thanked her and hurried away before she could realize she'd made a mistake.

I was meeting Peter in the Ash because most of the staff there knew me. There was nowhere safer in London, and, more important, less likely to judge you. We were using the book symbol to help us recognize each other. Just like Tom Hanks and Meg Ryan in *You've Got Mail*. Given that his name was Peter, the choice had been obvious.

Peter had been sweet but brief over the last few days of messaging, insisting he made a much better impression in person. He'd told me he was thirty-two (good start), and that he'd found my card in a 1999 *Pokémon* annual (slight red flag) that he'd bought for his nephew (a relief). All in all, I could allow myself to feel optimistic.

I checked in with the JEMS chat like I'd promised.

MARIA: have you got there OK?

EVIE: I'm just heading up the stairs now. He's already here

JEREMY: who do you think it is?

EVIE: Peter?

SARAH: didn't you go to see Hot Widower's daughter in Peter Pan before Christmas?

EVIE: is that relevant?

SARAH: I'm just saying. Peter. Peter Pan. A bit of a coincidence if you ask me

I paused on the corner of the staircase. Was she seriously suggesting it might be Ben?

He does have your number.

And hadn't Ben been at the bar when the message arrived? I found myself thinking of how pink his ears had been on his return, almost like he was worked up about something . . .

I shoved the thoughts away. Of course it wouldn't be Ben waiting there for me. We'd only just ventured over the line into friendship, a miracle in itself. Sometimes I genuinely had to remind
myself that I wasn't actually living in a rom-com.

> EVIE: it's not Ben. We're just friends. Besides, I wouldn't even
> want it to be him

> MARIA: so you're friends now. Don't tell me you haven't
> thought about it even a little bit

I headed into the third-floor bar. There were a couple of staff
members huddled together at the curtain, giggling and peeking
through into the restaurant. You never knew when there might be
a celebrity at the Ash. Normally, however, the staff tended to remain pretty cool about it. As I approached, I saw one of them was
the blond waiter who'd witnessed Monty sliding out of a women's
bathroom stall headfirst like a seal. *Oh, no.*

His eyes widened as he spotted me and nudged the girl he'd
been chatting with. She wasn't quite as quick to hide her interest.
Oh, God, does everyone know about what happened in the toilets?

The waiter stepped forward, hands behind his back. "Miss Summers," he said. "What a delight to see you again. We've put you in
the Director's Booth."

The Director's Booth? It was only one of the most exclusive loca-
tions in the club, after the VIP area. Was all this because of my
date? I felt a surge of excitement.

Who on earth would warrant this reaction? What if Peter was
some big shot, and that's why they'd let him up here? I tried to
think of famous Peters as I followed the blond waiter through the
crowded restaurant. I doubted Peter Capaldi would message a
stranger and lie about his age.

Peter Andre? He might.

Booths lined each side of the restaurant; the waiter led me to
the only one that had a privacy curtain. It didn't bear thinking
about what that privacy might be used for, considering this was a
club that kept body oil in the loos.

At first, all I saw was the broadsheet-sized menu held up in front
of the man's face.

"Miss Summers has arrived, sir," said the waiter.

For a wild, bewildering second, I thought: *What if it actually is Ben?*
My heart convulsed as the menu was lowered.

What. The actual . . .

"You," I said to him.

"Red." NOB grinned.

He folded the menu with tanned hands. *He'd* been the cause of
everyone's excitement? He might be *the* Ezra Chester, but he wasn't
that exciting. Not once you got to know him, at least. My heart was
still hammering. *It's the shock,* I told myself. Nothing to do with
what I'd been thinking just a moment before.

"Oh, hang on." NOB tapped his phone to light up the screen
and then balanced it against a striped popcorn box in the center of
his table. "That's better."

The screen had a title page on it.

It read:

PETER PAN

"I'm John," the waiter said to NOB, and received zero response.
"Right, then, I'll just . . ." He started to tug at the curtain, realized
I was standing in the way, and pulled it around me. "I'll leave you
to it, then." With a last, lingering look for NOB, he did the professional melt-away.

I rounded on NOB. "*Where* have you been? You've ignored

every message I've sent you. You tell me to work harder, then make me believe you aren't bothering to write. When you finally do deliver, you don't even let me know!"

"Not every message," NOB said, ridiculously blue eyes sparkling. *Have his teeth been whitened?* He was wearing a gray suit so well cut that it folded around his chiseled edges like it was an envelope and he was the card it was made for. "You look stunning, by the way."

"I . . ." He had a way of disarming me that was just downright annoying.

"Sit down, Red."

My knees wobbled and I caught the table, pulling myself into the booth opposite him.

"Is this a joke?"

"I got your text," he said calmly. "'I'm done'?"

Had he done this to punish me for my message? He'd *catfished* me?

"Did you bring me here just to humiliate me?"

"I wasn't sure you'd even come."

"Well, I didn't know it was you, so . . ." I gestured to my dress. It was the nicest one I owned. Forest green, with a black lace overlay. And I'd wasted it on an arsehole.

"You said you were done with our deal, Red. Though, given you're here, I'm assuming that wasn't strictly true."

"You didn't give me much choice," I said, refusing to feel guilty for my fib. "I can see your tan, Ezra. You've been on holiday, leaving me to deal with Monty and the producers on my own. I did the only thing I could think of."

"It was a writer's retreat," NOB insisted. "After Monica and the breakup, I had to get away. I actually *wanted* to get those pages done for you. The longer I was away, the more I realized why that was. I knew I had to tell you. This seemed a fitting way to do it. Peter. *Peter Pan.* The book you took from the bookstall, remember?"

So the name did have significance.

"Tell me what, Ezra?" I asked. A writer's retreat? Could I believe that? He *had* delivered the pages.

He fiddled with his glass. "You . . ." he began, and trailed off.

"What?" I asked irritably. NOB shifted in his seat, his smooth forehead glistening ever so slightly. Wait . . . was NOB *nervous*?

He took a steadying breath. "You're not wrong about rom-coms, Red. Because, if you were, then I wouldn't have fallen for you."

It took me a moment to remember to breathe. "Don't be cruel, Ezra."

"You don't believe me," he stated, as if unable to believe it himself. "Okay, let's start small. 'I'm just a boy, standing in front of . . .'"

"Stop it."

"Red, I'm serious. *Evie*," he said as I stood, yanking the curtain back. I was a few feet away when he called out, *"Please."*

There was something so plaintive, so un-NOB-like about the word, that it stopped me. Other diners were staring. I turned around to find that NOB had followed me out of the booth.

"I really do like you. Do you need me to shout about it? Because I will." He threw his arms wide and raised his voice. "I like you, Evie Summers. I've fallen for you. In fact"—he lowered his voice—"I've been falling for a while."

I saw John the waiter eyeing us from across the restaurant, a look of *Here we go again* resignation on his face. The same waitress who'd passed us earlier was beside him. She had her hands over her mouth, eyes round and doelike, like she'd never seen anything as romantic.

"Oh, for goodness' sake." I pushed NOB back into the booth and onto the seat, yanking the curtain closed before sliding in next to him. "That was mortifying."

"That was pure rom-com." NOB grinned. The smile fell away when he saw my thunderous expression. "Why is it so hard to believe that I like you?"

"Because you're *Ezra Chester*. You date the Monica Reeds of this world, not Evie Summers from Sheffield," I said. It wasn't that I thought I was particularly hideous, but this was *NOB*. He was all about status and appearances. He wouldn't even let me read his script because I was just an assistant.

And yet he was staring at me like he couldn't understand what I was saying. "I'm not with Monica. I'm here, with you. Telling you that I like you. Go on a date with me. *One* date. That's all I'll need to convince you."

He seemed so sincere, and he wasn't giving up. Exactly how far was he willing to take this? Could I somehow use this to get him to show me the script?

"Just *one* drink," I said grudgingly. "And we'll do it right now."

"It's a start." As NOB flashed that Hollywood, all-is-right-with-the-world smile of his, John stuck his head through the curtain. He didn't look happy.

"Just in time—we'll have just *one* bottle of your merlot," NOB told him.

"Okay, let's hear this," I challenged him when the waiter had retreated.

"You're adorable. You make me laugh. And you're just about the only person who doesn't take my shit," NOB reeled off, a little more easily than I'd been expecting. "And," he said, "you like me. Admit it."

I found him attractive, but I was hardly alone in that. It didn't mean I *liked* him.

Even if, I had to concede, there was more to him than I used to believe there was. The roadside rescue. Ziggy. If pressed, I might even admit that his messages weren't entirely infuriating.

"No," I said anyway. "I really don't, Ezra."

He flinched, and I felt a flash of guilt.

"Don't tell me you haven't enjoyed these last few months. I

have. Talking to you has been the one highlight of a crappy start to the year. You *like* me, Red."

I wanted to deny it, but the truth was, there was a small part of me that at the very least appreciated him. As maddening as he was, there was something very straightforward about Ezra Chester. What you saw was very much what you got, and it was appealing.

He inched closer to me along the booth, as if sensing weakness, blue eyes eager.

"I think we might have something here, Red. Tell me you don't feel it too."

I remembered being in his kitchen the day we'd made our deal, when he'd looked at me as though really seeing me for the first time. It had been like standing in a spotlight. Compared to that, the look he was giving me now was a tractor beam, pulling me in.

Someone made a brisk gap in the curtain. John. He placed a tray with glasses and wine on our table with a flourish and started to uncork the merlot.

"We need a moment here," NOB said to him.

"Oh, it won't take long, sir." John poured a drop of wine into NOB's glass, clearly in it for the long game, only to find the bottle plucked from his fingers.

"Thank you, John," I said, as NOB fluttered his fingers to usher him away.

The waiter snatched his corkscrew back and didn't bother to close the curtain behind him.

"You were saying?" NOB said to me.

I glanced away from him across the restaurant, needing a moment. A new arrival caught my eye.

"Oh my God," I said. *"Ricky."*

"That's not my name."

"No," I said, lowering myself down in the seat. "Ricky. My ex. He's here."

Chapter 29

Dicky

```
INT: THE DIRECTOR'S BOOTH, THE ASH—SATURDAY,
FEBRUARY 2, 8:13 P.M.

NOB lounges against the purple leather of
the booth, lit by a miniature spotlight.
Beside him, EVIE sinks down so her chin is
level with the table as NOB looks at her in
amusement.
```

"There's a story here. Tell me." NOB started to rise to his feet. "Or I could just ask your ex."

I pulled him back down. "Okay, okay."

Glancing back over to Ricky, I saw who he was with. Jodi.

"Oh, *shit.*"

If she saw me out with NOB alone, she could have the entire industry believing we actually were dating. Come to think of it, why were she and Ricky here alone . . . ?

"Still waiting."

"Fine." I kept it short. "Ricky's my ex. We were together for two years. He got a job as an assistant at our rival agency and left me. He told me . . ." I stopped.

"What, Red? Here." He slid my drink toward me and I took it with sweaty palms. I'd managed to avoid Ricky for over twelve months. My job was everything to me, and yet I'd purposely missed events I knew he'd most likely be at. Still, in an industry this small, we were bound to bump into each other sometime or other, and the Ash was the industry's nexus point. Especially for someone like Ricky, who wanted to be seen. "Breathe," said NOB. I took his advice and inhaled the wine.

"He told you . . . ?" Did he really care about this?

"He told me that he wanted a bigger life. A more exciting one." I swallowed more wine, cheeks burning. *It's not like NOB is learning anything he doesn't already think himself.* "And he couldn't have that with me. I wasn't enough. So he left me." It took only seconds to say the words that had haunted me for a year. *I just want more,* he'd told me, and in that instant the boy I'd loved became just another person telling me I wasn't good enough.

NOB cocked his head at me.

"Ricky is a dick weasel."

My laugh was strangled. "My friends call him Dicky."

"Well, don't look now, but Dicky's spotted us. He's coming over. Up you get."

I straightened. *Oh, no, oh, no.* NOB topped up my glass just in time for Ricky and Jodi to appear at the edge of our table.

"Evie! I thought that was you. Ritchie wasn't sure, but you're hard to miss, aren't you?"

I forced a smile at Jodi and made myself look at my old boyfriend. He'd upgraded his round tortoiseshell glasses for designer ones, and he'd changed his hair so that it was parted on one side and curled. *Is that a perm?* He smiled at me, showing the small, gappy teeth he'd always said he hated but which annoyingly made him look mischievous and fun.

"Evie," he said, like I was an old acquaintance. "Where's Monty? Don't tell me—he's got you keeping his seat warm while he gets here." Ricky's small eyes were merry, like we were sharing an in-joke.

"I'm here with a client, Ricky," I returned, satisfied to see him twitch at the name.

He looked from me to NOB, and his curiosity was clear even through his studied nonchalance. Jodi was less subtle, moving closer to the table, eyes on the prize.

"It's Ritchie," he said, holding his hand out to NOB. "And of course I know who you are. No introduction needed." This was pointed at me. "*So* great to finally meet you, Ezra." Once he became an assistant, he'd stopped joining in with using NOB's nickname, saying it didn't feel right.

"Sure," NOB said, picking up his glass.

Ricky swiftly dropped his hand, not yet defeated. "Can I be a total geek and say how much I loved *A Heart Lies Bleeding*? I know you shouldn't share your number with someone you've just met. Okay, it's fifteen. I saw it fifteen times."

Ricky's "I'm such a geek for you" act normally worked like a charm. Though I knew he rarely watched a film more than once. "Really, Ricky?" I couldn't resist saying. "Fifteen times?"

His eyes narrowed but remained focused on NOB, waiting for his reaction.

"I wouldn't be surprised if your real number was far lower," NOB said.

The fight-or-flight sirens in my head trailed off as Ricky tried to decide how to respond to this. Before our deal, NOB had done this kind of thing to me countless times. He was an expert at making you feel like you had to earn *his* attention, not the other way around. Seeing him do it to Ricky was, I had to admit, kind of fun.

"Jodi, FTD," Jodi cut in. She used her agency's initials, expecting NOB to know of its prestige. If he did, he certainly didn't look like he cared. She stepped close to Ricky and squeezed his arm, her blond hair floating around her shoulders. Wait, were Ricky and Jodi a *thing*? Could this get any worse?

"We're actually out celebrating Ricky's promotion to agent," Jodi said. Ricky's eyes met mine.

"Congratulations," I told him, feeling like I'd somehow set my-self up for that one.

It shouldn't have stung this much. His promotion had always been inevitable. Once he set his mind to something, there was no stopping him. When we'd met, he'd been a barista called Ricky. He'd loved attending work events with me, I thought to be sup-portive. Then he started talking to more people there than I did, always seeming to know everyone's name in the room. Six months before he'd broken up with me, he got his first job at our rival agency and became Ritchie. Ricky told me it was just business, nothing personal. That it shouldn't affect our relationship. He al-ways, I was realizing, knew exactly what to say.

"Oh, it's not that exciting," Ricky dismissed. "To be honest, I've been doing the job for a while." He shrugged, enjoying himself. "Once you've saved a few deals, got to know a few producers, peo-ple assume you're already an agent. Now I have the business card, I guess that makes it official."

He produced a card and offered it to NOB, who ignored him and took out his phone. It was so rude, I almost loved him for it.

"Ritchie's already signed his first client," Jodi said. NOB stifled a yawn.

"I'm *so* giddy about him. Alessandro. Insane talent." *Ricky* had been the agent to snatch Alessandro away from me? I'd been trying to convince myself that Alessandro was Monty's loss, but this time it didn't work. I'd found him, and *Ricky* had gotten there first. *How dare he?* "He's the kind of top-tier talent I'll be representing. Of course," he said directly to NOB, "I'm always looking for more."

Is he really trying to poach NOB right in front of me? As rage kindled in my chest, I noticed a small smile playing on NOB's lips, as though he found Ricky amusing.

"You know, it's funny we should bump into you," Jodi said. "There's a hilarious cheap knockoff Ezra Chester script going around at the moment. Someone's blatantly tried to rip off your style." The amusement vanished as NOB's mouth thinned. When he didn't respond, she looked irritated. "If I didn't know any better . . ." She eyed me up first, then NOB, her meaning crystal clear. "I'd say we'd just interrupted something."

"You have, actually," NOB said, leaving her stunned. *Insulting.* "We were just about to go through to the VIP area to celebrate Evie's invaluable help on my latest script. I really couldn't have done it without her." I flushed a little at this, pleased. Ricky looked green. "You should join us. Let's make it a double celebration."

"Good assistants can take years to train," Ricky jumped in. "So no wonder Evie is the best."

I flinched. *Did he really just say that?* This was the boy who would talk me down whenever I was nervous. I used to adore his way with words. He always made it sound like we were meant to be together. So when he'd told me I wasn't enough for him anymore, I'd been floored. *Just as he'd known you would be.* I blinked back tears, but I wasn't upset, I was fuming.

Before I could retort, NOB threw something at Ricky. "Here." Unfortunately, it was his VIP card and therefore wasn't big enough to do any significant damage. "We'll catch up with you. You should get in a bottle of"—he glanced at the menu—"the Ash special-edition Dom Pérignon."

"Of course." Ricky's gappy teeth showed. "And then we can talk about your career options." *Ask for forgiveness, not permission:* That was Ricky's motto.

"Can't wait," NOB deadpanned.

When they were out of sight, I prodded him. "You'd better be up to something," I said.

"That was just step one."

He snapped his fingers to call the nearest waiter over. John, who searched around desperately for another colleague to take his place.

When it was clear he was on his own, he slowly made his way to us and switched on a smile.

"Yes, sir?"

NOB started to pat his pockets. "My VIP card has gone missing. I had it when I came in, but I'm wondering if I left it in the gents . . . There was a guy in there with a perm. Maybe he knows where it is."

John paled, his eyes flicking to me. I shrugged, wondering where NOB could possibly be going with this.

"I'll . . . I'll speak to the maître d'," he said, defeatedly. "Deepest apologies, Mr. Chester." The curtain swished in his wake.

"Exactly what *are* you up to?"

"Come on, Red. Don't you want to pay Dicky back just a little bit?" His eyes flashed.

Ricky's parting words had haunted me for a year. I was just starting to shake them off, and now he was back in my life again, happily using me to make another connection.

Would I like to see him get some comeuppance?

"Let's do it."

The second floor of the Ash was separated into the Projection Booth bar and the Screening Room, the impenetrable VIP area. The Screening Room's thick metal door had started life in a bank vault. It was flanked by staff who filled their suits like they moonlighted as cage fighters.

We were waiting in the Booth as John entered, trailing behind the maître d'.

"So much for this place being exclusive," NOB said, gesturing toward the doors.

"I can assure you, Mr. Chester," said the maître d' in a broad Huddersfield accent. "If anyone was in there using your card, I'd know about it."

On cue, a waitress stepped between us all to get to the doors, carrying the champagne and NOB's pass. We all watched as NOB plucked the black card off her tray. The maître d's face turned bone white. John started to move discreetly toward the staircase.

"Well, *I'm* certainly not in there," said NOB. "Step two," he muttered to me as the maître d' pulled out his walkie-talkie.

"We have a Code Black situation. Can all staff with Interloper protocol security training please make their way to the Screening Room *now*."

A minute later, we'd been pushed back to a "safe distance" and NOB had claimed the champagne bottle "for the distress." About five staff members had assembled in front of the metal vault door, standing straight-backed. The maître d' indicated to them to turn their flashlights on and then put his finger on his mouth. He held his arm up straight and then swung it low toward the VIP area.

The bouncers heaved the door open.

"Go, go, go!" the maître d' shouted, and they all filed through after him one by one, swinging their flashlights.

We spied Jodi and Ricky inside the dimly lit room, cowering as the spotlights hit them and the staff huddled around them.

Ricky called out in relief when he spotted us in the doorway. NOB waved at him.

"See," I heard Ricky say. "We're with him."

When the crowd of staff members turned to us, NOB went from waving to an exaggerated shrug, as if he had no idea what Ricky was talking about.

Jodi took a step away from my ex, distancing herself. Seeing the confidence slide off Ricky's face was priceless.

"What now?" I said to NOB.

"Now for step three." He grinned. He took a swig of the champagne, pulled me in close, and kissed me.

Chapter 30

Ezra

INT: GIL'S COFFEE HOUSE—SUNDAY, FEBRUARY 3,
11:30 A.M.

BEN and ANETTE are sitting at their usual
table, reading. The door to Gil's opens.
They both look up, see that it's a stranger,
and drop their gazes again. There are two
empty mugs of hot chocolate in front of
them. BEN glances at the third mug by the
chair next to him. It is still full, though
the whipped cream is now puddled on the
table. He drags his attention back to his
copy of *National Geographic*. ANETTE looks up
briefly from her book, eyeing her dad with a
knowing expression. The door to Gil's opens.
Both father and daughter look up.

I relaxed when I saw Ben and Anette were still here. I made sure
they'd seen me, then fired off a message to JEMS. I'd overslept this
morning. It was as though everything over the last few months—
the agency being at risk, the meet-cutes, then encountering Ricky—
had finally caught up with me. Once the thrill of seeing my ex get
his comeuppance had faded, last night had become yet another
failed meet-cute—despite what NOB had insisted, I hadn't been
convinced by our drink. *Or that kiss.* And with only two weeks to go
until the deadline, I was running out of chances to find Mr. Happy
Ending. I'd fallen into bed utterly spent, waking late to find JEMS
full of unread messages about my date with Peter, two missed calls

from Maria, and a photograph from Ben's phone: three hot choco-lates, sent just after ten a.m. After that I'd rushed all the way here.

EVIE: I'm so sorry guys! I slept in

SARAH: finally! You had us worrying. I do have wedmin to be getting on with, you know

JEREMY: when you add "min" to words it gives me a mingraine

MARIA: I'm glad you're OK, but in the future an "I'm not dead" text after a blind date would be appreciated. So . . . was he Mr. Happy Ending?

EVIE: he was NOB

MARIA: WHAT??

EVIE: he told me I could stop searching. He said he'd fallen for me

JEREMY: what a dick

MARIA: that man. He will do anything to stop you from finding someone just so he doesn't have to finish his own bloody script!

SARAH: how many times do I have to tell you, Evie? You CAN stop searching. I've already found you the perfect plus-one for my wedding!!

It should have been reassuring to see my friends instantly jump to the same conclusion that I had last night—the one that had made me head straight home after the Ash. *Of course* NOB had been lying to distract me from meeting someone. He was dragging his heels about finishing the script, and my lack of success with the meet-cutes was the perfect excuse. The smoking-hot screenwriter doesn't fall for the assistant in real life. And yet a part of me wished my friends hadn't been *quite* so certain he wouldn't.

Enough with the self-pity. I had to focus on finding my real Mr. Happy Ending so I could prove NOB wrong about rom-coms and then rub his face in it. No more distractions, no more excuses. I'd do two meet-cutes a day if I had to.

So why are you still thinking about that kiss?

As I reached the table, Ben stood up. He waved and I lifted my hand—before seeing Xan return Ben's gesture from across the room.

"I'm so sorry I'm late! You're not going, are you?"

I quickly lowered my arm.

"We waited for you," Anette said, pointing to the now-cold mug of hot chocolate left on the table. The flake listed in the melted cream. Ben raised his dark brows at me.

"It's still good," I said, sitting down and sipping the cold, sweet liquid. I tried not to gag. *"Yum."* I looked up at Ben. He really was quite tall. "Could you stay for another round?"

"I don't know. What do you think, Anette?"

"It wouldn't be much of a celebration without us."

I was staring at them both, utterly confused, when Xan appeared at our table with a ginormous frosted cake full of rainbow-colored sprinkles.

Anette slipped on a brightly colored paper cone hat. "Congratulations, Evie!"

"Whatever for?" I asked, astonished.

"For getting NOB to finish the script!" Anette grinned. "We knew you could do it."

Ben blew on a party blower he'd produced from somewhere.

"This is amazing, thank you." I'd told Ben last week that refusing to do the meet-cutes had worked. He must have thought it was all over. I was so touched I almost didn't want to correct them. "But NOB hasn't quite finished yet."

Ben removed his party blower. "You still have to meet someone?" he asked.

"Yes," I said. For such a little word, it felt strangely hard to say.

"There's still time," Anette said. I very much hoped Ben hadn't noticed the look his daughter gave him when she said that.

"I'll just leave this here, then," Xan said, placing the cake down. "Can I tempt any of you with my latest orange smoothie mash-up? This time, I've used avocado and raw—"

"No," all three of us said.

"Coffee it is, then." Xan did a "to each their own" shrug as he left.

"Make a wish," Ben said, handing me the knife. He pulled Anette close, resting his chin on her shoulder, hooded eyes on me. It was kind of adorable.

I thought about what I wanted. To meet someone, surely. If this was a rom-com, two weeks would be more than enough for two people to fall for each other. *One Fine Day. Two Weeks Notice. Moonstruck.* In real life, it felt like an impossible time frame. And even if I was successful, after Ricky, I didn't want to risk actually falling for . . .

Why am I still thinking this way? Sod *Dicky.* I'd spent a year believing I wasn't good enough for him. After his behavior at the Ash, it was time to start accepting that *he* wasn't good enough for *me.* I had two weeks left. NOB was so close to the finish line. My promotion, saving the agency—it was all within reach. And all I had to do was meet one single man and I could have everything I'd always wanted. That's what I should wish for.

But is that all you want?

"I'm aging here." Anette giggled as her dad tickled her.

"Okay, okay, I've got one," I laughed, slicing into the cake and seeing it had rainbow layers.

I wish I could be a writer again.

"Red! Hey, Red!"

I looked up in shock. NOB was waving at me from the doorway. What was going on? NOB? *Here?* In Gil's? That just felt . . . *wrong* somehow. How had he even known where I'd be? Then I remembered my excuse for leaving last night—that I had to be up early to write up the meet-cute, as awry as it had gone. He'd pressed me for details—I thought to make sure I was definitely writing my report—but I hadn't imagined for one second he'd turn up.

Yet here he was, standing over us, grinning that dazzling, too-white smile of his.

"Ah, the famous Gil's. This is the place you do my reports? It's so . . . *provincial*. Hard to believe we're still in London."

"What do you want?" I asked, seeing Ben and Anette's identical scowls.

NOB held his hand out toward Ben.

"I'm Ezra, *awesome* to meet you. And you are?" After a pause, Ben shook his hand. It was like that moment in *Ghostbusters* when the streams crossed.

Anette was gaping at Ezra with frank fascination.

"I know who you are, you're N—"

"Ben," said Ben quickly, saving me.

"Why are you here, Ezra?" I asked. "I'm with my friends. Can't it wait?"

"Sorry to interrupt your . . . lunch?" NOB said, taking in the half-eaten cake. "I'm here about our date, Red. You left last night before we could put something in the diary."

Ben's eyebrows shot up.

"There is no date, Ezra," I told him, wondering at Ben's reaction. I had complained about NOB frequently, it was probably that.

"*You're* the screenwriter," Anette said, apparently undeterred.

"My reputation precedes me," NOB said, pleased.

"The one that can't write."

Ben choked on his coffee.

Anette ate a forkful of cake, humming to herself. NOB looked at her, perturbed. I gave Ben a pleading glance. After a moment, he nodded, retrieving Anette's book out of her backpack, along with what looked like a photographer's autobiography for himself. NOB was frowning at them both, then his eyes widened. He turned his head toward me. *Oh, no, don't you dare . . .*

Silently, he mouthed the words *Dull Dad?*

Oh, no. He remembered the report about Anette's school play. Streams well and truly crossed. He had to leave.

"Don't you have a script to write?"

I mouthed *Behave* to him and checked to make sure Ben hadn't seen. He was studying his book with an intensity it probably hadn't done anything to deserve.

"That's why I'm here." Before I could protest, NOB slid into one of the chairs opposite us like he owned the place. "Ah, perfect," he declared, eyeing the remains of cake. "May I?" He helped himself to a huge slice without waiting for a reply. When Anette signed furiously at Ben, he tapped her book, then concentrated firmly on his own.

"First of all, that wasn't for you," I said, tugging the plate from NOB's hands. "Second, you do realize that cake is one giant glutenous carb, don't you?"

"That's kind of the point." He scooped the slice from the plate, took a deep breath, and pushed half of it into his mouth.

"What are you doing?" I said, exasperated.

A throat cleared. It was Xan, with a large coffee. He looked between NOB and Ben and then at me. NOB gagged as he swallowed. "That's full-fat milk and caffeinated, right?"

"That is what you ordered," Xan replied, heading off with a roll of his eyes.

"What's going on, Ezra?"

NOB took a huge gulp, shuddering at the taste.

"I'm showing you I'm serious about my feelings for you."

Ben's page tore a little as he turned it.

"You really don't have to," I said. It wasn't going to get him anywhere.

"Come on, a guy would have to be a total loser not to notice how great you are." NOB glanced over at Ben and winked. *Why did I have to send him that stupid report?* Because I'd been mad, and embarrassed, and I hadn't known then that Ben and I might become friends.

And if NOB didn't leave soon, there was a chance we never would.

"There's only one way I'll stop," NOB said as he took another bite. "Agree to go out with me."

"I said no, Ezra." He held up a finger, swallowed, and pulled at the waistband of his jeans as if they were already getting tighter. I'm sure it was just chance that this allowed him to flash his abs. I saw Ben move as if to place a hand on his own stomach, then shake his head before returning to his book.

NOB banged a fist against his chest to dislodge the cake, chugging more of the coffee and groaning like it was toilet cleaner. At this, Anette tugged her hearing aids out and placed them, pointedly, on the table, before leaning back over her book. How had our lovely celebration come to this?

"Please, Red. I can feel my arteries clogging. Forget about your doubts for a moment and remember it's just me, Ezra, asking you for one little date."

What had Maria said? That he was just distracting me from finding Mr. Happy Ending? This seemed like an awful lot of effort to go to.

Of course, a small voice said, *if it turns out NOB is telling the truth about his feelings, that would prove I was right about rom-coms. He'll have to finish the script.*

And saying yes would also get him to leave.

"You're killing me, Red." He wiped his mouth. "Have it your way." He readied himself for more cake and I held up my hand. Anette glanced up.

"Okay," I said, and she watched me say the word. Ben stopped, mid–page turn. Anette seemed like she was about to speak and Ben caught her eye, shaking his head pleadingly at her.

"You're serious?" NOB said, swallowing.

"One date," I told him, wondering at Ben and Anette's exchange.

His multicolored grin was one part triumphant, two parts relieved. "That's all I'll need," he said. "Now if you'll excuse me, I need to purge."

Nothing escaped Anette. She signed something to her dad that I was fairly sure was "Me too."

As I watched him stride through the café, drawing no small number of stares, there was the tiniest part of me that felt . . . curious.

Movement caught my eye. Ben was helping Anette into her coat before putting on his own.

"You're going?" I asked.

"Anette wants to see her friend Bea," he said. Anette's next signs were brisk. "She says thank you for a lovely morning."

From her expression, I doubted that was a direct translation. I felt like I'd disappointed her somehow. I tried to thank her in return, but she was refusing to look at me.

"If there's even the slightest possibility he's telling the truth, I could get him to finish the script," I said, desperate to explain but feeling I was somehow making it worse. "If there wasn't only two weeks left . . ." Anette still wasn't looking at me.

Ben took her hand. "Good luck with your date," he said. "I really hope it's what you want."

I was left alone to puzzle over what that could possibly mean.

Chapter 31

Makeover Montage

INT: EVIE'S KITCHEN—WEDNESDAY, FEBRUARY 13, 9:55 A.M.

EVIE is leaning on the kitchen unit, looking at a pink cardboard cake box with a dubious expression on her face. There's a delivery slip taped to the side. She pulls it from the envelope to read it.

Red. I've never been one for flowers. You've subjected me to what passes for your "food," I thought I'd treat you to mine. Behold, in honor of our date today, this gluten-free vegan date cake from Soho's best bakery. It's a revelation.

A car is coming to pick you up at ten a.m. sharp. Get ready to be swept off your feet. Can't wait to give you your surprise later.

Ex

I peeked inside the box and winced. In a way, it was kind of sweet that NOB had sent it to me. Even if it was a dense brown log. I double-checked the time in his note. Ten a.m.—was that right? We were supposed to be meeting tonight. At least I wasn't expected in the office. With only five days to go until the deadline, Monty had holed up in the Ash where he had easy access to nerve-steadying alcohol and could fire regular messages at me asking where the ending was. I'd crossed my fingers and promised him it was all under control. And maybe it was. NOB's enthusiasm certainly hadn't waned.

The only thing he'd tell me about our date was that he had a surprise for me. Half jokingly, I'd asked if it was the script, and he'd replied with a wink. Now I couldn't stop myself from wondering if it really *was* the script. Maybe it was already finished. The date would be worth it for that.

I longed to ask my friends for their advice, except they didn't know about tonight. No matter what happened, I would tell my friends everything. Just, *afterward*. They'd already let me know exactly what they thought about NOB's "feelings" for me. They didn't believe him. Which was completely understandable. I just wanted to approach the date with a clear head. For the past week I'd exhausted myself doing daily meet-cutes, determined not to let NOB distract me, if that was indeed his game, and none of them had led anywhere. As much as I had tried to caution myself against it—part of me was pinning my hopes on this date. I wasn't ready to let my friends— with the very best of intentions—remind me how foolish this was. It wasn't like I was in any danger of falling for NOB. But it would be foolish not to at least find out if he'd fallen for me . . .

Besides, I had enough judgment to contend with already. Last Sunday at Gil's, I'd bought hot chocolates and brownies, hoping to get things back on track with Ben and Anette after NOB's interruption the week before. I'd sat there for almost two hours, until the hot chocolates had gone cold. Ben and Anette never showed.

I heard the click of heels against linoleum.

"What on earth is that, my duck?" I moved so Jane could get to the drawer.

"It's supposed to be a cake."

"How utterly without joy. Speaking of which, you haven't seen

Belinda, have you?" Belinda was Jane's Ourgasm 3000™, a supersleek vibrator that was apparently the best she'd ever had.

"Have you checked the dishwasher?"

She pulled a face. "It's empty. I hope she turns up, I've missed her. Right. I'm off. Good luck tonight! I'm out, so you have the place *completely* to yourselves. I've even cleaned the swing."

I shut the lid on the cake, my appetite suddenly waning. "Thanks, Jane, but it's only the first date."

"Exactly!"

RED: thanks for the cake

EZRA: I knew you'd love it. Just wait until your surprise. See you soon, Red X

I stood in the building the cab had dropped me off at, none the wiser about what to expect. Was this the date? I'd brought my dress with me, just in case. I wasn't even sure where I was. There'd been no signage out front. Inside, every hard surface was white and glittered like diamonds, interspersed with cherry-red soft furnishings. It was like being inside a mouth in a toothpaste advert.

"Hi," I said to the pristine twentysomething boy on the front desk. "I'm supposed to be meeting Ezra Chester, is he here?"

A man stepped out through an opening in the plush red curtain that hung behind the desk. Fifties, tanned, bald, dressed fully in black from loafers to black-rimmed glasses. He looked me up and down, then clasped his hands.

"Ezra! My best client. You must be Evie," he said in a soft Scottish burr. He whipped a hand out. "Gary. So lovely to meet you."

I shook it, perplexed.

"You've no idea of the treats we have in store for you."

"I really don't," I told him.

Gary gave me a once-over. "Come on, let's get you out of that *coat*." My beloved duffel coat didn't deserve that tone. It was snatched off me before I could protest, and I was wrapped in a brilliant white gown.

"Where's Ezra?"

"He will be here to collect you at five p.m. sharp."

"But that's seven hours away!"

"I know, it's not much time, but somehow we'll have to fit it all in."

"Fit all what in?" I asked.

"Why, Evie." Gary pulled a cord to draw back the curtain, revealing the kind of salon that had clients, not customers. "Your makeover, of course."

He'd booked a *makeover* for me? That was presumptuous, hugely insulting, and so . . . *NOB*. My fingers twitched, my first thought being to tell my friends. But of course I couldn't. So I messaged him instead.

RED: is this my surprise?

EZRA: Doesn't every great rom-com have a makeover montage?

But this was real life, and what I'd *wanted* was the script, not a makeover. Especially not one that lasted *seven hours*. Cosmetic surgery took less time. By the time Gary had returned with a trolley, I was fuming.

"Okay, you wee red-haired siren. Let's take a look at you."

"Actually, I'm just going to go. There's been a huge misunderstanding." *I thought NOB might be a decent human being.*

Gary rested an elbow on his hip. "Of course. This is one of the most exclusive salons in London, I'm absolutely incredible, and everything is paid for up front. Why wouldn't you walk away from such an opportunity? Though aren't you just the tiniest bit curious to see exactly what Ezra has lined up?"

I narrowed my eyes. "Let me see the list." He handed me a brochure and I almost dropped it when I saw the prices.

"It's just the ones that are circled."

"Most of them are circled."

Gary smiled. "Yes. Did I mention that he'd paid up front . . . ?"

A plan began to form.

"Can I have a pen?" Reluctantly, he handed me one and stood there tutting as I went through the list. "Nope. No way. Absolutely not. No wax. *Olive oil hydrating wrap?* You aren't basting a turkey. Okay, that one's fine." I handed it back to him and when he saw what was left his face fell.

"Gary," I told him, "you're the best, aren't you? Work with what you've got."

He removed my hair elastic and shook my curls out. They sprawled over my shoulders in a formless mass. I honestly couldn't remember the last time I'd had them cut. Gary took a step back, then another, as if he were still too close to see them all. He clapped his hands for attention, raising his voice. "I need some backup!"

The first thing they wanted to do was dye my hair.

"I don't think so."

"It's going to look so natural you won't even notice. We're going to tame and enhance."

"So my hair is both too much and not enough?"

"*Now* you're getting it."

I thought it over. Normally I wouldn't even consider getting my hair colored, because in London that cost around the same amount as a small car. Plus, after years of merciless adolescent teasing, it had taken a lot of time and effort to achieve the love I now had for my red curls. And yet, this was supposed to be a makeover, and I wanted to make an impact, and it was free . . . I made Gary show me the exact shades he was using before I'd agree.

"Only seven more hours of this," he said as he mixed the dye. "Lucky me."

The thing about montages is they're sped up. I had to sit through every bum-numbing minute. In the movie version, it was unlikely you'd see the half-hour phone call with my mum about my bridesmaid dress and the part where I ate a sandwich.

"Now the makeup!" barked Gary, a mere four hours later, and a girl with a pixie cut and porcelain skin lugged a huge silver trolley over. He spent the next two hours creating a blank canvas of my face by obliterating every freckle. He worked all the way down to my shoulders, and when I strained I could see my skin was now a smooth creamy color. Then, artfully and with great care, he painted a new face over mine.

Another hour later, Gary wiped his brow. "Okay, we're done." His team gathered round to look, their expressions telling me nothing. Gary had covered the mirrors "For the big reveal." He shooed them away. "Evie, darling," Gary said, "I knew I could see a minx inside you, and, by God, I think we've coaxed her out. I believe you're ready for the final touch."

I was pushed through some heavy curtains into a changing room. On a cushioned seat was a large hexagonal box with a toffee-colored satin bow.

"What is this?" I called to Gary, who was hovering on the other side of the curtain.

"Just put it on!"

I tugged at the ribbon and removed the lid. Resting on layers of crisp cream tissue paper was a puddle of material such a dark shade of green, it was almost black. I stroked it. My fingernails were the exact same shade. The fabric was a cool whisper against my skin as I lifted the dress out of the box, the skirt pooling on the floor. Beneath it was a pair of black patent heels with red soles and silk bows at the ankles. There was also underwear. Extremely *supportive* underwear.

Suck it up, Evie. It will be worth it.

"I'm ready," I called.

Gary instantly whisked the curtain aside. He did a double take when he saw me, hands fluttering to his mouth.

"There you are, you *minx*," he said. "Now, stand right here and close your eyes."

I let him maneuver me into position. "Three, two, one."

I looked. He'd wheeled in a full-length mirror. The whole team had gathered in behind me, and a couple of other clients as well. For the first time in my life, no one would have been able to tell that I was blushing.

"Oh my God."

Gary was close to tears.

"Do you like it?"

The girl who looked back at me was not Evie Summers. This Evie had been poured into a dress that flowed over every curve like smoke. Her sleek hair lay in a gleaming coil over one bared shoulder, the color a beautiful burnished red and gold. The exact shade teenaged me would have longed for. She had pale, almost translucent skin, huge sapphire eyes, and a dark crimson mouth. She was, I had to admit, beautiful.

She just wasn't me.

"Thank you," I said, in lieu of more adequate words.

Gary kissed the air next to each cheek.

"You look like a dream," Gary said.

Yes, the one where the handsome prince tells the girl he's fallen for her and then has her made into an entirely different person.

Somehow, I wasn't surprised to find NOB had arrived in a limo.

"Wait," he ordered from the backseat before I could get in. He took a moment to look at me. His mouth curved into a slow, satisfied smile. "Evie Summers, there you are," he said.

"What do you think?" I did a twirl in my heels, feeling my right ankle threaten to give.

"Absolutely stunning," he said. "It's a whole new you, Red."

I exhaled slowly, feeling my makeup-stiffened cheeks resist my smile. "I just wanted to thank you."

"You're welcome," NOB said, pouring two glasses of champagne.

"I spent my entire life being a wallflower, and you've got me to bloom."

He eyed me a little warily. "Glad you think so. Are you ever going to get in?"

"It's just that it took this makeover for me to finally realize how beautiful I am."

A few seconds passed.

"You aren't really happy, are you?"

"You think? Of all the insulting, misogynistic, arrogant things to pull, Ezra!" I exploded. He almost dropped the glasses. "I'm only here to tell you, in person, that our date is off."

"I wanted to give you something to write about!" he burst out. I stared at him in bewilderment. He shuffled closer to the door, looking at me in earnest. "For your meet-cute."

"*What* meet-cute?"

"This one. *Ours.* Call it *Two Weeks Notice. The Proposal.* Whatever. I'm it."

"You've been watching rom-coms?" *Which one of us is Sandra Bullock?* That wasn't important.

"All the ones you recommended."

I was about to respond when something dawned on me.

NOB was offering to help me fulfill the final stipulation of our deal. Exactly as I'd hoped.

"You do realize that if you're my Mr. Happy Ending, you have to finish the script?"

His blue eyes were crystal clear and guileless. "I realize I'm offering to be the last meet-cute you'll ever need." He shuffled back to make room on the seat. "Aren't you the least bit curious?"

I considered my options. Leave now, head held high, telling him he can forget the script. Or . . . I sighed, throwing my bulky satchel into the car first and inching the dress up over my knees so I could climb onto the heated leather.

"Relax," NOB said, smiling again as he handed me a glass of champagne. The high shirt collar beneath his dark blue suit was almost priestlike. Never had a man looked less holy. "If you don't like what I say next, I'll take you straight home. The makeover was only step one of my surprise. I wanted to do something for you, the woman who got me to write a rom-com. It had to be something fitting." Hope welled up inside me. *Was it the script after all?* "I thought, what could be more appropriate than a red-carpet premiere?"

"What?" I fluctuated between disappointment and excitement. I'd always wanted to go to a film premiere, but in all my time with Monty, he'd never let me. I also *really* wanted that script.

Ezra drained his champagne. "I knew you'd love it."

"Is this my surprise?"

"It's part of it." I breathed out in relief. The script was still a possibility. "Look, I made a stupid mistake with the makeover, I get that. But *please* don't give up on me just yet." There was a note of urgency in his voice. For all the world, Ezra seemed completely sincere. "I need you to know," he continued, "things are different. With you. *I'm* different." Frustration and earnestness warred on his face. "Please believe that."

"Ezra," I said, "tell me you aren't about to give me the 'you're special' speech, because that's straight out of the rom-com playbook and I won't fall for it. Especially not from you."

"Red," he said smoothly. "The thought never even crossed my mind."

Chapter 32

Hollywood Miss

EXT: THE RED CARPET, ODEON, LEICESTER
SQUARE—WEDNESDAY, FEBRUARY 13, 6 P.M.

EZRA holds his hand out for EVIE and pulls
her from the car in one smooth motion. She
stands beside him and he puts his arm
around her waist. Security ushers them
toward the red carpet, which is sectioned
off from the public. EZRA whispers
something in EVIE's ear that makes her
smile as he guides her toward the cameras.
The look she gives him is cautious but
thoughtful.

I blinked the flashes away so I could absorb as much of the scene as possible. The moment we stepped onto the red carpet, a wall of noise hit us. This was no small film. A vast poster hung down the Odeon's frontage, but from where I was standing, I couldn't read it. Huge glass jars with white church candles burning inside them lined the carpet. Crowds of photographers pressed in from all sides. I found myself unable to move, startled by another flash and the sheer volume of this many people in such a small space. Ezra— NOB—startled me by tucking a finger beneath my chin, making me look up.

"You are stunning," he said. "Let them see that."

I pulled away.

"I'm freezing." My teeth chattered, partly through the cold, but also from nerves.

I startled when he slid his hand behind my back, posing for the cameras with an ease that spoke of years of practice. *Ezra Chester has his arm around me.*

How many times had he done this? There would have been the worldwide premieres for his film, of course, and that night when he'd won the Oscar, but the rest . . . he must have been with Monica, who'd have walked the carpet like she owned it. The flashes were so bright, I could barely see. *Flash.* "Ezra." I badly wanted to keep moving, but he held us there for a few more seconds as he glanced behind us.

"You're fine, Red." When I tried to speak again, my throat tightened on his name. *Flash.* I stumbled in the stupid heels. *What if my friends see these pictures?* The thought hadn't even occurred to me before I saw the crowds. Just how big was this film? *Flash.* I couldn't do this. I didn't belong here. *You just don't have what it takes.*

"You've got this, Red." NOB's smile was easy and laid-back—for the cameras, I realized—but his eyes were firmly on me. "When it was my first time on the carpet, I felt exactly the same."

"Really? *You* were nervous?"

"I was completely terrified. Do you trust me?"

Not even a little, I wanted to say. But NOB was holding his hand out to me, his blue eyes gentle. Tentatively, I took it. "Follow my lead. Look over there, now to your left, down, at me, back at them." I did as he said, and my breathing eased. "Now at me, down again, and at me. Still at me. Only have eyes for me." I swatted his arm. His smile widened. "Come on."

This wasn't about being seen. I had wanted to attend a premiere for as long as I could remember. I might never get another chance like this. *You can do this.* The tide of panic began to recede—and I had *Ezra* to thank for it.

I focused on my feet. How many incredible writers had trod this same path? People who'd helped make the world a little brighter, a little easier to understand. I used to imagine what it might be like to attend my own premiere the way other people dream about their weddings. To sit in the red seats. Feel the reaction of the audience around you, knowing it was for your story, your words. It had been all I'd ever wanted.

A woman wearing a dark bomber jacket and an earpiece told us to keep moving. I stepped out from under the weight of NOB's arm at my waist. He called after me, but I spotted someone I recognized from an HBO series. The actors were arriving. I hadn't missed the screenwriter, had I? I hoped I'd recognize them, whoever they were.

I stood on tiptoe. "Can you see them anywhere?" I asked NOB, who'd hurried to catch up.

"Who?" He whipped his head round, checking behind us.

"The screenwriter!"

"He's right here." NOB pulled me close. "And I only see you."

"That's another fine line."

His lips curved. "But I walk it so damn well."

"Move along, please," the same woman said to us as she passed. I tried to, but Ezra's—*NOB's*—arm was still around my waist.

"What would be so bad about us being together, Red?"

She returned to us. "Sir, madam, you need to move."

"Just a moment," NOB said to her. "I'm trying to understand why this stunning, infuriating woman still refuses to believe that I'm mad about her."

"I see," said the woman, bemused. "Madam, might I suggest you accept that sir is smitten, so we can all get on with our lives?"

His blue eyes searched mine, desperate for an answer. Despite myself, I felt goose bumps rise. *Could this be real? Could Ezra Chester genuinely like me?* He wasn't running away at the prospect of having a meet-cute with me. He was the one asking *me* to stop running.

"Red, I know that Dicky made you feel like you'd never be good enough for anyone. But, frankly, fuck that guy," NOB said, flashing me a grin. "He's an idiot. And so is that Dull Dad. You are more than enough, Red. You're everything. I'm standing here, wanting to be with you. You can have everything you've ever wanted. All you have to do is say yes."

There were a lot of things I hadn't anticipated when I'd entered into our deal. That someone would genuinely fall for me. That *Ezra Chester* would fall for me.

Or that there would ever be the slightest possibility that I, Evie Summers, might even think about falling for him.

The security guard's walkie-talkie buzzed and she spoke into it urgently. "She's here?" She looked at us. "Yes, we're clear here. *Aren't we?*" she shot at us.

"We are," I said.

Ezra smiled—not a Hollywood grin, but an open, honest smile, full of relief.

"Are you ready for your surprise now?"

Hope danced in my chest. It was the script, it had to be. *You can have everything you've ever wanted.*

"Definitely." He pulled me closer to him, sliding his hand along the silky material at my back. Without warning, he dipped me, Hollywood style, and kissed me right there on the red carpet. It was—in so many ways—the perfect kiss.

So why, as lights exploded around me, did I hear Ben's voice saying "I really hope it's what you want"?

Somehow, the noise around us intensified. I broke away from Ezra and tipped my head back, to see the world topsy-turvy. Ahead, a space had cleared for the actor who had just arrived.

I couldn't breathe.

Standing only meters away, dressed in a floor-length red lace gown, poised and stunningly beautiful, as always, was Monica Reed.

She'd seen the whole thing.

NOB pulled me upright, and I stepped away from him in shock.

"It's her film," I said, the force of the realization driving all the breath from my lungs. I searched his face. "Was all of this for her? The *makeover*. The kiss. Was it to make her jealous?" *Tell me*, I willed him. *Tell me it's not true.*

"Red . . ." There was a flash of something in his eyes. *Guilt.*

I blinked away sudden tears, not knowing if they were hurt or humiliation or both.

"This is just what I promised you," Ezra said, swiftly recovering. "Your surprise, remember?"

"Kissing me in front of your ex-girlfriend?" I asked, incredulous. It couldn't be further from what I'd wanted. "She was right. You're a child, Ezra. Grow up."

His eyes became flinty. "I did this for *us*. For the script. Surely you get that? I told you how much I needed your meet-cutes to keep me going. I just needed the final one so I could finish, and you weren't doing so great on your own. I've been nothing but honest with you. I've given you something to write about. This was our *deal*, Red. It's not like you aren't getting exactly what you want, either. I'm saving your job."

Every breath was painful, like I had something sharp wedged in my lungs.

Someone cleared their throat. It was the security guard.

"Are we done here?"

"Oh, we're done," I said.

I took one last look at NOB and lifted my dress to walk away. A move that had all the potential to look fantastically dramatic, if my ankle hadn't chosen that exact moment to give way, sending me sprawling across the carpet.

I considered just lying there until everyone had gone into the cinema, but someone took my hand and pulled me up.

Monica.

Her eyes were unyielding, almost challenging. "Come on. Falling's the easy part. Show them how you get back up."

I leaned on her as I took my heels off. Cameras flashed around us. "Thank you," I said. "And I'm sorry. Congratulations on the film."

Gathering what little dignity I had left, I fled.

NOB: What do you want me to say, Red? I didn't think you'd react that way. It was supposed to be a great happy ending for you

NOB: Red, what's the difference between tonight and what I did for you with Dicky?

NOB: Do you need me to admit I made a mistake? Fine. I made a mistake

NOB: You're in luck, Red. Even though you didn't meet anyone, I have decided to finish the script. You're welcome. All I need is for you to write about our meet-cute as if it ended how it should have done. That's "happily ever after," if you're still unsure

NOB: Red, just give me the damn meet-cute

YOU MISSED A CALL TODAY AT 8:03 P.M. FROM NOB

YOU MISSED A CALL TODAY AT 9:45 P.M. FROM NOB

YOU MISSED A CALL TODAY AT 11:03 P.M. FROM NOB

RED: no more meet-cutes. I'm finally done

Chapter 33

Piece of Cake

INT: EVIE'S BEDROOM—THURSDAY, FEBRUARY 14,
6:42 P.M.

EVIE sits slumped on her bed, eating a tub
of ice cream, in the same dress she wore to
the premiere. It's loosely tucked into her
pajama bottoms. Her hair is slightly flat
on one side. She's removed most of her
makeup, but there are black smudges under
her eyes.

I'd called in sick today for the first time in years. After everything
that had happened last night—and the three months preceding
it—I needed a break to figure it all out.

I'd had a call from Monty earlier, informing me that NOB had
complained about my lack of commitment. Didn't I know that the
deadline was four days away? He needed the ending for the meeting with Intrepid Productions on Monday. The one he hadn't in-
vited me to. Didn't I realize the consequences if he turned up
empty-handed? I confirmed that I did indeed fully comprehend,
and then put the phone down.

I'd existed in a state of constant anxiety since learning the
agency could go under, every day being wound tighter and tighter,
and last night, after what NOB did . . . Something in me had
snapped. I was a disconnected phone line as far as my worries were
concerned. *Try again later, caller. Evie isn't home right now.*

I ate another spoonful of cookie-dough ice cream and saw another message had arrived.

MARIA: I thought you'd want to see this, my love

Even from almost two hundred miles away, Maria's friendship spider sense was second-to-none. I clicked the link, my half-formed smile faltering. It was a *Bitch About It* column:

RED CARPET RAT

There are some things you just don't do. Get engaged at a friend's wedding. Upstage the star of the movie at their own premiere. Yes, Bitches, that's what Monica Reed's desperate ex Ezra Chester, 33, attempted last night when he brought a mystery date to her premiere. "It was a pathetic attempt to get her back, but it fell flat—literally!" a close source said, referring to the moment his blond date landed face-first on the carpet. And who helped her up? Only Reed herself. What a queen.

The only shot of me was, of course, one where I was facedown on the carpet at Monica's feet. At least I was unrecognizable in that smoky dress with my new sleek hair. *Blond indeed.*

MARIA: you're going to think I'm crazy for asking this, but is this you?

I stared at her message. I'd promised myself I'd tell my friends the truth, and I wanted so badly to go to them for comfort—if I even deserved it after hiding everything from them. But after what happened, I couldn't face them knowing I'd actually let myself believe even for a second that NOB liked me. Not when they'd never have let me go in the first place if I'd checked in with them. I'd been such a fool. A blob of ice cream fell onto my dress, trailing a milky-white line down the dark green silk. I wiped at it before answering.

EVIE: what?? Of course not! I was at home watching Netflix, you know me

MARIA: I just wanted to check. You know you can tell me anything, right?

EVIE: I know

Crisis averted. My spoon hit the bottom of the tub. I rolled off my bed in search of more.

There was nothing left worth eating in the freezer. I opened the fridge, willing to take anything as long as it was bad for me.

My eyes landed on the date cake NOB had sent me. I pulled it out and slammed it down on the counter. A choked sob escaped me. I put a hand over my mouth, blinking away tears.

I wasn't crying for NOB. It was what he'd done, and the fact that I'd responded to it. I had finally been starting to drop the defenses I'd built after Ricky. NOB had said a few kind things, and for the first time in a long time, I'd been open. It had taken a moment, but I'd been willing to let him in. NOB shouldn't get to be the example for what would happen if I dropped my walls.

My breathing steadied and I was left staring at the stupid *so not* an actual cake. It didn't even have the decency to be bad for me. I picked it up anyway and took it with me to my bedroom, breaking off a chunk as I went and shoving it into my mouth.

Oh.

Oh, God.

It was so . . . dry, and yet, at the same time, moist. With a chemical aftertaste. Like trying to eat furniture foam dipped in wallpaper paste.

I ran to the loo and spat it straight into the toilet, heaving. As I straightened, I caught sight of myself in the mirror.

Tear-streaked face. Flat hair. Mascara smudges. Half my freckles still covered by makeup. I barely recognized myself. I'd been so *proud* of myself for getting NOB to write. In the end, NOB had got exactly what he wanted. He'd broken through his writer's block. Despite what he said, he didn't really need me to finish the script. Soon enough, people would once again be singing his praises all over Hollywood. And what did I get? My job. A promotion. I should really be happy.

I flushed the toilet, feeling a rush of satisfaction as the cake was sucked away down the U-bend. *So long, NOB.*

That felt . . . *good.* I threw another chunk down. It landed with a lovely, heavy *thunk.* I pushed the button. *Flush. Goodbye, arrogant arsehole. Thunk.* I *should* be proud of myself. *Flush.* I'd got NOB to write. *Thunk.* The meet-cutes had led to so much more than I could have dreamed of. *Flush.* The book group. *Thunk.* Steph. *Flush.* Writing again. *Thunk.* Ben and Anette . . . *Flush.*

Another piece landed. *Thunk.* So take *that*, you arrogant. *Flush.* Number one. *Thunk. Boychild! Plick!*

I pushed the button down again. No resistance, no flush. I tried a few more times. Nothing. The last bit of cake squatted at the bottom of the bowl, refusing to budge. Closing my eyes, I tried again. *Flush.*

Oh, thank God.

Wait.

Why were my toes wet?

I looked. The bowl had filled all the way up to the top and water was pouring over the edge, that last piece of cake now bobbing on the surface like a little brown log.

I leaped back, holding the plate like a shield.

Surely the water should have stopped pouring out by now.

The cistern groaned alarmingly.

I kicked off my soaking slippers and stood barefoot in the water.

"Oh, *ew*." Grabbing the towels off the radiator, I tucked them around the bottom of the toilet. They'd barely soaked up the water before more poured out.

"Stop!" I shouted at the toilet. "Please, just stop! I've had a really bad time and I really, *really* don't need this."

It didn't respond to emotional pleas. *What do I do?* I searched around wildly for something—anything—that might help. Relief hit me when I spotted the handle of the toilet brush sticking up from beside the toilet.

I grabbed it and was so startled when it started to buzz that I dropped it straight into the bowl.

Then watched as Jane's Ourgasm 3000™ disappeared down the U-bend.

I paced the hallway. The toilet was still pouring out water and I'd done everything I could to extract Belinda, including using the actual toilet brush, which had at least managed to turn her off. It was time to call someone for help. A plumber would be the obvious choice. *Hi, I need a plumber because my toilet is blocked. With what, you ask?*

I shuddered. No way. After three months of meet-cutes ending with a red-carpet nosedive, I was at maximum humiliation. That left Jane. Maybe she had some friends who'd know what to do. Even if I did have to explain that her pride and joy was now stuck in the U-bend.

Each attempt to call sent me to voicemail. "If you need me, I'm probably tied up somewhere. Later, my duck!"

The list of people I knew in London suddenly seemed very small. There was Steph, but I doubted she wanted to spend her Valentine's Day with her hand down my toilet. And, sadly, Monty, who was two up on me when it came to toilet messes he'd needed rescuing from, and still wouldn't see that as a reason to reciprocate.

Which left only one option.

EVIE: I'm in trouble

As mortifying as it was, I explained the whole situation, even saying that the cake had been a gift from NOB. I just left out exactly why.

EVIE: I am so sorry for interrupting your Valentine's Day with this

SARAH: we're between courses of our M&S dine in for two. Jim said he's just glad he didn't choose the chocolate pudding

EVIE: you told him?!

SARAH: I still don't really understand why NOB would get you a cake

MARIA: David said you should call a plumber

EVIE: does everyone know?? I can't! What will they say when I explain that my loo's blocked with cake and a vibrator??

JEREMY: you are a single girl alone on Valentine's Day, they probably get calls like this all the time

EVIE: viable alternatives please

JEREMY: who ya gonna call? Hot Widower!

EVIE: not helpful, Jeremy

MARIA: actually, I think he might have a point. Doesn't he live near you?

EVIE: he doesn't want to see me

SARAH: trust me, that man will answer your call

The pool of water had now reached the hall. Unappetizing clumps of cake had washed up onto the cream carpet, looking exactly like something that would emerge from an overflowing toilet. Sarah was wrong about Ben. He'd left me alone in Gil's last week and hadn't even responded to the photo of the hot chocolates I'd sent. I didn't know if I could handle being let down by Ben again. Especially when he already thought everything I did was a spectacle. This would just show him he was right. The proof was literally in the pudding.

Chapter 34

- - - - - - - - - - - - - - -

Round the Bend

INT: EVIE'S FRONT DOOR—THURSDAY,
FEBRUARY 14, 8:23 P.M.

EVIE tucks her dress more securely into her
pajama bottoms and straightens her
cardigan. Her hands fly to her hair before
she shakes her head, clearly deciding it
can't be salvaged. Taking a few deep
breaths, she opens the door. There's a
tall, broad-shouldered man standing on her
front step with a toolbox in his hand,
facing away down the street.

"Thank you for coming."

Ben turned, eyes widening as he caught sight of me. I hadn't
expected him to get here so soon and there'd been no time to do
more than slip a cardigan on. *What must I look like?*

"No problem." He held up his toolbox. "I'm sure this won't take
long."

I stepped back to let him in. "Best take your socks off too," I
advised, as he shrugged out of his thick navy jacket and hung it on
the "come hither" finger hook in the hall. He pulled his jumper
over his head. He wasn't wearing his usual shirt. Just a simple blue
T-shirt that stretched over his broad shoulders.

"Shall we . . . ?" Ben said, and I startled.

"Oh, yes, sorry. It's down the hall." I turned and led the way,
hurriedly trying to tuck more of my dress into my pants.

"Where's Anette?"

"She's feeling well enough to have a sleepover at her grandparents' tonight." Ben's voice was friendly but bland. Like we were passing acquaintances.

"She's been ill?" I asked, crab-walking around the wet towels.

"Didn't you get the—" He paused. I turned back. He was staring at a brown clump perched on the damp carpet.

"It's cake," I said.

Ben looked deeply relieved.

He headed inside the bathroom first, bare feet splashing on the tiles. I hovered behind him.

"Can I help?" In reply, Ben placed his toolbox into my arms.

"Do you know what the problem is?"

To give myself better odds of him actually turning up, I'd told him only about the flooding, not the cause. I flicked the handle of the toolbox.

"If I had to hazard a guess," I said nonchalantly, "it's full of cake."

The only sound to be heard was the steady falling of water from the edge of the toilet bowl.

"Right," said Ben evenly. I decided it was best not to tell him about Belinda too. She might have been dislodged by the toilet brush, a chance I was willing to take.

Ben cocked his ear, listening to the choking noises the cistern was making, his face thoughtful. He pulled on some rubber gloves and I raised my brows.

"Don't worry, I can fix this. It won't take long."

"Don't tell me," I joked, shifting my knee against the toolbox to keep it from tipping off the bath. "You've seen this kind of thing before."

He almost smiled. "You name it, Anette has probably stuck it down a toilet at some point."

We were both being very adult about this. I kept ahold of the box as Ben searched for the valve to turn the water off (there wasn't one) and said things like "I'm going to have to rig the float to stop it," and I nodded like I understood.

"So . . . this cake," he said after a while, a hand deep in the cistern.

I sighed, changing which leg I had propping up the toolbox. We could have gone this whole time without ever having to talk about it.

"It was stupid, I know."

"What happened?" he asked mildly.

The man was elbow-deep in my toilet, what more harm could the truth do at this point? "I went on the date with NOB. It turned out to be a mistake. And not just because of his terrible taste in gifts."

His warm brown eyes met mine. "And the script?" he said softly. "Is your job okay?"

It was nice of him to ask, considering where his hand was right now. "I'm not sure." Maybe NOB would still write the ending. Maybe everything would be okay, and I would become an agent just like I always wanted. I just wished I felt happier about that prospect.

Ben nodded and returned his attention to the tank. "There you go." He stepped back. It was such a relief to see the water had finally stopped running.

"Now I just need to remove the clog," Ben explained. *Ah. That.*

He set to work with the plunger he'd brought with him, the overflow sending little brown islands spinning across the floor. He stepped back. A wodge of date cake bobbed on the surface.

"We have a floater," he said. I pulled my face. "Sorry, dad humor. It's ingrained." He scooped it out and deposited it in the bath.

"There's something still in here." He peered into the bowl. I winced, clutching the toolbox and preparing myself for the worst.

"Are you absolutely sure?" I asked, plaintively. *Oh, please just sod off, Belinda.*

Ben considered the toilet regretfully. "I'm going to have to go in." He bent down low, pushing his hand in. Water poured over the side, soaking his T-shirt through. I found myself observing the interesting way the material stuck to his chest before remembering it was loo water.

Then he leaned over too far and slipped, his chin dipping perilously close to the surface.

"Ben!" Unthinkingly, I jerked forward to help him and a wrench fell out of the toolbox onto my bare toe.

"Shit!" I hopped on one foot and slid, feeling the whole room tilt and the toolbox leaving my fingers. "Ooof!" The breath was knocked loose from my body. Firm hands were at my back.

Ben had caught me.

He gently lowered me to the edge of the bath, ignoring the toolbox that had upended inside it.

"Owww." Tears burned my eyes.

"Let me look." Before I could stop him he was crouched, one knee on the wet floor, tugging his gloves off so he could hold my foot. My leg shot out on reflex, knocking Ben square on the jaw. He went backward, grabbing my ankle and taking me with him as he slid down onto the wet tiles.

We were lying nose-to-nose, with me on top, both slightly out of breath.

"What did you do that for?" I yelped.

"You kicked me!"

"You tickled my foot!"

Unexpectedly, Ben started to laugh, his entire face lighting up. And there, shivering, as I lay on top of him, my heart began to pound so hard I was sure he could feel every beat. But this was *Ben*. The man who'd run a mile every time it looked like he might be caught up in one of my meet-cutes. Who'd left me sitting in Gil's last Sunday alone.

"Ben," I said, suddenly feeling something.

"It's the plunger," he said quickly, extracting it.

Bzzz. We both looked toward the toilet.

"Evie," he said. "What is that?"

I blushed furiously, pushing myself up to standing. Fantastic. As if Ben needed any more reasons to judge me. "I bet you aren't even surprised by any of this," I said, raising my voice over the buzzing.

"What do you mean?" he asked, standing too. And just like that, I was *mad.*

"I heard what you said about me to that woman, Samantha, before Christmas." *Bzzz.* "'She's always making a public spectacle of herself,'" I said, mimicking his deep voice. "Well, here's your validation." I flicked wet cake from my ruined dress to the floor.

"I remember what I said," Ben replied, remaining annoyingly cool. He tugged the gloves back on.

"You're not even denying it!"

He sank to his knees, cocking his head and listening.

His voice strained a little as he reached back into the U-bend. "That woman keeps trying to get me to prevent Anette from taking her hearing aids out in public so she has a chance to be 'normal.' Right from the very first time you met Anette, you've always treated her like she's just how she should be. And because of the things you do, when she looks at you, she sees that it's okay not to care about what people think. Around you, she doesn't have to be 'normal.' She's just herself. *That's* the conversation you were overhearing. Screwdriver."

I scrambled to straighten the toolbox and handed him the first thing that looked like one.

"But . . . you don't really like me. I keep messing things up."

"Now, *where*," said Ben, frowning as he used the end of the screwdriver to try to dislodge the clog, "did you get that idea?"

Bzzzzzzzzz. Bzzz. Bzzzzz. Bzzzzz. Oh, God. He'd switched her to some kind of turbo function.

"You weren't at Gil's last week," I said, somewhat weakly.

"We messaged you," he said. "What else can possibly be in here?" he mumbled.

"You did?"

"We sent photos," Ben said. He cocked his head. "A*ha*!" He yanked his hand out, wielding something triumphantly. It took him a full two seconds to realize he was brandishing a vibrator at me, on the maximum setting.

- - - - - - - - - -

While Ben took a shower, I sat on my bed to update my friends on Clog Gate, as it would henceforth be known.

Ben is in my shower.

I pushed the rather distracting thought to one side on seeing I had over fifty messages.

SARAH: EVERYTHING IS RUINED. I'M CANCELING THE WEDDING

EVIE: what's happened? Is everything OK?

SARAH: the stupid photographer has broken his stupid leg, dancing at someone else's stupid wedding! He's canceled with two days to go!! Jim is threatening to have one of his cousins step in!!!

EVIE: I'm so sorry, Sarah. Isn't there anyone else?

I pressed a hand over my thundering heart. While I couldn't have been more relieved to find Sarah was just being Sarah, I would also like to live to a ripe old age.

Without looking, I knew what Sarah's response would be.

SARAH: Evie, you have to ask Ben

EVIE: it might not be as easy as that

JEREMY: Hot Widower!

SARAH: I'm begging you. Remember how you ruined my hen do? You owe me big time. He's far more talented than an actual wedding photographer

MARIA: I agree this does seem like a perfect option if he's free, but didn't Evie say he was camera shy these days?

I slipped a pair of jeans and a jumper on as I considered what to do. Ben had already done so much for me.

He might have said he was no longer a photographer, but I knew part of him still loved it. Which meant there was still a chance he could find his way back to it, regardless of what had happened to make him stop. As small as it might seem, maybe this wedding could help. This could be my chance to return his kindness.

I'd do it.

I decided I'd show up for Ben.

EVIE: OK, I'll try

SARAH: great! That's all sorted then. Good thing I didn't overreact

JEREMY: !

EVIE: I can't promise anything

SARAH: it's fine, I know he'll say yes to you

MARIA: good luck, my love

I hovered outside the door of the loo, listening to Ben singing the title song from *Singin' in the Rain*.

"Do you want a hot chocolate?" I called, before realizing I was offering him more brown liquid.

The singing stopped. "Yes. Thank you," he called.

Clearly he had a strong stomach. "I've left a top on my bed for you."

A few minutes later, Ben padded into the kitchen behind me, his dark hair wet and fluffy from where he'd half dried it with a towel. He was wearing my old Sheffield University hoodie, and it looked far better on him.

"Is that a *Brick Park* quote on your wall?" he asked. "'Make it mean something'?"

"Yes," I said. "My dad had it made for me." So Ben could quote my favorite film, no big deal. I added extra marshmallows to his drink.

"Your hair," Ben said.

I touched it self-consciously. It had gone straight back to its natural curl as soon as the water had hit it. "The styling's all come out," I said ruefully.

"I like it that way."

I smiled, handing him the Gil's-branded mug. "Here. Happy Valentine's Day. Thank you for spending it unblocking my toilet."

He laughed, then swapped his mug for mine. "Chip," he said, pointing at the one he was now holding.

Once we'd settled on the sofa together, I spooned marshmallows into my mouth for strength before I began.

Here goes.

"There's something I want to ask you."

Ben blew on his drink, watching me with his steady eyes.

"Are you busy this weekend?"

He stopped blowing. "Just the usual. Why?"

"It's my friend Sarah's wedding." I got my words out as quickly as possible. "I know it's not what you're used to, and it's just a wedding, well, it isn't 'just' a wedding to my friend, which is why this would mean so much, and of course Anette is welcome too."

Ben sat up straighter, something like hope on his face. I carried on, encouraged. "Sarah will reimburse any costs, and pay you, of course, and the accommodation is already sorted because the original photographer had a room." I glanced at my phone. Sarah had been firing details at me for the last fifteen minutes.

"You're asking me to be the photographer," he said slowly, sinking back into the chair.

"You'd be doing me another huge favor, and I know you've already pulled a sex toy out of my toilet this evening, but it would really mean a lot to Sarah."

And the thing is, I willed him to know, *I think it might be exactly what you need.*

Ben remained very still. *Come on, Ben, take a chance. Please.*

He stood.

"I'm sorry. I can't."

"Wait, Ben . . ." I called after him. He was already backing out of the door.

"Thank you for the drink."

I stayed curled up on the sofa as he collected his things, wondering if I'd done the right thing. He passed by the living room on his way out and stopped. For a moment, I thought he might say something.

"Ben?"

But the only response was the front door closing.

It was close to midnight when I received his message.

BEN: I've spoken with Marc. Here are his contact details. He'll appreciate the work. I'm sorry, Evie.

Chapter 35

Full Monty

INT: THE ASH—FRIDAY, FEBRUARY 15, 6:23 P.M.

EVIE sits at a table in the third-floor
bar, a guarded look on her face. There's a
dress bag hung over a suitcase next to her.
MONTY is by the bar on his phone, waving a
waiter toward where EVIE is sitting. It's
JOHN, who slows down on seeing EVIE.

I'd almost said no when Monty told me to meet him in the Ash. I
was traveling to Sheffield tonight for Sarah's wedding tomorrow.
But my mind started churning with possibilities. Monty had never
taken me for a drink before. Perhaps this was his version of an exit
interview after I'd hung up on him yesterday. Or maybe NOB had
been so pissed off with me he'd told Monty everything. Or perhaps
he'd refused to write the ending after all because I hadn't sent him
"our" meet-cute. All in all, Monty had any number of reasons to
fire me. I couldn't go to Sarah's wedding with it hanging over my
head.

When John appeared, presenting a bottle of champagne at me
before pouring, I allowed myself to relax. It seemed doubtful that
Monty would celebrate firing me, at least not with me there. We
were three days out from the official deadline. Was it too much to
hope that NOB had delivered? If only Monty would end the call
and tell me already.

John finished pouring in silence. Something told me he was still sore about what happened last time I was here. "I just wanted to thank you," I said. "You always handle things so beautifully, no matter what we throw at you. I promise less drama from now on."

He seemed to soften a little. "Don't worry," he said, turning to go. "In this place, you're not even the worst of it."

Monty still wasn't finished, so I took out my phone and once again checked the photos that had come through this morning. The first was a selfie: Anette with flushed cheeks, a snotty nose, and Ben's hand holding a temperature gauge to her forehead as she drank from a steaming mug. The next picture was of Ben on a white chair next to her bed, relaxed and unguarded with his head down, dark hair drifting into his eyes as he read aloud from the copy of *Peter Pan* I'd given her for Christmas. The image made my heart ache a little.

Apparently Anette had been in charge of sending them last Sunday, but hadn't. My gut told me it was because I'd gone on the date with NOB. Anette had been so keen on setting me and Ben up, she probably saw it as a betrayal. The toilet incident had been good for something at least. There'd been a message from Anette along with the photos this morning. "I'm sorry NOB gave you a cake that looked like poop." Which was mortifying, given Ben must have told her what happened, but, on the whole, worth it if it meant she'd forgiven me.

Monty sat back down, belly easing over his belt. There was a sheen to his forehead as he snatched up the champagne flutes and thrust one into my hand.

"Chin up," said Monty. "We're celebrating."

"Celebrating what?" I asked, desperate to hear him say it.

"Your script, of course," Monty said, and I wondered if all the pressure with the agency had finally got to him.

"Ezra's script, you mean," I said.

Monty wiped at his top lip and rocked forward in his seat, giving me a wink. "I confess I didn't see it at first." I gulped my champagne. "You were both very cunning, submitting it all through Ezra. You really do go above and beyond for your job, Evelyn. It was when he sent the part about the hen do that finally did it for me. I remembered you saying something about why you were out of contact for the weekend, and then the next thing, I'm reading about a girl on a hen do that's clearly you. Ezra's a genius, but characterization has never been his strong point." The bubbles popped like cap-gun pellets in my throat. "So I fished that old script you wrote out of my filing cabinet, and the styles matched." Monty hit the table with the meaty part of his palm. "That's when I knew."

"I don't understand."

"You've been giving him the scenes," said Monty, as if pleased as punch he'd figured it out. "You know. The hen do. The drink spilling. The smutty book group." What did he mean? *The meet-cutes?*

No, no, no. This wasn't true. NOB had used me for *inspiration*. He hadn't taken my words. Why would he? He was an Oscar winner. He was . . .

He was a man who'd pretended to fall for me to get me to write him his *happy* ending. My breath came out in short bursts, like I couldn't draw in enough air.

Monty carried on, oblivious. "If I hadn't already twigged, the ending would have given it away. The one he's given me for the producers is miserable. He's clearly tried to write it by himself. It's missing a woman's touch, if you know what I mean. He needs you to sprinkle your magic on it before our meeting at Intrepid on Monday."

He reached for his bag and slipped the script out, placing it in front of me. There it was. The thing I'd all but begged NOB to show me.

The script I'd apparently already read.

I held it, barely feeling the paper against my fingers as I peeled back the first page. *The Drink Spill.* It was the opening of my meet-cute, complete with NOB's (largely insulting) tweaks.

```
FADE IN

INT: COFFEE HOUSE, EAST DULWICH—SUNDAY,
DECEMBER 2, UNGODLY HOUR (10 A.M.)

CHERYL—midtwenties, blond hair down to her
shoulders, a long dress, heels—stands in
front of the counter tapping her foot, full
of nervous energy.
```

All of my meet-cutes were here. The drink spill at Gil's. The bookshop. The road trip. Every excruciating moment of the last few months. All of it. It had been reformatted into a script, some liberties had been taken with the narrator's appearance, but that dialogue, the description, was almost all mine. *Pages will be sent when they're good and ready,* NOB had told me, buying himself time to make any necessary changes. After the first few reports, NOB had pretty much encouraged me to describe every meet-cute like a script. Each time demanding more dialogue. The second half of the script was almost word for word what I'd sent to NOB, but with a new character wedged in: *him.*

"How does it end?" I heard myself asking, but a part of me already knew.

"Terribly," Monty said. "The screenwriter tells the assistant he's fallen for her. He sweeps her off her feet with a kiss on a red carpet and she breaks his heart. It's like he's never seen a romantic comedy. Given the photos from Monica Reed's premiere, I suspect he might be writing from experience." He gave me a knowing look and I tensed, waiting for the blame. Only finding out his assistant got involved with his client and caused a public scene wasn't Monty's concern. "The producers hate it. They want a happy ending. We wouldn't want a lover's quarrel to tip us off course now, would we?"

The room spun, my vision tunneling. A few pages slipped to the floor. NOB had fashioned himself as the romantic hero and me as the woman who broke his heart. And *this* was why Monty assumed I hadn't written the ending?

"The producers have asked for a more satisfying finale before they'll accept it, and it all needs a bit of a polish," said Monty. He was eyeing me, realizing, perhaps, that his assistant wasn't reacting quite how he'd expected. "You've taken the script so far, Evelyn, it's time to close this. Ezra really appreciates everything you've done. If only agents could get writing credits, eh?"

Everything came back into sharp focus.

"But I can't write," I said. "You told me that yourself."

Seven years had passed and the memory of that meeting was still painful. Fresh to London at twenty-two, I'd sat in front of William Jonathan Montgomery the Third, feeling like I was teetering on the brink of a great change, and knowing how proud my dad would be. Here I was, at Dorothy Taylor's old agency. A poster of *Brick Park* hung on the wall.

Monty had wanted to meet me to discuss the script I'd sent him. The one I'd poured my heart and soul into and burned through my savings to finish. It had been a film for all the girls who, like me, had taken their emotional education from the school of Nora Ephron; it was about a father who knew the moment he was going to die, and lived his life as if he didn't. It was sentimental and needed more work, and maybe that script wouldn't have been the one that sold, but it was a first step. One I would have taken, had Monty not said the words that broke me. Seven little words that had reached into the fissure that appeared when my dad had died, and cracked it wide open.

You just don't have what it takes.

It turned out he'd only called me in to offer me the role as his assistant because his last one had just walked out. He told me he admired the enthusiasm I'd displayed in my cover letter for the agency. I'd been desperate and still reeling when I accepted.

I'd thought of Monty's words so many times over the years it had become a mantra. As I sat in front of Monty now, I wondered how much power they still had over me.

He downed his champagne and poured more. "Maybe I was a little hasty back then." His words were flippant, unhurried, like they meant nothing to him.

I wanted to fold time. Bring together this moment with the one where he'd stripped away my confidence, so they were touching. *Don't give up,* I wanted to tell my younger self. *Don't put your self-worth in someone else's hands when you're at your most vulnerable. Listen to the people who love you.*

"You should be proud of yourself," Monty said, going to give me more champagne and seeing that I'd barely touched my glass. "The producers love your script so much they only want your ending, not Ezra's. Not that they'll know it's yours, of course. You've seen to that. Ever the professional, red-carpet mishaps notwithstanding. All grist to the mill!"

The enormity of what NOB had done fully sank in. He'd been manipulating me from the start. He'd stolen my words and passed them off as his own. As my anger built, I kept coming back to the question *why*. He couldn't have known when we made that deal that I'd end up sending him the material he could use for the script.

"Don't think there won't be rewards," Monty said. I knew that tone. He thought my silence meant I was holding out on him, as if this was a negotiation. "Of course, once the agency's back on its feet . . ." He knocked his glass against mine. "Evelyn Summers: Junior Agent. How does that sound?"

His words barely registered.

"It's my script," I said quietly.

"Yes, well, you're my assistant. About to take the next step, if you keep playing your cards right. Helping writers is what you do."

"No, this is actually my script, Monty," I said, my voice growing stronger. "Ezra stole it."

His hand shook as he tipped the last of the champagne into his glass, and it dawned on me that Monty knew exactly what NOB had done. "Evelyn Summers: Agent, then. How about that? And what the producers don't know won't hurt them."

He really believes I'm going to do exactly as he says. And why wouldn't he? I always had before.

I thought of everything I'd been through, all the work I'd put into my career over the last seven years, constantly trying to prove myself to a man who'd said I wasn't good enough. And now, after three months of neglecting everyone I loved, the humiliations, the constant attempts to "put myself out there," believing it was all worthwhile because NOB was finally getting somewhere, only for him to pass my words, my *life*, off as his own . . .

Now it was time to Be More Evie.

"I'm done," I said. As soon as I heard myself say the words, I knew they were true.

I was finally done taking Monty's shit.

"But you haven't even finished your champagne!" Monty said, eyeing my glass.

"No, I mean, I'm done," I said calmly. "Tell Sam-and-Max the truth, or I quit. I'll get a job somewhere else."

There was a heavy pause. When Monty spoke again, all the joviality was gone from his voice. "That hasn't worked out well for you before. It's so hard to get on without a good reference."

I stared at him. All those jobs I'd gone for, and no one had wanted to hire me. I thought it was because I wasn't ready. But it was because of Monty.

"What?" Monty shrugged. "You were a good assistant, Evelyn. Do you know how hard that is to come by? I wasn't about to just let you go. You should be flattered."

I knew then that I was never going to be made an agent, no matter what I did. Monty didn't want to work with an equal.

"I deserve credit for my script," I said flatly. "Give it to me and I'll finish it."

"That just isn't possible," said Monty. "I'm sure we can ask about getting you a script-editing credit. Your name could still be on the big screen."

I stood, pulling the handle up on my suitcase.

"Monty," I said calmly. "You know what I want. I have a train to catch."

"You're being childish, Evelyn."

John was standing behind the curtain. He'd heard everything.

"Wait," I heard Monty say. I turned back. He straightened his tie and ran his fingers through his graying hair, tugging at his jacket as if it would cover his protruding belly. "If you leave now, that's it. You know I can make sure no one will hire you. You are nothing without—"

"No, Monty," I cut in. "*You're* nothing without me." I turned back to John, who was looking at me anew.

"Miss Summers," he said grandly, draping my duffel coat around my shoulders as if I were one of the club's celebrity clientele. He leaned in, gave me a little wink, and said, "Bravo."

Chapter 36

- - - - - - - - - - - - - - -

Plus Two

```
INT: ROSEHILL MANOR, SHEFFIELD—SATURDAY,
FEBRUARY 16, 1:15 P.M.

EVIE and MARIA stand in front of a wide
floor-length mirror in a room with large
arched windows. They're wearing their
bridesmaid dresses and studying their
reflections with a resigned air.
```

We fussed with each other's ruffles, trying to pat them down, to no avail.

"Does my dress look okay to you?" I asked Maria, turning very slightly for her by shuffling my feet one way and then the other. For dresses with this much material, they were awfully constricting.

Maria cocked her head, examining me.

"I guess," she said finally, "it depends what you mean by 'okay.'"

I snorted. My mum had passed the dress along to Maria to give to me this morning, and had clearly worked her magic. It looked exactly as it should, except it felt even heavier than before, and it was certainly easier to zip up.

Maria's gray eyes were sharp. "Are *you* okay, Evie?"

"Of course."

Other than confirming NOB had delivered his ending, I hadn't breathed a word to her or any of my friends about anything else that had happened. Not about the date with NOB, or his betrayal, the stolen script, quitting my job, or the fact that I was going to have to move back into my old room at Mum's at the end of the month . . . *But I will*, I told myself. This weekend belonged to Sarah. There would be plenty of time after for talking about how I'd blown my life up.

"Is it NOB?" she pressed. NOB had turned up at my flat this morning after I'd ignored his repeated demands for the ending, refusing to leave until Jane told him I was out of town at a wedding.

"It's this dress, actually. I'm worried I'll fall face-first going up the aisle."

My eyes slid to hers, remembering the *Bitch About It* article she'd sent me.

"I'm here if you need to talk about anything," she said, tucking a dark strand behind her ear. "No judgment."

"He's hit the deadline." I forced a smile. "There's honestly nothing left to say."

I was saved from further questions by two boys screaming as they tore down the hallway.

"If anyone can deal with those two terrors, it's Sarah," Maria said. They were cute as anything, with their big brown eyes and dark twists of hair like their father's, but definitely a handful. We both had a moment of thinking back to the hen do.

"And she has us to provide the wine if it gets difficult," I added.

Maria held on to my shoulders, our ruffles catching on each other like Stickle Bricks. "Evie Summers," she said, eyes on mine. "You're going to be just fine."

I nodded, blinking away tears.

We both jumped as a woman I recognized from Jim's side of the family burst into the room. "It's Sarah!" she said, and I knew that look of fear all too well. "You're needed." The woman clutched her pearls and withdrew, presumably in search of a stiff drink.

"Are you ready for one last Mathers Meltdown™ before she becomes a Johnson?" I said.

"Let's go help our girl."

We hiked up our ruffles and hurried as quickly as the dresses would allow.

"Shuffle, shuffle, shuffle," Maria instructed me. "Quickly!"

I stifled laughter, even as I broke out into a sweat in the smothering material.

"Move like your life depends on it!" Maria told me, elbowing me quiet.

We burst through the double doors into the room where Sarah was getting changed.

"What's the matter?" Maria panted. We both frantically searched the light, airy space for signs of catastrophe.

There was only Sarah, standing in front of a long mirror, looking absolutely stunning. Her hair gleamed white gold in its bun. Her gown brushed the floor, the beautiful expanse of ivory accented only with the slim band of sparkles at her waist. Every inch of her was elegant and tasteful, apart from, just maybe, the diamond crown.

"Just having a bit of fun." Sarah beamed. She opened her arms wide. Maria and I exchanged looks before stepping into her embrace. "Thanks for putting up with me through this," she said, holding her head back to protect her hair. "I know I can be a tad neurotic."

"You? Never," Maria said. I buried my smile in a ruffle.

The boys tore past again, roaring at the tops of their voices.

"Oliver, Adam, what did I say to you?" Sarah hollered. The noise immediately ceased.

"Sorry, evil stepmother," they choroused.

Maria and I were both braced for her reaction. "Stop looking so worried!" she said. "I told them to call me that. And I've threatened to take them with us on our honeymoon if they don't behave." Her smile grew wider. "Jim's surprised me with a *very* romantic luxury week away in the Maldives. We aren't going to Center Parcs! Well, not until the summer, anyway."

"Knock, knock." Jeremy stuck his head around the door.

"Jeremy," Maria said, aghast. "What on earth is that on your head?"

Jeremy adjusted his peach hat without comment. It looked an awful lot like it had been made from one of the ruffles on our dresses.

Sarah's smile was beatific. "I wanted him to look as adorable as you guys!"

"What?" Jeremy said. He arranged the hat over his curls, and, against all odds, it suited him. "Consider my lack of complaint my wedding present."

"Is he here now?" Sarah asked him, suddenly all business. He nodded and she turned to me, eyes glittering with excitement. "Evie, remember how I promised you a plus-one?"

"Vividly," I said, heart sinking.

Sarah nodded toward the door. "Well, go on, then. He's out there waiting for you."

I looked to my friends for help, but Maria and Jeremy studiously avoided eye contact. So they'd known about this. Straining to hide my lack of enthusiasm, I lifted my dress and slowly shuffled into the hall.

Standing in front of the entrance, looking a little nervous and wearing a gray shirt with a matching tie, was Ben. He held his old camera in one hand; holding on to his other hand, and beaming, was Anette. She wore a beautiful red-and-white dress with a big red ribbon around the waist that matched her glasses. I couldn't help but notice she was also wearing her Union Jack wings from her school play.

Ben was my plus-one? I could have protested. Said all the usual excuses. *He wouldn't want to date me.* And yet, seeing them both, the words caught in my throat. Everything was upside down right now, but Ben and Anette being here somehow made sense. When Ben lifted the edge of his mouth in a smile, my heart lifted too.

"He got in contact this morning," Sarah said quietly from behind me. My friends had all gathered at the doors so they could watch. "Marc gave him my number."

"Okay, but who was the real plus-one?" Jeremy muttered.

"Shut up," Sarah replied. She whispered, "Jim's youngest cousin, Roger. I've moved him to the kiddies' table."

"Isn't he married?"

"Twice divorced. Well, nearly."

"Shhh," Maria urged them softly.

I walked to meet Ben and Anette, trying extremely hard not to waddle.

"You came," I said.

"I had a little help with changing my mind," Ben said.

Anette grinned at me and winked.

Maria, Jeremy, and I waited at the head of the aisle as the string quartet played Pachelbel's Canon in D. Anette went first, the honorary flower girl, tossing gold rose petals and prancing as the guests all cooed in delight at her.

"Here we go," Maria breathed. We fixed our smiles in place. Every guest's eyes turned to us and their *ooohs* trailed off as our dresses came fully into view. I caught sight of a self-satisfied smirk in the crowd: Beth, in a long white dress (which Sarah was no doubt going to kill her for).

"Come on, you tragic beauties." Jeremy stood between us and linked our arms so we could lean on one another. "Let's get this over with." I had a sudden image of us all doing this at age eighty, and, despite everything that was happening, my life seemed less terrible.

A flash lit up the aisle. Ben. Our eyes met briefly. Even from here, I could see the tense set to his shoulders. I noticed Anette keeping a close watch on him as she scattered rose petals. *Okay?* she asked him. His face cleared. *Okay,* he signed back, and carried on. Photo by photo, I saw the tension start to fall away. *Okay,* I thought.

When we finally reached the top of the aisle, Sarah had appeared. Unlike our awkward shuffle, our friend glided down the aisle like it was a stage built for her. She radiated light as she basked in everyone's attention as though fueled by it. Then she reached Jim, and it was like no one was watching at all.

"Sarah Mathers," Jim said, looking down at his petite bride. "When my friends told me to try dating again"—a few whoops, mainly from men holding babies—"never in my life did I think I'd meet someone as incredible as you."

Sarah's pale cheeks turned a wedding-appropriate shade of rose gold.

"You have been my person to lean on when I've needed it most, and you've brought more love into my boys' lives than I thought possible."

Maria handed us tissues. Jeremy tried to wave her away and then took one anyway, dabbing his eye. "Dust," he whispered.

"And I promise I will spend the rest of my life loving you," Jim continued, "through thick and thin, and every PowerPoint presentation." There was knowing laughter from at least half the guests. My friends and I smiled at one another.

Sarah exhaled slowly. "Jim," she said. "You and your boys are the best thing that's ever happened to me. I never thought I could love someone so much . . . who has such terrible taste in clothes."

Jim laughed, wiping his eyes and squeezing Sarah's hands. Unobtrusively, Ben caught the moment.

"When I pictured my perfect family, it wasn't this," she continued. It was Jeremy's turn to squeeze my arm as we all wondered what she was going to say. "Because," she said, "I never imagined I would be this lucky."

"My heart," Jeremy uttered. And my eyes went, completely unthinkingly, to Ben.

Ben was taking photos of jiving grandparents on the dance floor. His usually serious face was alive as he moved around them, grinning at the show they were giving for his camera. I sipped at my drink, not realizing that my glass had got caught in a ruffle until the material was in my mouth. There was laughter from nearby.

Jeremy and Maria were both resting their chins on their hands with faux-dreamy looks in their eyes. Anette was grinning at me. We were sitting at the high table, gearing ourselves up to attempt to dance in these dresses—and, in Jeremy's case, that hat—the tablecloth strewn with crumbs from our dinner, and tiny crystals that caught the candlelight.

"What?" I asked.

Jeremy made a sign with his hands and Anette passed him the wine.

"Jeremy," Maria reprimanded. She was mollified when she saw Anette was clearly loving it. Jeremy did the sign for "thank you" and clinked his replenished glass against her juice.

"Show her, kiddo," Jeremy said. Anette hopped off her seat and leaned against me so she could show me the picture she'd taken.

It was me, looking at something across the room, my expression open, cheeks flushed and eyes sparkling.

"*What?*" I asked again, baffled.

"I can't believe I'm saying this," Jeremy said, "but Sarah was right. She picked you one hell of a plus-one."

I looked at Anette pleadingly. "Jeremy doesn't mean it like that." Sarah had confessed that Ben had no idea he was my "plus-one." If he thought this was a setup, it wouldn't go down well.

"I know," Anette said. "We're your plus-*two*."

Before I could say more, the opening chords to "Love Machine" by Girls Aloud blasted across the dance floor.

"Oh, God," Jeremy said as Sarah materialized in front of us, grinning determinedly, somehow still looking elegant, even with the diamond crown.

"Come on, you boring lot. Time to dance."

Gamely, and not a little tipsily, we let Sarah pull us up to the busy dance floor.

Maria and I tried to outswirl each other, throwing the material of our dresses around in lieu of being able to move our legs. Sarah stood in the middle of us, lifting her skirts and swaying. Jeremy did a twirl with Anette, who was now wearing his hat, and ended up bumping up against Sarah, causing her tiara to fall off and roll away along the floor.

Jeremy raced after it, returning it with a sheepish expression. Sarah took it from him and set it on her head, purposefully askew. "What?" she asked, seeing our surprised expressions. "We got married, didn't we? This is the part of the wedding dedicated to fun. Did *any* of you read my presentation!"

There was a flash of white in the crowd and Sarah tracked it like a hawk after prey.

"Beth!" she called, following her work colleague. "I want to introduce you to someone. His name's Roger . . ."

The song switched to something softer.

"Come on." Maria took my hand and we made a good go of twirling in our dresses until David tapped her on the shoulder, towering over everyone on the dance floor. "Can I steal her?" he asked me.

"She's all yours," I said. He gently pulled her away. I looked for

Jeremy, but he and Anette were shimmying toward the bar, where a cute barman was serving.

I was on my own. I moved to the edge of the dance floor, enjoying the way Maria and David had eyes only for each other as they danced.

Then Ben was next to me, taking a photo of them.

"They look so happy, don't they?" I said. If I could find someone to look at me the way they looked at each other after twelve years together . . . I hadn't forgotten what Maria said at Sarah's hen do, but that look meant they were doing something right.

Ben hung his camera around his neck, turned to me, and held his hand out. It took me a second to register what he meant.

"Oh," I said. "Yes."

As we stood on the LED flooring, the music changed to Frank Sinatra's "The Way You Look Tonight." Ben fumbled around with the ruffles on my back, trying to find somewhere to put his hand. I laughed a little. "I'm not sure this dress was exactly what Frank had in mind when he sang this."

He stepped a little closer and tripped. "Sorry!"

"It's okay." I yanked the material from under our feet.

David and Maria danced up to us; Maria was standing on David's toes to avoid tripping over her own ruffles. "Don't mind me. I just need to make a quick alteration to Evie's dress," she said, as David leaned her in toward us. "Your mother told me this should work." Her fingers touched a point at my neck, my waist, and somewhere on my back. Then she reached under my arms. "Maria!" I gasped, as she yanked hard and David pulled her back, taking the entirety of the top layer of my dress with them.

I looked down. I was now wearing a pale gold A-line dress that hugged my waist perfectly, the skirt swinging against my legs. "That's better." Maria grinned. "To the bar!" she ordered David, who danced her away from us.

The music switched to Elvis Presley's "Can't Help Falling in Love." I narrowed my eyes in suspicion. Sure enough, Jeremy and Anette were at the DJ's booth, grinning at us. I shook my head at them both.

When I turned back to Ben, he was holding out his hand again. He pulled me to him, placing his other hand in the small of my back. All my nerves were concentrated on the weight of that hand, and his fingers against my skin, as if there was no material there at all.

"You were right," Ben said. "About today. Being here. Taking photographs. Thank you. I . . . I don't think I would have done it without you."

"You're welcome," I said. "Though I suspect Anette played a big part."

He smiled. "She made one very persuasive point."

"Which was?"

Ben's fingers tightened on mine. Ever so gently, he pulled me closer, the gap between us becoming an inch, a centimeter, a breath. His mouth started to form a word. But I never got to hear it.

"Red." The shout rang out across the dance floor. There were annoyed gasps and the crowd parted to make room as someone pushed their way through.

My heart shoved its way into my throat.

"Red, babe," NOB called, approaching us. He was wearing jeans and a leather jacket, his hair all over the place. "Your meet-cute is here. Better late than never, right? DJ! My song."

"Lady in Red" started playing. Every single person on the dance floor was watching as NOB held his arms wide, waiting for my embrace.

Ben's hands dropped away, leaving me cold.

"Ben . . ." I willed him to see I hadn't planned this, but his attention was on NOB. His jaw set. He didn't say anything, just nodded as if he shouldn't have expected anything different, and walked away.

"Bye, Ben," NOB said to his retreating back.

"What are you doing here?" I demanded.

"I'm getting it right this time. I couldn't stay away from you, Red."

"You think you can just turn up at my friend's wedding after what you did?"

He stepped closer to me, lowering his voice. "I know I owe you a huge apology."

What could he possibly say to explain himself about the script?

"You have to know," NOB said. "Everything I said to you, it was all real. I'm sorry I didn't get things right at the premiere. I should have told you then, but I just couldn't deal with how I was feeling about us." He paused, searching my face. "The truth is . . ." He raised his voice again. "I love you, Red."

And that's when I saw that my friends had shuffled to the front of the crowd, their faces full of horrified disbelief.

Chapter 37

- - - - - - - - - - - - - - -

Splat

INT: THE BAR, ROSEHILL MANOR—SATURDAY,
FEBRUARY 16, 9:03 P.M.

EVIE pulls NOB through a set of double
doors at the back of the room. A heavy set
of curtains divides the room. She pushes
through them into an empty bar area.
There's a table stacked with champagne
glasses and bottles of prosecco, and a vast
cake on a plinth next to the table. The
cake stands almost two meters tall. Between
all eight of its vast tiers are lavish,
intricate layers of icing flowers that
trail down its sides. The cake culminates
in an icing castle complete with figurines—
a princess and a prince, kissing. Both EVIE
and NOB are momentarily distracted by it.

It was quieter in here, away from the music, though it sounded like things had picked up again in our absence. *Thank goodness.* I'd deal with NOB, then go and apologize to my friends.

And Ben.

"What the hell are you doing here? Really?"

"I love—"

I held up my hand. "Cut the crap, Ezra. Despite what little you did manage to write, you are *not* my romantic lead."

A muscle in NOB's jaw flickered, as he clocked what my words meant and considered how best to play this.

"You know, then," he said, finally dropping the pretense. "I'm here for the ending. Monty sent me. He thinks we've had some sort of lover's quarrel and suggested I surprise you."

"Because the last time went so well?"

"I didn't want to see you get fired, Red," he insisted, almost convincingly.

"I already quit." I gritted my teeth. "Don't pretend you're doing this out of kindness. You stole my work and faked falling for me to get me to finish it. You're an arsehole. I can't believe I ever thought you could be any different."

NOB pulled a face and grabbed a bottle of the prosecco to pour himself a glass.

"I want the ending, Red."

"It's *Evie*," I spat. NOB flinched. "You came all the way from London just to tell me this? You've wasted a journey. I'm not giving it to you."

"Don't flatter yourself, Red . . . *Evie*." He held up the bottle and champagne flute in mock submission. "First I went to Monica's, but she wouldn't have me, so I came here." He finished his glass, then plonked it on the side and drank straight from the bottle. His eyes traveled to the eight-tiered cake. "Tacky weddings aren't really my scene."

I clenched my fists. There was something different about him. The messy hair, the sneakers. "Are you drunk?"

NOB shrugged. "It's a free bar. What's your problem, anyway?" Something ugly passed over his beautiful features. "Your writing is the reason the producers love the script so much. That's a good thing, isn't it?"

"They don't even know it's mine!" I exhaled slowly, trying to keep my voice down. "Why did you steal it, Ezra?"

NOB chugged at the prosecco, wiping his mouth. "You really want to know?" he said.

"*Yes.*"

"When you came to me with the addendum that day, I was working on another script. I've been writing it this whole time."

It took a moment for this to fully sink in. "Another *script?* But . . . But you had writer's block," I said. "I thought I was helping you with the meet-cutes. Sending you inspiration."

"You thought I had writer's *block?*" NOB's tone was incredulous. *"Me?"* He took another swig of prosecco. "Okay, I did, a little. But not for long."

"It was three years," I said.

"Whatever. It's why I signed on for that rom-com. I needed *something.* I admit it, I was desperate. Then it was like I relaxed or something. The moment I signed Intrepid's contract, an idea for a film hit me that was so good, so much more my brand, I knew I had to write that instead. Once I sold the script for it, I'd be able to pay back Intrepid for the rom-com. Everyone would be happy. Except," he sighed heavily. "Monty was too hung up on the rom-com deal to see my vision clearly."

He waved the bottle widely. "Then you came along and offered to secure me the three months I needed to finish working on my script. When the producers kept bugging me for my rom-com idea, I gave them yours—a rom-com with not just one meet-cute, but all of them." He laughed. "I never thought they'd actually buy it. Giving them what you wrote about the meet-cutes was only meant to keep them off my back. When they loved the pages, I just kept giving them more. It bought me time to get my script ready to take out to L.A."

"Your writer's retreat," I said drily as the pieces fell into place.

"If it helps you feel better . . ." NOB tipped his bottle, finding it empty. He picked up another. "No one wanted my script. It's Monty's fault. I had to put the script out under a pseudonym so he wouldn't know I was shopping it behind his back. No one took me seriously. *Me.* Ezra Chester."

As I rubbed my forehead wearily, a memory came to me.

"That night in the Ash," I realized. "The cheap Ezra Chester knockoff screenplay Jodi was talking about . . . it's *yours*." Then I remembered Monica's cryptic comment on New Year's Day. *You really have no idea, do you?* She'd known all about it. The plagiarism. His other script. I wondered if it was why she'd broken up with him. I let out a laugh. "I honestly didn't think I'd find any of this funny."

He sneered. "That *knockoff* being rejected is the reason I had to pretend to fall for you."

I sobered. "How so?"

"When I came back from L.A., the rom-com was all I had left. Then *you* said you were done with our deal. I knew you were bluffing, but I still needed the ending. I had to make you believe that you'd already won, so I faked falling for you. You were so desperate to meet someone, I thought you'd buy it far quicker than you did." He sidled close to me. "We had fun, didn't we? It wasn't *all* lies." I looked at him sharply. "Look, Evie. You need this script just as much as I do. Just write the ending."

"Only if you give me credit," I said.

"Sure. If you write the ending, I'll name you as cowriter," he said.

"Full credit, Ezra."

"I can't," he whined, his eyes begging. "I need this too much. Come on. Your career is down the toilet. It will take you a *day* at the most. Just write the damn script!"

The words rang out across the room and the whole thing suddenly struck me as spectacularly ridiculous. I started to laugh, quietly at first, then found myself unable to stop.

"What's so funny?"

"You." I gasped, holding my sides. "Shouting at *me* to write the script. Now you know how it feels, at last."

NOB was giving me a look that suggested he thought he'd finally broken me.

I composed myself, straightening my dress. "Come on, Ezra. Time for you to go."

"No way."

"You heard her." I turned to find Ben standing near the curtain.

"This has sod all to do with you, Dull Dad. Go home."

Ben's eyes darkened.

"Leave. Now."

"Why does he even care?" NOB asked me. "Didn't he reject you? In the meet-cute," he explained to Ben.

"Ezra, don't," I said, desperate to stop him talking.

"You know, the one with the school play." His words filled the curtained room, making it seem suffocatingly small.

Ben turned to me, brows raised, silently asking if this was true.

"I was mad at you," I said softly. "I wrote it before . . ." Before the cottage, before the Valentine's Day rescue, before we danced.

"And now it's part of my film," NOB said.

"*Your* film?" Ben said quietly.

"He submitted what I wrote about the meet-cutes for the script, but I *swear* I had no idea that's what he was doing."

"I heard that much." Ben's expression was impenetrable as his eyes slid to NOB. "So it's not part of 'your film,' it's part of Evie's. You stole it."

I stared at him. He didn't blame me?

NOB just rolled his eyes. "She's an assistant, isn't she? She *assisted* me. That's what she does." He returned to his prosecco. "And she really goes above and beyond, if you know what I—"

"You absolute *nob*." I stepped toward him, but Ben stood in my way.

"He's not worth it, Evie."

"It's okay, Ben," I said, glaring at NOB. "I can handle him."

NOB grinned, delighted. "She sure can," he goaded, slamming the bottle down. Now it was Ben's turn to take a step toward him. "Come on, Dull Dad, show us you're not just a boring twat."

I forced myself between them. "Stop it!" I demanded.

But NOB danced around me and pushed Ben's shoulder.

"I'm not doing this with you," Ben said evenly. "Get out. Now."

NOB shoved him again, harder this time. I called out a warning as Ben skidded back toward the mountainous cake. There was a *thud* as he knocked against the plinth.

All eight tiers wobbled.

The kissing figurines at the top tilted slightly to one side . . . and stilled.

I breathed out in relief. "Okay, that was too close. Ezra, you *really* need to go."

NOB was giving Ben a considering look. "You know, it's true what they say about redheads," he said, casually. "All fire. I'm only sad I didn't get to find out if she screws anything like she kisses—*oof.*"

Ben rugby-tackled him from the side.

Oh, God, oh, no. NOB flew backward, arms cartwheeling. He put a hand out to catch himself, but the only thing behind him was the cake.

There was nothing I could do but watch as NOB's right arm and shoulder went straight through the bottom tier.

There was a moment of perfect stillness, all of us too stunned to react.

Then the cake started to shake as NOB tried to extract himself.

"Stop moving! It might still be salvageable," I said, desperately. Maybe if we turned the cake around, we could hide the giant hole . . .

Ben held out his hand to help NOB up. "Come on," he said.

NOB made as if to take his hand—only to fling a huge chunk of sponge into Ben's face.

"Right," Ben said calmly, wiping cream from his eyes. Then he launched himself at NOB and they both careened backward into the cake, knocking the whole thing off its plinth and onto the floor with an audible *splat*.

Ohmygodhowisthishappeningohnononono.

They both leaped up, slipping and sliding as they grabbed on to each other's shoulders and wrestled in its ruins.

"For goodness' sake, both of you stop it!"

NOB took a foot-long turret that had once been part of the icing castle and whacked Ben across the back. Ben retaliated by lifting up the whole second tier and dropping it onto NOB's head.

"You are grown men!"

NOB went down, scrabbling around in the cake as Ben plucked some icing flowers and started pelting him with them. With both hands, NOB seized the biggest turret and thrust it toward Ben like a javelin. Ben grabbed hold of the other end, yanked him to his feet. Grunting with the exertion, the men played tug-of-war until the whole thing broke in two, sending them both sprawling back down onto the cake-smeared floor.

Something splatted hard against my chest. *"Oh!"*

Cold cream slid down inside my dress.

This is a complete and utter disaster.

"Come on in, there's plenty of room for everyone." There was a man's voice coming from beyond the curtain. It was the DJ. *What's he doing here?*

"It's time to witness the new Mr. and Mrs. Johnson cutting the cake. And what a cake it is too, folks! Drum roll, please!"

Please, no.

The three of us froze. Ben and NOB on the floor amid the destroyed cake, me standing over them, a tableau of despair.

As the curtain was drawn back, I closed my eyes.

Three. Two. One.

"Is someone going to explain to me why there are two men in the middle of my wedding cake?"

"Oh, no," I heard Jeremy say. "They were meant to jump out of the top."

"Not the time, Jeremy," Maria replied, faintly.

I looked. The entire wedding party looked back. I couldn't meet my friends' eyes.

Sarah was holding the prince and princess figurines. They were snapped apart.

"You," said Sarah, all cold fury, jabbing the princess at NOB. "Get off my cake and get out of my wedding." NOB looked as if he might try to charm her but thought better of it. He stood, swiped a bottle of prosecco from the table, and went to saunter through the curtain. Jeremy wrestled the bottle out of his hands and elbowed him through.

"And *you*." Sarah pointed the prince at Ben. She shook her head. "You were supposed to be the good one."

"I am so sorry, Sarah," Ben said, leaping up and sliding a little, eyes anywhere but on me. He tried to wipe away the icing that was covering him from head to toe, before realizing it was futile. "I will pay for all of this. There's no fee for your photos. I'm sorry."

Anette broke away from Maria's side and walked over to her dad, avoiding standing in the chunks of cake that had fallen off him. She held out her hand. "Come on," she said heavily, rolling her eyes at the crowd as if he were a naughty child. "This is exactly why we have the no-sugar-before-bed rule."

There was a little laughter at this.

Shoulders slumped, and with one last apologetic look toward Sarah, Ben limped with his daughter through the curtain.

Alone now, I finally faced my friends.

"Evie," said Maria. "How could you?"

"I'm sorry," I began. I'd ruined things for Sarah. *Again.* My friends deserved an explanation. And yet I couldn't help looking to where Ben and Anette had disappeared.

"Grovel later," Jeremy told me. "Go get him now."

I met Sarah's eyes, then Maria's. Jeremy held the curtain back and, hoping Sarah and Maria would forgive me, I gave him a grateful smile and dashed past before anyone could say another word.

Ben and Anette were halfway down the hall, heading for the foyer. "Ben, wait."

He didn't slow. I hurried to catch up with them. "This was a mistake," he said, without turning. "We shouldn't have come." My stomach twisted. Anette tugged at his hand.

"Was all of today a mistake?" I asked.

Ben stopped at the double doors, head bowed. Anette looked up at him. "I shouldn't have agreed to be Sarah's photographer," he said.

"Why not?" I demanded.

"Because. Life made sense before we met you, Evie. We were doing just great until you came along."

"Dad," said Anette.

He pushed through the door. *That is* it. I stormed after them into the foyer.

"You should still be a photographer, Ben," I shouted after him. A staff member behind the front desk put his finger on his lips, and I lowered my voice. "I thought that working this wedding might help you get back to doing what you love. I just wanted to help."

Ben signed something to Anette. She signed furiously back, but her dad simply gestured to the doors we'd just come through. She jutted her chin before heading back through them, the music briefly pulsing into the foyer as they closed behind her.

"You don't get to interfere in people's lives like that, Evie."

He still wouldn't face me, so I stood in front of him, my arms folded. "You want to talk about interfering? That fight back there?

Trying to get NOB to apologize? And what about the balloons? Sarah's hen do? I don't need you to keep rescuing me, Ben."

"You could have fooled me. Maybe if you weren't so busy attempting to meet a man you don't actually have any interest in dating, you'd have time to focus on more important things."

I blushed furiously, raising my voice. "What is it that bothers you so much about these meet-cutes, Ben? At least I'm doing something with my life. You're stuck in a rut. Going to Gil's every single Sunday. Telling yourself that you're no longer a photographer when you so clearly are. And you know what else you are? You're a coward, Ben. You aren't willing to take a chance on something you love, even when it's right there in front of you."

I saw the rapid rise and fall of Ben's chest and he took a step closer to me. "Something I love?" he asked quietly.

"Yes," I replied, flustered.

"Evie?" It was Maria, the anger cooling on her face when she saw us standing there together.

Anette followed behind her, dragging a bag. "I got your camera stuff, Dad." When Ben didn't answer, she did the *okay* sign. He shook himself and went to meet her, shouldering the bag and taking her hand.

They reached the main doors and, just for a moment, Ben hesitated, as though he might say something, before pushing through them and out into the night.

I felt a warm hand on my arm.

Maria. But I couldn't face her right now.

"Come back inside," she said.

"I can't. I'm sorry I lied to you. I'm sorry I ruined everything." I wiped my eyes and backed away. "Enjoy the rest of the evening. I love you. Please just tell everyone . . . If they ask, tell everyone I'm sorry."

Chapter 38

JEMS

```
INT: EVIE'S CHILDHOOD BEDROOM—SUNDAY,
FEBRUARY 17, 7:23 P.M.

EVIE is burrowed deep in her duvet in a
small single bed, working on her laptop.
She's surrounded by tissues. She keeps
checking her phone, then putting it back
down again. There's a knock on the door and
EVIE's mother enters, holding a tray with a
pot of tea and some jam on toast.
```

I gave my mum a watery smile as she entered, but kept my swollen eyes on the screen so I could finish ordering the removal van. I'd already let Jane know I was moving out at the end of the month. She'd offered to let me pay her next month's rent once I got a new job, but I was no longer sure what I wanted. *Welcome to rock bottom, Evie.*

My mum settled the tray down on my old bedside table.

"I've brought you a snack," she said. "And some tea." She poured some for us both, then plonked the plate in my lap and handed me the cup, forcing me to sit up. "I think you should try speaking to your friends," she told me.

I sighed, biting into the toast. My stomach growled and I realized it was the first thing I'd eaten all day. I devoured the whole piece.

"They aren't talking to me. Mum, I ruined Sarah's wedding, and I lied to them about NOB." I'd told my mum everything, and had to practically confiscate her bus pass to prevent her from going to find him. "Sarah barely forgave me for her hen do. They'll never forgive me for this. I don't deserve it."

"Are you sure?" my mum asked, ever the optimist. She busied herself with getting my jumper and jeans out of my case and laying them out on the bed. As if this would somehow encourage me to change out of my pajamas.

Today was the first day since I'd moved to London that the JEMS group chat had been silent. "I'm sure," I said, tearing the second piece of toast in two. My mum put a bra and my brush on the little pile on my bed, glanced over at me, then added some deodorant and a toothbrush.

"I really think you should at least try to speak to them. After all, it would be rude to leave them waiting."

It took me a few seconds to register what she'd just said. "What?" I asked.

"Especially when they've all made such an effort to be here," my mum said.

I scrambled up, grabbing my clothes. "Mum!"

I entered the living room to find my friends all squeezed onto my mum's squashy two-seater sofa, holding cups of tea.

"Hi," I said, trying a smile. Sarah was in the middle, somehow retaining her bridal glow in a smart shirt with faded jeans. Jeremy nodded at me. I couldn't read Maria's expression.

"Evie," said Jeremy formally. "Come in. We all have something to say to you. It won't take long."

"Because I have an early flight," said Sarah.

I shuffled inside, dread churning in my stomach. I could hear my mum in the kitchen, making a lot of noise to indicate she was giving us privacy, though not so much that she couldn't listen in. I searched Maria's face for clues as to how this was going to go. When no one spoke, I rushed to fill the silence.

"I know how awful I've been," I said. "I should have told you about NOB. I should never have let it go that far yesterday. Sarah, all of you, I'm so sorry."

"You have been a terrible friend," Sarah said bluntly. "You destroyed my cake. We had to get a dozen Victoria sponge cakes from Tesco. Jim's sister took the rest of my wedding photos. But what's worse," she said, voice softening, "is that I wanted my *best friend* at my wedding, Evie. You *left*."

"I'm so sorry, Sarah," I said, appalled at myself. "I've been awful. Totally thoughtless. I wasn't there for you."

"You haven't been there for months," Maria said.

"Completely self-absorbed," Jeremy added.

"And *lied* to us," Maria finished.

"I know," I said, distraught at the hurt in their expression. "I won't do it again. And I promise nothing really happened with NOB. Maria, you saw that photo of me on the red carpet. That pretty much said it all."

"We've all seen the photo," Jeremy assured me.

"I should have told you the truth," I said miserably. "But I knew what you'd say. And you'd have been right. It was all over before Sarah's wedding, I promise. I had no idea he would turn up yesterday. I should never have spoken to him. I should have made him leave straight away." I looked at each of my friends in turn. "I know I don't deserve it, but . . . do you think you can ever forgive me?"

I held my arms tightly around myself, bracing myself for what they'd say. They were my family. I didn't know what I'd do without them.

"Absolutely not," said Sarah and I fought back tears, throat burning. I'd messed things up too badly.

Jeremy elbowed her.

"We were all ready to talk terms. The silent treatment. Drinks on you for a year. The whole works," said Jeremy. He gave the tiniest of smiles. "We made a list."

"Then your mum got in touch," said Maria.

"She explained everything to us. We know what that cockhat did to you with the script," Jeremy said. He looked at Sarah. "Incidentally, that's what I'm calling that thing you made me wear during the wedding."

"We also know you quit your job," said Sarah, ignoring him. "And that you're moving back in with your mother." She wrinkled her nose. "You made it really hard to hold a grudge."

I stared at them all, hardly daring to believe it. "Does that mean . . ."

"Get over here," Jeremy ordered. He and Maria stood up. She held out her arms, eyes shimmering.

There was a pause. "Fine," Sarah said, standing too. "Though you're paying for that cake."

I found myself in the center of a hug I'd been needing for a long time.

"You guys," I said, my mouth buried in someone's hair. "You really had me terrified for a minute there."

"We know," Jeremy said.

They pulled me down onto the small sofa between them.

"Thank you for being here for me. *Again*," I said. "I know it's my fault for keeping things from you, but even though we've seen each other, I've really missed you."

"Evie Doris Summers," Maria said in a tone that brooked no argument. "Of course we're here. You stop the world when your friend needs you."

The tears I'd been holding back started to flow. I'd been so focused on what I wanted, that I hadn't been there for them. And here they were, turning up for me.

"The things I'd say to that man if I ever saw him again," Maria seethed, eyes going distant. "Thinking he can just steal your script and pass it off as his own. What an arrogant, entitled *arsehole*."

"He's worse than that," said Sarah. "He's yet another man who's being allowed to take credit for a woman's work as if it's nothing. And it *isn't* nothing." She looked at me. "So what are we going to do about it?"

"I don't know yet," I confessed. "I've told him and Monty I deserve credit, and they've both refused."

"Maybe," said Sarah, her voice uncharacteristically gentle, "it shouldn't be their decision."

"Whatever you decide to do," Maria told me, holding my hand, "we're so proud of you. You're writing again, and those a-holes can't take that away from you."

I laughed, dabbing at my eyes with my sleeve. "I don't intend to let them."

Jeremy reached into a canvas bag by the sofa. "We did have another reason for being here." He put something on the table.

Anette's camera.

"We need to show you something," Maria said.

Sarah turned the camera on and pressed play on a video. Anette came into focus. She was wearing the red-and-white dress from the wedding and looking over her shoulder. I could hear Ben's and my voices raised in anger through the doors behind her.

"Hi, Evie, I hope you find this," she said, coming close to the lens, her voice hushed. "I have to be quick, but I wanted to tell you something. It's about my dad, Benjamin Michael Williams." She enunciated his whole name. Jeremy got out his phone. "And that's this. The thing is, there used to be three of us, and we took on the whole world together. Then a bad thing happened and it was just the two of us. The bad thing scared him. He didn't want it to happen again, so we stopped having adventures. This kept his awesome daughter safe, but, after a while, he forgot that to live is an awfully big adventure." She pointed a small finger at the camera. "That's you, Evie. You're the adventure." She whipped her head around. I could clearly be heard shouting, *"You're a coward, Ben."* I flushed. Jeremy raised an eyebrow. "Uh-oh. Got to go. Remember: Benjamin Michael Williams." The screen went dark.

I sat staring at it for a moment. Maria put her arm around me, giving me a moment to process it.

"Do you want to look him up?" said Jeremy. "Maria made us wait for you to decide."

Did I? I might never even see Ben again. *So why do I still want to know?* I nodded. Jeremy showed me his phone, and we all huddled around.

He'd already found a website for *Benjamin Michael Williams Photography.* There were more of those brilliant, heart-stopping images I'd seen before. "He's displayed in galleries all over the world. Look at the prices on these things!" Jeremy said. My friends all ushered me out of the way so they could ogle. "Evie." His tone was reverential. "Your boy's rich."

They all looked at me. "He's not my boy," I said. "I'm serious!"

"I can't believe it!" Sarah exclaimed. We all looked at her. "*The* Benjamin Michael Williams took my wedding photos!"

"You didn't know who he was until one minute ago," said Jeremy.

"Still," Sarah preened. She put a hand on my leg. "Evie, one day, I might even forgive you for destroying my cake," she said generously.

"Thanks, Sarah."

Jeremy was still fiddling with his phone when he went very still. "There are some articles here," he said, his tone serious.

"What is it?"

"They're about his wife."

"I want to see," I said. Somehow I had the feeling Anette wanted this too.

He handed the phone to me. *Tragedy in the Alps.* The article was dated just over three years ago. As I read, the final pieces of the Ben puzzle clicked into place. Chloe and Anette had been traveling with him on a shoot. Ben had been up in the mountains on the day it happened, and Chloe and Anette had stayed behind in the village where the crew were based. He was late coming back, and Chloe and Anette had gone to get some dinner. It was no one's fault. They were crossing a road and a Jeep slid toward them, brakes useless on the ice. Witnesses said that Chloe managed to get Anette clear before the car hit her. She died right there on the road. Ben wouldn't even have known until he'd returned, hours later.

My dad had died on his way to see one of my short films. It hadn't been my fault, I knew that now, and yet it was one of the reasons I'd stopped writing. Chloe had died while Ben was taking photographs. This was why he'd stopped. Until I'd pushed him to start again.

"I called him a coward," I said, numbly. Jeremy gently prized the phone from my trembling fingers. "I said really awful things to him. Unforgivable things." My friends all squeezed me tightly.

"You did. But you meant well," Sarah said.

"Thanks, Sarah." I knew she meant well too.

"What are you going to do?" Maria asked.

"How can I expect him to forgive me?"

"You know how I feel about love." Jeremy pulled back from the huddle. "You can keep all the flowers and the heart-shaped boxes of chocolates. When a man comes over to unblock your toilet, *that's* romance."

"What do you mean?" I sniffed.

"He might surprise you," said Jeremy.

After my friends had left, I curled up on my mum's sofa holding Anette's camera. I turned it on again, curious about the photos she'd taken at the wedding, wondering if there was one of me and Ben before it all went so horribly wrong.

I must have clicked back to the beginning of the memory card because the photo that came up was a few years old. It was of Anette, Chloe, and Ben, grinning into the camera. Chloe's hair was lighter than Anette's, but their smiles matched. They looked so happy, so unaware that their little family was about to change.

They were sitting in Gil's.

My hands felt too rubbery to keep holding the camera.

My mum stuck her head into the room. "Is it too soon for cake?"

"Yes," I said.

She gave me a plate with a little brownie on it and sank into the sofa beside me. She lifted her arm so I could lean into her.

We both looked at the photo.

"What a beautiful family," she said.

"I was so terrible to him," I said. "I said he was stuck in a rut. I didn't even mean it, not really. I love our breakfasts in Gil's. Why did I say that?"

She took my brownie and bit into it. "Sometimes, when you've had a trauma, you try to control whatever you can to prevent it from ever happening again."

"You didn't," I said. The sofa was draped in a throw she'd made. There was a keyboard along the back wall so she could practice for her lessons. The brownie was from her latest baking class. For as long as I could remember, my mum was always trying new things, always moving, never staying still.

"I did, in a way," she said. "I did everything I could to make sure any change that happened in my life after your dad passed was down to me, and me alone. It helped, but it also took a long time for me to come to terms with the fact that there will always be things that are out of my control. You have to learn to embrace that."

I thought about my life before my deal with NOB; how much

time I'd dedicated to work, to a job that I loved and resented in equal measure. About how I still had the same friends, whom I loved, but that I hadn't tried to make new ones in London. How I'd taken fewer risks with love after Ricky. How I'd stopped writing after Monty had told me I didn't have what it took.

"After Dad, I chose the Ben route, didn't I?"

"Oh, love. We all do what we have to in order to get through things. But I hoped that one day you'd be more open to life again. I just want you to be happy, and I feel like these past few months you've been happier than I've seen you in a long time. Change can be a very good thing."

She offered me the rest of the brownie and I took it. "I still wish I could change what I said to Ben yesterday," I confessed. "But I can't help believing he really does need to start taking chances again. Do you think he could ever learn to do that?"

"Who knows?" said my mum. "Maybe he already has."

MARIA: have you decided what you're going to do about your script?

EVIE: I have. It turned out to be an easy decision in the end

JEREMY: and Hot Widower?

EVIE: him too

SARAH: you've got this

EVIE: I know. But knowing you're all here for me helps. You make me feel very lucky.

SARAH: that's sweet, but you're still paying for my cake

Chapter 39

The Ending

```
INT: BOARDROOM, INTREPID PRODUCTIONS—MONDAY,
FEBRUARY 18, NOON

MONTY, NOB, and SAM-AND-MAX are seated at
the end of a large table. The walls are all
made of glass and you can see through into
the next room, where there are colorful
round chairs, people playing table
football, and a margarita machine. Everyone
has a copy of the script. MONTY looks
confident. NOB is wearing sunglasses. The
door opens, and EVIE enters.
```

". . . just a bit of polishing, that's all, but I think we can all agree this version is more than acceptable—" On seeing me, Monty fell silent. He wrestled his face back into his usual easygoing smile, though his eyes were like nail guns, pinning me from across the table. I could see him desperately trying to figure out why I was here.

NOB tilted his chin downward, dipping his glasses to look at me as if he couldn't believe my nerve. I held his gaze, daring him to say something. Instead, he flipped his glasses into place and leaned back in his chair, gazing at the ceiling. He hadn't shaved for a few days and he was wearing a cap—designer, but still very un-NOB.

Sam-and-Max, on the other hand, were all smiles as they welcomed me in and gestured me to a seat.

"Was there something you wanted, Evelyn?" Monty asked, as though slightly embarrassed for me.

"She's here to discuss the ending," one of the producers said, leaning back in his chair, fingers interlocking across his chest. "She emailed us yesterday to say she had a solution, one she's already discussed with you. We're all ears."

The look on Monty's face was pure relief. *She's come to her senses,* it said.

"Actually," I said, heart hammering but determined, "I'm here to discuss the whole script."

The relief flickered between panic and uncertainty before professional calm took over. "I'm afraid this is my fault," Monty said smoothly. "I gave her some extra responsibility and it went to her head. Evelyn, this is no longer your concern. This sort of behavior is exactly why I had to let you go."

"You're no longer with the agency?" one of the producers asked, focusing on me.

"I'm—"

"She's been sacked," Monty said, cutting me off.

Sam-and-Max looked at each other. One of them steepled his fingers on the table. "Then I think we're all wondering why you're here."

Monty looked grimly satisfied as he stared at me across the desk. "Why waste our time? Let's call security now."

I stood. It was now or never.

"I'm here because this is my script," I said, picking up a copy. The calmness in my voice surprised me. "I wrote it. And it should have my name on it."

My old boss turned an off shade of puce. "Call security! I'll do it, shall I?" He strode to the door and yanked it open.

"Wait."

Monty looked around wildly for who'd spoken. It was NOB. He was standing up, his sunglasses in his hands. "She's telling the truth."

What? NOB looked like he might actually throw up, but he remained standing.

"Don't be so modest, Ezra," Monty said, his voice pitchy. "Perhaps it's time you took a break. All the big names do, it's nothing to be ashamed of. Starting right now."

"That script is Evie's. At best, I assisted on it." He managed a smile; it looked painfully raw. "And not particularly well."

Sam-and-Max were frowning. They looked to each other, some silent communication passing between them.

"He's tired. The deadline was too much. He doesn't know what he's saying," said Monty, half leaning on the door. "That," he said, pointing to the pages in my hands, "has an Oscar winner's name on it, just like you wanted, not some *assistant's*." He eyed the producers. "Isn't that what's important here?"

"If you need proof," I said, "I can tell you how it should have ended."

"Security!" Monty cried down the hall.

"Sit down, Monts, you old fool," NOB snapped. "The script is Evie's, and you know it. She did it." He addressed the producers. "All that warmth you loved? Those characters? The *fresh voice* you couldn't get enough of? It's all Evie. You could have given me another three years and I wouldn't have accomplished anything half as good as what she did in three months. She's a natural. Only some arsehole stole her words so she has no idea."

"She clearly did her job too well," Monty tried, refusing to give in. "She has you believing she's done the hard graft. I ask you, can anyone really quantify how much help writers receive?"

"I have all her emails, Monts," NOB said to him. He turned to the producers. "I'll send you everything she sent me. You'll find I pretty much lifted what she wrote word for word. I'll return the money too. It was time I downsized anyway." Finally, he looked at me. "For what it's worth, Evie, I'm sorry."

His honesty didn't completely make up for what he'd done, but I nodded at him.

NOB mimed dropping a mic, slipped his glasses back on, and left.

Monty's eyes were locked on his client's retreating back, face slack. Sam caught Max's eye and drummed his fingers on the table, and, after a heavy pause, Max nodded.

"The ending," said Sam to me. "What were you thinking?"

— — — — — — — — — —

"Evie," said Max, welcoming me back into the room. After I'd laid out a version of the script where the assistant got her happy ending, they'd sent me away so they could discuss their options. The excited expression on Monty's face was disconcerting.

"We don't choose our partners lightly," Sam began. "We wanted Ezra Chester's name on Intrepid Productions' next project."

I nodded. It was what I expected.

"But we keep coming back to the fact that we adore this script."

Hope unfurled in my chest, almost painful in its intensity.

"And that we started this business taking chances," Max said. "We chose the name Intrepid for a reason."

They smiled at me.

Sam held out his hand for me to shake. "Welcome to Intrepid, Evie. We're sure the news that we're bringing on brilliant new female talent for our rom-com will be met with relief."

I could barely breathe. In an instant, that pile of papers on the table became a future I hadn't dared to imagine. And there was one person I wanted to share it with most. Unfortunately, unlike the assistant in the script, I'd realized my feelings too late.

Monty was nodding furiously. "What better publicity could we ask for than 'the assistant wrote the movie'? It's a real rags-to-riches story."

"We're going to need to speak to your agent."

"I always knew she had it in her. I was the one who discovered her, you know. No need to ask me twice." Monty laughed, waving his hand. "Yes, Evelyn, I will represent you. And at William Jonathan Montgomery and Sons, you'll be our number-one client. All-star treatment."

"Thank you," I said to the producers, those two words holding so much weight I almost buckled. "And I represent myself."

"Surely you don't mean that, Evelyn," Monty blustered. "This is what you've always wanted. I remember what you said all those years ago. I'm your dream agent. You can't say no to that."

I looked at him. "Maybe I was a little hasty back then," I said. At this, Monty finally slumped into his chair, defeated.

EVIE: guys . . . guess who's finally going to be an agent.
Though I only have one client

SARAH: I can't keep up. I thought we could all stop pretending you don't want to be a screenwriter now?

MARIA: tell me you did it!! Aljsdkajdklajs!!

JEREMY: come on, Evie, the suspense is killing Maria

EVIE: I did it! My name is going to be on the script. I'm a writer!

MARIA: that's our girl

JEREMY: 🎉

SARAH: FINALLY

EVIE: there's still one more thing I need to do

Chapter 40

Gil's Take ~~One~~ ~~Two~~ Three

```
INT: GIL'S—SUNDAY, MARCH 10, 10 A.M.

EVIE enters the café, eyes zeroing in on
her usual table. There are strangers
sitting there. She bites her lip and
heads to the counter. XAN is serving.
```

I stood in the queue, occasionally looking around for two familiar faces on reflex. There'd been no sign of them for three Sundays in a row. They used to come in during the week now and again, Xan told me, but recently he hadn't seen them at all. Still, I'd been here every weekend, buying hot chocolates and waiting. Just in case.

You're stuck in a rut. Going to Gil's every single Sunday.

Ben hadn't replied to any of my messages so I'd tried calling, only to hear an automated "This number is currently unavailable" message. Which probably meant that all my messages had been flung into a void.

It was time to accept that Ben and Anette didn't come here anymore.

"Three hot chocolates?" Xan asked me.

"Actually," I said, "just a takeaway cappuccino today."

I headed to the end of the counter to wait, trying to dispel the sadness that had settled over me like snow. I had so much to be happy about. These last few weeks had been a complete whirlwind.

I'd signed my contract with Intrepid Productions (after a few solid rounds of negotiations, of course). They'd given the script the go-ahead. I'd polished it until it shone, just like I'd been doing for years at the agency, and when I was finished, I finally admitted to myself why editing had been the best part of my old job. It had been as close to writing as I thought I'd ever get. I'd miss the writers, but leaving the agency had been like letting out a breath I hadn't realized I'd been holding.

The money I'd negotiated for the script was good enough that, if I wanted to, I could buy somewhere to live. I'd paid Jane until the end of the month, but now I had options. My future was wide open; all I needed to do was take the first step. After all, writers can be based anywhere. Even Sheffield. I could go home.

And yet, so far, I hadn't. The only thing I had done was buy my mum a dog, which, in honor of Ziggy (*i.e.*, the best part of NOB), she'd named David.

"Cappuccino for you, Evie," Xan called. He slid the takeaway cup along the counter.

"Xan, this is empty."

"Is it?" said Xan, his eyes widening.

Frustrated, I pulled the lid off to show him. There was something curled inside. I tugged it out.

It was a film ticket for a showing of *Brick Park* at the Prince Charles Cinema in Soho at noon today.

Chapter 41

The Meet-Cute

```
EXT: THE PRINCE CHARLES CINEMA,
SOHO—SUNDAY, MARCH 10, NOON

EVIE looks up at the white box sign above
the glass doors. It bears the letters BRICK
PARK—SOLD OUT. She frowns, then walks into
the foyer and heads to the counter. When
she shows her ticket, the staff nudge one
another and smile, some standing on tiptoe
to see her. One of them asks her to follow
him downstairs.
```

I trailed down the stairs after the boy, wondering if I'd imagined the reactions to my arrival. Maybe the team here, like me, was curious about other Dorothy Taylor fans. There were criminally few of us. I'd been baffled but touched when Xan had given me the ticket, trying to remember when I'd mentioned loving the film to him.

"I know you guys love your cult classics," I said, handing my ticket over. "But no one has ever heard of this film. *No one.*"

"You'd be surprised." The boy pushed the doors to the theater open for me. "Step this way."

Every seat was empty.

"Isn't it sold out?" I asked.

"Yes," the boy said, closing the doors behind me.

I took my seat, choosing the very center, *i.e.,* the best spot for perspective and audio. Though I was the first to arrive, the lights dimmed straight away. I wished I'd had the sense to buy popcorn.

It took me a few seconds to register the image that had appeared on the screen.

It was me.

What. The. Hell?

I looked around, but I was still on my own.

The picture had been taken at Gil's. I was on my laptop, lost in whatever I was writing.

Someone walked in front of the screen.

"Hi," Ben said.

"Hi," I replied, heart aching sweetly at the sight of him.

His thick, dark hair was wavy and loose. He wore a T-shirt under his jacket. No shirt in sight.

"What is this, Ben?"

"I needed to tell you something."

"I've been going to Gil's. You could have told me there. Only I haven't seen you around," I said.

"I've been working," said Ben. "It requires a bit more travel than my old job."

"I messaged you."

"I know. It turns out Marc still prefers shoots where the reception is almost nil."

"You . . ." I paused, realizing exactly what this meant. "You took a chance."

He smiled. "Someone told me I was stuck in a bit of a rut. Turned out being yelled at by a bridesmaid after ruining her friend's wedding was exactly what I needed."

"Why are we here, Ben?" I asked, standing and beginning to make my way along the seats.

"I thought it would be better in person."

"What would?"

"Telling you how I really feel about you."

I stopped at the steps. "But I know how you feel," I said. "You made it perfectly clear when you thought I'd made you part of a meet-cute."

"I was an idiot," he said. "When you said you were doing them for work, that it didn't have to be real . . . I was afraid that if I was just another meet-cute, it might not be as real for you as it was for me."

That's why Ben hadn't wanted to get involved in my meet-cutes?

"It's real for you?"

"Earth-shatteringly," he said.

My heartbeat was in my throat as I took the steps, one at a time.

"What about everything you said at the wedding?" I pushed.

"I acted like a jerk. I'd just destroyed your friend's wedding cake and I said some stupid things. Like how life made sense before I met you. The truth is, things haven't felt this clear to me in so long. I'm sorry, Evie." All those times I'd wished I could change what I'd said to him, I'd never thought he'd wanted to say something different to me too. "After my behavior, Anette was under the impression that you might need some convincing. She suggested a speech. I've always been better with pictures." He gestured to the screen.

Another image appeared there, and I stopped still. This one was of Anette and Ben, pulling their tongues out behind me as I write on my laptop, oblivious. The next was of me and Ben. I'm looking at something across the café, and Ben . . . Ben's looking straight at me. In the next I'm lifting up the Union Jack wings saying I know how to fix them—and Ben's face is full of wonder.

These were all the photos Anette had taken of us over the past three months. All except the one where I was standing beneath the streetlamp, holding my red umbrella in the rain. The one Ben had taken. I wasn't posing. My hair was frizzing. And I looked beautiful.

The final photo was from the wedding. Ben and I, dancing. My face was tilted up toward him. He was holding me close. The corner of his mouth was lifted in a crooked smile at whatever I was saying, as if it was only him and me in the room.

The look in Ben's eyes, it was almost like . . .

"According to a certain meddlesome seven-year-old," Ben said, "I couldn't just tell you I loved you."

I pulled my eyes away from the photo. "You . . . what?"

"I love you," he said simply. Ben loved me? "The way you are with Anette. Your warmth. Your stubbornness. Your kindness. Your passion. Your hair . . . *Especially* your hair. Your willingness to make a public spectacle of yourself." That smile again. The one that looked like it was only half there, but to a connoisseur of Ben's smiles, it was everything. "For how brave you are. I love you, Evie Summers."

Ben *loved* me.

There was something about seeing it up there on the big screen that made it harder to deny.

"I thought, after everything, you deserved your very own meet-cute."

He'd remembered. How long ago had it been that I'd described this moment to him? The cinema. The film. I'd just never imagined that the only other person in the cinema would be him.

"You booked the whole cinema."

"I hear rom-coms require a grand gesture," he said.

My foot hit the bottom step. "Let me get this straight, Ben. After months of avoiding being one of my meet-cutes, you've created one of your own?"

"I have."

I began to cross the carpet toward him.

"And even though you still don't know if it's real for me, you're standing there, willing to tell me that you love me?"

"I decided to take another chance," he said.

I closed the gap between us. "Then you should know," I said, looking up at him. I saw him hold his breath. "It really paid off."

"Evie," Ben said gravely. "I'd like to kiss you now."

"Has anyone ever told you"—I laughed—"that you talk too much?"

He lifted his hand to my cheek, placing his other on my lower back, and pulled me to meet him.

"Better?"

I looked up into those hooded brown eyes, full of light, and warmth, and *love*. As sure of me as I was of him. Then I gave myself to the absolute wonder of his mouth on mine.

Epilogue

The Drink Spill

```
FADE IN

INT: GIL'S COFFEE HOUSE, EAST
DULWICH—SUNDAY, UNGODLY HOUR (10 A.M.)

EVIE SUMMERS—late twenties, freckled, red
curls down to her shoulders, a bright
yellow 1950s-style tea dress, Doc Martens—
stands in front of the counter tapping her
foot, full of nervous energy. ANETTE
WILLIAMS runs across the café to tug the
back of EVIE's cardigan. EVIE turns around
and ANETTE jumps, startled.
```

"Cut!" yelled Greta, the director.

"Sorry, sorry," I said to her. I darted forward and waved so Anette could see me. She went bright red and burst out laughing, and the actress—a gorgeous up-and-comer—laughed too, giving her a quick hug before returning to her mark. Anette slipped between the lights and cameras to return to our side. Ben ruffled her hair.

"If you're going to bring people to the set, you need to keep them under control," Greta called.

"I will, I'm sorry, she's just so excited."

"I didn't just mean the kid," said Greta, her eyes roaming to a point somewhere behind us.

I turned to the three people who were currently hogging the snack table.

"Evie, Evie, Evie. The snacks are free!" Jeremy called.

"I'm proud of you," Maria called, running her critical eye over the baked goods.

"Does the actress really have to wear Doc Martens too?" Sarah asked, sipping a Diet Coke.

"I love you guys," I said. "So glad I brought you."

Ben placed a kiss on my forehead. "It's funny to think we're watching the moment I first started to fall in love with you." He pointed to the actor playing him, whose brows weren't nearly dark enough, in my opinion.

"When I made a child throw up," I mused. "How romantic."

"Actually, it was when you came and sat back down with us. That's when I knew: This woman will make me brave." I nudged him with my elbow and he chuckled. "It's true. Look at what you've achieved. Take a moment to fully appreciate this." He gestured to the set. "You did it, Evie."

I looked over at the actors who were absorbed in their scripts, learning my words. "My dad used to tell me that whatever I wrote, I should make it mean something."

He smiled that crooked smile I fell in love with. "Imagine how proud he'd be of you now."

"Quiet on set! Three." Greta mimed two and then one, putting her finger on her mouth. Ben put his arm around me as we watched the actors begin again.

Okay? Ben signed to me. *Okay?* Anette signed too, then grabbed our legs in a fierce hug.

Okay, I signed, and I couldn't have meant it more.

Acknowledgments

First of all, hello, my fellow acknowledgments readers! Thank you for reading this far (thank you for reading full stop). I always love reading the acknowledgments for that little bit of insight into who the author is, which makes it doubly strange to now be writing my own. Thankfully, they're not about me, but the brilliant people I'm lucky enough to know.

A huge thank-you to the team at Putnam and Penguin Random House. To my amazing US editor, Margo Lipschultz, fielder of panicked phone calls, giver of sound advice, editor extraordinaire, thank you. Sorry about the poo scene. And Tricja Okuniewska—thank you so much for all your incredible hard work.

Thanks also to everyone else at Penguin Random House who has championed and worked so hard on this book. I couldn't hope for a more enthusiastic and dedicated team.

Publicists extraordinaire Alexis Welby and Bonnie Rice. Marketing moguls Ashley McClay, Jordan Aaronson, Emily Mlynek, and Brennin Cummings. Thanks so much for everything you do. This book wouldn't have gotten anywhere without you.

And I owe thanks to Vikki Chu, Tal Goretsky, and Anthony

Ramondo, who dressed my words up in such a gorgeous cover, and inspired me to step up my game to be worthy of it. You've made it so I get to actually see Evie and Ben in real life. Thank you. Thanks too to Kristin del Rosario for the adorable interior design, and Claire Winecoff for managing the production-editing process so seamlessly.

To all the fabulous people at Penguin Random House dedicated to putting this and many other books into readers' hands—thank you!

And everyone else! A huge, huge thanks to:

The team at Orion. To the inimitable Sam Eades, who acquired this. Thanks for taking a chance on me, Sam. Thanks also to Katie Brown, who has run with this novel and helped me get it across the finish line. Special thanks to the rest of Team Trapeze: Phoebe Morgan, Anna Valentine, and especially Shyam Kumar for all his hard work. Thank you for taking such great care of this book.

Gillian Redfearn for being there from the start. Your capacity for generosity always astounds me. Anyone who has you fighting in their corner is very lucky indeed.

Diana, for telling me to "Be More Evie."

Cat Web for the lasagna. You are a kind and brilliant soul.

Richard Roper for being a much-needed sounding board when I was up to my ears in deadlines.

My flatmates, Nat and Chris, and Luna (aka Pounce-o, Dog-Dog, Goose, etc.). For the wine and reassurances and furry hugs (that last one is exclusively Luna). Sorry that I never clean the bathroom. I've been writing this book.

Anna Boatman—and *The Vampire Diaries*, for bringing us together. I'm sorry I didn't show you the book until it was done. Your opinion matters a whole bunch to me.

Charlotte Cray. Like Maria, your tough love packs a punch,

and I wouldn't be the same without it. You are a balm for the soul. Thank you so, so much.

Claire Fraser, all-round awesome human and friend. Thank you for believing in me, for telling me I could do this, and for saying I am "100 percent perfect" as I am. For you, I am including the word "tits" in my acknowledgments. Thank you, my love.

All my friends back "home" in Manchester, for being there from afar: Ellie Devlin, Liz and Alex Holt, Rebecca Mortimer, Paul Hughes, Rob Byron, Michael Monks, and Amanda Browning. Your support means everything.

Quick side note: Gil's is based on Ezra & Gil's in the Northern Quarter of Manchester, UK, which you should absolutely visit if you're ever in the area. I can't guarantee a meet-cute, but I can say for sure that you will eat incredible food (try the beans on toast—trust me, it's delicious and the perfect hangover cure).

And, finally, thank you to my family:

My grandma, Dorothy Parkinson, who's a writer too. Dorothy Taylor was named for her. Thanks, Gran.

My aunt and uncle, Julie and Damian. You told me to put you in here, but I would have anyway. And my cousins Abi and Holly, because I know you'll never let me forget it otherwise. You're my favorites.

Mandy and Josie—thank you for being so proud.

My sisters, Louise and Victoria. Through thick and thin, I'm so lucky to have you both in my life.

Grace. One day, you'll out-Anette Anette.

And to my parents, Dawn and Barry. For always having faith in me. Thank you, you're my absolute heroes. I literally and figuratively wouldn't be here without you.

Lastly, to the man who told me I wasn't good enough—thanks for the inspiration.